THE CHINATOWN HOUDINI BANDITS

A Broken Lawyer Novel

Donald L'Abbate

Also by Donald L'Abbate

"Was it Murder?"

And

The Broken Lawyer Series

'The Broken Lawyer"

"A Murder Under the Bridge"

"For One Man's Honor"

All proceeds from the Broken Lawyer novels are donated to charity.

To learn more,
visit Donald's website at
WWW.DLABBATE-WRITER.COM

Contents

DEDICATION

This book is dedicated to the people in Alcoholics Anonymous and to the organization to which I am eternally grateful.

A SPECIAL THANKS

I want to give a special thanks to my neighbor and friend, Mario Badagliacca, who suggested using the Chinatown tunnels in one of my stories. It was his suggestion that led me to research New York City's Chinatown history that is very much a part of this book. So, thank you Mario.

I also want to thank Joy A. Lorton, Typo-Detective, whose excellent proofreading and editing skills make my works readable.

And, of course, I want to thank my wife, Rose, who patiently reads through the drafts, corrects my plot errors and offers helpful comments.

CHAPTER 1

Sometimes things happen for reasons that you can't understand at the time. That's the way it was the day Connie announced there was a Mr. Jia Li Fang at her desk asking to see me. With my office on the second floor of a commercial building on Mott Street in New York City's Chinatown, I don't usually get very many walk-in clients. I'm a criminal defense lawyer and most of my clients come to me by way of the city's 18B Panel attorney assignment program for indigent clients. When Legal Aid can't or won't handle a criminal case, the 18B Panel assigns it to private lawyers like me. The pay isn't great, but the work is steady.

I do get some better paying private clients on referrals, but working in Chinatown and being Irish, I definitely don't have walk-ins. My Chinese clients come from the friends I've made in the neighborhood, including old man Shoo who owns Shoo's Restaurant. I had my first office in Chinatown in the backroom of that restaurant. I know it may sound strange, having a law office in the backroom of a Chinese restaurant, but it was cheap, and I'll leave it at that for now.

Connie escorted Mr. Fang into my office, then left, closing the door behind her. He was an elderly gentleman. If I had to guess, I would have said somewhere in his eighties. He was wearing a Tang suit, a type of traditional Chinese jacket with a straight collar. It was the style favored by the older Chinatown residents who kept to their traditions more so than the younger generations who preferred western styles. Chinatown was that way, a mixture of the old and the new, but mostly the old. Although most residents spoke English, they all spoke Chinese.

I asked Mr. Fang what I could do for him and how it was he happened to come to me. He smiled, nodded his head and said a friend suggested I might be able to solve a problem he might have. I couldn't help but notice the emphasis he had put on the words "might have." It was Mr. Fang's subtle way of saying he wasn't sure he trusted me yet and until he did, I wasn't going to get the whole story.

I wasn't surprised, I had been working in Chinatown long enough to know it was a small closed society, and I, a Caucasian, didn't fit in. I had managed over the years to make friends and find local clients, but most were second and third generation Chinese Americans. But even with them, when push came to shove, I wasn't Chinese and that was it. Old man Shoo was the only contact I had with the older generation, so I suspected he was the one who had sent Mr. Fang my way. It didn't really matter who sent him; he wasn't going to stay long if he didn't think he could trust me.

I waited for Mr. Fang to tell me more, but he sat staring at me. It was a test of wills to see who would speak first. I'm pretty pigheaded, so we were getting nowhere, and I figured the meeting was a bust. Not that I cared. I was busy enough as it was, and I wasn't going to waste time playing games. If Mr. Fang didn't tell me why he was in my office, I was going to show him the door. At least that was my attitude until Mr. Fang reached into the satchel he had hanging from his shoulder and put a pile of cash on my desk. Apparently, Mr. Fang had sensed my growing impatience and was sending a message of his own. The pile of cash was certainly large enough to keep the meeting going, and since Mr. Fang had now put the ball squarely in my court, I needed to respond.

I offered Mr. Fang a cup of tea. Offering a cup of tea is a sign of respect to the older generation, and Mr. Fang graciously accepted my offer with a simple smile and bow of his head. I asked Connie to bring us some tea, knowing she understood the drill and would serve the tea in the Chinese tea service I kept in the office for just such occasions. The set had been a gift from a wealthy Chinese client, and I had been told it was a very fine antique tea set. Mr. Fang seemed impressed. At least so far. As I grabbed the teapot to pour the tea I was hoping Mr. Fang wasn't expecting me to perform a full Chinese tea ceremony. I've attended those ceremonies many times, and they require skills and dexterity far beyond my abilities. All Mr. Fang was going to get was a cup of tea without pomp and circumstance.

Mr. Fang sipped his tea and smiled, seemingly pleased with the tea or my feeble offering, or both. Now the ball was back in his court, and I waited for him to say something. I was getting tired of the game, but the pile of cash on the desk was holding my attention. Finally after two sips of his tea, Mr. Fang asked if I was familiar with the incident earlier in the week on Mott Street. Obviously we were going to do this his way, the hard way. I said that I assumed he was talking about the bank robbery, and he simply nodded his head.

What I knew about the incident was limited to what I had read about it in the *New York Post*. The Citibank on the corner of Mott Street and Chatham Square had been held up by three masked gunmen around midmorning. As the gunmen exited the bank, they crossed paths with two New York City cops on street patrol. A gun battle ensued, and fortunately, neither cop was injured, but one of the suspects had been wounded. The three suspects ran up Mott Street into the basement of a building and disappeared. Their disappearance had been sufficiently mysterious for the media to dub the trio the "Houdini Bandits."

I glanced at the pile of cash on the desk, which I was starting to think could be the proceeds of a crime, and therefore, much less attractive, and I asked Mr. Fang if he had robbed the bank. He laughed and said, "No, No. I'm much too old to do such a dangerous thing." Before I could ask my next question, Mr. Fang said simply, "It was my grandson. I think. You see, leaves emerge from where they should not." I wasn't sure what that meant, but it didn't matter. Mr. Fang hadn't robbed the bank, so the money setting on my desk wasn't the proceeds of a crime.

CHAPTER 2

Before I tell you anything more about Mr. Fang and his possible bank robbing grandson, I should mention a few things about myself. Not that you care, and not that I feel like sharing my life with you, but it may help you understand where I'm coming from. I'm a criminal defense attorney, and I work out of an office on Mott Street in New York City's Chinatown. I'm also a recovering alcoholic. As you might suspect, alcohol has played a large role in my life. Actually, alcohol came close to ending my life, at least professionally, but it didn't.

I didn't leave law school wanting to be a criminal defense attorney. When I started out I wanted to be a prosecutor, and for a while I was. My first job was as an Assistant DA in the Manhattan District Attorney's Office. I was a golden boy with a promising career until things went south. It seemed my badass mouth and booze are like oil and water; they don't go together well. They got me thrown out of my job. With nowhere else to turn, I became a criminal defense attorney. For the first few years things didn't go so well, mainly because I was still drinking heavily, but then things changed. I got sober in AA and will hopefully remain a card carrying member of the organization for the rest of my life. At least that's the plan.

Just for the record, getting sober wasn't originally my idea. I was quite content to stagger along through my chaotic life, but the Administrator at the 18B Panel, from which I was getting all my clients, and upon whom I depended to earn a living, threatened to have me disbarred if I didn't go to AA. I figured if I got disbarred and I still wanted to live with indoor plumbing and eat regularly, I'd have to get a real job that likely involved physical labor which wasn't exactly up my alley. But that wasn't what convinced me to go to my first AA meeting. I went because I knew that was the only way I could keep doing the one thing I loved most, practicing law. I love the law more than anything. Well, maybe not as much as Gracie.

Gracie is my longtime girlfriend who insists I not refer to her as my girlfriend. I don't know why that is, but I've tried to honor her request. For years I have racked my brain trying to figure out what to call her. Calling her just a friend isn't accurate; she's more than just a friend. But then what can I call her? I could call her my partner, but since we're both lawyers, it makes it sound like we're a law firm. I thought about calling her my faithful companion, but that makes her sound like a dog. Simply calling her my companion makes me sound like an old man and calling her my roomie isn't any better. I tried calling her my main squeeze, but that just got me a punch in the arm. So, I'm back to calling her my girlfriend, which is okay as long as Gracie doesn't find out.

Gracie is an Assistant District Attorney working in the Special Victims' Unit. I've known her from the old days when I worked in the DA's Office. We had a relationship back then that went south with the rest of my life when I was drinking heavily. After I sobered up, we got together again and have been basically living together ever since. You may find this strange, but I still have my own apartment, even though I don't spend many nights there. So why do I keep it? That's a good question. It's one of those questions I don't ask myself because I'm not sure I'd like the answer.

But enough about me, at least for now. Mr. Fang was still sitting across from me, and the pile of cash was still on the desk. I was struggling to understand who Mr. Fang wanted me to represent, him, who hadn't robbed the bank, or his grandson who "might" have robbed the bank. Either way it was going to be a tough job because there was no case pending against either one of them. Not that you had to wait for an arrest to hire a lawyer. But generally speaking, you have to be pretty sure you committed a crime or there's a good reason for you to be charged with one.

I asked Mr. Fang why he thought his grandson was one of the bank robbers. I thought it was a natural question under the circumstances. But the question seemed to take Mr. Fang by surprise. He just stared at me for a moment, and then he sipped his tea. When he finally answered, all he said was, "I have my reasons." I'm sure he did, but that wasn't good enough for me. I'm not one to look a gift horse in the mouth or anywhere else for that matter, but I wasn't going to take Mr. Fang's money on his hunch that his grandson might have been involved in a bank robbery.

I tried explaining that to Mr. Fang, but when I finished, he insisted that I at least look into the matter for him. I suggested he hire a private investigator and offered to introduce him to my investigator, Tommy Shoo, but Mr. Fang declined. He said he preferred having me represent him and his grandson, and if I thought the services of an investigator were necessary, I should hire one and he'd happily pay the bill. It seemed clear that Mr. Fang wasn't going to let this thing go, and I hated to think what might happen to him if the next lawyer he chose to consult was ethically challenged. There was a great deal of money setting on the desk, and I knew a few local ambulance chasers who'd sell their souls for a lot less. If you're thinking I was just looking for a way to keep the money myself, you'd be wrong.

What I did was offer to investigate the situation, using my contacts and Tommy Shoo. I figured a $5,000 retainer would cover the fees. That was about one-tenth of the amount of money piled on my desk. If the investigation failed to turn up evidence that Mr. Fang's grandson was involved in the bank robbery that would be the end of it. On the other hand, if we determined he was involved, then I'd talk with Mr. Fang about representing the kid, and we'd work out the terms.

My proposal met with Mr. Fang's approval, and he carefully peeled $5,000 off the pile of cash, leaving it on the desk and returning the remaining cash to the satchel hanging on his shoulder. With that settled, I asked Mr. Fang his grandson's name. For a minute I thought he wasn't going to tell me, which would have been the end of the whole deal, but then he said his grandson was Joey Chung. He said it like I should know who he was, but I didn't. I asked where Joey lived which I thought was a natural follow-up question, but Mr. Fang didn't seem to think so. That's when I told him if he wasn't going be open with me, I wouldn't be able to help him. He thought about it for a minute and took another sip of tea. Then he said, "Confucius Plaza." Confucius Plaza is a coop complex north of Chatham Square built in 1975 exclusively for Chinese Americans. It has 762 apartments and a fifteen-foot-high bronze statue of Confucius at the front of the complex. So, now I had a name and an address, and that seemed to be all I was going to get. But it was enough for now.

I had Connie draw up a retainer agreement while Mr. Fang finished his tea. Once the tea was done and the retainer agreement signed, Mr. Fang thanked me, bowed and left the office, his satchel containing the better part of $45,000 in cash hanging casually on his shoulder.

Mr. Fang, walking around with all that cash, wasn't surprising. In Chinatown, cash is king. You probably think it all comes from the illegal gambling, the drug trafficking, the human trafficking, and of course, the sale of counterfeit goods. Yeah, those businesses generate hundreds of millions of dollars a year in revenues, but even the legitimate businesses prefer dealing in cash. As I said, in Chinatown cash is king, especially with the old-timers who tend not to trust the bankers. Maybe they're smarter than the rest of us.

I used to wonder where there was more cash, in Chinatown or in the Federal Reserve Bank a few blocks away. After spending all these years in Chinatown, I'm betting it's in Chinatown.

CHAPTER 3

Shortly after Mr. Fang departed, Tommy Shoo, old man Shoo's grandson and my private investigator, arrived to report on a drug case he was investigating for me. The client was a girl with a mysterious past who was charged in a major drug case. Her name was Jenny Shao. Jenny had recently turned eighteen, and she was charged with multiple counts of drug possession with intent to sell, all Class A- felonies carrying prison terms of eight to twenty years. Although Jenny was in serious trouble, she wasn't being very cooperative in her defense. For one thing, she refused to tell me anything about herself or her past. For another, she refused to talk about her involvement with the Asian Empire street gang and how she got herself into this jam. All of it made defending her a challenge to say the least. That was why I had gotten permission from the 18B Panel Administrator to hire Tommy Shoo to do some investigating.

From what I saw at my two meetings with Jenny at the Rose M. Singer Women's Jail at Rikers Island where she was being held pending trial, she didn't appear to be a drug addict. I've interviewed enough addicts at Rikers to know when a prisoner is coming off drugs. Actually the signs are easy to spot. There's the sweating, the chills, the goose bumps, the muscle spasms, the watery eyes, and the nasal congestion. Often there's vomiting involved so you don't want to sit too close. But Jenny exhibited no signs of withdrawal, and from what I could see, she didn't have any track marks. She was calm, her eyes were clear, and her face wasn't puffy. If I had to bet, I'd put my money on her not being an addict. As for her being guilty, I had no idea and she wasn't helping me decide. All she would say was that she hadn't done anything wrong. How many times had I heard that before?

According to the arrest report, Jenny didn't have a criminal record, at least as far as the NYPD had been able to determine. That was in her favor, but it didn't mean much. It might help in a bail application, but even if the arraignment judge granted bail, Jenny couldn't afford to post it. She was an indigent defendant, meaning she had no money, and that was why the 18B Panel Administrator had assigned her case to me. Jenny, like all my 18B clients, was going to be locked up at Rikers until her trial.

Whatever details I knew about Jenny's case came strictly from the arrest report and the newspaper stories, and there were plenty of those. Jenny's arrest wasn't a simple one-on-one bust. No, Jenny was picked up in a huge citywide action conducted by the NYPD, the Drug Enforcement Administration and the FBI. It was a lengthy and well-executed operation called Asian Dragon. Aimed primarily at stemming the growing Chinese drug trade, its main targets were the Zheng Organization, operating out of Brooklyn, and the Asian Empire, a street gang operating in Manhattan's Chinatown, and the Chinese neighborhoods in Flushing.

Working secretly for months, the Task Force had compiled a list of people and locations, and in a series of coordinated early morning raids, the Task Force arrested over two hundred people, Jenny among them. Not since the Jade Squad, a NYPD operation in the 1980s, took down the leadership of the Flying Dragons and the Ghost Shadow street gangs, had Chinatown seen such a dramatic law enforcement operation.

Jenny was arrested in an after-hours joint on Pell Street along with seven others, mostly members of the Asian Empire. She wouldn't tell me why she was at the club, who she was with or why she was arrested when other patrons weren't. The fact that some patrons weren't arrested and Jenny was, told me Jenny was either a target on the cops' radar, or she was with the wrong crowd. I needed to know which it was, and I was hoping Tommy could provide those answers.

Tommy had spent the better part of a week trying to find out who Jenny Shao was, where she came from and how she was involved with the Asian Empire. Unfortunately, he wasn't able to come up with very much information. It seemed Jenny had no digital footprint, at least none that Tommy's computer wizard, Linda Chow, was able to find, and if Linda couldn't find one, it didn't exist. Linda was a computer genius. She could hack into any system in the world and access every database ever created. At least that's what Tommy claimed. But what do I know? I'm computer illiterate and happy to stay that way. When Linda is working on one of my cases, it's better for me if I don't know anything about anything. It's called plausible deny-ability, or some such thing. It means while Linda is hacking her way into places she shouldn't be, I can sit there dumb as a stump, and hopefully, not get disbarred or sent to jail. So far it's worked.

According to Linda, there were only two reasons why Jenny wouldn't have a digital footprint. One, Shao wasn't her real last name; or two, she was in the country illegally. I figured it was both. So if Jenny wasn't going to help, how was I going to defend her? Of course, that might not be a problem because if Linda figured out Jenny was here illegally, it wouldn't take long for the Feds to reach the same conclusion. Rather than try her in New York, it was easier and cheaper to simply deport her. Once those proceedings started, she'd no longer be eligible for 18B representation, and I'd be done with the case. As much as that would solve my problem, something about deporting her bothered me. It wasn't because I thought people shouldn't be deported; it was something about this kid. I had a feeling there was more to her story that I needed to know.

The address Jenny gave police when she was arrested was an old tenement building on the East Side. It was the same rundown, slum neighborhood I lived in when I was drinking and couldn't afford to live anywhere else. Tommy had tried interviewing Jenny's neighbors, but they weren't very cooperative, so he hadn't learned very much. One elderly woman, who lived on the same floor, said four people seemed to live in the apartment. Two were men; two were women; all were Chinese. The old lady identified Jenny from her mug shot as one of the tenants and said Jenny had recently moved out, but she didn't know where she had gone. She said Jenny was friendly, would always say hello, ask how she was doing, but the other three kept to themselves.

No one else in the building had anything to say about Jenny or the other occupants of the apartment. That was typical for the neighborhood. People kept to themselves or were too drunk or strung out to notice anything. I knew how that was. I grew up in Hell's Kitchen on the West Side where it was the same story. People kept to themselves because it was safer not knowing anything. If any of Jenny's neighbors knew anything, they weren't going to talk. So, where to now?

Tommy said he was trying to set up a meeting with one of his contacts in the Asian Empire gang. His guy wasn't really a member of the gang, more of a fringe player which was why he hadn't been picked up in the big sweep. But he knew a lot about the gang's members and activity, so Tommy was anxious to talk with him. Of course, the guy was nervous with all that had gone down, and he was being overly cautious. Tommy hoped he could work out a sit-down with the guy in a day or two. The way things were looking, that could be our best lead.

Tommy is what they call in Chinatown an ABC, American born Chinese. After his parents were killed in the 9/11 attack, he and his brother were taken in by their grandfather, old man Shoo, and raised in Chinatown. Growing up in Chinatown, they were totally immersed in Chinese culture. They both speak Cantonese fluently and can get by in other dialects. As a result, Tommy has access to people and information in Chinatown that I could never have. In Chinatown, I'm a foreigner in a foreign land, but Tommy is a native son. Or, almost a native son.

I told Tommy to keep working on Jenny's case, then I filled him in on our possible new case with our "maybe" bank robber. Once Tommy agreed to take the job, I went into my desk drawer and peeled $3000 from the roll of bills Mr. Fang had left earlier, and Tommy signed our standard contract. Tommy was going to be busy for the next few days.

CHAPTER 4

The Citibank robbery had been splashed all over the newspapers and the local TV stations. As far as bank robberies go, this one wasn't a big deal. What made it so fascinating was how the three suspects escaped.

From what I had read, the robbery was a run-of-the-mill job. Three masked and armed men had entered the bank at approximately eleven o'clock. They ordered all of the patrons and bank employees to lie on the floor, and while two of the perpetrators kept an eye on them, the third entered the vault and loaded over $300,000 into a duffel bag. The trio then exited through the bank's side door onto Mott Street. As soon as they were gone, the bank security guard exited through the bank's front door and ran into two NYPD officers on patrol on Chatham Plaza. The two officers raced around the corner onto Mott Street just in time to catch a glimpse of the three suspects crossing the street. When one of the cops yelled for the suspects to stop, two turned and opened fire on the cops. Taking cover behind a parked car, the cops returned fire, moving toward the suspects, using the parked cars for cover. Gunfire continued back and forth, and it was believed one of the suspects was wounded in the leg.

Here's where the story got intriguing. The suspects were last seen entering a sidewalk staircase to the basement of the Golden Wok Restaurant. Believing the suspects were trapped in the basement, one cop kept watch over the street entrance to the basement while the other went inside the restaurant to cover the inside basement access. Then they waited for reinforcements. By the time the SWAT team arrived, the local media were on the scene broadcasting live, and that ultimately created a big problem for the NYPD.

With the TV cameras trained on the building and the SWAT team, reporters on the scene chatted excitedly with anchors back at the studio about the impending raid. Viewers watched and listened as an NYPD negotiator tried to coax the three bandits out of the basement. When that failed, the SWAT team went into action.

It was all very dramatic, watching the SWAT team storm the basement and waiting for them to emerge with the three suspects in custody. But then it got embarrassing when the SWAT team came out empty-handed. There was no trace of the suspects. They had apparently vanished. Unfortunately for the NYPD, all of this was playing out live on every local TV station and in front of every news agency. No one could remember anything as embarrassing happening on live TV since Geraldo Rivera opened Al Capon's safe.

The big question was "*Where did they go?*" Speculation was rampart, and of course, the talking heads all had their theories, most of which centered on a secret tunnel.

It's been long rumored that a web of secret tunnels existed under all of Chinatown. I know for a fact that at least one such tunnel exists. I had a client who used the tunnel to pull off a pretty good stunt. I've never been in any of the secret tunnels, so I can't say for sure others exist. But I wouldn't be surprised if they do.

Chinatown's history is one of intrigue mixed with violence. In the early 1900s, there were the infamous Tong Wars, and Doyers Street, which curves sharply as it runs from Pell Street to Chatham Square, was known as the "Bloody Angle." It was so named for the murders that took place on the street. Supposedly the tunnels were used to escape from the cops, but also as a place to bury the bodies that nobody wanted found. That was all I knew of Chinatown's history at the time, but it was about to change.

I wasn't sure the cops believed a web of tunnels still existed, but there was no other way to explain the three suspects vanishing. Unless one of them was David Copperfield, a secret tunnel was the only way they could have escaped. So once the SWAT team secured the crime scene, the NYPD Emergency Service Unit went to work examining the basement. Unable to find the trio's escape route, their disappearance remained a mystery.

The newspapers continued to follow the case which they christened the Houdini Bandits case, but there was no news on how the suspects made their escape. Specialists from the FBI were called in to examine the basement for trap doors or escape hatches, but so far none had been found.

I know the cops and the FBI don't always tell the media the truth and sometimes they hide information. If Mr. Fang's grandson was involved, I had to find out what the cops really knew. Fortunately for me, the investigation hadn't been turned over to Major Crimes, but it was being handled by the detectives at the Fifth Precinct. I think the department, embarrassed at having lost the suspects in a basement with no apparent means of escape, was hoping to limit its embarrassment by keeping the case in the local precinct. Not that the embarrassment was going to end anytime soon.

Whatever the reason for keeping the investigation at the precinct level, it was good for me. I have my own contact in the Fifth Precinct, Detective Richard Chen, who I've known for years. I wouldn't call us close friends, but we get along well enough that over the years we've done each other favors. Chen is a good cop and a good man. Being a good cop, he wouldn't do anything shady and wouldn't share confidential information with me. But being a good man, if he sensed injustice being done, he'd drop a hint or two to put me on the right track.

I wanted to know a little bit more about the Citibank robbery, so I invited Detective Chen to have lunch with me at the Worth Street Coffee Shop. The Worth Street Coffee Shop is my unofficial second office. It's located across the street from the courthouse, so it's a convenient place to meet clients and witnesses before going to court. It's also a good place to meet people who might not want to be seen with me in their official capacity, if you get my drift. I knew Chen wouldn't be comfortable talking to me at the Fifth Precinct station house and he probably wouldn't want to be seen entering my office, so the Worth Street Coffee Shop was the perfect neutral place to meet. Just two friends having lunch.

CHAPTER 5

The Worth Street Coffee Shop is also a deli, a good New York City deli that serves good deli sandwiches. If you're not familiar with New York City delis, you might not know that a genuine deli pastrami or corned beef sandwich comes piled with an inch and a half to two inches of meat. Anything less isn't a real deli sandwich; it's just a sandwich and, trust me, it'll disappoint you. Pastrami and corned beef are meant to be eaten on thick rye bread, or on a club roll, smothered in deli mustard. If you don't have the right amount of meat in the sandwich, it just doesn't taste right. The sandwich has to be accompanied by a good kosher dill pickle and a side of coleslaw. That's a New York City deli lunch, and I feel sorry for anyone who's never had one.

I had a client who moved to South Carolina tell me about a local sandwich down there called a pulled pork sandwich. She swears it's just as good as a New York deli sandwich, but I refused to believe it. Besides, I'm Irish, so corned beef, not pork, is part of my heritage, or so I thought. But not long ago my friend sent me a couple of articles saying that corned beef and cabbage is not the traditional Irish meal; it's lamb, or bacon and cabbage. The switch to corned beef came about because the Irish immigrants in America in the late 1800s couldn't afford lamb, so they substituted the cheaper corned beef, or bacon, in its place. She had me on that, and I was forced to find a pulled pork sandwich in New York City. Much to my surprise, it wasn't hard to find a place that served pulled pork sandwiches in Manhattan. I admit it was a good sandwich, but it was no New York deli sandwich, that was for sure.

Anyway, I met Detective Chen at the coffee shop, and we both ordered pastrami sandwiches and coffee. It had been a while since we last spoke, so while waiting for our food to arrive, we did a little catching up. But my life doesn't change much and apparently neither does Chen's, so the catching up was over pretty quickly, and I got down to business.

I told Chen I might have a client who might have had something to do with the Citibank robbery. Even with all the "mights" thrown in, Chen still wanted to know more about my client. I explained that I didn't have a real client yet, and I didn't know if my potential client had anything to do with the robbery. Chen gave me a curious look and asked if this was all a joke. I assured him as incredible as the story sounded, it was no joke.

Our sandwiches arrived, and we took a break in our conversation. Given the girth of a good deli sandwich, it's difficult to eat and talk at the same time. There are some people capable of doing so, but generally they're ill-mannered slobs, and it's not a pretty sight. Chen and I munched away quietly.

Deli sandwiches are served cut in half, so when you finish the first half of the sandwich you can take a break. Maybe munch on the pickle and eat some coleslaw. It's also a good time to converse before tackling the second half of the sandwich. I can't say I was surprised when Chen asked again if this was a joke. I explained the situation as best I could without violating attorney-client privilege. I know I said that Mr. Fang wasn't yet a client but when he spoke to me, he did so because I was a lawyer, and he had the right to expect our conversation was privileged.

My explanation, as crazy as it was, satisfied Chen and while he said he couldn't give me a lot of the details, there were some things he could share. That was, if I agreed to surrender my client if and when I got a client, and if the client had anything to do with the bank robbery. The conversation was turning into something from Alice in Wonderland or maybe an Abbott and Costello routine. But what the hell? The whole situation was crazy.

I asked Chen right off if he had any suspects. Chen said no one in particular but they suspected the robbery was an inside job or involved someone from the armored truck company that transported cash to the bank. There was an unusually large amount of cash in the bank vault on the day of the robbery because a contractor working a nearby construction site had ordered a cash payroll. It was unusual to have a cash payroll and only someone working in the bank or someone working the armored truck delivering the cash that morning would have known about the extra money.

They had checked out the bank employees, and so far, no one had jumped out at them. They were still checking the armored truck company's employees, and they were starting to look at the contractor's people as well. Chen was sure that somewhere down the line someone who knew about the extra cash had given the information to the perpetrators. It was just a matter of finding that person.

There was something else puzzling about the robbery. According to several confidential informants, the job had been done without Hip Sing sanction. No crimes in Chinatown, except petty street crimes, are committed without tong sanction. At least not if the perps plan on keeping all of their body parts attached.

That sort of control over local crime isn't unusual in a ghetto. It's how things were in Little Italy when the Mafia ran the neighborhood. But those days are pretty much gone. Little Italy is becoming more and more a part of Chinatown, and the FBI crackdown on the Mafia three decades ago reduced it to a bunch of wannabe gangsters. In recent years, the Mafia has rebounded a bit as the FBI has focused its attention on terrorism and homeland security, but it's not like it was in the days of Don Corleone, and the odds are it never will be again.

But the Mafia wasn't my problem at the moment, the Citibank robbery was.

Chen wasn't sure that all three robbers were Chinese. None had bothered to wear masks, but they wore wide-brimmed hats and sunglasses. They were also smart enough to keep their heads down, and with the wide-brimmed hats, their faces couldn't be seen on the surveillance cameras. None of the customers or any of the bank employees was able to give the cops much of a description. Most said the perpetrators were Chinese, but some said they were Hispanic. Chen said the lack of witness details was likely due to what he called "gun distraction." I had heard the term before. It describes people's tendency to focus their attention on the gun when confronted by an armed perpetrator.

Since the robbers knew about the tunnels, Chen assumed they were locals. But locals who went against the tongs had to be crazy. Damn crazy, if you ask me. If Mr. Fang's grandson was involved in the robbery, being arrested and going to prison might be the least of his problems. If the tong got him before the cops, it wasn't going to be pretty.

If there was any good news, it was just that the bills were new and the serial numbers were all recorded. A bill alert had been issued, so if any of the bills were deposited in a bank or reached the Federal Reserve System, Chen's office would be notified. That in itself wouldn't help identify the robbers, but it would give the cops a place to start looking for them. Of course, if the robbers were caught with the money in their possession, then that would be the ball game.

As for physical evidence, there wasn't much, just some shell casings from the shoot-out and some blood evidence. The Crime Scene Unit had swept the bank and the bank's vault but came up empty. The three men had been careful not to brush up against any furniture, walls or doorways. Not that Chen had expected to find anything useful. Sorting through the hundreds of fingerprints you'd typically find at any commercial establishment wasn't likely to produce any helpful leads.

The Crime Scene Unit did collect shell casings on Mott Street where the shoot-out with the patrol officers had taken place. All totaled, CSU recovered thirty-two shell casings, all 9 millimeter calibers. The two patrol officers said they had fired a total of twelve shots. The location of the shell casings and an examination of the cops' weapons confirmed their story. That meant the perps had fired twenty shots at the two cops.

CSU also found and documented blood splatter and a trail of blood drops on Mott Street and the adjoining sidewalk. The findings were consistent with the claim that one of the robbers was wounded in the shoot-out. The patrol officer who fired the shot claimed he hit the robber in the lower leg. Blood splatter and bullet damage found on the bumper of a car supported his claim. Based on the physical evidence, CSU believed the bullet struck the robber in the calf and went through the muscle, hitting the car bumper. The blood drops began at the same location and continued in a straight line for approximately twenty feet down Mott Street. Then the droppings ended. CSU and Chen believed the wounded robber realized that he was leaving a trail and had dressed the wound to stop the bleeding. Blood samples collected at the scene were run through DNA databases, but no matches were found.

That was it as far as physical evidence was concerned. I was anxious to get to the next part of the story, the basement escape, but Chen apparently didn't share my interest in moving on quickly. Instead he picked up the second half of his sandwich and started eating. I can't say that I blame him; after all, the next part of the story was the embarrassing part. The part where the NYPD lost three bank robbers in a locked basement. I can't say I'd be anxious to talk about that if I was in Chen's place. Following Chen's lead, I picked up the second half of my sandwich, and the two of us ate quietly.

As I savored the final bite of my sandwich, Chen downed the last of his coffee and resumed telling his story. The two patrol officers chased the trio of suspects down Mott Street, taking cover behind the parked cars as they advanced. The last they saw of the suspects was when the suspects entered the basement of the Golden Wok Restaurant through the sidewalk stairwell. The patrol officers approached the basement entrance cautiously. The staircase went down to what appeared to be a heavy steel door. If the officers tried entering the basement through that doorway while the armed suspects were still in the basement, the officers would be sitting ducks.

Sizing up the situation, the officers wisely decided to wait for backup to arrive before trying to enter the basement from the street. One of the officers then kept watch over the street entrance to the basement, while the other officer went into the restaurant to find out if there were other entrances and exits from the basement. The restaurant owner said there was a staircase to the basement in the kitchen, but it was locked from the inside. Checking the story, the officer found the door locked but taking no chances, she kept it under surveillance until the SWAT team arrived.

Chen said he arrived on the scene at the same time as the SWAT team. A cadre of heavily armed officers wearing body armor formed a semicircle around the sidewalk staircase leading to the basement. Then Chen and the lieutenant who headed up the SWAT team, along with three other members of the SWAT team, went into the restaurant's kitchen and spoke with the patrol officer guarding the door. After hearing what she had to say, they were then convinced that the three suspects made a big mistake and were trapped in the restaurant's basement.

For the next two hours, while the local TV stations broadcast events live, members of the NYPD's Hostage Unit tried to coax the suspects into surrendering. When that didn't work, the SWAT Commander organized a raid plan. Breaching the sidewalk entrance would be too dangerous, so the plan was to enter through the kitchen doorway. The NYPD Emergency Services Unit was called in to evaluate the best way to remove the door quickly and without putting officers at risk. In less than twenty minutes, the ESU people worked quietly to remove the hinge pins, attached pull handles to the door and were ready to pull it down. With the SWAT team standing by and ready, the door was pulled out and two flashbang grenades were tossed into the basement. Flashbang grenades, or stun grenades as they're sometimes called, are non-lethal explosives that produce deafening noises and blinding light, all of which work to disorient anyone in the vicinity of the explosion. Before the smoke from the grenades even started to clear, the SWAT team rushed down the stairs.

It wasn't long before the SWAT team reported the basement was clear; there was no one found in the basement. With the TV cameras rolling, and the commentators excitedly explaining how the three bandits were about to be marched out of the basement in handcuffs, the SWAT team came up from the basement onto the sidewalk empty-handed.

At that point, the white shirts, as the big boys from police headquarters are called, all slipped away and headed back to One Police Plaza. They had shown up for only one reason, publicity. Had things gone right, they'd have been front and center talking to the media, but as things turned out, they wanted no part of the operation. That left Chen and the SWAT team Lieutenant to argue who would do the press conference. Neither one wanted the honor of standing there trying to explain what had happened. In the end, Chen lost the coin toss and was forced to face the media.

The media coverage was brutal, especially the *New York Daily News*, which proclaimed "BANDITS ESCAPE WHILE NYPD WASTES THREE HOURS SURROUNDING EMPTY BASEMENT TALKING TO THEMSELVES." Chen said after the fiasco no one in the department wanted to be associated with the case. Usually a bank robbery case is turned over to the Major Case Squad, but the Commander of the squad made it clear he wanted nothing to do with the case. So poor Detective Chen was left holding the bag. The Houdini Bandits were all his.

In the days following the robbery, Chen brought in the ESU team to examine the basement for possible escape routes. When they came up empty, Chen called in a favor and got the FBI forensics unit to conduct its own investigation. Again, nothing.

I asked Chen about the rumored tunnels and if they might have played a part in the escape. He said he had heard rumors about the tunnels for years, but only once had he actually seen one. That was the tunnel my client allegedly used in robbing and killing a Triad boss. Of course, no one was ever able to prove it was my client who committed the crime, but the FBI did eventually find the tunnel where the murder took place.

Chen said if that tunnel existed, there could be more tunnels as of yet undiscovered. There were law enforcement agents who believed that Chinatown's counterfeiting rings had a network of secret underground rooms, accessed through basements and subbasements throughout Chinatown. Rooms large enough to store counterfeit goods and even house factories. Some agents believed these subterranean rooms were connected by a series of tunnels. It sounded far-fetched, but Chen said he couldn't ignore the possibility. After all, Chinatown was famous for hidden rooms, secret passages and even tunnels, and it would explain how his suspects got away.

Chen was working all angles, but so far nothing was popping. None of the local hospitals or doctors had reported treating a gunshot wound. Of course, that didn't mean anything. In New York City there were plenty of places to have a gunshot wound treated without it being reported to the police. It just cost a lot more money doing it that way. Chen had his people put pressure on all the known "off the books" doctors, but none would admit to treating a lower leg bullet wound.

None of the stolen cash had yet been reported by any bank. That didn't mean the robbers weren't spending the cash; it just meant none of it had passed through a bank yet. If and when it did, tracing it back to the robbers would be difficult, but not entirely impossible. I thought Chen's take on that was a bit too optimistic, but given the mess he was in, I figured he was clutching at straws.

That was all Chen had to say, and it hadn't been much. Most of it I already knew from reading the papers. I didn't think Chen was holding out on me; I figured he told me all he knew. It seemed the robbers had pulled off a pretty good crime which made catching them tough. Normally that wasn't a big deal. NYPD would investigate the crime until the trail went cold, then the case would be filed with all the unsolved cases. But in this instance with all the publicity the case had received, there was no way it was going to quietly fade away. Chen would be on the hook for a long time.

Now that Chen was done telling me his side of the story, I knew what was coming next. He wanted to know about my client, or should I say my potential client? I told him the whole thing was very fuzzy, and I wasn't comfortable talking about it. At least not yet. But I promised I'd get back to him if things firmed up. I felt sorry for Chen, but there wasn't much I could do other than pay for lunch.

CHAPTER 6

My fascination with the Chinatown tunnels took a back seat the following day when the New York County grand jury returned indictments against 114 of 201 suspects arrested in Operation Asian Dragon, including Jenny Shao. Eighty-six of the suspects arrested were illegal immigrants and turned over to ICE for deportation. The remaining eleven unindicted suspects, presumably the heads of the drug cartel, had been charged in Federal Court where the penalties are more severe. My problem was that I had no idea how I was going to defend Jenny Shao. She wasn't talking, and Tommy wasn't coming up with any information to help in her defense. Now arraignments were being scheduled, and I was going to have to do something. The best I could do under the circumstances was to plead her not guilty, then play duck and cover.

From what I could tell, Jenny was in the bottom tier of defendants and not one of the District Attorney's primary targets. Her name made the newspapers just once, two days after Operation Asian Dragon, when a list of all two hundred and one defendants was published in the *New York Post*. Since then only a couple of dozen names made it into print, and Jenny's name wasn't one of them. In these types of cases, the District Attorney likes to strike while the iron is hot, and he can get the most favorable press coverage. That means pulling out all the stops and going after the most notorious defendants first. Since the Feds had the top tier defendants, the District Attorney had to be content with the next level down, but he couldn't politically afford to slip much further down the line. He needed some quick convictions before the public lost interest or before the Feds grabbed all the headlines.

The DA wanted quick convictions, preferably without a trial, but getting quick convictions wasn't always easy. The top-level dealers could afford top-notch defense attorneys who would often drag out cases waiting for the publicity to die down. Then if there was a trial, there was always the risk of a not guilty verdict, especially if witnesses disappeared or juries were bribed. So, it was in the DA's interest to get quick, clean guilty pleas. The best way to make that happen, without having to give away the store, was to get a lower level suspect to roll over on the bosses. Not an easy task in itself, but a lot less difficult when you had a couple of dozen potential rollover candidates to work with.

Even though Jenny hadn't confided in me, I knew instinctively that she wasn't a big enough fish for the DA to try to turn. The seven clowns she was arrested with were all low level Asian Empire gangbangers, who Tommy had assured me were all bottom feeders. If Jenny was involved with the Asian Empire, it was only with the lowest ranking members, and she certainly wouldn't have any information worth trading. No, her best bet was to lay low and wait for the DA to lose interest in the case. Once the top tier defendants were put away, the pressure to get convictions would be off, and the media would lose interest. That's when the DA would look to clear the books and start offering better plea deals. That's what happens in big cases like this one. It's simply a matter of practicality, and it pays to know the ropes.

Everyone arrested in Operation Asian Dragon had been charged with the same long list of crimes. The list was a wish list more than anything else. It made for good media coverage and good publicity for the NYPD, the Mayor and the District Attorney. But once the dust settled and after the drug lords had been put away, the DA still had to deal with the dozens of remaining defendants, knowing damn well he couldn't make cases against some of them, at least not on the pending charges. That was why I was certain at some point I could get the charges pending against Jenny reduced even without her cooperation. But I could do better if I had her cooperation.

The key was to delay proceedings for as long as possible. Yes, that meant Jenny remained in jail pending trial, but the alternative was a quick trial followed by a really long prison term. If I worked things out as I hoped to do, in the end Jenny would plead to a misdemeanor and be sentenced to time served. That was the best-case scenario, but to make it happen I needed

Jenny's cooperation. That's why I was heading back to Rikers to talk with her again.

I've made hundreds of trips to Rikers Island. Given my choice, I prefer to go by way of subway and bus and avoid taxicabs. I hate riding in taxicabs. Always have, and always will. I call it a "thing." Gracie calls it an irrational phobia. She keeps telling me to get over it, but even if I could, which I doubt, I won't. Yes, in case you hadn't noticed I'm pigheaded and proud of it. Of course, I'll never admit that to Gracie, and if you tell her I said that, I'll never talk to you again. So why am I going on like this? Because on the day in question I had to endure another terrifying taxicab ride, this time at the hands of Nicholas Karadopolous. Yes. I take names, and I record them in my little book, which isn't so little anymore. The only thing I can say about the ride was, as a recovering alcoholic, it's important that I find something to be grateful about every day and getting out of that taxicab in one piece was something to be grateful about. Of course, when you think about it, it could have gone the other way. I could have gotten out of the taxicab and gone directly into a bar.

When I finally sat down with Jenny, I tried to impress upon her the seriousness of her situation, but she just looked at me and said nothing. I told her she had been indicted, and if we didn't come up with a defense, she was facing twenty-five years in prison. That didn't seem to bother her, so after a while I just gave up and told her I'd see her at her arraignment. I left my card and said if she changed her mind and wanted to talk, she should call me. I wasn't holding my breath on that one.

I left Rikers feeling depressed. This kid's life was just beginning, and for some reason, I couldn't fathom, she was about to throw it away, and there was nothing I could do to stop her. I needed some therapy of my own, so on my way back downtown, I called my AA sponsor, Doug. Doug is also a lawyer, but he's smart. He doesn't practice criminal law; he practices business law and makes money. I don't call him for legal advice, just cheap therapy. Whenever I feel I'm starting to go off the rails, I know it's time to call Doug

CHAPTER 7

When I got back from Rikers, Tommy was waiting in my office to report on Joey Chung, Mr. Fang's grandson, and the news wasn't good. Tommy had Linda Chow run a complete computer search on Joey, but very little turned up. Other than a juvenile conviction for petty larceny, Joey's record was clean, and he apparently kept a low profile. With nothing turning up on the computer, Tommy was forced to do some old-fashioned legwork. Armed with a photograph of Joey provided by Mr. Fang, Tommy had spent the better part of a week touring Chinatown looking for Joey or someone who knew where he was.

He'd staked out Chung's apartment in Confucius Plaza and interviewed Chung's neighbors, but no one had seen him in a while. One neighbor told Tommy about a club where Joey usually hung out, and Tommy put a man on the club, but no Joey. Tommy was beginning to suspect Joey might have skipped town.

That's what Tommy was telling me when Connie announced that Mr. Fang was on the phone and needed to talk with me. He said he was at Shoo's Restaurant, and it was imperative that I meet him there in ten minutes. When I asked him why, he said, "All things are unknown before they are known. It is extremely important that you come now." Then he hung up. The phone call at least confirmed my suspicion that Fang had come to me on the recommendation of old man Shoo. But why the sudden urgency to meet, and why at Shoo's place?

Walking down Mott Street to Shoo's, I told Tommy what I had learned from Chen, and we both concluded that Joey was with Mr. Fang at Shoo's. Tommy wanted to join the meeting, but I thought it best if I went in alone. If Joey wanted to meet, it meant he was involved in the bank job, and I didn't want to spook him and chance him taking off. I figured it hadn't been an easy job convincing Joey to meet with me, and I didn't want to blow the whole thing up. Tommy would wait outside, and I'd call him if and when I needed him.

As I walked through the front door, old man Shoo came out of the kitchen and with a smile and a nod of his head, he pointed me toward the backroom. There I found Mr. Fang and a young man seated at what had been my old desk. Mr. Fang bowed his head and invited me to take a seat. A pot of tea and three cups were on the desk, and Fang filled each cup up, offering the first to me. With a simple bow of my head, I accepted the cup and waited for Fang to serve himself and the young man that I presumed was his grandson, Joey Chung. Joey looked to be in his early twenties. He was thin; you might even say skinny. He was also on the short side, but good looking. He was also obviously nervous, and his hands shook as he sipped his tea.

The tea ceremony completed, Mr. Fang formally introduced his grandson. Here's where things got interesting. Generally I never ask a client if they're guilty. Why? Because if the client wants to take the witness stand and testify, I can't allow that client to lie. If I know that the client is guilty and allow him or her to say otherwise, we're both in deep shit. Besides, a client may be guilty of something, but not necessarily to the degree they're being charged. So that's why I make it a practice not to ask a client if they're guilty.

In Joey Chung's case, it was different. We wouldn't be sitting in Shoo's backroom carrying on a conversation if he hadn't been involved in the bank job. He hadn't been charged; he wasn't even a suspect, so why hire a lawyer unless he had something to do with the crime? But I wasn't going to assume anything, so I said simply, "What can I do for you?"

Joey looked at his grandfather who nodded his head, then turning to me, Joey said, "I helped rob the bank." Okay, now we were on the same page, and it was time to get serious, but first things first. I asked Joey if he wanted me to be his attorney, and when he said yes, his grandfather pulled a wad of cash from his satchel and put it on the table. Tempting as it was to simply take the cash, I couldn't. I told Mr. Fang that Joey needed to sign a retainer agreement, and if he, Mr. Fang, was going to be paying the bills, he needed to sign it also. Mr. Fang nodded in agreement, and I suggested we walk to my office and complete the paperwork. That's when Joey blanched, and Mr. Fang said, "No."

Now I was confused. Was he refusing to sign a retainer agreement or refusing to come to my office? When I asked Mr. Fang to explain, he said it wasn't safe for Joey to be seen entering a lawyer's office, and that's why we were meeting in secret at Shoo's. Playing dumb, which I do well, I asked why he thought it was dangerous for Joey to come to my office. I figured that I knew the answer, but I wanted to hear it from Mr. Fang and Joey, so I'd know we were all on the same page. Mr. Fang nodded to Joey, who said that if the other two guys found out he was talking with a lawyer, they might kill him.

"Might" wasn't the word I would have used, but it was still a good reason to be cautious. I knew there was more to it than that and so did Mr. Fang. It was a Chinatown thing. No crimes are committed in Chinatown without the Hip Sing Tong getting a share of the proceeds. I knew that, and I was sure Mr. Fang knew it too. I could tell by the look in his eyes. It was the only time thus far that I had seen any emotion in those eyes, and what I saw was fear. But if he didn't want to talk about the possible tong involvement at that point, he must have had his reasons, and that was okay by me. We wouldn't talk any further about the risk Joey faced until I heard Joey's story.

I suggested that I prepare the paperwork, and then we'd meet again at Shoo's in an hour and start working. Mr. Fang, who had recovered his composure, nodded. At the risk of ruffling his composure, I said that I wanted a $75,000 retainer. That didn't seem to faze him; he simply nodded.

I picked up Tommy outside of the restaurant, and together we walked back to my office. I told Tommy what had happened and that I'd be representing Joey. Since Tommy was already on the case, I didn't have to worry about client confidentiality. Anything I told Tommy was covered under the attorney-client privilege. Back at the office, I had Connie draw up the retainer agreement, then I grabbed a yellow legal pad, some pens and headed back to Shoo's.

CHAPTER 8

Back at Shoo's, you could say it was like old times sitting there at my former desk. But it was different, this time I wasn't drunk and there wasn't a bottle of scotch in the desk drawer. Even though it hadn't been that many years since I sat at the desk drunk, in reality it was a lifetime ago. I still remembered well those days of alcoholic drinking, the loneliness, the pain, and the self-loathing that went with it. I remember because if I don't, I'll probably drink again. So, I remember those days, and I go to AA meetings, and I share my experiences with other alcoholics like myself looking to stay sober.

I'll tell you candidly that sitting at my desk on that day, I felt the tingle I used to feel just before I opened the drawer and pulled out the scotch bottle. I knew what that meant. As soon as I was done with Joey and Mr. Fang, I'd call my sponsor, Doug, and before day's end, I'd go to a meeting. But first there was business to attend to.

Mr. Fang and Joey arrived right on time, and they were ushered into the backroom by old man Shoo. Joey was wearing a sweatshirt with a hood pulled over his head, and he looked nervous. Mr. Fang, on the other hand, had apparently regained his equilibrium and was wearing his inscrutable game face. There was no telling what was going on in his head.

I explained to both of them that before we got down to business, they needed to sign retainer agreements. That way there would be no question that I was Joey's lawyer, and everything said from then on would be covered by attorney-client privilege. I explained the terms of the agreements Connie had typed up earlier and gave copies to Joey and Mr. Fang to sign. Joey, apparently not satisfied with my explanation, asked his grandfather why he had to sign an agreement. Mr. Fang, handing Joey a pen said, "The palest ink is better than the best memory." You couldn't argue with that.

Joey signed the agreement without reading it which wasn't unusual as most clients don't bother reading it. But Mr. Fang read it very carefully before signing it. Then he opened his satchel, removed a pile of money and set it on the desk. There were fifteen bundles of $50 bills, making a total of $75,000. Counting the money would be rude; besides, I had learned long ago that Chinese businessmen don't cheat that way. A debt is a debt, and one doesn't welsh on a debt.

I thanked Mr. Fang with a nod of my head and put the stack of bills in my briefcase. Then I said to Joey, "So, tell me your story."

Joey had one hell of an interesting story. He was essentially what I call a knockabout. He'd inherited a large sum of money when his parents were killed in an automobile accident. At the time he was nineteen years old and a freshman at NYU. His parents' deaths had hit him hard, and he quit school, intending to go back in a year or two. But as time passed, he lost interest in school and just about everything else other than partying. With all the money he inherited, he didn't need to work. He sold his parents' condominium in Soho, bought himself an apartment in Confucius Plaza and began living the life of a playboy. He hung out in the after-hours clubs in Chinatown, dabbled in recreational drugs, and dated a lot. In other words, he was generally wasting his life.

Two years ago, his stock account took a big hit, and he was forced to adjust his lifestyle downward. An adjustment he didn't care for. That's when he became acquainted with Bobby and Billy Cha, who hung out at his favorite after-hours club providing drugs to patrons in need.

As far as Joey knew, the Cha brothers weren't part of any organized street gang or tong. Although they sold drugs, did some loan sharking, and dealt occasionally in counterfeit goods, their operation was small enough to stay under the radar of both the NYPD and the local Chinatown gangsters. At least up until now.

With his lifestyle in jeopardy due to his diminishing funds, Joey turned first to his grandfather for help. Mr. Fang disapproved of Joey's lifestyle and refused to give him any money. That's when Joey turned to the Cha brothers, looking for a way to earn some cash. He started selling small quantities of drugs to people in the after-hours clubs. It was no biggie, and the bucks weren't big, but it was enough to keep Joey happy. When Bobby and Billy offered get Joey more involved, he turned them down.

Then things changed for the Cha brothers. The Asian Empire discovered they were working its territory and issued a warning. They cut off the pinky fingers of both brothers and threatened to remove more body parts if the brothers didn't cease and desist their operations. Sufficiently frightened, the brothers abandoned their businesses, content to live on money they had stashed away earlier. But when that money started to run out, they came up with the plan to rob a bank. When they approached Joey about joining them, he refused. There was no way he'd do anything like that.

Joey said he turned them down because he knew what would happen if he got caught. At seventeen, he and a high school buddy had stolen a car, gotten caught and wound up with a record. Fortunately, his parents had understood and with the help of a good lawyer, he had gotten off as a juvenile offender and hadn't wound up spending time in jail. But the experience had been enough to keep him basically on the straight and narrow since. He didn't consider selling small amounts of recreational drugs to adult friends a crime, but robbing a bank was definitely a no, no.

After being approached and turning down the Cha brothers, Joey didn't hear anything further about the bank job for a few months. Then two weeks ago, he met up with Bobby and Billy at the club, and they told him the bank job was on, but they had a problem. The way the job had been planned, it was a three-man operation, but their third man had just escaped the country and gone back to China before being arrested on a murder charge. You would have thought that was enough to scare Joey off, but apparently it wasn't. The two brothers convinced him it was a quick and easy job that would net him over a hundred grand.

The brothers had an insider at the bank. Her name was Nancy, and she was a teller at the Citibank on Mott Street. She was also a regular at one of the clubs where the brothers sold dope. One night Nancy's money ran out before her need for a fix, and she offered Bobby Cha information about one of the bank's customers in exchange for a little smack. It seemed this particular customer, CT Builders, a local construction company, was one of the last of the bank's customers to still pay its employees in cash. That was probably because most of its employees were illegal aliens, but it didn't bother the bank manager.

CT Builders was a relatively small company, but it occasionally managed to pull down a big job and when it did, the bi-monthly payroll could exceed $300,000. CT Builders paid its employees every two weeks on Friday. On the Monday before payday, the CT bookkeeper would call the bank's manager and order the cash. One of Nancy's jobs was to prepare the transfer order, and that was how she knew when and how much the payroll would be.

When CT Builders had a big job, the amount of the payroll usually exceeded the amount of cash the bank kept on hand, and the bank manager would call the Federal Reserve Bank the day before the payroll was due and order cash delivered the following morning. The next day the cash would be delivered by an armored car and stored in the vault until armed guards from CT Builders came to pick it up.

The information Nancy gave Bobby that night was good enough to buy her a hit of cocaine and to get Bobby and Billy interested in robbing the Citibank. They scouted out the location, concluded it was an easy score and then went about planning the job.

The bank had two entrances, the main door on Chatham Square and a side door on Mott Street. The bank was relatively small, and it had only one security guard, an elderly man, unlikely to pose a problem. Bobby, the supposed brains of the operation, saw it as a three-man job. The plan was for two to enter through the Chatham Square entrance and one through the Mott Street entrance. Once inside, they'd quickly overpower the old security guard, and they'd get all the customers and bank employees to lie on the floor in the middle of the bank where they could keep an eye on them from the doorways. Then while one man guarded the Chatham Square entrance and the second man guarded the Mott Street entrance, the third would go into the vault and load the cash into a duffel bag. They'd leave the bank by way of the Mott Street door and blend in with the ever-present Mott Street crowd.

If the job was done correctly, the Cha brothers figured the whole operation would take less than six minutes. So, even if someone managed to trigger a silent alarm, they'd be out of the bank before the cops could respond. All they needed was the word from Nancy that CT Builders had ordered a large cash payroll. Bobby kept supplying Nancy with enough cocaine to keep her on the line while he and his brother recruited their third partner.

When Joey said he wasn't interested in the job, the brothers found someone else. But the day Nancy told them a $325,000 payroll had been ordered for delivery, their third man took off for China. In desperation, the brothers again approached Joey. This time they were more insistent, and Joey, figuring it was a quick, easy job, agreed to join them. But he did have one condition; he wouldn't carry a gun. That condition was the only smart thing Joey did. The brothers agreed to the condition, and Joey was assigned the job of collecting the cash from the vault.

On the day of the robbery, things initially went as planned. The trio sat in a coffee shop across from the bank and watched as the armored truck delivered the cash for the payroll right on schedule at ten o'clock. That gave the Cha brothers and Joey a two-hour window before the armed guards from CT Builders arrived to pick up the money.

At eleven o'clock, the bank appeared to be relatively empty, and that's when the three went into action. They entered the bank, and while Billy made his way to the Mott Street door, Bobby walked up to the security guard as if to ask a question. Joey just walked toward one of the teller cages. Then Bobby pulled his gun, held it to the security guard's head and told everyone to raise their hands. He then took the guard's gun and put it in the waistband of his pants.

In the meantime, Billy who had also pulled his gun told everyone to come into the center of the bank and lay on the floor. As they did that, Joey jumped over the teller counter and went into the vault. He opened the duffel bag he had carried folded up inside his jacket and began loading it with cash. The money was on two shelves, neatly banded and stacked.

Joey figured they were out of the bank and on Mott Street in less than five minutes. It seemed everything had gone as planned. But then they heard cops yelling at them. Billy turned and started shooting at the cops who fired back. Bobby joined in shooting at the cops, and the three of them ran across Mott Street, Joey still carrying the duffel bag with the money in it. Just as they were getting to the other side, Billy yelled out he'd been hit in the leg.

It wasn't a bad wound, and he was able to keep running. They ran down the sidewalk on the south side of Mott Street, using the parked cars for cover.

When Bobby noticed Billy leaving a trail of blood, he stopped and told Billy to bandage his leg while he kept the cops pinned down. Joey was beginning to think they were finished, what with the cops shooting at them and more cops likely to arrive at any minute. But once Billy had wrapped a piece of his shirt around his leg wound, Bobby said to follow him, and he led them down a set of stairs into a dark basement. Bobby turned on the lights, and Joey saw stairs leading up to a doorway. He figured they'd make their escape that way. But he was wrong.

Bobby told Joey to sling the duffel bag over his shoulder and grab his hand. He then said to hold onto Billy with his other hand. Joey had no idea what was happening; then Bobby turned off the light and the basement went pitch black dark again. Bobby started moving very slowly, pulling Joey and Billy along. Joey couldn't see anything; it was too dark, but he heard a squeaking, like a big door or panel moving. Then he felt a cold breeze, and as he moved forward being pulled along by Bobby, he heard the squeaking noise again, this time behind him.

After a minute, Bobby stopped and a light went on. They were in a tunnel. Bobby said to sit and take a rest. Joey unslung the duffel bag and sat on the damp floor. Bobby examined Billy's leg; it was a clean through and through wound, nothing to worry about. They sat for a while, laughing and congratulating each other on their success, then Bobby led them through the tunnel and they ended up in the basement of an old tenement building on Bayard Street.

Bobby counted the money. It was $345,000, so each share was $115,000. But Bobby said it was too dangerous to spend any of it, so he'd store it until it was safe, then they'd split up. They waited in the building until it was dark outside, then the three of them left. Joey went home to his apartment and decided it might be wise to get lost for a while. He had been spending the last week or so with a girlfriend in SoHo avoiding his usual haunts, just in case the cops were on to him.

He hadn't seen either of the Cha brothers since the robbery and didn't know if they were still around.

Joey was done talking. Now he and his grandfather were looking to me to tell them what to do.

CHAPTER 9

I explained to Joey and his grandfather that the only way Joey could help himself was to turn himself in and roll over on the Cha brothers. He'd also have to help recover the money. If he did that, he'd have credibility with the District Attorney and leverage to cut a better deal. It was unlikely he'd get away without doing some prison time, but hopefully not more than a year or two. Joey didn't look happy, so I reminded him he had committed an armed robbery, and if convicted, he could be sentenced to twenty-five years in prison.

Joey said if I was able to get him a good deal, he'd give up Billy and Bobby Cha, but he didn't know where the money was. Then he asked what would happen if he didn't turn himself in but waited until he was arrested to cut a deal. I said he'd lose some of his leverage, and he'd wind up with a longer prison term. Of course, Joey pointed out he might never be arrested, and turning himself in could be a stupid thing to do.

He had a point, but not a good one. Every criminal thinks his crime is the perfect crime. But in today's day and age, there are hardly any perfect crimes. Sooner or later nearly everyone gets caught. The few who don't get caught are the really smart guys, and the Cha brothers didn't strike me as being really smart.

Joey thought about all of it, then he pointed out that if the Cha brothers found out he'd turned on them, they might try to kill him. That was a misconception that needed to be corrected. Joey had to be told that given the opportunity, there was no doubt the Cha brothers would try to kill him. I hadn't clarified that yet because I thought it added a negative tone to the conversation. Talking about being killed tends to upset people, especially when they're the one winding up dead. In a conversation where you have both good and bad news, you don't want to bring up the bad news right away because if you do, people tend to focus on it and not listen to the good news. Not that going to prison was good news, but it was certainly better than being killed by the Cha brothers. But now that Joey had brought it up, we needed to talk about it.

It was also time to talk about that "thing" we hadn't talked about at Shoo's Restaurant the first time I met Joey. The Chinatown thing, or to be more accurate, the Hip Sing Tong thing. It was more bad news for Joey. It wasn't only the Cha brothers who might be looking to put him in an early grave. If the Cha brothers hadn't cleared the robbery with the Hip Sing Tong, which would have included sharing the stolen money, the tong wouldn't be happy, and we all knew what happens when the Hip Sing Tong is unhappy. I could tell from the look on Joey's face that the job hadn't been sanctioned, and now he realized he was in bigger trouble than he thought. Even if he didn't turn on the Cha brothers, he'd still have a target on his back.

As I explained the facts of life in Chinatown to Joey, Mr. Fang sat quietly nodding his head. As expected, nothing I had said came as a shock to him. He had known all along that the tong would take revenge; he simply hadn't wanted to talk about it before Joey was committed to turning himself in. It was a smart move on his part.

I saw two ways to avoid having Joey killed by the Cha brothers or by the Hip Sing Tong. One was to have him locked up in protective custody, which in most cases gave him a better than fifty-fifty chance of staying alive. Rikers Island isn't the most secure place in the world, and prisoners being held in protective custody have been killed. The second option was to have Joey released on bail, then hidden by his grandfather. I was sure his grandfather could do a better job of hiding Joey than could the Department of Corrections. Naturally, Joey and his grandfather favored option number two. I asked Mr. Fang if he was willing to put up bail money, or at least pay the bond fee, presuming I could cut a deal with the DA. The old man nodded and said he was prepared to put up as much as one million dollars if need be. I have to say I was impressed. I've never had a client willing to put up that much money for anything.

The first thing I had to do was call Chen and set up a meeting with him and someone from the DA's Office. Not just the riding ADA assigned to cover the Fifth Precinct, but someone with authority to cut a deal. If we got the terms I wanted, then Joey would turn himself in. If the DA played hardball and wouldn't agree to our terms, I'd meet again with Joey and his grandfather, and we'd go over our options. Until he heard back from me, Joey was to lay low and keep off the streets. More importantly, he wasn't to have any contact with the Cha brothers.

Joey didn't want to chance being seen with me, so he and his grandfather left Shoo's Restaurant first, then I left a few minutes later. Joey was being smart. Once word got out, and it would, that a suspect had been arrested in the Citibank case, the Cha brothers would know they were in deep shit, and it would be obvious who put them there. They'd probably go underground, run, or kill Joey. Or maybe all three. Not to mention what the Hip Sing Tong might have in mind for Joey's future, so it was good that Joey was taking precautions to keep himself alive.

When I got back to the office, I put in a call to Detective Chen. I explained the situation and told him I wanted to set up a meeting right away with him and a senior member of the DA's staff, someone with the authority to cut deals. Chen said he understood what I wanted, and he'd get back to me as quickly as he could.

It didn't take long. Twenty minutes later, Chen called back and said Marty Bowman, a Deputy District Attorney, would meet with us in his office in an hour. I said I'd be there.

It was good news. I knew Marty Bowman and had dealt with him on a big case not that long before. Marty was sharp, but also practical, and he'd know a good deal when he saw one.

I figured Marty was available to meet sooner, but he wanted to talk with Chen before I arrived. That was smart, and it didn't worry me. First of all, there was nothing I could do about it. Besides, I knew Chen was anxious to get his hands on the suspect, so he wasn't about to say anything that could torpedo the deal. In fact, I was counting on Chen supporting my demands. It's always better being in the majority in a two on one situation than being in the minority.

CHAPTER 10

The DA's Office is a short walk from my office, so I arrived early enough to drop in on Gracie before meeting with Chen and Bowman. Gracie was surprised to see me and asked what I was doing in the building. I said that I was there to meet with Marty Bowman to try and arrange a surrender deal for my client. I had talked to Gracie about my meetings with Mr. Fang, so she knew what I was talking about. I asked her if she had any advice and she said, "Be nice to Marty. You owe him from last time."

That wasn't exactly true. The last time I had a case with Marty, my client walked on a murder charge, but my client was innocent. Of course, it didn't hurt that Marty's star witness, his only good witness, was killed on the day he was scheduled to testify. Just for the record, my client didn't have anything to do with the witness' death. Nor did I for that matter.

I would have argued with Gracie, but I didn't have the time and, besides, arguing with Gracie usually gets me nowhere. Instead I gave Gracie a kiss and told her I'd see her later at home.

When I reached Marty Bowman's office, I found Detective Chen seated with a nearly empty cup of coffee in front of him. Apparently, as I suspected, he had been there a while, and he had filled Marty in on why we were meeting. Both men stood, and we shook hands.

Marty said it was good to see me again, and I said the same back. It wasn't a lie; I liked Marty and it was good seeing him. Of course, that could change if he gave me a hard time. You wouldn't be wrong in calling me a fair-weather friend, at least when it comes to prosecutors.

I decided to set the tone for the meeting right away, and I announced my client was ready to surrender and tell everything about the Citibank robbery, including the identities of the other two suspects and how they managed to escape. Marty asked about the money and looked a little skeptical when I told him my guy didn't have any of the stolen money.

Chen chimed in and asked my client's name. I said, "Not so fast, my friend. First, there are some conditions we need to agree on." I laid out our demands, which I had written on a yellow legal pad to make sure I didn't leave anything out. I started with bail. I wanted assurances that the DA would support my bail application and wouldn't claim any bail I asked for was insufficient. If, for some reason, the judge ordered my client held in custody pending trial, I wanted assurances he would be held at a facility other than Rikers Island and in protective custody. I wanted all charges against my client dropped. I knew that was a reach, so it was only my opening bid. Robbery with a weapon is a violent felony, so it carries heavier charges and longer prison terms than non-violent felonies. To get Joey's prison sentence to less than a four-year minimum, I needed to have the charges reduced to a Class E felony, and that would be a real gift.

Marty listened, taking notes as I spoke. When I finished, Marty sat back, looked up at the ceiling to let me know he was thinking, then he laughed and said, "No way we drop the charges, especially when we haven't recovered the money." I knew that would be an issue, but Joey said he didn't have the money, so there wasn't anything I could do about it.

But the news wasn't all bad. Marty hadn't objected to the bail or possible protective custody, so we were only negotiating over the charges. Still, I couldn't just give up on the charges, so I acted hurt and looked to Detective Chen for a little support, knowing the pressure he was under to arrest someone. Especially with the newspapers carrying stories of the Houdini Bandits daily.

Chen sighed and then he said to Marty, "You know, we might never solve this case without help from Jake's client." Marty shook his head; it wasn't his problem.

Then Marty reminded me that my client and his friends had robbed a bank of over $300,000 while armed with deadly weapons. That meant my client was facing a charge of robbery in the first degree, a Class B felony that carried a maximum sentence of twenty-five years in prison. There was no way in the world he could justify dropping those charges.

Joey had sworn to me he wasn't carrying a gun, but I didn't know if he was telling me the truth. Legally it didn't make a difference; if one member of the group was armed, all participants were guilty of armed robbery. The only reason to bring it up was to make Joey seem more sympathetic.

Figuring Chen had seen the video from the bank's surveillance cameras, he'd know if all three suspects were armed or not. It was time to find out if Joey had told me the truth. Looking at Chen, I said very confidently that my client was the one perp without a gun, then I held my breath. Chen said nothing, so I figured I was still on solid ground. It was time to push my luck. Looking at Chen, I said, "Isn't that right, Detective Chen?"

Chen nodded and confirmed my claim. I looked at Marty who was staring at me with that "So what?" look on his face. I said although not having a gun himself might not make a difference legally, it did say something about Joey. Marty wasn't impressed. He sat patiently waiting for me to make a counter demand now that he had rejected my first demand.

The problem was I didn't have any maneuvering room left. There are only three degrees of robbery. Joey was charged with first degree, which was the highest. The lowest, third degree robbery, is a Class D felony which was what I was shooting for. But if I asked for the charge to be reduced to third degree, Marty would want to settle in the middle at second degree, and that was a Class C felony. I was more or less trapped in a corner.

Rather than offer a compromise and seal my fate, I said that my guy is really shaky, and I can't guarantee he's going to hang around if he doesn't get what he wants. I said that, hoping it would make Chen nervous, and it did. He leaned in toward Marty and said he really needed this guy. Marty needed Joey as well, and he wasn't about to blow the deal. This was more about posturing than principle.

Marty had a pretty good idea I was looking to cut a deal for robbery in the third degree, and he wasn't going to agree to it so easily. But he knew in order not to kill the deal, he had to leave the possibility open. That meant he had to let me out of the corner I was in. He sighed, did the ceiling stare again, then offered robbery in the second degree. He acted like it was killing him to make the offer. That put the ball back in my court and now, unlike before, I had a shot at the deal I wanted.

One thing I learned negotiating plea deals is to never rush, particularly when you have an advantage. With that in mind, I figured it was a good time for me to stare at the ceiling. I don't know what good comes from staring at the ceiling, but Marty seemed to like doing it, so I thought I'd give it a try. I get bored quickly and not finding anything particularly interesting on the ceiling, I looked Marty in the eye and said, "Make it robbery in the third, and we have a deal."

This time Marty didn't look at the ceiling which I took as a bad sign. My gut was telling me he was going to turn down the deal. He seemed about to speak when Chen asked if he could have a minute with Marty alone. I figured Chen had picked up the same negative vibe from Marty as I had, and he was hoping for a chance to save the deal.

I walked out of Marty's office and sat in the chair alongside his secretary's desk. Marty's secretary is a sweet young kid named Mary Patricia. In case you couldn't guess, she's Irish, so we have kind of a bond. It seemed, however, that Mary Patricia didn't appreciate the bond we shared because she just sat there typing away and ignoring me.

I was trying to think of something clever to say when the door to Marty's office opened, and Chen invited me back inside. Not having thought of anything clever to say to Mary Patricia, I simply smiled and said, "I'll always remember our time together." Mary Patricia just grunted. Apparently, she didn't treasure the moment as much as I did.

When I walked into Marty's office, he looked pained, like maybe he had gas or something. I was going to suggest he take a good antacid, but I thought better of it, and simply took my seat and waited. Obviously, Marty wasn't happy with what he was about to say, and he wasn't in a hurry to say it. Finally, after staring at the ceiling, he said that he'd drop the charge to robbery in the third and agree to bail and protection terms, provided my guy gave him everything on the other two perps, and he helped to recover the money by telling the cops all about the tunnels.

I hadn't seen that last condition coming. I was pretty sure Joey didn't know anything about the tunnels other than the one he had been in. But the deal was too good to pass up, so I figured we'd take it, and Joey and I would become experts on the Chinatown tunnels. How hard could it be to find out about these damn tunnels? Enough people were talking about them. It would just be a matter of talking to the right people.

I told Marty it sounded good, and he should have Mary Patricia type it up, so I could take it to my client. Marty said that was fine, but the deal was only on the table for twenty-four hours. If he didn't have a signed copy back by then, the deal was off. That was okay.

I couldn't agree to the deal on the spot because I had to run it by Joey first. But I also wanted to leave myself a little wiggle room on the terms. I had just scored a big win, so any attempt to sweeten the terms wasn't likely to go over well with Marty.

We had an agreement on the big terms, and it was being reduced to writing, so there wouldn't be any issues later. But we hadn't agreed yet on the sequence of events. Naturally, Joey would have to turn himself in soon, but how soon after that he had to name his fellow felons, and how soon we had to come up with information about the tunnels, was still up in the air.

Timing in life is everything, and getting Joey protection was paramount. Marty understood that Joey wouldn't name his coconspirators until he was protected, but we needed the protection immediately. Once word got out that the cops had a suspect in custody, the Cha brothers would know they were toast, and they'd go looking for Joey. Not to mention Joey making the top ten most wanted on the Hip Sing Tong hit list.

I didn't see the protection issue being a problem; it was the tunnel thing that worried me. I assumed Joey didn't know much more about the tunnels than I did, so we were going to have to do some digging to keep that part of the bargain, and I wanted as much time as possible. Rather than make Marty suspicious by trying to negotiate a timetable at that point, I delayed signing the agreement.

Chen seemed disappointed. I think he wanted to see me and Marty exchange the secret handshake used to seal plea deals. If that's what he was waiting for, he'd just have to wait a little longer.

CHAPTER 11

Chen and I left Marty's office together. On our way out of the building, I asked why he and Marty were so interested in the Chinatown tunnels. Rumors about the tunnels had been circulating for years, but as far as I knew, the NYPD never showed much interest in them. Besides, as far as I knew, no one was sure that they existed and, if they did, how widespread they were. Chen confirmed that was true, but the NYPD Intelligence Division believed a web of tunnels did exist and was being used by smugglers and counterfeiters to store and run goods. Chen had seen nothing supporting that belief, and he had no idea how the Intelligence Division arrived at it. Thus far, the only person who seemed to have actual knowledge of the tunnels was my client, and that was why Chen was able to convince Marty to take the deal.

That wasn't good news. I hadn't thought information about the tunnels was linked that tightly to the deal. I figured Joey would tell him what he knew which was really nothing other than where he entered and exited the tunnel, and that would be it. But if it wasn't enough, we'd be in trouble unless I found out a whole lot more about the damn tunnels. I had a former client who had used the tunnels, but he was in the witness protection program, and I had no way of finding him. I couldn't call the US Marshall Service and say, "I need to talk to Mr. Haung. Could you give me his new name and phone number, please?" I did hear from him occasionally, but the letters came without return addresses and were rerouted by the US Marshalls, so I never knew where they actually came from.

Outside the building, Chen and I parted ways. As soon as I was clear of him, I phoned Mr. Fang. I told him to meet me at Shoo's as soon as he could and to bring Joey with him. Then I called Tommy and told him we needed to find out everything we could about the Chinatown tunnels. Other than the tunnel used by our former client, Tommy didn't know of any other tunnels and wasn't sure any others existed. I assured him there was at least one more tunnel, and I needed to know if there were more. He said he'd start working on it and get back to me. In the meantime, he suggested I talk to his grandfather.

Walking to Shoo's, I was making sure that I wasn't being followed. Detective Chen was smart enough to know I'd go see my client to discuss the terms of the deal. If he wanted to jump the deal, he'd just follow me and make a quick arrest. I didn't think Chen was that kind of guy, but he was under a lot of pressure to find the Houdini Bandits, so I was being cautious. If I thought I was being followed, I'd walk past Shoo's and go to my office.

The streets of Chinatown are always crowded which makes it difficult to tell if you're being followed. I used all the tricks I knew which weren't many. I'd stop occasionally to look in a shop window, using the reflection in the glass to check people behind me. I crossed the street at mid-block a couple of times, checking to see if anyone was following me. Then there was the old standby trick of stopping suddenly and quickly turning around to see if anyone else stops. It's not very subtle, but it's effective. Or so they say. I haven't caught anyone following me, so I can't confirm that it works. I can confirm that when you do it on a crowded street, people bump into you and you'd be surprised at the language they use.

By the time I got to Shoo's, I was convinced no one was following me. Inside the restaurant, old man Shoo was watching from the kitchen door and nodded toward the backroom. Mr. Fang and Joey were already there waiting for me. I explained the terms of the deal. Knowing the question of bail was on both their minds, I made it clear that whether Joey was granted bail was strictly up to the judge, and there was no guarantee he would. The agreement simply said the DA wouldn't ask that Joey be held in custody pending trial, and he wouldn't object to our bail request.

Mr. Fang said he understood, but he wanted to know what would happen if bail was denied. How would Joey be protected from the Cha brothers and the Hip Sing Tong? Joey hadn't said a word, but he had gotten very pale, and I had the sense he was thinking about backing out of the deal.

I said if bail wasn't granted, then Joey would be put in protective custody to keep him safely out of the reach of the Cha brothers and the tong. Mr. Fang questioned how safe his grandson would be, and I assured him the DA had a vested interest in protecting the one and only star witness. Of course, if bail was granted, then Joey's safety would be up to Mr. Fang, who said that wasn't a problem; he'd provide a safe house.

Truth be told, I was more worried about Joey's safety if he was granted bail than if he wasn't. I knew how he'd be protected in jail, but I had no idea what Mr. Fang had in mind. I didn't want to know the details, but I wanted to be sure both Mr. Fang and Joey understood how serious the situation was.

I told Mr. Fang I trusted his judgment, but I needed to be sure he understood the seriousness of the situation. Joey was only getting a deal because he was rolling over on the Cha brothers. Once the news broke that Joey had turned himself in, the Cha brothers would do everything they could to make sure Joey never testified against them. That included putting out a contract on his life. Mr. Fang asked if it was a serious concern, and I assured him it was. There were plenty of gangbangers out there eager to earn money and fame by assassinating a turncoat witness. Mr. Fang said I needn't worry because Joey's safety was his primary concern, and he'd make sure Joey was safe.

I didn't ask for details because, frankly, I didn't want to know. If the Cha brothers, or members of the tong, showed up at my door asking where they might find Joey, we'd all be better off if I didn't know.

When I finished explaining the terms and answering questions, I said that I thought it was the best deal we'd get, and Joey should take it. Mr. Fang looked at his grandson, who didn't seem overjoyed at the terms, and told him he should take the deal.

I knew from the look on Joey's face he wasn't certain what he should do. I guess he'd been hoping that he'd get off with no prison time, even though I told him that wasn't going to happen. There was no way an armed robbery charge would be reduced to a no prison time charge, not unless he could produce Jimmy Hoffa's body, and even then, it would be a stretch.

I explained again if things went as well as expected, he'd only be sentenced to one year, which meant he'd wind up serving less than nine months. Considering he was facing a maximum prison term of twenty-five years, that seemed like a damn good deal. Mr. Fang nodded in agreement, and Joey said he'd take the deal.

I said I'd work out the surrender terms, but Joey should be prepared to turn himself in the next day. However, first, I needed to know everything he knew about the tunnels. Regrettably, he knew nothing other than he had entered the escape tunnel through the wall to the right when coming into the basement from Mott Street. It was dark, so he never saw how Bobby accessed it.

Once inside the tunnel, they moved quickly, and he didn't pay attention to details. He thought they may have passed an entrance to another tunnel, but he wasn't sure. When they got to the end of the tunnel, they went through a doorway into a basement, up some stairs, and out onto Bayard Street. He didn't know the address of the building. He only remembered it being somewhere in the middle of the block between Mott Street and the Bowery.

Obviously, Joey wasn't going to be any help in finding out about the tunnels, but Marty Bowman didn't need to know that. As long as I could come up with information about the tunnels, we'd be okay. I was counting on Tommy to do his usual magic and get me some answers.

It was time to arrange for Joey's surrender. I called Marty Bowman, told him we had a deal, and I was prepared to surrender my client to Detective Chen at the Fifth Precinct the following morning under a couple of conditions. Marty, of course, was a little pissed off that I was tossing in some conditions, but he listened patiently and discovered the conditions were reasonable. I wanted assurances there'd be no leaks to the press of the arrest in advance and my client would be arraigned immediately after being booked. No one from the DA's Office or the NYPD would announce that a suspect in the Citibank case had been arrested until after the arraignment, and after my client was safely in custody. I reminded Marty that keeping my client alive was in both our interests.

Marty agreed to the conditions, but wanted to know when he could interview my client. I said once I was certain that my client was out of harm's way, he could have a face-to-face interview. But immediately after the arraignment, I would reveal to him and Detective Chen the names of the other two suspects, in addition to information where they might be found. Marty said that was fine, but he wanted a face-to-face interview. I said we could arrange a meeting to discuss the details of the crime. I was careful not to say anything about the tunnels.

Marty wasn't happy with the timing, but if I was giving him the names of the other two suspects, he was okay with delaying the interview.

I told Joey and Mr. Fang to meet me at Shoo's the next morning at nine o'clock. The restaurant isn't open for business that early, but old man Shoo is usually there, and he'd done similar favors for me in the past.

Then I gave Joey some final instructions. I told him to wear a suit and tie, and I suggested he make it an old tie and wear loafers because they'd take away his tie and shoelaces at Central Booking. They didn't want people hanging themselves in the holding cells; it gave the place a bad reputation.

I also told him to bring just one form of identification with him and leave his wallet, cash, wristwatch, rings, and everything else at his grandfather's place. The less he had with him, the less that had to be inventoried and the less that could be lost. It wasn't that I didn't trust the cops; it was the bureaucratic system I didn't trust.

Once Joey and Mr. Fang were gone, I worked things out with old man Shoo, then I called Detective Chen. I told him the surrender terms, got his word he'd abide by them, and I'd have my client in his office at ten o'clock the following morning.

The die was cast. Now the only question was if I could find out about the tunnels and what might happen if I couldn't.

CHAPTER 12

The following morning I met Joey and Mr. Fang at Shoo's as planned. Joey was understandably nervous, and Mr. Fang looked not surprisingly very calm. Mr. Fang was very much like old man Shoo. Inscrutable is the term I think that best describes the two of them. You can never tell by looking at them what's going on inside their heads. One thing is for sure, I wouldn't play poker with either of them.

Joey, on the other hand, was anything but inscrutable. You could tell by looking at him that he was scared as hell. It made me wonder what he had been like on the day of the robbery. This kid wasn't your typical violent felon. If he'd gotten thrown into the general population at Rikers Island, they'd eat him alive; that was why I had demanded that he be placed in protective custody if the judge refused bail. It was true; I was worried about the Cha brothers getting to him, but I was more worried about the scumbags he'd be with if not isolated.

I explained to Joey what was going to happen at the Fifth Precinct, then at Central Booking and, finally, in court during his arraignment. Then I gave Mr. Fang the name and phone number of a bail bondsman I know. I suggested he might want to use the man because it would be easier and faster to get bail posted using a licensed bail bondsman than putting up the cash himself. Mr. Fang nodded and put the card in his jacket pocket.

Joey had followed all my instructions and suggestions, and other than looking like he was about to vomit, he was ready to go. After another cup of tea to help calm Joey's nerves, we walked over to the Fifth Precinct station house on Elizabeth Street.

It wasn't a long walk, at least not for me. I can't say the same for Joey who was turning paler the closer we got to the station house. I told him as bad as things might be, they probably weren't as bad as he was imagining. That was something I knew from my own experiences as a recovering alcoholic. Joey could have benefited from a visit to AA. Unfortunately, we didn't have time to stop in at an AA meeting, so my little nugget of wisdom would have to do.

Entering the Fifth Precinct, I wasn't surprised to see Marty Bowman on hand to greet us, along with Detective Chen and half a dozen other detectives. Not that Bowman usually hangs out there, but this was a special occasion. Looking around, I asked Chen where he was keeping the brass band. I don't think he was amused.

Figuring Chen and Bowman wanted to get down to business, I said, "This is my client, Joseph Chung, and he's here to surrender himself in connection with a recent robbery." I was careful not to use the work "bank" or to give the date of the robbery. Chen, knowing the conditions of the surrender, simply read Joey his Miranda rights while placing handcuffs on his wrists.

I told Joey not to say a word to anyone about anything until he saw me again in a few hours at the arraignment. Then, as two cops led Joey away, followed by Chen and Marty, Mr. Fang and I left the precinct. Marty had promised to call me as soon as Joey's case was put on the arraignment calendar. If things went as planned, Joey would be arraigned in Criminal Court early that afternoon and, hopefully, he'd be out on bail by evening.

Walking back to the office, I asked Mr. Fang if he had arranged a safe place for Joey to stay while on bail. Mr. Fang said yes, then started telling me where, but I cut him off before he got very far. I explained it was better for all of us if I didn't know where Joey was hiding out. Having no idea how vicious the Cha brothers were, but knowing they were no choir boys, ignorance could be lifesaving for all of us. I didn't mention the Hip Sing Tong because Mr. Fang was well aware of its reputation for vengeance.

Although my concerns may have seemed selfish, I was sure Mr. Fang understood this was a situation where what's good for me is good for Joey. Although I can't say I've ever been tortured, I don't think I'd do well if I was. Maybe I could hold out if it involved Gracie, but other than for Gracie, and maybe Doug, I would probably give it up pretty quickly. So the less I knew, the safer Joey would be.

Before you judge me, consider what you would do if someone started pulling out your fingernails or cut off your pinkie finger. Try looking at your hands while you're thinking about that. I'll bet you're not so brave anymore, are you? You see, I'm just being honest when I say I don't think I could hold out very long.

When we got to Bayard Street, Mr. Fang and I went our separate ways. But not before we arranged to meet later in the Arraignment Part at the Criminal Courts Building. I promised to call Mr. Fang with the time of Joey's arraignment as soon as I heard from Marty.

CHAPTER 13

I had some time to kill before the arraignment, so I decided to drop by Shoo's Restaurant and chat with old man Shoo to see if he knew anything about the tunnels.

I found Shoo in the kitchen sitting on his stool reading a Chinese newspaper. His stool was strategically placed so he could keep his eye on the restaurant's front door and on his cooks who, as usual, were screaming at each other. I've never figured out why they were always screaming at each other, and it never seemed to bother the old man who just sat there reading his paper. I should mention that the kitchen was where the customers' bills were settled and where the cash was kept in a drawer next to the old man's stool. It hadn't been that long ago that he reluctantly started accepting credit cards, but he still preferred cash. The waiters were instructed to encourage customers to pay cash, and when a customer paid cash, the old man added two bucks to the tip. It worked out well for everyone; the waiters got more money, and old man Shoo saved the credit card company fee.

When I walked into the kitchen, the old man looked up from his newspaper and smiled, bowing his head slightly. I liked the old man, and I felt he liked me. He offered to feed me, but I had just eaten. I did accept his offer of a cup of tea, and the old man shouted instructions to the chefs. Then he and I went into the dining room and sat at a quiet table near the kitchen door where the old man could keep an eye on things.

He didn't speak very much English, but it was enough for us to get by. I always suspected he understood more than he let on, and on a few occasions over the years, those suspicions proved true. He was smart, and he was shrewd, and like the other old-timers in Chinatown, he never let you know what he was thinking. The only time I ever saw any real emotion on the old man's face was at the hospital the night Tommy had been shot while doing a job for me. It was a bad time for all of us, but especially for the old man. As I said, I'd never seen him show emotion before that, and once Tommy was on the mend, I never saw it again.

When the waiter brought our tea, I bowed my head to the old man in a show of respect. Then I took a sip of my tea. I had learned a lot about Chinese culture over the years, enough to know it would have been rude to start asking questions before I sipped my tea. With the niceties out of the way, I asked the old man if he knew anything about the tunnels. He said he had heard about them many times, but he had only actually been in one. Actually, he didn't say that in so many words. What he said was, "I hear, lots talk, but I see only one." I asked when and where he saw the tunnel, and he said it was years ago, and it was under Doyers Street. Then he smiled and said, "You go look. Now tunnel Wing Fat number five Doyers."

I figured he was referring to the Wing Fat Shopping Arcade under Doyers Street. It's said to be part of the old tong tunnel system, the only part known to still exist, although much of it had undoubtedly changed from its original form. I had never been in the arcade, but I heard it described as being long, narrow and dangerous for strangers. I decided that I needed to have a look at the place for myself, but first, I wanted to know what else Shoo knew about the tunnels. I pressed the old man for more information, but he said that was all he knew. I trusted he was telling me the truth, but I was pretty sure some of his old pals knew a lot more. As well as the old man and I got along, he wasn't about to bring his old buddies into the conversation just because I asked. No, for that to happen, I needed to go through Tommy. I made a mental note to give Tommy a call, and then I graciously thanked the old man for his hospitality and help and headed over to Doyers Street.

It's a short walk from Shoo's Restaurant to No. 5 Doyers Street, which is easy to miss because it's just a big red unmarked door squeezed between The Taiwan Pork Chop House Restaurant on one side and a wine and liquor store on the other. There was some signage over the doorway, but it was mostly in Chinese. I had passed that door hundreds, maybe thousands, of times and never gave it a second thought. It was just a door. But now the door had my attention. It was a heavy steel door with no glass, the type of door meant to keep people out, not invite business customers in. I suspected it wouldn't be any more inviting inside, and I was right.

Once through the door, I went down a winding flight of stairs into a long narrow corridor with a low ceiling and overhead fluorescent lighting. The corridor couldn't have been more than four feet wide. It was hardly what I'd call an arcade. It was more like an underground hallway except it didn't go in a straight line.

There were some business offices on both sides of the corridor and some unmarked doors as well. Given the history of the tunnel, it was eerie; I tell you that much. I passed one open door, looked in and saw four men who, when they saw me, just glared at me. I smiled and said hello, but they continued to glare at me. I don't think they were happy to see me.

I imagined what the tunnel was like a century earlier. Did the doors I was passing once lead to secret rooms, maybe opium dens and gambling joints? Was there a whole web of tunnels in those days as many claimed, and did those tunnels still exist? By the time I reached the far end of the arcade, my mind was spinning with possibilities. I exited the arcade onto Chatham Square through the lobby of the Wing Fat Mansion condominiums next to the OTB. The whole trip took me less than fifteen minutes, and the only thing I learned was that visitors weren't welcome in the Wing Fat Arcade.

I was hoping Tommy could put me in touch with someone who knew more about the rumored tunnels.

CHAPTER 14

Leaving the Wing Fat Arcade, I got a call from Marty that Joey would be arraigned in an hour at the Criminal Court Building. I called Mr. Fang and told him to meet me in court in half an hour, then I hightailed it back to my office to pick up Joey's file.

I expected everything would go along smoothly at the arraignment. On a felony charge such as the one Joey was facing, not much happens at the initial arraignment, and it's usually a quick affair. The defendant doesn't enter a plea until after the case has been referred to a grand jury and an indictment is returned. The only thing of significance on the agenda is the matter of bail. In Joey's case, I'd request bail, and under our agreement, Marty wouldn't object, so I didn't expect that to be a problem.

After the arraignment ended was when it would get interesting. Bowman and Chen couldn't wait to announce the arrest of one of the Houdini Bandits. I figured they would alert the press, and my suspicion was confirmed when I got to the courthouse and found the hallway outside the Arraignment Part overflowing with media people. Acting dumb, which for me wasn't much of a stretch, I found a newspaper reporter I knew, and I asked him what he was doing there. He said he wasn't sure, but his paper had been tipped off by the DA's Office that they'd be wise to cover the proceedings that afternoon. Then he said that he knew something big was going down because Marty Bowman was inside, and Marty never covered arraignments.

He was right about that. Arraignments were almost always handled by the rookie Assistant District Attorneys. They're simple proceedings, but they're a good way to give the rookies courtroom experience. The only time any heavyweights handle arraignments is to take a bow in front of the media. Today it would be a double bow, Marty and Chen.

Inside the courtroom, I found Mr. Fang seated in the front row. I sat beside him and told him about the press in the hallway. I warned him that if they found out he was Joey's grandfather, they'd hound the hell out of him. So if he didn't want that to happen, he shouldn't say anything during the proceedings or leave the courtroom when I did. When he left the courtroom, he should wait outside the building away from any crowds, and I'd call him on his cell as soon as I could. Mr. Fang nodded, acknowledging he understood and agreed.

Then moving inside the courtroom railing, I smiled at Marty and checked in with the calendar clerk. I wasn't surprised to find Joey's case was number one on the list. Marty Bowman wasn't about to sit around waiting for his case to be called, not when he had the press waiting for him.

Except for a couple of curious reporters, the rest of the media stayed outside of the courtroom. They knew Marty couldn't hold a press conference inside the courtroom, so they positioned themselves in the hallway and waited for him to emerge. I had just taken my seat at the counsel table when Detective Chen arrived. He nodded to me, then took a seat in the first row of the gallery.

When Joey's case was called, it was announced only as a charge of violating New York Penal Law, Section 160.15, robbery in the first degree. No mention was made of Citibank or anything else that would have indicated Joey was one of the Houdini Bandits. Of course, with Marty handling the arraignment, a smart reporter might put two and two together and get a jump on the media crowd. But looking around the courtroom, the two reporters who had chosen to sit inside remained glued to their seats. I guess they didn't get it.

When the Court Officers brought Joey into the courtroom, he didn't look any the worse for wear. He looked a bit more relaxed than he had when we surrendered him earlier at the Fifth Precinct. At least he didn't look like he was about to puke, which was good since he was sitting right next to me. I asked him how he was doing and cautioned him not to acknowledge his grandfather in the gallery. He looked puzzled, so I explained about the newspaper guys and keeping his grandfather out of the limelight. He thought that was smart, so he never looked back at the gallery even when we were done, and he was taken back downstairs by the Court Officers.

Judge Brown was on the bench. He was a decent judge, better than most, but not necessarily sympathetic to defendants. Under normal circumstances,

I would be a little concerned about him granting Joey bail, but I had Marty's agreement not to ask for remand, nor object to my bail application.

Marty upheld his end of the bargain and Judge Brown ordered bail at $250,000 cash or bond, which gave Mr. Fang the option of putting up the money himself, or he could pay a bail bondsman a 10% fee to put up the money instead. I had recommended Mr. Fang use a bail bondsman because it was faster and kept his name out of the loop, and he had agreed. So, earlier I had alerted a friend of mine, Sal Martinez, who owns A-1 Bail Service that a Mr. Fang might be contacting him. I had told Mr. Fang what he would need for the bond, and he was ready to pay the 10% fee in cash. That would certainly speed things along, not to mention making Sal a happy man.

The proceedings took less than ten minutes; then came the circus. Marty and Chen left the courtroom with me right behind. We were no sooner out the door when the media began hollering questions. Marty raised his arms to silence the crowd. Then he introduced himself and Detective Chen, saying he had a statement to read, after which he and Detective Chen would answer a few questions. The statement was short and to the point:

"This morning at approximately ten o'clock, Joseph Chung surrendered himself at the Fifth Precinct to face charges of robbery in the first degree in connection with the recent Citibank robbery. As of this time, two other suspects in the case are still being sought by police. In accordance with practices of the District Attorney's Office, no further details can be given at this time. If and when further information becomes available, the press will be notified."

Marty had barely finished reading the statement when everyone started yelling out questions. Again, Marty raised his arms to quiet the crowd, saying he'd take questions one at a time, and he pointed to a *New York Post* reporter in the front row. His question and the ones that followed were pretty much along the same line. *Did the police know the identities of the other two suspects, and what had they learned from Chung? How did the suspects escape? Did they use the secret tunnels? Had the money been recovered?*

Marty and Chen answered a couple of the questions, but to most questions they responded, "No comment at this time." The media, finally tired of not having their questions answered, turned to me, only to get the same answer. That was enough. They all packed up and left the three of us standing alone in the hallway.

I handed Chen a piece of paper with the names, Bobby and Billy Cha, along with the names of places where they liked to hang out. At least until now. Once news of Joey's arrest hit the street, which was probably happening as we stood there, the Cha brothers were likely going into hiding.

Chen read the names and said he knew the brothers. Not personally, but by reputation. Their names had come up in a number of investigations, and although they hadn't been arrested recently, Chen seemed to recall them having a record. Chen pulled out his cell phone and called the station house. The manhunt for the Cha brothers was now officially underway.

I told Marty we'd be arranging bail for Joey that afternoon. I asked him to keep Joey somewhere safe and out of Rikers until we arranged for his release. Marty said he had expected as much, and he had already made arrangements to keep Joey under guard in a cell in the basement of the Criminal Court Building, away from the regular holding cells. He'd be released from there as soon as bail was posted.

Leaving Chen and Marty, I called Mr. Fang and told him I'd meet him at A-1 Bail Service in twenty minutes. Then I called Tommy to let him know the word was out on Joey.

CHAPTER 15

Under most circumstances, cash is a wonderful thing, and that's how it was at A-1 Bail Service. My buddy, Sal Martinez, was thrilled that his $25,000 fee was being paid in cash. So thrilled he agreed to reduce his usual collateral demand from 75% of the bail amount to only $25,000 if put up in cash as well. Sal nearly fell out of his chair when Mr. Fang pulled out his satchel and plopped down the added $25,000 on Sal's desk.

Sal looked at me with a shocked smile on his face, and I told him that in consideration of all that cash, we wanted fast service, and by 'fast,' I meant immediately. Sal got the picture and said he'd draw up the bond right away, and he'd have it posted within the hour. As I said, cash is a wonderful thing.

After leaving Sal's office, there was nothing left to do except wait for Joey's release. I guess I was nervous because I asked Mr. Fang if he had arranged a safe place for Joey to stay, forgetting I had asked him about it earlier that morning. Mr. Fang apparently remembered me asking, as well as cautioning him not to tell me any details, because he replied simply that he had.

Connie called on my cell to let me know Joey's arrest was on the news. My name was also mentioned as Joey's attorney. Connie thought that made me "cool," as she put it. I didn't think so; I thought it just made me a target. It also meant I'd be wise to avoid my office until Joey was safely tucked away in his hiding place.

If the Cha brothers had heard the news, they were probably looking for Joey already and following his lawyer was one way to find him. I would have gone to Shoo's or the Worth Street Coffee Shop to wait for the call that Joey was being released, but too many people knew those were my hangouts.

After explaining the situation to Mr. Fang, I asked if he knew somewhere we could hang out without attracting attention. He said he knew just the place and led the way to a small tea room on Pell Street. We were greeted at the door by someone I took to be the owner. He and Mr. Fang exchanged a few words in Chinese, then the man escorted us through a curtain into a backroom. There were two tables and a couple of chairs, and the man invited us to sit.

A few minutes later, a young girl arrived with tea and red bean buns.

If you visit Chinatown, I promise you'll find it fascinating. Cross onto one of Chinatown's three original streets, and it's as though you left New York City and entered another land.

However, no matter how often or how long you visit, there are parts of Chinatown, like the backroom of the tea parlor where I sat with Mr. Fang that you'll never be able to see. After years of working on Mott Street, I was still an outsider, and always would be. Yes, I had been granted access to places generally off-limits to outsiders, and I had been made privy to some of Chinatown's secrets. But it was all on a very limited basis, and none of it resulted from my own initiative. That's just the way it is in Chinatown.

CHAPTER 16

We were each working on our second cup of tea when my buddy, Sal, from A-1 Bail Service called to say Joey's bail had been posted, and he'd be released at the Criminal Courts Building in less than half an hour. I called Marty Bowman and told him Joey was about to be released on bail, and I was prepared to bring him to the DA's Office for a short debriefing within half an hour. However, I wanted Detective Chen to accompany us, along with a couple of officers, to ensure Joey's safety. Marty agreed and said he'd arrange for Chen to meet me at the Criminal Courts Building.

I explained to Mr. Fang we'd be going to the DA's Office, after which he would take Joey to the safe house. I'd arrange for the NYPD to accompany them there, but as I had explained earlier, I wouldn't go along because it was better if I didn't know where Joey was staying.

It was important that Joey not leave the safe house. I reminded Mr. Fang of our conversation and my warning that the Cha brothers were likely to put out a contract on Joey's life. Mr. Fang assured me he understood the seriousness of the situation. I didn't think it was necessary to remind him that the Hip Sing Tong would probably be looking for Joey as well.

Fearing Joey might get bored and leave, Mr. Fang had promised to stay with Joey in the safe house to ensure that didn't happen. As an added precaution, I had Linda Chow, Tommy's computer wizard, cut off Joey's cell phone service. Not only couldn't Joey use the phone to make calls, any incoming callers would be told he was no longer in range, and the GPS locater would show him somewhere in the Atlantic Ocean. It's amazing what Linda can do on a computer.

Mr. Fang assured me the landline telephones in the safe house had been disconnected, and there were no computers or Internet service. As for his own cell phone, he'd keep it on his person at all times during the day and lock it in the safe at night. Joey would be in a communication dead zone.

When we got to the holding cells at the Criminal Court Building, Detective Chen and two uniformed cops were waiting for us. We could see Joey behind the glass partition as he signed the inventory sheet and retrieved his driver's license and tie. I smiled at seeing he had taken my advice and traveled lightly. With the paperwork taken care of, Joey was officially released on bail.

Our little entourage moved quickly around the corner and into the District Attorney's Office on Hogan Place. I was surprised to find Marty Bowman waiting for us in the lobby. He was obviously anxious to talk with Joey.

In the elevator on the way to a conference room on the sixth floor, I told Marty I wanted a little time alone with my client before the interview began. It was a reasonable request and one Marty should have expected, and probably did expect. Still, he had to show his annoyance. It's all part of the game. He gave me an angry look, and I shot one back at him and we were done. Gracie has a name for that sort of thing. She says it's the alpha males "squaring off." I say it's "having fun."

Joey, Mr. Fang and I were ushered into the conference room and told we had ten minutes. I looked at Marty and said I'd call him when we were done. He got the message, nodded and closed the door.

I just wanted Joey to get comfortable in the room. I told him to keep his answers to Marty's questions short and to the point. I didn't want him elaborating because that's usually how people get themselves into trouble. I summed it up by saying, "Just stick to the facts, no opinions or speculation and if you don't know, say you don't know. Lastly, if I start to talk, you shut up right away. Got it?"

Joey nodded his head. He got it. He looked relaxed, which was the look I was going for. Nervous clients do stupid things. But then again stupid clients do stupid things, even when they're relaxed. But Joey wasn't stupid. Unless, of course, you consider robbing a bank stupid.

I asked Joey one last time if he was ready, and when he said yes, I opened the door and called down the hallway to Marty.

Marty, Detective Chen, and two ADAs entered and took seats around the long conference room table. Then I got nervous because Joey looked too relaxed. He was sitting a bit slouched down in his chair, his one arm casually slung over the back of the adjoining chair.

Being too relaxed isn't as bad as being too nervous, but it's not good either. I needed to correct the situation, and I knew just how to do it.

When Marty started to ask Joey a question, I raised my hand and stopped him. I said that before we begin with the questions, I wanted to set the ground rules and make sure certain conditions had been met. That sent Marty off on a tantrum, which is what I intended. I wanted Marty yelling, so Joey would see firsthand that Marty wasn't his friend.

I knew how Marty operated. If I hadn't lit his fuse, he'd have been sweeter than candy when he started questioning Joey, and if Joey was too relaxed, he might think Marty wasn't a threat. Now, hopefully, he would know otherwise.

Letting Marty vent, I glanced at Joey who was obviously getting the message. He was no longer slouched in his chair. Rather, he was sitting bolt upright with his arms on the table and a serious look on his face.

I told Marty to calm down. I just wanted to remind him that the interview was limited to the details of the robbery and didn't include information about the tunnels. That's when I told Marty that Joey's knowledge of the tunnels was very limited, and I would be providing additional information later about the tunnels.

Marty threw me a nasty glance, but he didn't object. He just shuffled the papers on the table in front of him, then smiling sweetly, he asked Joey his first question.

The interview lasted a little more than an hour, and it went well enough that I never interrupted the questioning. When Marty finished with his questions, Detective Chen had a few of his own. After Joey answered those questions, Marty said he was satisfied, and as long as I promised to give him information on the tunnels, he'd reduce the charge against Joey from robbery in the first degree to robbery in the third degree.

We hadn't yet agreed on a sentencing recommendation, but I didn't think it was the time to push the issue. There'd be more conferences before we were done, and I'd be in a better negotiating position after the Cha brothers were in custody and, hopefully, the bank's money was recovered. Recovering the money makes the cops look good, and it makes plea bargaining easier.

Chen called in the two plainclothes cops who would escort Joey and Mr. Fang to the safe house. I stepped aside with Joey and Mr. Fang and gave them some last-minute instructions, after which they left. I was getting ready to leave myself when Marty said he and Chen wanted to know what was going on with the tunnels. Apparently, the damn tunnels were a bigger part of the deal than I had expected.

The three of us sat back down at the conference room table. Marty wanted to know where we stood on the tunnels. I told him at the moment I didn't know anything more other than what Joey had said during the debriefing. I assumed what he said was true, and that he and the Cha brothers escaped using a tunnel in the Golden Wok's basement. That was it. I suggested maybe the NYPD should take another look at the basement.

I reminded Chen that the last time we had a case together involving a tunnel, it took the NYPD and the FBI over a week to find it. Chen wasn't happy with my comment, but what could he say? It was true.

Marty then asked how I planned on providing additional information on the tunnels if my client didn't know anything more. That was a good question and one I didn't want to answer with a simple, *I'm looking around for answers*. Instead, I said that I had a couple of contacts who I believed knew about the tunnels and were willing to talk to me. That was the truth, although what and how much they knew about the tunnels wasn't clear. I mean, everybody in Chinatown claims to know something about the tunnels, but it doesn't mean they actually know something.

Fortunately, Marty didn't push me on it. He simply asked when I'd be getting back to him with some information, to which I answered "soon."

In my experience, "soon" is a fabulous word. It's so relative. Ask anyone who's had to deal with a delivery man or a repairman. "Soon" can mean minutes, hours, days, months, or even, under certain circumstances, years. I love to use the word when answering questions, but I hate hearing it when I'm the one asking the questions.

Anyway, Marty didn't make a big deal out of it; he only asked me to get back to him as soon as I could. As for Chen, he offered his help if I wanted it. I said that I appreciated the offer, and I'd let him know if I needed his help.

On my way back to the office, I called Tommy and told him finding out about the tunnels was a high priority. I didn't know how we'd do it, but I figured if anybody could do it, Tommy could.

CHAPTER 17

The day after Joey's arraignment, I had hoped to start looking for tunnels, but I couldn't because Jenny's arraignment was scheduled for that morning. Thankfully, it went off without a hitch which isn't saying much since not a lot can go wrong at an arraignment. Unless your client suddenly jumps up and confesses, things usually go smoothly. I had one client who insisted he wanted to plead insanity. We both knew he wasn't insane, and I counseled him against making the claim. At his arraignment, believing we were on the same page, I entered a plea of not guilty on his behalf. That's when he jumped up and confessed to kidnapping the Lindberg baby and killing Jimmy Hoffa. He then danced around imitating a chicken until the Court Officers handcuffed him and dragged him off. I had to explain to him later at Rikers that there was a big difference between criminal insanity and acting like an idiot. I don't think he understood what I was telling him because during a court conference, he kept insisting to the judge he was insane, or as he put it, "cuckoo." Of course, the judge wasn't buying it, and in the end, he wound up doing more time than he would have had he kept his mouth shut.

But back to Jenny's arraignment. I still wasn't sure what I could say in Jenny's defense, so I had simply entered a plea of not guilty on her behalf. The matter of bail wasn't an issue because Jenny couldn't afford to make bail, even if the judge granted it. The whole proceeding took less than ten minutes.

Talking with the arraignment ADA afterwards, I learned that the person in overall charge of the Asian Dragon cases was Sarah Washington. That was good news. I knew Sarah well, having worked with her on numerous cases over the years. Sarah was sharp, a good lawyer and fair. I was sure she and I could work out a good deal, but I needed Jenny to cooperate and give me something to work with.

After the arraignment, I spoke briefly with Jenny, or I should say to Jenny because she had nothing to say to me. I told her again she was in big trouble, and she needed to talk to me. She still didn't respond, so I said I'd see her at Rikers in a couple of days.

Once the Court Officers had taken Jenny back down to the holding cells, I was done, and I decided to drop by Sarah's office to let her know I was representing Jenny and to see where things stood. My plan was to keep Jenny's case off the trial calendar for as long as possible. With Sarah having so many defendants to deal with, I was sure she wouldn't mind me slow walking the case. She'd know I was doing it to get a better plea deal after the bulk of the cases were resolved. But someone was going to be last, so why not Jenny?

Whenever I go to the District Attorney's Office, I stop by Gracie's office to say hello. It doesn't matter that I just saw her that morning when I left her apartment, or I'm going to see her for dinner that night. It's just something I've done for years. I hate to think what would happen if I didn't stop by, and Gracie found out about it. Let's just say I've grown very fond of certain benefits that come with cohabitation, and I don't want those benefits withheld.

I was about to stick my head into Gracie's office when her secretary said Gracie was in a meeting upstairs. Upstairs being the place where the big boys roamed. I once dreamed about being up there myself. Of being one of the big boys, maybe even the District Attorney. I was actually on my way there when my love of booze put an end to the dream. I wonder how many dreams of mine have died in bottles of booze. I may have destroyed that dream, but I'm sober and that's what counts.

I asked Gracie's secretary to tell Gracie I had stopped by, then I made my way to Sarah Washington's office. Sarah had recently been appointed Senior Assistant District Attorney in the Trial Division, and she was responsible for prosecuting all of the Asian Dragon cases. All, that is, except the thirteen cases brought in Federal Court. Those cases were being handled by the US Attorney's Office. That still left Sarah with a boatload of cases, and even with the staff she had as Senior ADA, prosecuting all those cases wouldn't be easy.

That was why I was hoping to take advantage of the situation to cut a deal for Jenny. But first I needed to set the groundwork, and then I needed Jenny's cooperation.

When I walked into Sarah's office, she looked up and asked, "What the hell do you want?" I knew Sarah was under a lot of pressure, but I never expected that kind of welcome. Maybe it wasn't a good time to visit. I thought about leaving, but instead I said, "I just dropped by to say hello and maybe discuss a little business." Sarah just grunted, never looking up from the papers on her desk. Not sure what to do, I said, "Who the hell are you, and what did you do with my friend, Sarah Washington?" I figured I had nothing to lose.

Sarah started to laugh, and she apologized for being so "abrupt" with me. I told her she hadn't been abrupt; she had been downright rude. I should know because I'm the king of rude. She laughed again and asked what I wanted. Now that we were back on friendly terms, I said that I had a defendant in the Asian Dragon cases, and I wanted to talk about my client's situation. I explained Jenny's situation and my thoughts about keeping her case off the trial calendar for as long as possible. Sarah agreed it was a good strategy, and she said if I kept making pretrial motions, she'd consent to adjourning Jenny's case.

Sarah wanted to know more about Jenny's personal situation, but unfortunately, since Jenny wasn't talking to me, I couldn't give her any information. Rather than confess that my client wasn't cooperating, I said we'd talk about it in due course. I'm not sure what "in due course" means. I've heard some very smart people use the phrase, so I thought I'd throw it in at that point. Sarah just nodded and I assumed we were good for the time being.

Now I had to come up with a bunch of pretrial motions, none of which were likely to be granted, but all of which would delay a trial. I hate using such a tactic because I don't like playing the system, but as long as Jenny refused to cooperate, I didn't have much of a choice. I'd do whatever I could to protect her and hope at some point I could get through to her.

That night at dinner, I told Gracie what I was doing. Gracie agreed I would be abusing the system, but she didn't see that I had much of a choice. I was doing the best I could under the circumstances, and it was my duty as a criminal defense lawyer to do no less. I felt better hearing that come from Gracie, but I still wasn't comfortable with the plan.

In her job with the Special Victims' Unit, Gracie often deals with female victims who refuse to cooperate or are too scared to cooperate. I asked her if she had any advice on how I could handle Jenny. She said I needed to be patient, which isn't my strong suit, and I needed to win her confidence. I asked how I was supposed to do that, and Gracie said I'd have to figure that one out on my own. There are times when Gracie sounds a lot like Doug.

CHAPTER 18

Tommy walked into my office, and the first thing he said was that we had a meeting with Professor Jack Wu at NYU in an hour. I had no idea who Professor Wu was or why we were going to meet him. Seeing the puzzled look on my face, Tommy explained. Professor Wu was a friend of Linda Chow, Tommy's computer whiz partner. That was all well and good, but it didn't explain why we were meeting with him.

The reason, Tommy said, was because Professor Wu was an expert on Chinatown's history. If I wanted to know more about old Chinatown and the tunnels, Professor Wu was the man to see. It made sense. If we're looking for the tunnels, it wouldn't hurt to know where, when and how they were built.

New York University is spread out in over ninety buildings, mostly in Lower Manhattan with the bulk clustered around Washington Square Park. Professor Wu's office was in the University's History Department on the fourth floor at 53 Washington Square South. On a nice day, it's a decent walk from my office on Mott Street to Washington Square Park. But on a rainy day like the one we were having, it's not so nice, and Tommy insisted on taking a taxicab. Me, I'd rather walk miles in the rain than ride one block in a New York City taxicab. But I didn't have time to walk, so we took the taxicab.

Amazingly we made the relatively short trip without incident. At least none that I was aware of having because I had my eyes closed the whole time. Tommy used to make fun of my "thing with taxicabs," claiming it was irrational. That was until I challenged him to show me a single taxicab that doesn't have scars from a collision with something. Thus far, he hasn't been able to do it. I think the first thing a driver does on pulling out of the garage with a brand-new taxicab is to drive into something. It's like an initiation for the taxicab.

But as usual, I digress. Professor Wu's office was small and cluttered with books and papers. He greeted us warmly, offering us tea or coffee as he cleared room on the two guest chairs so we could sit. Two of the office walls were lined with bookshelves filled with books and files. The wall behind the professor's desk was what some people call a "brag wall," filled with diplomas, certificates and photographs of the professor with presumably prominent people. I say presumably because I only recognized a few of them.

The professor was of Chinese descent, but he spoke without an accent. I'd later learn he was third generation Chinese, and much of what he would tell us came from stories told by his grandparents and even his great grandparents. From what I could gather by reading the "brag wall," Wu had degrees from Yale and Harvard and was recognized by many as an expert on the history of the Chinese in the United States.

I was impressed. All I wanted to know at that point was if he knew anything about the Chinatown tunnels, but I had promised Tommy I'd let him take the lead so I kept my mouth shut. In case you haven't noticed, I'm not big on patience, so it would probably surprise you that the first meeting with Professor Wu lasted nearly two hours without him talking about the tunnels. The meeting would have gone longer except the professor had a class to teach.

The man was absolutely fascinating, and I got hooked on his stories. Chinatown's history was a hell of a lot more interesting than I thought, and if I was going to learn about the tunnels, I'd first have to understand that history.

Chinese immigration to the United States began in the middle of the eighteenth century, with a small number of immigrants settling on the west coast. By the middle of the nineteenth century, a wave of Chinese immigrants arrived in California, enticed by the famous Gold Rush. But when the dream of golden riches gave way to reality, many moved east to New York City, settling in the slum area of the Lower East Side of Manhattan then known as Five Points.

Five Points covered much of what later became Chinatown and Little Italy, and it was notorious for its violence. In the mid-1800s, it was home to several criminal gangs. Criminal gangs such as: Forty Thieves, the Bowery Boys and Dead Rabbits, to name three. The story of these gangs is portrayed in the Martin Scorsese movie, *The Gangs of New York*, set in Five Points, in the mid 1880s.

The early Chinese immigrants arriving in New York City settled on Mott Street and the community grew around it. In 1880, the area bounded by Pell, Mott and Doyers Streets would get the name Chinatown in an article in the *New York Times*.

In keeping to themselves and maintaining their customs, the Chinese immigrants were viewed by many as odd and dangerous. This image wasn't helped by their willingness to work for cheap wages. Fueled by a growing resentment against the Chinese immigrants, Congress in 1882 passed the Chinese Exclusion Act, barring any further immigration of Chinese people. The Act would have a heavy impact on the social structure of the Chinese communities because it barred the immigration of wives and children of Chinese workers already in the United States.

In New York City's Chinatown, which at the time had a population of seven thousand, there was an estimated one hundred fifty men for every forty women. The ban remained in effect until 1943, at which time it was lifted and a quota for Chinese immigration was established.

With an overwhelmingly male population, Chinatown was rumored to be a den of male inequity and was labeled the "bachelor's society." Claims of opium dens, prostitution, illegal gambling, and slavery were widespread. Many of the rumors were true, but they didn't define the entire Chinatown population.

To protect themselves from growing hostility, the residents of Chinatown banded together as they had in China in organizations and societies called tongs. Many of these tongs were benevolent and trade organizations, but others were criminal enterprises.

The reaction of New York City's Caucasian population to the rumors of what went on in Chinatown was a mixture of disgust and fascination. Eventually, fascination outweighed disgust, and a growing number of New Yorkers visited Chinatown to eat in its ever-increasing number of restaurants. Cooks created dishes meant to appeal to the Caucasian population, dishes such as chop suey and chow mein.

Food wasn't the only thing attracting New Yorkers to Chinatown. Gambling, drugs and prostitution were openly offered by criminal elements ruling Chinatown during the early decades of the twentieth century.

We were just getting to the tongs and the infamous Tong Wars when Professor Wu said he had to leave to teach a class. I was going to suggest he skip the class but thought better of it. He didn't strike me as someone who took responsibility lightly. Instead, we made an appointment to see the professor again in his office the next afternoon. I would have preferred the morning, but I was busy. I was going to see Jenny at Rikers.

CHAPTER 19

The following day proved interesting in more ways than one.

I don't know why, but that was the day Jenny decided to confide in me. Maybe I had worn her down, or maybe she was finally scared by the reality of her situation. But whatever the reason, she opened up to me. Her last name wasn't Shao; it was Shum. Shao was her great grandmother's maiden name, a name she figured wouldn't turn up in any computer search since the woman had lived and died in a small city in the middle of China.

Jenny had been born in San Francisco to first generation Chinese American parents. Her father was an orthopedic surgeon, with a very successful practice. Her mother was a tenured professor of economics at Golden State University. The family lived in a townhouse bordering Lafayette Park in the posh neighborhood of Pacific Heights. So what the hell was this rich kid from San Francisco doing living in a slum in New York City under an assumed name?

After telling me about her parents, Jenny stopped talking and looked away. I was afraid she was going to close down again, so I stopped asking questions. I figured talking about her parents had upset her, and I'd give her a minute or two to compose herself. Finally I said, "Just tell me why." She looked at me and, with tears running down her cheeks, she said, "My father threw me out of the house." Wow! I wasn't expecting that one.

I was fairly certain Jenny wasn't a drug addict, and she didn't appear to be pregnant, so I couldn't imagine why her old man would throw her out. Admittedly, I have a limited imagination when it comes to raising kids, never having had any of my own. At least none that I'm aware of. Some of my drinking years are a bit foggy, but there haven't been any paternity suits brought against me.

Still confused, I again asked Jenny, "Why?" She explained. Three years earlier, when she was 15, she fell in love with an 18-year-old Chinese boy from San Francisco's Chinatown. His name was Shing Lew, and he was a Chinese national in the country illegally. Knowing her parents wouldn't approve, she tried to hide the relationship, but somehow they found out about it and forbid her to see Shing. But Jenny was in love and met with Shing in Chinatown almost daily, at times skipping school. It wasn't long before the two started having sex.

Jenny claimed that for the first year and a half she didn't know Shing was a member of the Golden Dragons, a Chinatown street gang. I wasn't sure I believed her, but it didn't matter if I believed her or not. She said when she learned Shing was in the gang, she confronted him, and he promised to quit the gang. Although that was probably a lie, it turned out not to matter.

At the time, the San Francisco PD had Shing under surveillance and in one of those chance things, a detective working the case had been a patient of Jenny's father. He recognized Jenny from the pictures her father kept on his desk. Fearing that Jenny would get swept up when Shing was arrested, the detective alerted Jenny's father to the situation. Eventually his good deed would backfire when Jenny warned Shing about the cops. But I'm getting ahead of myself here.

Jenny's father was a no-nonsense man. The same day he learned that Jenny was still seeing Shing, he enrolled Jenny in a girls' boarding school in Texas. When Jenny arrived home that evening, she found her parents waiting for her with her bags packed. Her father confronted her with surveillance photographs given to him by his detective patient. Then in a very calm and controlled voice, he told her that her behavior had become totally unacceptable and since she could no longer be trusted, she had to attend the school in Texas.

When Jenny protested, her father said it was either attend the school or leave his house. Jenny looked to her mother, but her mother backed her father. After screaming obscenities at both of her parents, Jenny ran from the house, vowing never to return.

With nowhere to go and no money, she called Shing, and they arranged to meet at a hangout in Chinatown. On her way there, Jenny stopped at an ATM hoping to get some cash, but her father had acted quickly and canceled her bank card. She then tried her credit card with the same result. Frustrated, she tried calling Shing only to find her cell phone service had also been terminated. She was on her own; the only one she had now was Shing.

When the two met, Jenny explained what had happened and she told Shing about the surveillance photographs. They spent the night in a flophouse hotel in the Tenderloin District. The next morning, Shing picked up some cash, and they left town on a Greyhound bus. Stopping for a day or two along the way to rest and pick up some clothes, they traveled to New York City. Once in the city, Shing hooked up with the Asian Empire, and they moved into an apartment on Elizabeth Street that they shared with two other gang members. Shing got her an identification card with the name Jenny Shao, and her new life began. That had been a year and a half ago.

As hard as it had been to get Jenny to start talking, the words were now pouring out faster than I could take notes. It was as though an emotional dam had burst, and now everything she had been holding inside was rushing out in torrents. I wanted to give her a break, but I was afraid if I did, she might clam up again, so I encouraged her to continue.

Life with Shing in New York City wasn't exactly what Jenny had hoped for. Most nights, he'd leave her in the apartment around ten o'clock and not return until nearly dawn. Then he'd sleep most of the day. When she asked for money, he gave her very little and did so grudgingly. Finally realizing that she was trapped, Jenny got a job as a waitress in a Chinese restaurant on Pell Street. It wasn't a great job and it didn't pay much, but without a Social Security card, there weren't many jobs she could get.

She hated her life. Shing continued to ignore her, and the two men with whom she and Shing shared the apartment treated her badly. She said they never touched her or anything like that; they just ignored her most of the time. But they would scream at her if she disturbed them.

Jenny's only friends were two girls she met while working at the restaurant. She wanted to invite them to visit, but Shing wouldn't allow it. He said she should keep to herself; it was better that way.

After a couple of months living in the Elizabeth Street apartment, Jenny demanded they move into a place of their own. Shing said he'd think about it. That night when she returned from work, she found her clothes in the hallway in plastic bags and the lock on the apartment door changed. After she pounded on the door, a stranger answered and screamed at her to go away.

With no place to go and very little money, she called one of her friends from the restaurant who took her in. They worked out an arrangement on the rent, and that was where she was living when arrested. The apartment was a tenement slum. It had two bedrooms. Jenny and her girlfriend shared one of the bedrooms, and the other was shared by three guys. The three guys kept pretty much to themselves, but Jenny admitted knowing they were members of the Asian Empire gang. She never spoke to them other than to say hello, and she never mentioned knowing Shing to them.

I asked her about her own gang status and how she happened to be with so many Asian Empire gang members the night she was arrested. She swore she wasn't a member and had nothing to do with the gang. The night of her arrest, she had gone to the club on Pell Street with another friend from the restaurant. It was the first time she had been in the place and, although she had never met most of the people there, she figured they were members of the Asian Empire. I didn't know whether to believe her, but I wasn't going to challenge her at that point because I didn't want her clamming up again.

I said nothing and waited for Jenny to talk. After a minute, she asked me if I knew what happened to Shing because she hadn't seen or heard from him since she was thrown out of the Elizabeth Street apartment. I told her all I knew was that he wasn't on the list of defendants scooped up in the Operation Asian Dragon raid. I couldn't tell if she was relieved or angry at the news. I didn't want to believe she still had a thing for Shing, but she struck me as one of those kids that, in the words of the old song, falls in love too easily.

I could tell the kid was emotionally drained. She had hit the bottom of the well. I'm not the touchy-feely type, but I felt sorry for the kid and was almost tempted to put my arms around her and comfort her. I say almost because I'm not sure I had it in me to do it. Besides, it wasn't going to happen, not with the Correction Officer watching us through the window in the door. The last thing I needed was to be accused of fraternizing with a prisoner and a young one at that.

I assured Jenny I would do everything I could to get her the best deal possible, but that meant she'd have to stay at Rikers a little longer. I knew it wasn't going to make her happy, but if she couldn't post bail, there wasn't anything I could do about it. I suggested contacting her parents, but Jenny said no, she didn't need their help. Like hell she didn't, but it wasn't my call.

I sat with Jenny a little while longer until I felt she was feeling better emotionally, then I told her I'd be back to see her once I had spoken to the ADA handling her case. She smiled, and for the first time since we met, she thanked me.

I figured all along that she was a good kid that had somehow gotten mixed up in a bad situation. Now I knew that my instincts were right, and that made keeping her locked up harder, but it was the only way I could get her a reasonable plea deal. Maybe I could lean on Sarah Washington; it was a long shot, but one worth taking. As soon as I left Rikers, I called Sarah and set up a meeting for the next day, then I went off for my second lesson on Chinatown's history.

CHAPTER 20

Tommy and I arrived at Professor Wu's office early and found him anxiously awaiting our arrival. He confessed that he was excited having such eager students interested in Chinatown's history. The course he taught at the university covered the history of China, with very little about Chinese migration and nothing specific about New York City's Chinatown.

He confessed that it was his fascination as a boy with Chinatown that attracted him to study Chinese history. I asked if he was raised in Chinatown. He laughed, and said no, far from it. He grew up in Westchester County, just north of New York City, and his early contacts with Chinatown were minimal, basically limited to those occasions when his parents took him there for dinner. But whenever he went, he was always fascinated by the sights and sounds of the area. Once he was old enough, he went to Chinatown on his own, often spending whole days just wandering the streets.

But when he went to Yale, his very active social life kept him from visiting Chinatown, even though the Yale campus in New Haven, Connecticut, wasn't that far away from New York City. Taking his Master's Degree and earning his PhD at Harvard also kept him away from New York City. But when he came to NYU as a professor of Chinese history, he was naturally drawn to Chinatown, only a few blocks from the campus. He was surprised to find that nothing had really changed in the years since he had been there. Chinatown still fascinated him as it had when he was a boy.

Over the past decade since arriving at NYU, he had researched and studied Chinatown's history. He had published articles, lectured at the Museum of Chinese in America in Lower Manhattan, and he even conducted tours of the area. But he admitted that he was the happiest when he could share his knowledge with interested people.

Class picked up where we had left off at our last session, the tongs of Chinatown. The word tong means, "a meeting place," and generally describes the community organizations first formed by Chinese immigrants in San Francisco to provide aid and protection. At the start, these tongs offered loans and shelter to newly arrived immigrants, mediated disputes, and provided mutual assistance to local merchants. Over time, some tongs turned to illegal activities, including gambling, drugs and prostitution. Not unlike the Italian mafia, these criminal tongs preyed on members of the local community, selling protection and loan sharking.

The earliest criminal tongs in New York's Chinatown were the Hip Sing Tong and the On Leong Tong. At the head of the On Leong Tong, formed in 1893, was Tom Lee, a businessman known as "The Mayor of Chinatown." Headquartered on Mott Street, the tong ran gambling, drugs and prostitution. Lee spoke passable English and eventually developed connections with New York City's powerful political machine, Tammy Hall.

The Hip Sing Tong came to New York from San Francisco in the 1890s. With headquarters on Pell Street, the tong also ran criminal enterprises controlling much of the vice. The leader of the Hip Sing Tong was Sai Wing Mock, better known as the infamous Mock Duck. To counter the On Leong Tong's growing political influence, Mock Duck allied the Hip Sing Tong with enemies of Tammy Hall, most notably a crusading Assistant District Attorney and a zealous minister, who claimed their mission was to rid Chinatown of its vices.

At the turn of the twentieth century, Chinatown was a sea of corruption, and the two tongs, one protected by the police and the other protected by the District Attorney's Office, offered gambling, prostitution and drugs. And the tongs weren't alone when it came to criminal enterprises. In 1904, a Jewish gangster named Mike Salter opened the Pelham Cafe in the heart of Chinatown's vice district. Protected by Tammy Hall, Salter would become a prominent and important player in Chinatown's criminal world.

Known as the uncrowned prince of Chinatown, Salter had been an election captain for Tammany Hall. Having done well for the bosses by stuffing ballot boxes, intimidating voters and similar illegal tactics, he was given permission to open his saloon at 12 Pell Street in the building known as the House of a Hundred Entrances.

It was during this era, while the tongs controlled Chinatown, that the tunnels were built. Used to hide gambling and smuggling activities, they also allowed rival tong members to move about Chinatown undetected.

Things were just getting interesting when the professor's phone rang. After a brief conversation, he announced he was needed at a faculty meeting, and we'd have to end our session early. He only had about ten minutes before the meeting, so he wouldn't start on a new topic, but he was glad to answer any questions Tommy or I had.

I asked if he had ever been in the tunnels himself. He said the only tunnel he'd been in was the Wing Fat Arcade, but a few years ago he had spoken with a man who claimed to have been in the tunnels. I asked if he had the man's name and address. He did, but as he searched in his desk for the information, he warned us that the interview was seven years ago, and the man was ninety-one years old at the time.

That wasn't very encouraging, but there was some good news. The professor had notes from the interview, and he offered to make me a copy.

Going to a file cabinet in the corner of the room, he took out a folder and left the office. A few minutes later he returned and handed me copies of his file. He said the man's name and address were on the second page. I thumbed quickly through the pages, noticing some diagrams I hoped were maps of the tunnels.

The professor had a busy schedule over the next couple of days, and he wouldn't be able to meet with us until the end of the week. I was eager to hear more about Chinatown's history, but I was anxious to track down this new source the professor had given us. Actually, Tommy was the one who would track down the source; I would just supervise the job.

In the taxicab on the way back to the office, I was so busy reading the professor's notes that I wasn't even bothered by the ride. That alone should tell you how excited I was about the notes.

The man Professor Wu had interviewed about the tunnels was Yue Ying Tso. At the time he was living on Elizabeth Street, but that had been seven years earlier, so the address could be stale. He could have moved or, even more likely, died. After all, he was ninety-one years old when Wu met with him. Either way, I figured that was something our computer wizard, Linda Chow, should find out quickly.

I did a quick calculation and concluded that Tso was born in 1915, which meant he would have been a young boy when the tunnels were supposedly widely used. So, if he was alive and if we could find him, it was possible he could have the information we needed. It was another long shot in a case filled with long shots and guesses.

That night was pizza and movie night with Gracie. It was my turn to pick the movie, and I had chosen one of my favorite war movies, *The Bridge over the River Kwai,* but I was so distracted by Wu's memo I couldn't get into the story. All these questions were popping up in my mind, and I wanted like hell to go over Wu's memo again. Gracie had fallen asleep halfway through the movie, which happens to be two hours and forty minutes long, but I didn't dare turn off the movie or try reading the memo for fear she'd wake up and catch me at it. If she did, she'd have a fit and she'd be right. I've made her watch the movie at least three times, so if I wasn't going to watch it again, the least I could have done was tell her to pick something she liked. It would have been a chic flick, but if I was reading the memo, it wouldn't have mattered.

Life is complicated, especially when you live with a woman, and even more so when the woman is Gracie. I love her to death, but she is a handful. Please don't tell her I said that.

Anyway, the movie didn't end until after midnight, and it was another half hour before we were in bed. Gracie went back to sleep, and I tried reading the memo, but my eyes kept closing. I was beat, and I needed sleep.

The next morning, I had a conference scheduled with Sarah Washington. I was going to push her for a plea deal in Jenny's case and if I was going get it, I had to be sharp. So, a little after one o'clock, I gave up trying to read the memo and went to sleep. That night I dreamed about tunnels, and before you go all Freudian on me, it had nothing to do with sex. Not unless the sex involved walking in a tunnel with a ninety-eight-year-old man.

CHAPTER 21

My conference with Sarah Washington didn't go as well as I had hoped. The prosecutions in the Asian Dragon cases were dragging on for longer than anticipated because, for some reason, the target defendants weren't cutting plea deals. No one knew for sure why they were holding out, but they were and that was screwing up my strategy. The media was following the cases closely and starting to show impatience over the lack of convictions. What the Mayor and the DA had hoped would be a publicity bonanza was turning into a calamity for both. The mayor was pressuring the DA to get convictions, and the DA was pressuring his staff. He had made it clear he didn't care who they prosecuted; he wanted convictions. If they couldn't nail the big fish, then the small ones would have to do.

That was how things stood when I met with Sarah to ask for another adjournment of Jenny's case. Sarah was sympathetic and said under any other circumstances, she'd agree to an adjournment, but her hands were tied. She was under strict orders not to grant any adjournments in any Asian Dragon case. That meant I'd have to ask the Court to adjourn the case, and with the DA opposing my request, I'd need a damn good reason for the adjournment. Unfortunately, my only reason for wanting an adjournment was so I could cut a better deal down the road, and that reason wasn't going to cut it.

The alternatives to an adjournment were a trial or a plea bargain. The DA had squat for evidence against Jenny, and the chances for an acquittal were good but not guaranteed. A lot depended on the public's interest at the time of the trial and with the media frenzy, the atmosphere wasn't favorable for an acquittal. Jenny's explanation that she didn't know the people she was with when she was arrested, and she didn't know they were carrying an ass-load of oxycodone, might or might not fly. But the only way to find out was to put Jenny on the stand, and that created more problems than I was ready to deal with. In the first place, there was the matter of her name and who she was. As soon as Jenny took the stand and swore to tell the truth, the first question would be to state her name. If she said, "Jenny Shao," she'd be committing perjury, and we'd both be in a world of trouble. Jenny for lying under oath and me for allowing a witness to lie on the stand. Technically it's called suborning perjury. It's a crime, and it could get me disbarred.

Talk about being between a rock and a hard spot. I liked Jenny, and I'd do everything I could to help her, but I wasn't going to commit a crime and risk being disbarred. I came close to being disbarred in my drinking days, and I vowed that I'd never let that happen again. I considered withdrawing as Jenny's lawyer, so the Court would have to give her time to get a new one, and the new lawyer would need time to come up to speed on the case. But I'd need the Court's permission to withdraw and for that I'd need a good reason. Usually attorneys ask to be removed from cases because the client isn't paying them. But I was being paid by the 18B Panel, so that reason wasn't going to fly.

I had to face facts. The options were narrowing, and there wasn't anything I could do about it. It was time to find out what kind of plea deal I could negotiate. I pressed Sarah, arguing that she didn't have enough evidence for a conviction, and she should drop the charges down to a misdemeanor. Sarah was no rookie; she knew I was boxed in; and she had the upper hand. But she's a good egg, and she wasn't going in for the kill, at least not right then. She said under the circumstances, there was no way she could reduce the charges to a misdemeanor, but she was willing to drop the more serious charges of intent to sell if Jenny pleaded guilty to simple possession. That sounded good; we were on the right trail, but the question was the quantity of the drugs.

Sarah said she couldn't drop down too far on the charge because her boss would never approve it. She suggested one charge of criminal possession of a controlled substance in the third degree. It was a Class B felony, but with a first offense, the sentence could be as low as one year or as high as nine years. It would also include five years of probation. Sarah said she'd recommend the minimum sentence, but that was just a recommendation, and it didn't stop the judge from imposing a stiffer sentence. We'd be rolling dice and with all the publicity these Asian Dragon cases were getting, I didn't like the odds.

I pushed to have the charge reduced to criminal possession of a controlled substance in the fifth degree. It was still a felony, but only a Class D felony, and on a first offense, the sentence was one to one and a half years. It carried the same minimum sentence, but it removed the risk of a much longer sentence if the judge didn't go along with the DA's recommendation. Sarah thought about it, but she said it would be a hard sell. She countered with an offer of criminal possession in the fourth degree, a Class C felony, with a minimum sentence for a first offense of one to five and a half years. With that charge, the odds of a judge approving a minimum sentence were better but still not guaranteed.

We were getting closer to a deal, but I still had another big problem to solve before I could work out a final deal. Under New York Criminal Procedure Law, the judge is required to order a presentence investigation on any defendant convicted of a felony, and he cannot pronounce sentence until a written report has been issued. An investigation into Jenny Shao was going to turn up nothing, and that would send up all sorts of red flags. There was no way we could reach a plea deal until we came clean, and I gave Sarah Jenny's real last name.

Not sure how to start, I simply mentioned that Jenny may have been known under a different name that wasn't in the record. Sarah frowned and asked me to explain. I could have done one of my usual tap dances around the subject, but I knew Sarah wouldn't buy any bullshit. Besides, she and I had always been straight with each other. I wasn't about to jeopardize our relationship, not when I had to come clean at some point anyway. I said, "Shao isn't Jenny's last name; Shum is." Sarah dropped her head into her hands and asked, "When were you planning on telling me this?"

I said I had planned on telling her earlier, but it slipped my mind. I don't think Sarah appreciated the humor because she sure as hell wasn't laughing. She wanted details about Jenny, and I gave her what I knew, which wasn't much. She asked me if there was anything in Jenny's past that would sink a sentencing recommendation. I assured her that I had checked Jenny out, and she was clean. In fact, her record was so clean it would definitely support a lighter sentence. Sarah seemed relieved and suggested it would help if

Jenny's parents cooperated and came for the sentencing. That I already knew and I told Sarah that I had discussed it with Jenny, but she didn't want her parents contacted. Sarah shrugged her shoulders. It wasn't her problem. It was mine.

Sarah was right; it was my problem. Was I going to follow my client's instructions and not contact her parents, or was I going to do what I thought best? It wasn't an easy decision to make. You probably have no idea what can happen when you ignore a client's orders. Well, I do. Unfortunately, I know exactly what happens since I've walked that plank a couple of times. You wind up arguing incessantly with the client, who becomes even more uncooperative than he or she had been before. It's an absolute nightmare.

So why did I do it in the past? Because it was the right thing to do for the client. In the end, the client realized that and was grateful. But in the interim, it was a living hell.

CHAPTER 22

That evening, Tommy called with good news. Yue Ying Tso was alive and well, at least as well as one could expect at ninety-eight years of age. He no longer lived on Elizabeth Street; he was in a nursing home in Flushing. Tommy hadn't actually seen him, but he had spoken to his son, who said his father was a bit feeble, but his mind was still strong.

He knew I'd want to see Tso as soon as possible, and when he hadn't been able to contact me, he checked my schedule with Connie, then arranged for us to see Tso the next morning. I told Tommy I'd meet him at the office at nine o'clock in the morning, and we'd go see Tso together.

Flushing was in the outer borough of Queens, technically a part of New York City, but no Manhattanite considered those outer borough people true New Yorkers. To me, traveling to Queens was like leaving the country.

The next morning, I met Tommy as planned, and of course, we argued over how we were going to get to Flushing. Tommy wanted to take a taxicab, and I wanted to go by subway. Since I was paying the bills, the argument was brief, and we went by subway.

The Sunshine Nursing Home was five blocks from the subway stop at Main Street. As Tommy and I walked to the nursing home, I remarked how much downtown Flushing was starting to resemble Manhattan's Chinatown. Tommy laughed and said he recently read that Mandarin Town, as Flushing's Chinatown was called, was larger and faster growing than Manhattan's Chinatown. I wanted to argue with Tommy, but looking around as we walked the five blocks to the nursing home convinced me Tommy was probably right.

The Sunshine Nursing Home was a five-story brick building with large windows, a center garden court, and a seemingly very accommodating staff. When we introduced ourselves to the receptionist, she said Mr. Yue Ying Tso was waiting for us in the sunroom, and she summoned a nurse who took us to him.

Yue Ying Tso was sitting in a wheelchair, and he smiled pleasantly as the young nurse introduced us. He was extremely thin and looked every bit ninety-eight years old, but his eyes shined with the intensity of a younger man, giving me hope that his memory was intact. When he spoke, his voice was shaky, but there was no hesitation in his speech.

When I said we were there to talk to him about the Chinatown tunnels, he smiled and said he remembered talking about the tunnels to a nice young man some years ago. As he recalled, the man was a professor. I don't know if seven years ago is considered long-term or short-term memory, but obviously whatever it was, Tso's memory was good.

I asked him if he had been in the tunnels and he said many times. Then he went on to explain. When he was a young boy, his mother worked in a laundry, and his father worked as a waiter in a restaurant two doors down from where they lived on Mott Street. On the nights that his mother worked late, which was often, his father would bring him to the restaurant, and he'd sit in the kitchen where an old cook named Chen Gao befriended him.

Apparently, the old cook loved to tell stories and in Tso, he found an eager audience. One night, about a year after Gao had been telling him stories about China and life in Chinatown, Gao said he had a special story to tell him. But first Tso had to promise never to reveal what he was about to hear. When Tso made the promise, Gao said he once worked for Tom Lee, the leader of On Leong Tong, and he was one of Lee's hit men called *boo how doy.* Then he told stories of the Tong Wars and the bloody battles fought on Doyers Street. Tso remembered the night Gao claimed he had been in the Chinese Theater on Doyers Street on the night when hit men sent by the Hip Sing leader, Mock Duck, killed four On Leong members. Telling the story in chilling detail, he said that he had escaped death by using one of the secret tunnels. Then, whispering in Tso's ear, he said that he and two other On Leong boo how doy attacked a Hip Sing laundry man with hatchets in retaliation for the theater attack.

That night, without revealing what Gao had told him, Tso asked his father if the old cook's stories were true. His father, inferring from the question that Gao had told Tso about his past, said the stories were true. Chen Gao had been a *boo how doy* for the On Leong Tong. And a fierce and important one, at that. Tso asked his father why Gao, who was so important, was now a lowly cook. His father explained that when the police cracked down on the crime in Chinatown, arresting as many members of both the Hip Sing and On Leong Tongs they could find, Gao went into hiding. Chen Gao disguised himself as a cook as he waited for the tongs to reorganize. But with the police constantly patrolling Chinatown's streets, Gao had accepted his fate, and he remained a cook.

The old cook continued regaling young Tso with stories that both fascinated and terrified him. One night when business in the restaurant was slow, the old cook took Tso into the basement and showed him a secret panel that opened into a tunnel. Together they entered the tunnel. Tso was in awe, seeing the tunnels that the old cook had talked about in so many of his stories. The tunnels used by the tongs to escape police and each other. But the tunnels hadn't been used by the tongs in twenty years.

Tso said he remembers that night in the tunnel with Chen Gao vividly, like it was yesterday. He had been so impressed that, from then on, whenever his father took him to the restaurant, he'd explore the tunnels. Occasionally he'd hear someone else in the tunnels, and he'd hide, his heart racing as he imagined a hatchet wielding gangster stalking him. But it usually turned out to be some old man hustling along with a package of laundry or groceries.

Recalling those days brought a smile to the old man's face. He took a sip from the cup of tea the nurse had brought him and asked if we wanted to hear more. Indeed I did. He smiled at me and bowed his head. Then he continued with his story.

He explored the tunnels two or three nights a week for two years. In time, he was able to travel the length and width of Chinatown underground. He laughed, saying, "Of course, in those times, Chinatown consisted of only three streets." But he could travel in the tunnels from the beginning of Mott Street to the end of Pell Street. That got my attention. Joey and the Cha brothers had escaped through the basement of a restaurant at No. 10 Mott Street. I asked Tso if he remembered the address of the restaurant where his father worked, and he did remember. It was No. 28 Mott Street.

I looked at Tommy. Maybe we were on to something. I asked Tso if the tunnel went as far as Bayard Street, which was where Joey recalled exiting the tunnel the day of the robbery. The old man said it was possible, but he couldn't say for sure.

I had brought along a street map of Lower Manhattan, and I handed it to Tso, asking if he could draw the locations of the tunnels on the map. He laughed and said he knew the tunnels from below ground only. Walking through them nearly ninety years earlier, he never knew for certain what was above. He recalled passing through a number of basements, but he didn't know the building numbers. He sighed and said much of what he knew about the tunnels back then eluded his memory now.

I was sure the old man was telling the truth, and he had shared with us everything he remembered about the tunnels. Both Tommy and I had other places we needed to be, but we didn't want to seem rude by rushing off. Besides, I admit that I was enjoying the stories. We sat and listened to Tso's stories until the nurse returned and announced it was time for his exercise class.

On the subway ride back to Manhattan, Tommy and I agreed the information from Tso, while lacking in detail, might still be helpful. We had a lot more work to do on Joey's case, but it would have to wait because I needed to turn my attention to Jenny Shao's case.

CHAPTER 23

The next morning I sat down with Jenny and explained we either had to go to trial or make a plea deal. Jenny, being an optimistic, dopey young kid, was convinced she'd beat the rap at trial because, as far as she was concerned, she hadn't done anything wrong. In some eyes, she may have been right, but in the eyes of the law, she was a coconspirator. As much as I hated to disillusion her, she needed to hear the facts of life. Yes, we might win at trial, and she'd go free. But the way the law was written, there was a better chance she'd be convicted. And if she was convicted, she'd spend the next fifteen years or more of her life in prison.

No one likes to hear they might be going to prison, and Jenny was no exception. As soon as I mentioned her going to prison, her face took on a hostile look, then it quickly faded, and she started to cry. Jenny wasn't as tough as she pretended to be, and I felt badly for her. There was no way Jenny would survive a long prison term. Being at Rikers awaiting trial was one thing; having the penitentiary doors slammed behind you is something else altogether. I'd known dozens of kids like her, and I saw what happened to them when they went into the system. Most came out hardened or broken, and none came out better off than when they went in. I didn't want that happening to Jenny, but I needed her to understand that a plea deal was the only way to ensure she wouldn't wind up spending the next fifteen years in prison. If Jenny was sent to prison, she was going to have a tough time of it.

I explained to Jenny, in excruciatingly vivid detail, what she could expect to face at trial and the numerous pitfalls involved. She was a stupid kid, but she wasn't dumb, and what I told her seemed to sober her as I expected and hoped it would. After considering what I had just told her, she asked about a plea deal. I had done enough with the doom and gloom, so I started with the best-case scenario, even though at the time it was a long shot. I said I might be able to have the charge reduced to a misdemeanor with no prison time, but I did warn Jenny that was a reach. A more realistic possibility was having the charge reduced to a Class E felony with no prison time, or a sentence of time served. But our best chance for either outcome was if Jenny's parents cooperated.

I thought for sure Jenny would agree and either call them herself or allow me to call them. But I was wrong. She outright refused to call them and ordered me not to contact them. I did my best to change her mind, but to no avail. Finally, frustrated and unable to think of anything else to do, I said goodbye to Jenny, and I told her to call me if she changed her mind.

All the way back to Lower Manhattan, I kept arguing with myself over what to do. I was in an ethical bind. I wanted to call Jenny's parents, but Jenny was the client, and she had ordered me not to call them. What should I do? Obey my client and probably see her go to prison, or disregard her specific instructions in the hope of saving her ass? Not to mention my own ass, which would be on the line if I ignored a client's specific instructions.

In situations like this, I often turn to Gracie, who usually gives me good advice. But I'll admit that sometimes my ego gets in the way. I think it's an alcoholic thing. When I drank alcoholically I knew everything, and there was nothing anybody could tell me. I was smarter than everybody else, and I knew better than everybody else. Unfortunately, when I got sober, I got dopey. Some people say I just wised up and that's probably true, but I don't like to admit it. Every now and then, that old superior thinking kicks in, and it's usually then that Gracie demands I go to an AA meeting or call Doug. If she's really pissed off, she suggests I do both, and she asks me to drop in for a visit with the Devil.

That night I asked Gracie's advice about calling Jenny's parents. I figured Gracie, being a woman and all, could probably relate better to Jenny than I could. When you're used to dealing with violent scumbag felons, dealing with an eighteen-year-old girl requires an adjustment in approach. A big adjustment.

I asked Gracie if she thought I should call Jenny's parents. She said as a lawyer her advice was to follow my client's instructions. "You can't get in trouble doing that," she reminded me, as if I needed reminding. Then she added that if I really wanted to help this girl, I'd call her parents.

I had just about made up my mind to call Jenny's father when Gracie threw a wrench into the works, and she asked me what I would do if Jenny's parents refused to cooperate. It was a good question and one that took me by surprise. It had never entered my mind that they would refuse to help Jenny. For some reason, I had this notion that parents always help their kids, no matter what. It was an odd notion because my old man had walked out on my mother and me when I was a little boy. I guess it was the love and loyalty my mother had shown me that made me think all mothers were like that. The truth was that I knew they weren't. I had handled enough domestic violence cases, both male and female, to know that the family bond isn't always what it should be.

But in Jenny's case, her parents were highly educated and successful people. And Jenny was just a mixed up jerky kid. Surely, they could understand and want to help their only child. Gracie said she wasn't so sure about that. I thought maybe Gracie's experiences in dealing with crime victims played a part in her thinking, but I couldn't discount her opinion. In the end, I decided to reach out to Jenny's parents, but I was prepared for them to turn me down. At least that's what I thought at the time.

CHAPTER 24

After my morning call with Mr. Fang confirming Joey was safe and behaving himself, I decided it was time to track down Jenny's parents. Obviously Jenny wasn't going to be any help, so I'd have to find the Shums on my own. First, I tried to get the Shums's home phone number, but it was unlisted. Disappointing, but not surprising.

Knowing Jack Shum was a prominent orthopedic surgeon, I figured how hard could it be locating him in San Francisco? After all, how many orthopedic surgeons named Jack Shum could there be? I was right; there was only one, and he was head of Orthopedic Surgery at the University of California San Francisco Hospital.

Finding Dr. Shum turned out to be a lot easier than getting him on the line. After allowing for the three-hour time difference, I called his office, only to find myself in one of those circular conversations that go nowhere and drive you out of your mind. This was the conversation:

"May I speak with Dr. Shum, please?"

"Do you wish to make an appointment?"

"No, I just want to talk to the doctor."

"May I tell him what it's about?"

"It's personal."

"Will he know what it's about?"

"Probably not."

"Can I tell him what it's about?"

"It's personal."

"Perhaps you'd like to make an appointment to see Dr. Shum?"

"No, I just want to talk to him, please.

"Can I tell him what it's about?"

At that point, my patience, which is marginal at the best of times, was worn very thin. I felt like saying, "Yeah, tell him his daughter is in jail on a major drug charge, and I'm trying to save her ass." But for Jenny's sake, I held my tongue, and I said simply that it involved his daughter. I hadn't intended to say that much, but the grand inquisitor left me with no choice. I thought if I had showed up in person at Shum's office, she'd have me on the rack by now.

After a short wait, a man, who identified himself as Dr. Shum, asked very abruptly who I was and what I wanted. Again, holding my tongue for Jenny's sake, I told him my name, explained why I was calling and asked for his help. Then, not to my surprise, but to my bitter disappointment, he said he had no daughter and hung up the phone.

At the moment, I was glad Gracie had prepared me for that kind of response from Jenny's father. If she hadn't, I might have concluded that I called the wrong Dr. Shum or Jenny was still lying to me about her name. But I knew neither was the case. When I told the grand inquisitor that I wanted to talk to Shum about his daughter, he immediately took the call, so I could safely assume he had a daughter. If he didn't have a daughter, why would he take the call?

Alright, so daddy dearest wasn't going to help Jenny, so that left mommy. I tried calling information for Mrs. Shum's telephone number, but it was unlisted. Jenny had said she was a professor of economics at Golden State University. I had Connie look up the telephone number of the Economics Department at Golden State.

Happily, this time around, there was no grand inquisitor, just one of those damn automated answering systems. *"If you know your party's extension, dial it now. If not, press 5 for our directory."*

Ten button presses later, I was finally connected to Professor Shum's line, only to get a recording that she was unavailable to speak and asking that I leave a message. At first, I was just going to hang up and try again later, but then I decided it might be better if she heard from me before she heard from her husband. I left a detailed message, along with my cell phone number, and asked her to call me as soon as she could.

With nothing else on my schedule that afternoon, I called Tommy and asked him if he wanted to go on a field trip. When he said yes, I called Detective Chen and arranged for him to be there as well. But before we went, I needed to talk to Joey.

Joey didn't have a cell phone, and there was no landline in the safe house. All precautions against Joey doing something stupid. Joey had protested vigorously but, in the end, he had to admit that he was prone to stupid behavior. The only way I could contact him was through his grandfather, Mr. Fang, who kept his own cell phone closely guarded.

Anyway, I spoke with Joey and got the information I needed. Then I met Tommy and Chen at the entrance to the basement at No. 10 Mott Street.

CHAPTER 25

When I arrived at the Golden Wok at No. 10 Mott Street, Detective Chen was waiting by the entrance to the basement, and he didn't look happy. I soon found out why. One of the squad's confidential informers had told one of Chen's detectives that a contract had been put out on Joey's life. It was a $30,000 deal which, in the scheme of things, was on the low end for a hit contract. But it was enough to draw a lot of action from the area gangbangers. The informer hadn't said who had put out the contract, but Chen assumed it was the Cha brothers.

The news wasn't good, but it wasn't unexpected. I figured all along that the Cha brothers would be looking to kill Joey, and it was why I had Mr. Fang arrange for a safe house. Later I'd call Mr. Fang and let him know about the contract. Since I had warned him it was likely to happen, it shouldn't come as much of a surprise. Still, I wanted him to know the threat was real, and he needed to keep Joey in hiding.

Even though the news of the hit was no surprise, it did worry me a little bit. Not so much for Joey, but for myself. A gangbanger looking to make a fast thirty grand might decide I was the quickest path to Joey. That was why I didn't want to know where the safe house was.

A $30,000 contract wouldn't attract a professional hitman, and that made matters worse. At least with a professional, it's quick, clean and good. The $30,000 guys are sloppy and slow. If you're going to be killed by a hitman, believe me, you want a high-priced professional doing the job. One shot and it's over. With these other bozos, they might have to shoot you five or six times before they kill you. How do I know that? A former client, Joey Bats, told me all about it. But that's another story.

While Chen and I were talking, Tommy arrived, and I turned my attention back to the matter at hand, finding the tunnel entrance.

The stairway leading to the basement was blocked off with yellow plastic police tape. The one with the words "CRIME SCENE. DO NOT CROSS" printed on it every couple of feet. It's not really much of a barrier; it's more of a suggestion and not a very strong one at that. I always thought the tape should have been red; you know, bureaucratic red tape and all that nonsense.

Chen lifted the tape, and we all ducked underneath and went down the stairs to the basement door. The door must have been locked because Chen started fumbling with a set of keys. Eventually Chen found the right key, and we all went inside.

It was dark, too dark for me to see anything, but Chen had come prepared with a flashlight. Using the beam from the flashlight, he found a light switch, and a couple of bare overhead bulbs lit up. They didn't give off much light, but it was enough for us to walk around without killing ourselves.

Eventually my eyes adjusted to the dim light, and I was able to see everything more clearly. The basement, like the building above it, was long and narrow. Pipes and electric wiring ran along the ceiling tacked to the exposed joists that held up the floor above.

There was a staircase along the far side wall toward the back of the basement that presumably led to the kitchen. The far back walls were lined with shelves holding boxes marked with Chinese characters and bags that I presumed contained rice. Chen said the boxes contained restaurant supplies and some cooking staples. The police and the FBI had examined them and the whole basement very carefully. He asked if I wanted to examine them myself.

I told Chen that I wasn't interested in anything in the back of the basement. I was interested in the area near the door we had come through. Chen asked why that particular area, and I explained that according to Joey, the exit into the tunnel wasn't far from the doorway. Chen asked how far and along which wall. I confessed that I wasn't sure because Joey wasn't sure.

When the door closed behind Joey and the Cha brothers, the basement went pitch black, and no one had a flashlight. Bobby told Joey and his wounded brother, Billy, to keep their backs against the wall. Then holding onto each other, Bobby led the way in the dark to the tunnel's entrance.

When I spoke with Joey earlier, I had him tell me the direction they moved and how far along the wall they went. He said they went to the right from the door about fifteen or so steps. That's when Bobby stopped, and Joey heard the creaking noise. I asked him if they made any turns along the way, and he said no, they moved in a straight line with their backs against the wall.

Following Joey's directions, I put my back against the wall to the right of the staircase. I moved along the wall, but it ended at the corner before I had walked fifteen steps. Joey must have been mistaken.

I examined the walls extending in both directions from the corner but found nothing. They were solid foundation walls. There was a joint in the side wall with some missing concrete, but Chen said the NYPD and the FBI had examined the joint and concluded it was solid. In fact, they had examined every inch of the basement walls and found nothing. That may have been true, but Joey and the Cha brothers got out of the basement somehow, and unless they had magical powers, there had to be a tunnel entrance somewhere down there.

CHAPTER 26

Disappointed that we hadn't made any progress in finding the tunnel entrance and since it was already past five o'clock, I was tempted to go straight to Gracie's place and not back to the office. But something inside me said I needed to go to the office, and I was glad I did. Professor Joan Shum had returned my call and could be reached at her office number for the remainder of the day.

It was only two-thirty in the afternoon, California time, when I returned the professor's call. She had left her extension number, which made reaching her office much less complicated.

Joan Shum answered on the first ring, making me think she might have been anxious to hear from me. I told her who I was and as I tried explaining why I was calling, she interrupted and asked if Jenny was okay. I assured her that physically she was fine, but her situation was not so good, and I explained what had happened.

When I finished explaining Jenny's situation, Joan Shum asked if I had called her husband. I wondered if she knew I had, and she was testing me or if she just suspected I had. Either way there was no point in lying. She'd find out the truth soon enough, so I said I had.

Joan Shum was a smart woman, so she had to know I wouldn't be calling her if her husband had been at all helpful. Nonetheless, she asked how he responded. For a moment I wasn't sure what to say. The woman obviously had doubts about her husband's attitude toward their daughter; otherwise, she wouldn't have needed to ask the question. But the fact that she asked the question meant she was holding out some hope that she was wrong. I knew she wasn't wrong, and I suspected she knew that as well. But what he had said about not having a daughter was so despicable, it might come as a shock to her. I didn't want her hanging up on me, and I wouldn't have blamed if she did after I told her what her husband said. Still, it needed to be said, and I said it.

There was a brief pause, then Joan Shum sobbed, a long and agonizing sob that said it all. I said nothing for the moment, giving her a chance to collect herself. Then I told her that Jenny needed her help. Through her tears, she asked what she needed to do. I told her it would help a great deal if she came to New York and made peace with Jenny. Without a moment's hesitation, she said that she would come as fast as she could.

Then I asked if she and her husband would post bail for Jenny. Joan had composed herself by that point, and she flatly said that she doubted her husband would agree to post bail. In fact, he'd probably object to her going to New York. She was prepared to defy him on that, but posting bail was another matter. I could understand where she was coming from. She said she would do her best to change her husband's mind, but he was a stubborn man so she wasn't hopeful.

Then she asked me to hold for a minute while she cleared her class schedule. When she came back on the line, she said that she could be in New York in two days. I said I'd make a reservation for her at a downtown hotel and get back to her with the details. She gave me her cell phone number and said if she wasn't able to answer, I should just leave a message. I gave her my cell phone number, and I told her to call if she had any questions.

That was it. I had no idea how this was going to turn out. All I knew was that Jenny needed the support of her parents, or at least her mother. Time would tell if I had done the right thing by calling her parents.

Later that night, I told Gracie about the conversation with Joan Shum. Gracie said I had done the right thing, and Jenny was likely to thank me once she realized her mother was there to support her. It all sounded good, but what was going to happen when Jenny found out her father had disowned her again? Gracie said she didn't know, but having one parent was better than being an orphan. Thinking back on my own life, I had to agree.

When my old man took a hike and never came back, I felt abandoned for a while, but my mother's love made me feel better. After all these years, I still remember her love and how it made me feel. So, I guess Gracie was right. The love of a mother can overcome the wrongs of a dumb ass bastard father.

It had been a long rough day and when my head finally hit the pillow, I thought I'd sleep like a log until the next morning. Boy, was I wrong!

CHAPTER 27

It was two o'clock in the morning, and I was sleeping peacefully next to Gracie when my cell phone rang. Groping in the dark to find it before the ringing woke up Gracie, I knocked over the lamp on the nightstand. That, of course, woke Gracie in a more frightening way than the ringing cell phone would have. So now I was trying to calm Gracie and answer the damn phone, all at the same time. It was Detective Chen.

Gracie turned on the lamp on her side of the bed and started yelling at me, making it difficult for me to hear what Chen was saying. I was fairly certain I had heard something about the Cha brothers and an arrest, but I couldn't get Gracie to shut up, so I got out of bed and locked myself in the bathroom. It was something Gracie had done a couple of times, so there was a precedent for the move. Of course, Gracie would later challenge my right to leave her in the midst of a conversation. I would have argued it wasn't so much a conversation as a lecture, but things had calmed down, and I have learned there are times when it's best to keep my comments to myself.

But the point I'm trying to make here is about the telephone call from Chen. His squad had been leaning on their confidential informers trying to locate the Cha brothers, but they had gotten nowhere. Then two nights ago, Chen received an anonymous tip that the brothers were hiding out in a deserted factory building in Long Island City. Chen had staked out the place and confirmed two men were living in the building, although he couldn't be sure it was Bobby and Billy Cha. But the odds were good enough to warrant a raid.

Earlier that night, Chen and his team raided the factory. The Cha brothers, heavily armed, refused to surrender and fired on the squad. In the gun battle that followed, one officer was wounded, and both Cha brothers were killed. Billy died on the factory floor in an exchange of gunfire. Bobby was shot and killed trying to escape.

Unfortunately, the money wasn't anywhere to be found and now with both brothers dead, it was anybody's guess where it might be. Failure to recover the money didn't affect Joey's deal directly. But Marty might have been open to a more lenient sentence if the money had been recovered.

The news was a lot to take in. After I hung up with Chen, I stayed locked in the bathroom a little while longer, trying to sort through it all. I figured if Gracie hadn't gone back to sleep, she'd be lying in wait for me, and there was no way I was going to get any peace and quiet anytime soon.

With both Cha brothers dead, Joey's odds of surviving went up. The Cha brothers' contract that was out on his life was worthless with no one left to pay it off. That was good news. Now it was just the Hip Sing Tong that had a reason to kill him. The bad news was that with the stolen money still out there, the tong's interest in Joey would be greater than ever.

It also meant that Marty Bowman was going to definitely want information about the tunnels because he had to figure that was where the money was hidden. Things weren't working out as I had hoped they would. With the recent field trip to the basement at No. 10 Mott Street a bust, I was hoping the capture of the Cha brothers would lead to something. Either recovery of the stolen money or information about the tunnels, or both.

Bobby Cha was the only one who knew where the stolen money was hidden; he was also the only one who could access the tunnel; and now he was dead. I'd have to find the money and the tunnels on my own and, so far, that wasn't going so well.

CHAPTER 28

The next morning Detective Chen called to let me know that his squad had just arrested Nancy Bellamy, the bank teller who had tipped off the Cha brothers about the cash payrolls. Joey hadn't known her last name, but it turned out there was only one Nancy working at the Citibank branch, and she fit the description Joey had provided. Chen had identified her as the insider some time ago but decided not to arrest her earlier, fearing for her safety. With the Cha brothers dead, the threat was gone, and the last suspect in the case was now in custody.

I called Marty and congratulated him on closing the Citibank case. I knew it wasn't actually closed, but it was my way of suggesting we were done, and we should all go home. I said all four perpetrators were accounted for, so the case was essentially over. All that remained was for Joey to plead guilty to robbery in the third degree, and that would be it. But Marty wasn't going for it. He said the case wasn't closed. There was still the matter of the missing stolen money.

I said it was a bank, how much could a couple of hundred thousand dollars mean to a bank the size of Citibank? Besides, it was insured.

I thought it made sense. Of course, I always think my arguments make sense. Marty didn't quite agree. He said there was also the matter of the tunnels. Not only was the money likely to be found in the tunnels, but the media wouldn't let go of the "Houdini Bandits" story until someone explained how the three had escaped from the basement. With the Cha brothers dead, that now fell to Joey. The NYPD and the DA's Office had suffered too much embarrassment over the case to just let it drop without an explanation.

If Joey or I couldn't provide the information, Joey wasn't getting the sweetheart deal. Third degree would be off the table, and he'd have to plead guilty to robbery in the second degree or go to trial. I objected but Marty wouldn't budge.

Coincidentally, Tommy and I had a meeting scheduled with Professor Wu that morning for another history lesson. The lessons were interesting, but if the professor couldn't give us something more about the tunnels, I didn't have time to listen.

Before leaving the office to meet Tommy, I called Mr. Fang and gave him the news about the Cha brothers. He was happy and relieved to hear of their demise and asked if that meant Joey could come out of hiding. I said it was best if Joey waited a couple of days to allow the news to get around. Until all of the potential gangbanger assassins realized the sponsors of the contract were dead and there'd be no payoff, it would be smart to keep Joey out of sight. Mr. Fang said he understood, and he'd keep Joey at the safe house for the time being. Then he asked if Joey could use the phone. He said it seemed very cruel to keep him so cooped up. I said it was probably okay, but he should use a burner phone just to be safe. When the old man said he had one handy, I wondered if perhaps Joey hadn't been so cooped up after all. But now that was water under the bridge.

I met Tommy on the corner of Mott and Canal Streets and since we had time to spare, we decided to walk to Professor Wu's office. Along the way, I filled Tommy in on recent events, and we tried to figure out what to do. All we knew for sure was there had to be an entrance to the tunnels in the basement at No.10 Mott Street. So it made sense to concentrate our efforts there. That is, if you ignored the fact that the best technicians from both the NYPD and the FBI couldn't locate the entrance.

Professor Wu welcomed us with open arms. He readily admitted relishing any opportunity to talk about Chinatown's history. Since he didn't have much of a chance to do so, Tommy and I were apparently fast becoming his favorite students.

I told the professor about our meeting with Yue Ying Tso and what we had learned about the tunnels, which at least confirmed that the tunnels had at one time existed. We needed to know if they still existed, and if so, how we could access them.

Wu said the existence of the tunnels in the early 1900s was well supported by historical facts. Tso's firsthand stories simply added another level of certainty. But neither history nor Tso's tales gave a clue whether the tunnels still existed and, if so, how many and where.

According to Wu, the only tunnels he knew were the Wing Fat Arcade and one other he had read about in a story about the Hip Sing Tong. Tommy and I glanced at each other, knowing the story was about a case we handled a couple of years prior.

The professor went on to say that while history wouldn't tell us if the tunnels still existed, it could give us clues where to look for them. Stories of murder and mayhem in the early days of Chinatown often involved escapes through the tunnels. Since much of the infrastructure of the area remained unchanged and with over 65% of the buildings being the original pre-1929 tenements, piecing together the stories might help us create a map of the tunnel system.

That made sense, so I told the professor to proceed with the history lesson. If nothing else, I'd get to hear a bunch of cool stories.

The Chinatown Tong Wars lasted for thirty years beginning in 1900 with the murder of Lung Kim, a Hip Sing Tong member, in an apartment at 9 Pell Street. The killer, Gong Wing Chung, was a member of On Leong Tong. Chung was arrested and charged with Kim's murder. A few weeks later, Chung's alibi witness and another Hip Sing Tong member were killed on Pell Street by the On Leong Tong.

With tempers running hot and assassination threats rampant, members of both tongs traveled cautiously, often using the tunnels. Wu believed both the Hip Sing Tong headquarters at 15 Pell Street and the On Leong headquarters on Mott Street were linked to the tunnel network. Wu couldn't be certain if the networks intertwined, but he said it made sense that they would.

Although he had no solid evidence to back up his suspicion, Wu believed Mike Salter's saloon, the Pelham Cafe at 12 Pell Street, across the street from the Hip Sing Tong headquarters, had multiple entrances to the tunnels. As he pointed out, the building was known as "the house of a hundred entrances."

The professor had two photographs of 12 Pell Street, one taken in 1906, and one taken recently. While a beauty shop now occupied the space once occupied by the Pelham Cafe, the building was unchanged. Most importantly, there was still a street entrance to the basement.

If Joey and the Cha brothers entered the tunnel at No. 10 Mott Street, it was only a block away from the Hip Sing headquarters, as well as the Pelham cafe at 12 Pell Street. From there, it was only one short block north to Bayard Street where Joey said they exited the tunnel. I made a note to check it out.

I asked the professor if he knew of any buildings along Bayard Street that might have had access to the tunnels. He said none of the buildings on Bayard Street had any historic significance in terms of the tongs and the Tong Wars. But nearly all the buildings on the south side of Bayard Street between Mott Street and the Bowery were the original tenement buildings. These buildings all had basements with sidewalk access, so he wouldn't have been surprised if one or two were connected to the tunnels. Of course, that was speculation on his part.

The violence of the Tong Wars was confined almost exclusively to the three main streets of the then Chinatown. Doyers Street with its sharp curve between Pell Street and Chatham Square was an ideal ambush location, and the frequent killings along the street earned it the nickname, "Bloody Angle." But the violence was hardly confined to the "Bloody Angle." Gunfire and hatchet fights broke out with regularity on Mott Street and Pell Street.

The violence wasn't limited to the streets. In 1905, the Chinese Theater at 5-7 Doyers Street, sometimes called the Chinese Opera House, was the scene of a massacre when several Hip Sing gunmen opened fire, killing four On Leong members. The shootings, bombings and hatchet murders that followed became so notorious that the boss of Tammy Hall was forced to intercede and broker a peace.

Professor Wu said he'd love to continue the lesson, but he had class, so we'd have to adjourn. That was perfect because with Jenny's mother due to arrive that afternoon, I had some work to do, and Tommy needed to start looking for the tunnels. I didn't know how or where he was going to do it, but that was his problem.

CHAPTER 29

Back at the office, Connie reminded me I hadn't finished the motion papers to suppress the evidence in Jenny's case. I was asking the court for an order keeping the DA from introducing the drugs and drug paraphernalia seized during Jenny's arrest because none of it was found on Jenny's person. It wasn't a strong argument, and I didn't expect to win, but I hoped it was strong enough for the judge to order a hearing. I needed to delay Jenny's case, and making the motion bought me some time, but I'd get a longer delay if the judge ordered a hearing.

It wasn't a difficult motion to write, but for some reason I couldn't get my thoughts together. It happens sometimes and when it does, I get frustrated and irritable. I say irritable; Gracie says obnoxious. I suppose it's a matter of viewpoint. I admit that I tend to take my frustrations out on those around me, so I'm not surprised that Gracie's viewpoint differs from mine.

That day I was taking my frustrations out on Connie who is no less tolerant and no less intimidated by me than Gracie. The fact that I employ Connie and sign her paychecks doesn't seem to matter. I think she realizes Gracie would never allow me to fire her, and that gives her lifetime immunity.

I'll never understand how I got myself into a position where two women have license to nag and yell at me, but I can only have sex with one. It's like being a bigamist without all the benefits. Even with full benefits, I don't know why any man would want more than one wife. I mean, I don't even have one, and never have, and look at the problems I've got.

But I'm rambling, so let me get back on track. The motion papers were not going well, and Connie, having learned from Gracie, ordered me to take a break and go to an AA meeting. In truth it was a good idea. I needed a break, and I needed a meeting.

I hustled over to the Lutheran Church on Mulberry Street just off Worth in time for the one o'clock meeting. It was a good meeting, at least for me it was. But then again, most are. I've been to some meetings that weren't so good, but some of that has to do with me. What you get out of a meeting depends on what you put into the meeting. That day I must have put a lot into the meeting because by the time it ended, I was feeling just fine.

Leaving the church, I was still pumped up from Professor Wu's stories that morning, and I decided to take the scenic route back to the office. As I wandered up Doyers Street, I could envision the battles that took place on the infamous "Bloody Angle."

Chinatown hasn't changed much over the years and one thing is for certain; things are not necessarily what they seem to be. A good example is the building at No. 9 Doyers Street. With nothing but a small "Chemist" sign hanging over the solid metal door, you'd never guess that inside was a swank cocktail lounge. The name of the place is Apotheke, and the drinks are served by bartenders in lab coats. I was there once with Gracie because she was curious about the place, but it's much too ritzy for my taste.

Back in my drinking days, I avoided places like that. Too many yuppies. I used to say that I liked drinking in the neighborhood bars with the local drinking crowd. But the truth is that back then I'd drink with anybody or with nobody. It was the booze that was important, not where I drank it or who I drank it with.

There was one place I went to a couple of times that was sort of like Apotheke. It's a place on East 10th Street in the East Village called the Blind Barber. During the day it's an old-fashioned barber shop, but at night it becomes a cocktail joint. They even have DJs. As I said, I went a couple of times, but it was way too sophisticated for my simple alcoholic tastes.

But getting back to my walk up Doyers Street. It dawned on me that the tunnels probably only still existed in the original old tenement buildings. When an old building was torn down to make room for a new building, as happened regularly, any tunnel entrances would have been demolished in the process. That could also be true when the buildings were modernized, as was also done frequently.

By the time I got back to the office, I was convinced the only way we'd find out about the tunnels was by finding the entrance at No.10 Mott Street.

But I didn't have time to worry about that. I needed to finish the motion papers. Fortunately, my meeting had put me in a better frame of mind, and I was able to knock out the motion in under an hour.

I had just finished when Connie announced that Mrs. Shum was on the line. I figured she was either at her hotel or delayed somewhere. It turned out she was at the hotel and wanted to know what was on the agenda. I said I'd meet her in the lobby in half an hour, and we'd talk and take it from there.

At my suggestion, she was staying at the Wyndham Garden Chinatown Hotel on the corner of Bowery and Hester Streets. It was a short walk from my office and not far from the Criminal Court Building. I called Gracie and told her I had a meeting with Jenny's mother and probably wouldn't be around for dinner. Then I left to meet with Professor Joan Shum.

CHAPTER 30

The Wyndham Garden Chinatown Hotel is well located, but it isn't very big. In fact, the lobby is rather small, so it wasn't hard to spot Mrs. Shum. She was seated on a couch near the front desk. As I approached, she must have guessed who I was because she stood and walked toward me smiling. I couldn't help but notice she was a very attractive woman. I judged she was somewhere in her mid-forties and still in good shape. There was definitely a strong family resemblance between Jenny and her mother, especially when they smiled.

Back in my drinking days, I definitely would have had a thing for Mrs. Shum, but since I got sober, I've managed to put a leash on my libido. Gracie doesn't mind me admiring other women, but God help me if it ever went beyond looking. But no problem. Mrs. Shum was my client's mother, and it was strictly business.

I wasn't sure whether to call her Professor Shum or Mrs. Shum, but I figured I couldn't go wrong with professor. I called her Professor Shum, and she called me Mr. Carney. That, of course, led to the "No, call me Jake" and "Call me Joan" routine. The name thing settled, I said we needed to talk, but I didn't want to do so in the hotel lobby, and I suggested we go to my office. Then noticing the time, I said to Joan if she didn't have any dinner plans, I'd be happy to take her to dinner, and we could talk while we ate. I knew that was a little bit forward. After all, we had just met, and she didn't know me from a hole in the wall but eating while we talked made sense. And, besides, I was hungry, and I didn't know how long our talk was going to take.

Joan accepted without hesitation, so either she trusted me, or she was very hungry, or maybe both. Anyway, I asked her if she had a preference for dinner, hoping she wouldn't leave the choice to me. I don't mind choosing restaurants, but I hate picking the cuisine. I mean, in Chinatown and Little Italy, you can't go wrong with any of the restaurants, but if you're in the mood for pasta, a dim sum restaurant isn't going to cut it. So I was happy when Joan said she preferred Italian. It was just a couple of blocks down Hester Street to Mulberry Street, and then we'd be in Little Italy.

It was a warm evening, so I suggested we walk, and I showed Joan some of the sights. It was a pleasant walk, and it gave us a chance to get comfortable with each other before we got down to business. Joan had been to New York City before, but never to Chinatown or Little Italy. She said New York's Chinatown was very much like the Chinatown in San Francisco, just a lot flatter. Little Italy, on the other hand, was nothing like San Francisco's Italian neighborhood of North Beach.

Turning the corner from Hester Street onto Mulberry Street, Joan was taken by the number of trattorias and small restaurants lining the street. She asked how, with so many restaurants, you pick one. I said that was easy; you tried them all until you found the best. She laughed and asked if I had done that. I said I had, and we were eating at Angelo's of Mulberry Street. She asked if it was the best, and I said it was as far as I was concerned. I explained that the place had been around since 1902 and if it had survived that long, you knew it had to be good.

Besides, Angelo's' menu offered dishes to please all tastes, from plain and simple to culinary adventures. Anything from simple pasta to rabbit in Madeira sauce, or as it's called on the menu, Coniglio Piccantino.

Joan claimed to be impressed with the menu, but said she wasn't that hungry and ordered Ravioli della Nonna. Not wanting to seem like a glutton, I skipped my usual antipasto dish, cold seafood salad and ordered the Spaghetti Aglio e Olio, spaghetti with garlic and oil.

While waiting for our food to arrive, I explained Jenny's situation. When I was done, Joan asked when she could see Jenny. I said as soon as the next day, but first I had a confession to make. I told her that I had contacted her and her husband against Jenny's wishes, and Jenny had no idea Joan was in New York. Joan said she understood and assured me I had done the right thing. For the last two years, she had worried every day about Jenny, not knowing if she was dead or alive. Now at least she knew her child was alive, in big trouble, but alive, and that was what mattered.

Joan, of course, wanted to know the status of Jenny's case and how I planned to keep her out of prison. It was a loaded question, loaded with the presumption that there was something I could do to keep Jenny from going to prison. I began by explaining that Jenny's use of a false name when she was arrested hadn't helped her situation and had set us back a bit. Once the DA had been told Jenny's real name, a new record search had to be conducted, and it was in the works. Any deal I planned on making with the DA was contingent on Jenny having no past criminal record. Jenny told me she was clean, but I needed to know that was true. Joan assured me that Jenny had no criminal record. I hoped that was true, but I was still skeptical. I liked Jenny and Joan, but I've been lied to by too many clients, and I've met too many parents who had no idea what their kids were into. I needed to see it in black and white.

Of course, Joan didn't see it that way. She was convinced that her daughter had no criminal record, and she asked again how I planned on keeping Jenny out of prison. I said, assuming the record search didn't turn up anything negative, I still believed Jenny's best chance of avoiding a prison term was delaying her case until all, or at least most, of the other defendants had been tried or had taken plea deals. The problem with delaying the case was that Jenny would remain at Rikers Island unless she made bail. When I said the word "bail," a troubled look crossed Joan's face. I figured that I knew why, but I'd wait for Joan to confirm my suspicion.

Joan said nothing for a moment, then she asked the odds of Jenny avoiding a prison sentence if I didn't delay her case. I said unless we delayed her case, the odds weren't very good. Then Joan asked how long I'd have to delay the case, and I admitted I couldn't be sure, but it was likely to be at least two months, maybe three, or even four. Joan winced and asked how much Jenny's bail would be. I said that depended on a number of things. First, since Jenny's ties to the community were minimal, anything negative in her record would weigh against the judge even granting bail. Assuming her record was clean and the DA didn't strongly object, bail could be set at anywhere from $25,000 to $75,000. I also explained it could be cash, which meant Joan would have to put up all the money, or she could get a bail bondsman to put up the money for a fee of ten percent.

That troubled look crossed Joan's face once more, confirming my earlier suspicion that bail was going to be an issue. Joan explained that she had come to New York against her husband's wishes, which I had thought was the case. Doing so wasn't easy, but she felt like she owed her daughter that much. But putting up bail against her husband's wishes was something else, and she wasn't sure she could do it. I realized this was a touchy subject, and I didn't think that moment was the time to press the issue, so I simply said I understood. Besides, I wasn't sure I could get bail for Jenny, so why talk about it?

When our food arrived, I figured it was a good time to change the conversation to something less stressful. I hoped it would take Joan's mind off of the problems. After all, they weren't going away, and there wasn't much else we could do to solve them that night. So why not enjoy our dinner? As we ate, I told Joan about Little Italy and Chinatown. She seemed relieved at the change of topic and looked like she was beginning to relax a little.

On the walk back to Joan's hotel, she asked what was next. I said if she was up for it, we'd go see Jenny the next day. I wasn't sure Jenny would be happy to see her mother, but I was hoping her attitude would change in short order. Of course, if I was wrong, Joan had traveled a long way for nothing, not to mention pissing off her husband. Joan was apparently thinking along the same lines because she asked me if I thought Jenny would be happy to see her. What could I do? I lied and said I was sure she'd be happy to see her.

Okay, I'm not supposed to lie. That's true. But sometimes lying is justified. Well, maybe not very often but sometimes. Anyway, I just wanted to leave Joan with positive thoughts, so she'd have a good night. What's so wrong with that? On second thought, don't tell me.

CHAPTER 31

The next morning I met Joan in the lobby of her hotel, and we took a taxicab to Rikers Island. I was surprised that my worries about Jenny's reaction to her mother's sudden appearance kept me from fretting about the taxicab ride. Except for the lurching back and forward caused by the driver's pointless acceleration and abrupt stops as we crept up the East River Drive in the morning traffic, the ride was uneventful. But not uneventful enough to keep the driver, Oswald Walker, and his taxicab from going on my list.

I know that I talk a lot about my taxicab list, but truthfully, keeping it is more of a mental health thing than anything else. I mean, there are 13,857 yellow taxicabs in New York City, and the taxicab companies change drivers as often as some people change their underwear. So what are the chances of me getting the same driver? Even if I did, what are the chances I'd find his name on my randomly kept and scribbled list? Can you picture some taxicab driver waiting at the curb while I go through twenty pages of names before deciding whether I'm going to get into his cab? If you can imagine that, you've never hailed a taxicab in New York City.

But back to Joan and our visit to Rikers Island.

As much as I tried to prepare Joan for what she was about to go through, I knew it wasn't going to help. Nothing I could say would prepare her for the ordeal she was about to endure. With my attorney identification card, I get into Rikers without too much of a hassle, but for everyone else, the process is long and depressing.

It took Joan about an hour and a half to clear security, and that was quick because there weren't many visitors at that time of morning on a weekday. On the weekends, it can take two to five hours to clear all of the security checks.

It's a multi-step process that begins at the Central Visit Building. Knowing the procedure, I gave Joan a quarter which she'd need for the locker where she was required to store her purse and all other items except her identification. After that, she'd have to remove her shoes and outer clothing and pass through a metal detector. In the meantime, she might be sniffed by the canine corps wandering around sniffing for drugs.

Once Joan cleared security at the Central Visit Building, she would be directed to a second security desk for the Rose M. Singer Center where Jenny was being held. At the second desk, they'd scan Joan's thumb, and then she'd be issued a Visitor Express Pass and directed to a bus that would finally take her to Jenny's jail. At the jail, she'd pass through a second metal detector, and if she had any personal items still with her, she'd have to put them in a locker at that jail.

But that wasn't the end of it. Next came the most humiliating part of the process. Joan would have to remove her shoes and socks if she was wearing any, open her mouth for inspection and bend over and pull her bra forward. After that, she'd finally be admitted to the visitors' area. That is, if she passed all the checks and didn't get sassy with any of the Correction Officers. I'm still trying to figure out why they call it a "Visitor Express Pass." If the process took any longer, it would qualify as a sentence.

Apparently, Joan behaved herself and got through the process, depressed and humiliated, but otherwise unharmed.

I usually meet with clients in one of the attorney meeting rooms, and guests aren't normally allowed. But if I know the Correction Officer working the desk, I give him a wink and tell him the person with me is my secretary, or someone working on the case with me. That usually does the trick, and it did that morning.

It takes about fifteen to twenty minutes after you finally check in for the prisoner to be brought to the attorney conference room. I was used to the waiting, but I figured for Joan it must have felt like a lifetime.

Finally, the door opened and Jenny came in. When she saw her mother, she froze. For a moment, the world stood still for the three of us. I didn't even breathe. I just watched and waited for Jenny to react. I didn't dare look at Joan. Then, after what seemed like forever but was only seconds, Jenny broke into tears and ran into her mother's arms. Both women were crying, and I didn't know what to do, so I sat down at the table and acted like they weren't there.

I hate it when women cry because very often I don't understand why they're crying. Take Gracie, for instance; she'll cry when she's sad, which is understandable. But she'll also cry when she's happy, which isn't understandable, at least not to me. So, how the hell am I supposed to react if I don't know if Gracie is crying because she's sad, or she's crying because she's happy? Do I comfort her, or do I give her a "that a girl" slap on the back? You know I'll be in the doghouse for at least a week if I get it wrong. So now you understand why I hate it when women cry.

Anyway, Jenny kept apologizing to her mother, and Joan kept saying it was okay. Finally, when the crying stopped, I said it was time to talk, and Jenny and Joan joined me at the table. Jenny asked about her father, and Joan brushed off the question, saying he was fine but busy.

Knowing it was a tender subject, I jumped in and said we needed to talk about strategy. I explained again where we stood and the strategy of delaying a trial. Jenny said she'd do anything to avoid going to prison, but she couldn't stand being there in jail much longer. With tears in her eyes, she turned to her mother and begged her to get her out of jail.

At that point, it wasn't my place to say anything. Joan had to make a decision, and it wasn't an easy one to make. I guess she could have ducked the issue for the time being by simply saying she'd talk to Jenny's father, but she didn't. She looked at me and asked what needed to be done to get Jenny out of jail. I think seeing firsthand what it was like at Rikers Island, Joan couldn't stand the thought of her daughter being held there.

I said that assuming Jenny's record came back clean, the judge in deciding whether to grant bail, looks at the risk of flight and whether the defendant poses a danger to the community. Clearly, Jenny wasn't a danger to the community, but she would be viewed as a flight risk. That's where her use of a false name would come back to haunt her. That and the fact that she had no ties to the community and no place to stay in the jurisdiction if bail were granted worked against her. But in the end, it was strictly up to the judge, and until I knew which judge would hear the application, I couldn't say more.

Joan asked if renting a place for Jenny to stay until this was all over would help. I said we needed to convince the judge that Jenny had no intention of fleeing the jurisdiction and simply having an apartment in the city could help, but it might not be enough.

Jenny started to cry, and Joan wrapped her arms around her. Then Joan asked if it would help if she promised to stay in New York with Jenny until the case was over. I said that might do the trick, but I wondered if she was prepared to make that commitment. I feared that sitting there seeing her daughter in a prisoner jumpsuit begging for help, might be blinding her to the reality of what would happen if she moved to New York for the duration of the case. There was no doubt in my mind that it would play havoc with her job, with her social life, not to mention what it would do to her marriage. I guessed none of that mattered to Joan because looking at her, I was fairly certain she had made up her mind to make the move. Jenny must have thought the same thing because she had stopped crying, and she was kissing her mother's cheek.

Before this was a done deal, I needed to make sure that if Joan said she'd move to New York, she wouldn't back out when reality overtook emotion. So before Joan said anything, I reminded her that it could take four months or more before I could clear Jenny's case. Then I said that she'd have to stay in New York all that time, with no breaks and no time off for good behavior. Her life would be in New York City, in an apartment with Jenny. I laid it out bluntly, trying to force Joan to consider the consequences of what she was proposing. I think that I was successful because she got a troubled look on her face. I don't pretend to know what she was thinking; after all, I'd only known the woman for one day, and God knows I don't understand women anyway. But I was pretty sure there was some conflict going on in her head. Having spoken to her husband, I could understand why.

Dr. Jack Shum wasn't happy that Joan came to New York for a couple of days. What the hell was he going to say when she announced that she was moving to New York for four months? Then there was the matter of the money. The cost of the apartment, the bail fee, the living expenses. Dr. Jack wasn't going to be a happy camper, that was for sure.

But Joan had apparently made up her mind because she said I should start doing whatever had to be done to arrange Jenny's bail. As for herself, she told Jenny she'd return to San Francisco that evening to work things out, and she'd be back by the weekend to stay. Jenny was still hugging her mother, and the two started to cry again. I was beginning to long for a good old fashioned violent repeat offender client. Not that I understood them any better, but at least they don't cry.

It was a tearful farewell but a happy one. Jenny was seeing light at the end of the tunnel; Joan had a plan; and I had my work cut out for me.

Getting out of Rikers is a lot easier than getting in. But only if you're a visitor and not a prisoner. As Joan and I rode the bus off the island, I suggested we take the bus and subway back to her hotel so we'd have more time to talk.

On the way, I told her bail could be high, and we might have trouble getting a bail bondsman to issue a bond. She said money would not be a problem, and then she asked me about my fee.

To be honest, I hadn't thought about that. If Joan stepped in and paid Jenny's bail, she'd no longer qualify for indigent defendant benefits under the 18B Panel. I mentioned that to Joan who said it wasn't a problem. Whatever the legal fee, she was prepared to pay it. It's not often that a lawyer hears a client say that, which led me to conclude that Joan was acting on emotion and probably not thinking through it all. I liked what she was saying, but I felt compelled to advise her that the costs she was looking at, including the rent and living expenses, were going to be quite a bit of money. With the bail and legal fees on top of that, it was going to run into a small fortune.

Joan just smiled and looking at me, said, "You're worried about my husband, aren't you?" I admitted that the thought had crossed my mind. Then Joan said, "My husband makes a very, very good living, but it's my family money that makes us rich." In other words, money wasn't a problem for Professor Shum. You've got to love an independent woman.

CHAPTER 32

After walking Joan back to her hotel and arranging to meet her when she returned from San Francisco over the weekend, I decided to drop in for a chat with Sarah Washington. Now that we had a game plan, it was time to test the waters and see if we had a chance of making a good deal. But first I needed to make sure the name thing had been straightened out.

I found Sarah at her desk buried in files. I'd brought coffee and donuts which, if you knew me as Sarah did, was a tip-off I wanted something. Sarah looked up from behind the pile of files and warned me I'd better be quick because she didn't have time to waste, and she wasn't in the mood for any bullshit. Perhaps it wasn't the best time to talk, but I was there and I had already sprung for the coffee and donuts, so I jumped right in.

I asked if that small issue, which I called an administrative matter regarding my client's name, had been taken care of. Sarah appreciates my humor, at least to a point. She laughed and said it was more like fraud. I said fraud is such a harsh term; I'd call it more of a misunderstanding.

Sarah rolled her eyes and shook her head. I got a little nervous, but then she said Jenny's paperwork had been corrected. I liked the term "corrected" because it meant the original entry was simply a mistake and not an intentional act of fraud by my client. That was good news, if you call facing twenty-five years in prison good news, but no additional time for fraud was good news.

But there was actually some good news. The record search of Jenny Shao had come up clean, so we were back to even. Maybe my plan could work out.

I told Sarah I was now in contact with Jenny's family, who had agreed to support her. In truth, it was only Joan who agreed, but saying her mother is on board and her asshole father had disowned her didn't set the tone I was going for.

Now that Jenny had her family behind her, I'd be applying for a bail hearing. Sarah raised her eyebrows, not a good sign. She asked if Jenny had any local family, and I confessed she didn't. But I pointed out that her mother was a tenured professor, and her father was a well-respected orthopedic surgeon. I thought it better not to mention that I, for one, didn't respect the bastard; besides, it didn't matter what I thought of him.

Naturally, knowing Jenny's family was from San Francisco, Sarah asked about local contacts. I assured her that arrangements were being made as we spoke for a place where Jenny would stay until the case was resolved. Her mother would remain with her, and I would vouch for both. Like my vouching for anyone carried any weight.

Sarah just shook her head. To be honest, I didn't expect her to be very enthusiastic with all of this, but at least she hadn't thrown the coffee at me. If it had been anyone else except Sarah, I think that I might have been wearing the coffee.

It didn't matter much anyway. It was the judge who'd ultimately decide if Jenny was granted bail. If bail was granted, I had no doubt the amount would be high with or without my vouching. But it might not be as high if the DA didn't oppose the application, and that was why I was sitting there with Sarah. It was way too early to ask for any favors. I was just laying the groundwork.

I couldn't do anything more until Joan returned. If she did. I didn't know how her husband would react to her plans, but he probably wasn't going to be very enthusiastic about her leaving him and spending a small fortune for a daughter he claimed he didn't have. I could envision the bastard killing her or, short of that, having her committed. I admit what Joan was planning to do was clearly crazy, but crazy was all we had.

The generals say you go to war with what you have and not with what you want. That was the case here. I wanted a rock-solid defense and a client out on bail. What I had was a scared kid with no real defense, a jackass father, and hopefully, a supportive mother with a lot of money. I've won some wars with less, but not with much less.

Sarah said that once I had something concrete in place we could talk. Until then, I should leave her alone and get my ass out of her office. I could have taken that the wrong way and been insulted, but Gracie has taught me to get in touch with my understanding side. You believe that, and I've got a bridge I want to sell you.

If you haven't figured it out by now, patience doesn't come to me naturally. I have to work at it, and to be honest, sometimes I don't care to. Doug, my AA sponsor, calls it a fault and tells me I need to work on it. I don't see it that way. As far as I'm concerned, as long as I limit my impatience to morons and assholes, there's no harm done. Doug says that's okay, but he and I don't always agree on who qualifies as a moron or an asshole.

Anyway, leaving Sarah's office, I stopped by Gracie's office for a chat. I knew she was anxious to hear how things went with Jenny's mother, and I needed some advice.

I told Gracie everything that had happened with Jenny and Joan, and then about my chat with Sarah Washington. Gracie thought things had gone as well as could be expected. Now I'd just have to wait and see if Joan came through as she had promised. If she did, Gracie reminded me I'd need to talk with Joe Benjamin and take Jenny's case out of the 18B Panel. That wouldn't be a problem; Joe would be glad to get the case off his watch.

The problem would be with Joan paying the legal fees and maybe thinking it entitled her to a say in the case. It didn't. No matter who paid the legal fees, the client is always the one entitled to make the decisions. Gracie was right; I needed to make sure Joan understood that, especially if there was a chance that Jenny's father might come around.

In my experience, I've found that doctors like to take charge, and you know how I feel about that. So if Dr. Shum suddenly discovered he had a daughter and decided to get involved in her legal defense, I saw nothing but trouble. Gracie, being the wise one, said I was projecting, and I should just wait and see what happens. Of course, she was right, but if I followed her advice I'd have to stop fantasizing about how I would humiliate Dr. Shum, and I was having too much fun to stop.

But that wasn't what I needed to talk to Gracie about. I had promised Joan I'd help her locate a place to stay, but I was hard pressed for time. In addition to Jenny's and Joey's cases, I had a full load of other cases that didn't leave me with a lot of free time to look at apartments. Besides, I wasn't comfortable spending so much time with another woman, so I asked Gracie to help out.

Gracie said she'd be happy to pitch in and suggested that when Joan arrived back in New York, I arrange a dinner, so we could all sit down together. It made sense, and I said I'd do that. Of course, since Gracie was doing me a favor, more or less, we'd be having sushi for dinner that night. If Joan liked sushi, I was in big trouble.

CHAPTER 33

I had just enough time after leaving Gracie's office to make it to Washington Park Square and Dr. Wu's office for another Chinatown history lesson. I found the lessons fascinating, but I wasn't so sure they were helping us find the tunnels. Tommy disagreed. He said if we knew how the tunnels were originally used, it could give us a clue as to where they were located. But Tommy wasn't putting all our eggs in one basket. He figured unless the tunnels ran under the street, they ran through or under the basements of the old tenement buildings.

Tommy figured that most of the old buildings remained intact, but some had been renovated and others demolished and replaced by new construction, which meant that the tunnels through or under those buildings would have been destroyed or at least blocked off. Working on that premise, Tommy had walked Mott, Doyers and Pell Streets, the original streets of Chinatown, making notes of the new or renovated buildings. It turned out that only a third of the tenements on those streets had been replaced by new construction, leading Tommy to believe much of the old tunnel system could still exist. The tunnels might not be connected now as they had been in the past, but it might not matter. If we could find out where the tunnels were accessed back when the old tongs ruled Chinatown, we might be able to find a way in ourselves. That's where Dr. Wu's history lessons might be helpful.

We took our seats across the desk from Dr. Wu, and he began the day's lesson.

The second Tong War broke out in 1909 sparked by a dispute over a woman named Bow Kim. Bow Kim, born in China, was sold into slavery in San Francisco for $3,000 to a man named Low Hee Tong, a member of the Four Brothers Tong. What made Bow Kim so valuable was the scarcity of Chinese women in America at the time, due primarily to the Chinese Exclusion Act of 1882. Essentially, all of the Chinese immigrants in America at the turn of the twentieth century had arrived prior to 1882 and were predominately male. It's been estimated that back then Chinese men outnumbered Chinese women by as much as a thousand to one.

Bow Kim was rescued from Low Hee Tong by a Christian missionary and eventually wound up in New York's Chinatown where she married Chin Lem, a member of the On Leong Tong. Somehow Low Hee Tong learned Bow Kim was in New York, and he demanded that she be returned to him, or he needed to be paid compensation. Chin Lem refused to surrender his wife or to pay a ransom, and his refusal was backed by the On Leong Tong. But Low Hee Tong refused to accept the On Leong's decision and turned for help to the Hip Sing Tong, an affiliate of his own Four Brothers Tong.

When negotiations over the matter broke down, a Hip Sing hatchet man hacked Bow Kim to death in her apartment at 15 Mott Street, triggering the start of the second Tong War. During the ensuing war, the On Leong headquarters was bombed, and both tongs suffered heavy casualties.

Eventually the violence subsided, and the two tongs coexisted in relative peace, although not without incident. Mock Duck, the flamboyant leader of the Hip Sing Tong, often seen walking with two guns and a hatchet, provided authorities with the addresses of gambling dens and brothels run by the On Leong Tong. In doing so, he omitted the addresses of the most profitable sites as a way of telling Tom Lee, the Hip Sing leader, that he could make matters worse.

The third Tong War was fought in 1912 over the opium trade. A year earlier, a raid on an opium den had uncovered a cache of letters disclosing opium rings operating in major cities across the country. The revelation caused a public outcry, and the FBI was called in to take action. Now, under pressure from federal authorities, along with local and state authorities, the tongs were forced to curtail their opium businesses. As the drug dealers came under more and more scrutiny, safe sale locations became rarer and rarer, and the competition between the tongs for those safe locations intensified. The war over the opium trade, like the earlier Tong Wars, eventually subsided, but not before both sides suffered heavy losses.

The last of the Tong Wars erupted in 1925. By then most of the prostitution and opium trade had been brought under control, leaving illegal gambling as the tongs' biggest source of income. The last war came about when Chin Jack Lem and several On Leong Tong members defected and joined the Hip Sing Tong. The defections resulted in violence not only in New York City's Chinatown, but in Chinese communities in Boston, Pittsburgh, Philadelphia, Detroit, and Milwaukee.

In 1925, Chinatown was a thriving community and the Tong Wars were proving costly, not only for the tongs but for the business owners and residents of Chinatown. The violence caused tourists to stay away, and some of the restaurants and chop suey joints were forced to close. With mounting community pressure and pressure from the federal authorities, the tong-controlled gambling moved to New Jersey, and the Tong Wars came to an end.

The stories, though fascinating, had nothing to do with the tunnels, and I was running out of time and patience. I asked Dr. Wu again where he thought that we could find an entrance to the tunnels. He said the only tunnel he knew that still existed was the Wing Fat Arcade. He reminded us that Mike Salter's Pelham Cafe at 12 Pell Street used to be known as the "House of a Hundred Entrances." That he believed was a pretty good indication there had been tunnel entrances at that building.

Although he couldn't be sure any tunnels other than the Wing Fat Arcade existed today, he was certain that back in the early 1900s, there were tunnel entrances at a number of locations. One of those locations was the On Leong headquarters at 83-89 Mott Street. A new building replaced the original building, so whether the tunnel entrance still existed he couldn't say.

The same was true for the Hip Sing Tong headquarters at 15 Pell Street. Whether the tunnels from the On Leong headquarters intersected with the tunnel from the Hip Sing headquarters was unknown but not necessarily unlikely. While the two tongs were at odds with each other and often at war, they shared a common interest when it came to escaping capture, smuggling, and hiding gambling and opium dens. The tunnels served those interests, and it made sense that the two tongs would share the space.

CHAPTER 34

After leaving Professor Wu, Tommy and I decided to walk back downtown, and along the way we brainstormed the matter of the tunnels. If the tunnels were still in existence and still being used, what would they be used for? One thing was for sure, they wouldn't be used for legal purposes. So who would use them and why?

Gambling, drugs and prostitution all came to mind. But other than druggies, who would want to go underground to gamble or get laid? It had to be something else.

We were walking along Canal Street, and I couldn't help but notice all of the shops had rack after rack of women's pocketbooks and showcases filled with watches, all knockoffs of expensive brands. It brought back memories of Tommy and I sharing the backroom at his grandfather's restaurant when he was selling Rollex watches. That's Rollex with two "L's", not with one. The difference being about $10,000 in price.

Why two "L's?" Because with two "L's," it's a cheap knockoff, a fake, but with one "L," it becomes a counterfeit item. Selling counterfeit items is a federal crime and can land you in prison. Selling knockoffs or fakes isn't illegal in New York so long as you have a vendor's license.

The simplest way to avoid a counterfeiting charge is to change the product's logo. So labeling a watch a Rollex distinguishes it from a genuine Rolex. That is, if you bother to look at it closely enough, and you're smart enough to know Rolex is spelled with one "L." Let's face it, you can't be very bright if you think you're getting a genuine $10,000 watch for $150, or a $2,000 Prada bag for $75.

Tommy was no longer in the knockoff business, but he kept in touch with some of his old partners so he knew the counterfeit product business was still booming in Chinatown. The crackdown by the Feds and the NYPD hadn't stopped the sales; it just changed the way the vendors did business. The fakes and knockoffs were still sold in the stores all along Canal Street and in Chinatown, but they rarely sold counterfeit goods.

Before the crackdown, vendors openly hawked the counterfeit goods, carrying with them a stock of items. That practice ended, and now the counterfeiters worked through hawkers, stock boys and lookouts. Tommy pointed out a guy carrying a laminated card, walking up to tourists. He was a hawker, and the card he was carrying displayed the goods he had for sale. If a customer was interested in an item, the hawker used a walkie-talkie to have his stock boy bring the item from the secured stockroom to an out of sight location. Usually it was the backroom of a store or restaurant. Someplace public enough not to spook the tourists, but still out of sight from any undercover cops.

The whole operation took place under the watchful eye of a "supervisor" and "spotters" who looked out for cops. The operation was the same as that employed by drug dealers who used stash houses and runners to keep their drugs away from the point of sale.

When we got to Mott Street, it seemed the number of vendors walking around with laminated cards had increased dramatically. Tommy said that was because Chinatown was still the counterfeit capital of New York City. He said there were numerous sites on the Internet advising where and how to buy both knockoff and counterfeit items in New York City, and all them mentioned Chinatown as the place to go.

Tommy hadn't been simply making small talk; he was making a point. The Chinatown tunnels would be an ideal place to hide the counterfeit goods, and a great way to transport them sight unseen. It made sense, and it was something the NYPD suspected, which explained why the tunnels were an issue in Joey's plea deal. This was the NYPD's opportunity to find a way into the tunnels, and that was worth a great deal to the cops. I worried that if we didn't come up with something that satisfied the cops, Marty would pull back on our deal.

Okay, so now we had a theory as to how the tunnels were being used, but we still didn't know if they actually existed and, if they did, where they were. Tommy said that was true, but there were two things we did know for certain about the tunnels. One, there was an entrance somewhere in the basement of the Golden Wok, and two, the only person we knew for sure who could access the tunnel was Bobby Cha. It made sense. There had to be a tunnel with an entrance in the basement of the Golden Wok Restaurant because there was no other explanation for how Joey and the Cha brothers escaped from the basement.

So if there was a tunnel entrance, we needed to go back there and find it. I reminded Tommy we had been there and hadn't found anything. Tommy said that was because we didn't have the right tools. Naturally I had to ask, what were the right tools? "Jackhammers," answered Tommy.

That might be right, but I doubted the owner of the Golden Wok would want us knocking holes in the basement walls. Tommy agreed that was probably true, but maybe not if it was the NYPD doing the knocking.

CHAPTER 35

That afternoon I got a call and when I saw the San Francisco area code, I knew it had to be Joan, and I got a little nervous. I was worried that Dr. Prick had convinced her that her plan to move to New York was stupid. I figured Joan wasn't going to be bullied into abandoning her daughter, but as an economics professor, she had to realize the plan had major economic issues and that was putting it mildly.

My fears proved to be unwarranted. Joan had called to let me know she had worked out everything on her end, and she'd be returning to New York the next day. She asked if I would reserve a room for her at the Wyndham Garden Chinatown Hotel, which I said I'd be happy to do. Once the details were ironed out, I invited Joan to have dinner with me and Gracie. She accepted the invitation, and we agreed to meet in the hotel lobby at seven o'clock the next evening.

After calling Gracie to tell her about our dinner appointment, I called Detective Chen. I laid out what Tommy and I had concluded about the tunnels and suggested we revisit the basement of the Golden Wok Restaurant, only this time with jackhammers. Chen wasn't at all enthusiastic about the idea. In fact, he called it crazy, or maybe he called me crazy, I'm not sure. I said before I put him down for a definite "no," I thought he should give it some thought, and we could discuss it over lunch in a couple of days. I had discovered some time ago that the best way to approach Chen was over a meal, and I'm not above using food to get my way. Look at how much sushi I eat just to get laid.

Chen said he'd think about it and then came the tip-off. He asked where and when I wanted to buy him lunch. I'm telling you, the man can be bribed with food. Not on anything big, of course, but on the little things.

I said next Monday at the Worth Street Coffee Shop at noon. Chen said he'd be there, and he'd be hungry. I knew right away this little adventure was going to cost me plenty, but if I got Chen to agree to jackhammer the basement of the Golden Wok, it would be worth every penny.

I was trying to figure out what to do next when Connie reminded me that I had a sentencing hearing in the Gomez case in twenty minutes. I had almost forgotten about poor Nathan Gomez. Nathan had been charged with disorderly conduct and indecent exposure for urinating in public. Normally these charges are handled as simple violations involving a small fine and maybe some public service, but Nathan was a serial urinator.

Nathan is a homeless drunk who, other than urinating in public, presents no threat to anyone. In fact, had it not been for Nathan's insistence on using Mrs. Saunders's flower urn in front of her shop on Christopher Street in the West Village as a urinal, he wouldn't be facing misdemeanor charges.

This wasn't the first time I had represented Nathan, but I was hoping it would be the last. As hard as I had tried to convince Nathan to piss somewhere else besides in Mrs. Saunders's urn, he just wouldn't listen. Mrs. Saunders, understandably upset over Nathan's choice of her urn as his urinal, pressured the police to do something. Unfortunately, they had no more luck talking to Nathan than I had, and they, too, were at their wits' end. Thus, the misdemeanor charge.

When I interviewed Nathan, all he would say was, "When I gotta go, I gotta go, and that place is close by." An explanation, perhaps; a legal defense, no.

That was what I faced when I met with ADA Marsha Winston to work out a plea deal. Obviously, we're all professionals, but I was still uncomfortable talking to a young woman who, truth be told, was young enough to be my daughter about some guy exposing his johnson..

But I had a job to do, so the first thing I suggested was dropping one of the charges. Either charge him with taking out his wee-wee or charge him with peeing in Mrs. Saunders's urn, but not with both. Marsha argued that he had done both, but I said he only took out his wee-wee so he could pee. I was beginning to feel like I was back in kindergarten, but I thought it was better to use those terms instead of terms I might have otherwise used had Marsha been a man.

I know what you're going to say because when I told the story to Gracie, she called me a male chauvinist pig. I'm sorry. Maybe I'm old fashioned or something, but my mother taught me you don't use certain language in front of a woman. In fact, she'd have washed out my mouth with soap if she caught me using "bad" language in front of a girl. That's how I was brought up, and it taught me a valuable lesson. If you eat Ivory soap, you vomit.

Why was it a valuable lesson? Because growing up, the only way I could get out of going to school was if I had a fever or I was vomiting. Simply feigning illness didn't do the trick. So when I wanted to skip school, I'd munch off the corner of the Ivory soap and wait twenty or so minutes. It was a nasty twenty minutes, but once I threw up, the cramps went away. Luckily my mother never noticed the bubbles coming out of my mouth as I vomited.

One other point. Some of you are surely thinking that I'm not shy using "bad" words when telling you my stories, but that's different. I'm not looking you in the face. If we were in the same room, I wouldn't feel comfortable using some of those words. Weird, right? Maybe it comes from eating too much soap as a kid.

But back to the pee king. We finally reached an agreement to drop the indecent exposure charge. Nathan would plead guilty to the misdemeanor, do fifteen days in the holding cells and that would be it. It wasn't a great deal but given the circumstances it wasn't all that bad. Dropping the indecent exposure charge was important because with that charge, Nathan could wind up being labeled a sex offender.

After I explained it all to Nathan, he agreed to the deal. I hoped Nathan doing time might convince him to change his bathroom location; besides, he needed to dry out.

We were due in Judge Moore's courtroom at four o'clock, and I was there fifteen minutes early as was ADA Winston. Nathan hadn't been held in custody and even though he had always showed up in court in the past, I wasn't sure he'd show this time. This was the first time he was going to be sent to jail, and I was sure he wasn't thrilled with the idea. But Nathan did show up. He was a bit drunker than he had been at previous court appearances but as he put it, he was preparing himself for jail. Drunk as he was, I was praying he wouldn't pee in the courtroom.

Wobbling only slightly but speaking clearly, Nathan pleaded guilty to the charge and, as agreed, was sentenced to fifteen days in jail. As he was escorted from the courtroom, he thanked me and gave a smile and a nod to

ADA Winston and to Judge Moore. I hoped he'd learned his lesson, but I doubted he had.

That night after Gracie got done calling me a chauvinist pig, I convinced her to have dinner in the West Village. Before picking a restaurant, I stopped into Mrs. Saunders's shop on Christopher Street and offered her $50 for the flower urn. At first she said it wasn't for sale, but I think she then realized who I was and why I wanted to buy it, and she accepted my offer.

The damn urn wasn't that big, but filled with dirt and flowers, it weighed a lot. Besides, knowing its history, I wasn't too happy to be carrying it around. Gracie spotted a construction dumpster a block away, and that's where the urn wound up. With any luck, I wouldn't be seeing anymore of Nathan Gomez and neither would Mrs. Saunders. At least she'd be seeing less of him, if you get what I mean.

CHAPTER 36

The next evening, Gracie and I met Joan Shum in the lobby of her hotel. Gracie gave Joan that once-over that married women give to possible competitors. It didn't matter that Joan wasn't competition; it was a reflexive reaction on Gracie's part. With the once-over finished and Gracie satisfied that Joan wasn't a threat, we moved on to the "small talk" portion of the program, closely followed by the discussion of where to eat.

Gracie asked Joan if she had a favorite food, and I began sensing sushi was in my future. But much to my surprise and delight, Joan said she'd love a nice big New York strip steak. If it wouldn't have resulted in severe bodily injury, I would have kissed Joan right then and there. But I knew better. All I could do was grin like the Cheshire Cat and suggest we grab a taxicab and ride down to Delmonico's on the corner of Beaver and William Streets.

Delmonico's is another iconic New York City restaurant. Actually, it's probably the oldest, having been opened by the Delmonico brothers in 1837. They boast that it's the oldest "fine dining restaurant in the country." I don't know about that, but it is the home of the world-famous Delmonico steak which I love.

Sadly, Gracie and I don't eat there as often as I would like. It's a little on the pricey side with everything ala carte, and Gracie isn't fond of red meat. Of course, I'm not fond of sushi, but we still eat a lot of it. I'm just saying; I'm not complaining.

When I suggested Delmonico's, Gracie gave me one of her looks. It was her, "Are you kidding me?" look which meant I'd better get a confirmation from Joan right away before Gracie tried to change her mind. Without skipping a beat, I said not only were the steaks great, but the restaurant was a top-rated tourist attraction with an interesting history. Luckily before Gracie could say anything, Joan said it sounded great. Gracie just gave me another one of her looks. It was the "no sex for you" look, but it didn't matter; we'd be eating at Delmonico's.

It was a great meal. Gracie and Joan talked about their jobs and about shopping, and all sorts of women's issues. I was mostly left out of the conversation, which enabled me to concentrate on the steak, the Delmonico potatoes, the roasted cauliflower, and the creamed spinach. If the word glutton comes to mind, you're not far off. But then again, you can't blame me. After all, it was Delmonico's, right?

After dinner, we walked around the Financial District and then hopped a taxicab back to Joan's hotel. When we arrived, Joan invited us for a drink at the hotel's bar. I would have declined, but before I could, Gracie accepted, and we all headed to the bar.

Joan and Gracie ordered glasses of wine, and I ordered my usual club soda. Being left out of the conversation this time wasn't as convenient until my cell phone vibrated, and I took a call from Tommy. He thought I should know that word on the street was the Hip Sing was paying big bucks to anyone who knew where Joey was.

That definitely was not good news. Excusing myself from the ladies, I went outside the hotel and called Mr. Fang. He was naturally alarmed and asked why the tong wanted Joey. I explained that with the Cha brothers dead and the money from the robbery still out there, Joey was the only link to the cash. Mr. Fang said Joey didn't know where the rest of the money was. But as I explained to Mr. Fang, the tong didn't know that and as long as they didn't, they'd want Joey alive which was better than wanting him dead.

Of course, once the tong found out Joey didn't know where the money was, they'd probably want him dead. I didn't say that to Mr. Fang. There was no sense in ruining his evening. Instead, I suggested he keep Joey inside and out of sight. I think he knew where this was going, and he agreed to keep Joey under wraps.

After talking with Mr. Fang, I returned to the ladies at the hotel bar. They were still jabbering away, so I took my seat alongside Gracie, sipped my club soda and waited. Apparently, I wasn't waiting patiently because Gracie threw me another one of her looks. In case you're wondering, Gracie has about fifty different looks she throws my way. All I know is that ninety-five percent of them mean I've done something wrong. As for what I've done wrong, well,

I've only been able to decipher about half of the looks. Using my powers of deduction, I figured the one she had just thrown me at the bar meant I wasn't being patient.

I wanted to roll my eyes and say, "*It's time to go,*" but I knew instinctively that would just get me another one of Gracie's looks, and I was already in the doghouse. Instead, I just smiled and looked interested.

Eventually Gracie and Joan ran out of things to say to each other, and they included me in the conversation. Joan announced that she planned on spending the next day, Sunday, searching for apartments. I said that first thing Monday morning, I would prepare and file a motion asking for bail.

Joan, of course, wanted to see Jenny on Monday, but I had a lunch date with Detective Chen, so I couldn't go to Rikers until mid-afternoon. Joan understood and said it wasn't a problem; she'd go see Jenny on her own. When I asked if she was sure about that, I must have looked concerned because she said I shouldn't worry. She knew the drill, and it wasn't a problem. She promised to call me after the visit and let me know how things were going.

With the scheduling out of the way, we called it a night, and Gracie and I headed to her place.

Later that night at Gracie's place, I told her what was going on with Joey and the tong. She naturally asked if I was in any danger. I didn't want her to worry, but I didn't want to lie to her either, so I said probably not.

The word "probably" is like the word "soon." It's open to a wide variety of interpretations, and its veracity isn't easily questioned. When you're in a jam, those two words, soon and probably, can prove to be invaluable. Of course, it all depends on whom you're dealing with. Telling a Mafia loan shark "soon" isn't likely to do much for you. Let's be serious. If you're in debt to a Mafia loan shark, it's money, not words, you had better come up with.

But once again, I wander. Gracie had asked a good question, and frankly, it was one I had asked myself earlier. There was a quarter of a million dollars at stake, which for me was a lot of money, but for the tong it was petty cash. Still, if it wasn't just about scaring off freelancers and they wanted the money, I could be in danger. It wouldn't be the first time the tong came after me; I just hoped it wouldn't wind up being the last, if you get my drift.

I'd try to be careful, but I had to face facts. I wasn't hard to find. I had no intention to go into hiding and joining the witness protection program seemed a bit extreme. So, I'd just live my life and pray. All I can say is that Joey was damn lucky I didn't know where he was.

CHAPTER 37

Monday morning, I drew up the motion papers to renew Jenny's bail hearing. I didn't mention the name change. I figured as long as Sarah Washington didn't call it to the judge's attention, it would slip by under the radar. If it was noticed at all, it was likely to be treated as a typographical error and nothing more. I had to fudge a bit on Jenny having a place to stay within the jurisdiction. I figured by the time we had the hearing, Joan would have found a place. If she didn't, I'd need to adjourn the hearing.

When the papers were finished and put in final form, I filed a copy with the court. Then I hand carried a copy to the District Attorney's Office and delivered them personally to Sarah Washington.

Jenny getting bail was a fifty-fifty proposition, even with Joan staying in New York. But the odds improved if the DA didn't oppose the motion, and I was counting on Sarah going along with the program. I was hand delivering the papers, so I could chat her up a little bit and maybe work out a strategy.

Sarah and I worked out deals in the past for clients that weren't nearly as deserving of sympathy as Jenny, so I wasn't expecting a problem. But when I handed the papers to Sarah, she gave them a quick once-over , and then she tossed them into her in-box without saying a word. That wasn't a good sign. My gut was telling me that something wasn't right, and I'd better find out quickly what it was. Rather than stand there staring at Sarah, I said that Jenny's mother was looking for a place for her and Jenny to live. Since her budget was practically unlimited, I had no doubt she'd have something in place long before the motion was heard. I smiled, trying to look casual, hoping my gut was wrong, and Sarah would suddenly smile back and say something I wanted to hear. But she didn't.

It was time to find out what was going on. I asked Sarah outright if she was going to oppose the bail request. She said that she didn't want to oppose it, but her boss was giving her a hard time. The arrests made during Operation Asian Dragon had gotten a good deal of positive press for the NYPD and the District Attorney. But so far no one was plea bargaining, and as a result, there hadn't been any convictions. The media was getting restless, and the District Attorney was getting nervous.

Rumors were starting to circulate that a fix was in, and that was why there were no convictions. According to more than one account, the Asian Empire had connections deep within the District Attorney's Office that were protecting the gang members. Of course, it wasn't true, but the District Attorney was still worrying that the rumors would hurt his reelection chances. The fact that he wasn't up for reelection for another two years didn't matter. Like most politicians, his biggest concern was always his reelection chances.

Not wanting to seem "soft" on the Asian Empire, the District Attorney had instructed Sarah to oppose any motion made on behalf of any suspect arrested during Operation Asian Dragon. It didn't matter that no one claimed Jenny was a member of the Asian Dragons. It was guilt by association at its worst.

When placed in a seemingly hopeless situation, I'm not above begging and have been known to do a pretty damn good job of it. A hangdog face almost to the point of tears is one of my specialties. I couldn't remember having used my pity routine on Sarah before, so I gave it a try. I thought that I was doing a pretty good job at looking sufficiently pitiful to warrant some mercy, but Sarah just went into a laughing fit. When she finally stopped laughing, she said I looked like I might have eaten some bad eggs at breakfast. Then she started laughing again. I guess I needed to work on my pity routine because that was definitely not the reaction I was going for.

Every time Sarah stopped laughing, she'd look at me and start rolling with laughter all over again. And I didn't even have my pity look on. All I could do was sit there embarrassed and wait for it all to end.

Finally Sarah's laughing fits ended, and we got serious again. Sarah said after our last meeting, she had read Jenny's file, and she could see why I was pushing her case. She had mentioned the case to her boss, and that's when she learned about the order to oppose all motions.

I could tell Sarah's heart wasn't in opposing the motion, but there was no way she or her boss would violate a direct order from the District Attorney. The best I could hope for was Sarah going easy with her opposition. Even with that, I'd have an uphill battle getting bail for Jenny.

I thanked Sarah and left. As I walked out of her office, I could hear her starting to laugh again. I'd have to rethink my pitiful look routine. Maybe I could try it out on Gracie. Did I even say that? What could I have been thinking?

Speaking of Gracie, I stopped by her office, but she was in a staff meeting. I was going to try out my pitiful look routine on her secretary, but I thought I could still hear Sarah laughing, and I decided to try it out in a mirror first.

Back out on the street, I gave Joan a call, but it went to her voice mail. I presumed she was already in process at Rikers, and her cell phone was locked up. I had hoped to let her know where we stood on getting Jenny out on bail before she saw Jenny, so she wouldn't get Jenny's hopes too high. But that wasn't going to happen.

CHAPTER 38

I should mention that since Saturday when Tommy told me the tong was looking for Joey, I'd been careful to make sure I wasn't being followed. I'm not sure what I would have done if I thought I was being followed, but I was being careful anyway. That meant not taking the most direct route to my destination. So, instead of heading directly to the Worth Street Coffee Shop two blocks away to meet Detective Chen, I decided to walk back to Mott Street, then to take Pell Street to Chatham Square and back to Worth Street.

The trip took about fifteen minutes, and I hadn't noticed anyone following me, and no one had dragged me into an alley and threatened my life. Either the tong wasn't interested in me, or it wasn't my turn yet. Either way, by the time I met Detective Chen at the Worth Street Coffee Shop, I had almost forgotten about the Hip Sing Tong.

I had learned over the years that when it came to a free meal, you could count on Chen arriving early. So I wasn't surprised to see him seated at my table in the back of the coffee shop sipping a cup of coffee. When he saw me approaching the table, he nodded, but he didn't smile. He didn't seem to be in a very good mood, and I knew why.

Chen was under a lot of pressure from One Police Plaza to recover the stolen bank money, but since the death of the Cha brothers in the Brooklyn shoot-out, he probably didn't have a clue as to where it was stashed. Now, with the Hip Sing Tong trying to find the money as well, Chen was in a real bind. If the tong got to the stolen money first, Chen's career was likely in the crapper.

This whole Houdini Bandits episode was proving to be a career killer for more than just Chen. By leaving everything at the precinct level, the top brass had succeeded in focusing all the attention there. But that focus was likely to shift upward if something good didn't happen soon. The only way to keep the focus from moving up the line would be to create a diversion by firing a few sacrificial lambs at the precinct level.

It was a shame. Chen was a good cop and a good man, who happened to be in the wrong place at the wrong time. Now he was a sacrificial lamb to be offered up for slaughter to protect the brass at One Police Plaza. He, the two patrol officers on the scene and the lieutenant from Special Services, would all take the fall on this one. There could be others as well, but who knew?

Politics suck, and that's one reason I'd never run for public office. The other reason is that I couldn't get elected. What with my big mouth and my history as a drunk, I wouldn't exactly fit the image.

None of this was good for Chen, but unhappily, it was for me. With Chen under fire from the brass, he needed to produce something to save his ass. Finding the tunnels would be a big break in the case. Maybe it wouldn't lead to recovering the stolen money, but it might garner enough positive media attention to get Chen out from under.

We ordered lunch and while we waited for the food to arrive, I again proposed to Chen that we jackhammer the Golden Wok basement to find the tunnel entrance. The last time I proposed doing that, he called it a crazy idea and said there was no way he'd do it. But this time when I proposed it, he didn't say anything. I was making progress.

Our food arrived and we stopped talking. Eating a good deli sandwich properly requires your full attention. If it's a genuine New York City deli sandwich, it's loaded with meat stacked almost an inch and a half high. When you bite into it, you need to be careful not to shift the bread too much, or some of the meat will drop out. Mustard can act as a lubricant, making it easier for the meat to slide against the bread, so you must apply pressure at key points to prevent shifting. You can always tell a tourist in a New York deli because they're the ones picking slices of meat off their plates with a fork. But don't fret. With a little practice and experience, you can be eating New York deli sandwiches like a regular New Yorker.

When we finished our sandwiches, we each ordered another cup of coffee, and then Chen said maybe jackhammering the Golden Wok basement wasn't such a bad idea. Then he confided that he was facing two choices. Either find the tunnels and the stolen money or retire from the force before he was demoted or fired.

With a couple of years to go before he reached full retirement benefits, early retirement was going to cost him a lot of money. But it was better than being fired, or even demoted. He needed to do something to get the brass off his back, and so far, my idea was the only one on the table. If he couldn't find the stolen money, the next best thing would be to at least find the escape tunnel.

Finding the escape tunnel would be a big media event. And if the NYPD Intelligence Unit was right and the tunnels were being used for illegal gambling, smuggling and counterfeit operations, the finding would be a huge media event and a major coup for the NYPD. It would probably be enough to save all the jobs at risk because of the Houdini Bandits.

I had high hopes for the plan, but I had no idea how to get the job done. For that I needed Chen's input. I asked him what we needed to do to make the plan work. He said the first step was to get approval from One Police Plaza. That he said was the hardest step. If approved, the rest was easy.

Once the plan was approved, he'd have the District Attorney's Office secure a search warrant, so the work could be done with or without the owner's permission. Of course, the damage would need to be repaired, so there was that additional expense to consider. Chen figured the whole operation could be concluded in less than three days, once it was approved.

I wanted very much to help Chen out, but there wasn't much I could think of doing. It was all riding on the brass approving the plan, and I had no way to influence anyone at police headquarters. All I could do at that point was offer moral support. I told Chen that I was working with Professor Wu trying to learn more about the tunnels, and I'd gladly share the information I had gotten from him. Unfortunately, the information had only been historical, and I had nothing on the present-day status of the tunnels.

I asked Chen about the tunnel used by my former client a couple of years back. It had been Chen's case, and that's how we met. He said that particular tunnel had been a short one running between two nearby buildings, neither of which was close to the Golden Wok. Besides, the tunnel had been filled and sealed. So much for that idea.

Chen knew if he proposed jackhammering the Golden Wok and nothing came of it, his fate was just about sealed. On the other hand, if the operation was successful, he'd keep his job and his pension. Those were the choices he was facing, and there wasn't much I could do to help him. Finally, he sighed and said he'd drop by One Police Plaza that afternoon and put the plan to the Chief of Detectives.

Later that afternoon Chen called and said he had spoken to the Chief of Detectives. The good news was, the plan to jackhammer the Golden Wok basement hadn't been rejected out of hand. After asking a bunch of questions, the Chief of Detectives said he'd bring the plan to his boss, the Chief of the Police Department. Chen was encouraged but not optimistic. He figured, given the NYPD bureaucracy, we weren't going to get a quick answer.

CHAPTER 39

Leaving the Worth Street Coffee Shop, I got a call on my cell from Joan. She was just leaving Rikers Island after visiting Jenny who was in good spirits. The reason she was calling was to ask me to look over a lease she was going to sign for an apartment in Lower Manhattan. She had gone apartment hunting on Sunday and found this place on Rivington Street, a mile or so north of Chinatown, and she had put down a deposit. My afternoon court conference had been canceled, so I told Joan to meet me at my office.

I don't do a lot of landlord-tenant work, but I knew enough about leases to know there wasn't much room to negotiate terms. It was basically a landlord's market, and the lease terms reflected it. The only terms in the lease favoring the tenant were the ones required by law, and those were few and far between.

When Joan arrived and showed me the lease, all I could do was point out the more onerous terms and make sure she understood what she was getting herself into. I thought the rent was astronomical at $9,000 a month, but Joan thought it was reasonable. After all, it was her money and her decision to make.

The term of the lease was six months, which was good. One way or the other, Jenny's case should be resolved by then. But because Joan had no job in New York, the landlord was demanding payment of the full lease rent in advance. That wasn't so good, but again it was Joan's money. I just wondered what Dr. Shum was going to say about spending $54,000 to house a daughter he didn't have.

To add insult to injury, the landlord wanted a two-month security deposit. That was too much for me to take. The lease was one-sided enough, without this bozo getting another $18,000 on top of the full rent. I mean, how much damage could two women do to the place? Alright, maybe I'm being a little sexist or naive with that remark. I have seen pictures of rooms trashed by druggies, but Joan hardly qualified as a druggie. As for Jenny, she was charged but nothing had been proven, and the landlord certainly didn't know anything about her case.

Joan was ready to pay the $18,000, thinking she'd get it all back at the end of the lease, but I wasn't so sure. Once these sharks got their hands on the money, getting it back would be like pulling teeth. It took a bit of doing, but I convinced Joan to let me call the landlord and negotiate. It took four phone calls to reach someone with authority to negotiate the lease terms.

The person I finally got on the line identified himself as "the in-house legal counsel for the owner's management organization." I wasn't impressed. When I explained my concern with the security deposit, Mr. In-house Legal Counsel explained it was a "value-based provision." I said he could call it whatever he wanted, but as far as I was concerned, it was highway robbery and probably illegal. But I said that I didn't want to jump the gun, and I'd get back to him after I checked it with my wife, who was in-house legal counsel for the District Attorney. I had elevated Gracie to spouse status, but she probably wouldn't mind given the circumstances.

In the end, Mr. In-House Legal Counsel accepted a $2,000 security deposit, which he agreed to hold in an escrow account. Then I told him to fax me new copies of the lease with the new security deposit, and Joan would sign it. He said I could just change the amount on Joan's copy. I think he understood from my laughing that wasn't going to fly. But just to make sure we were on the same page, I told him he needed to fax the copies, if he wanted to keep pretending that he was a lawyer who knew what he was doing. He grunted an okay, and hung up on me. How rude, especially when I was being nice.

The copies came via fax and Joan signed them. In two days she'd be a New York City inhabitant. Whether that would be enough to get Jenny bailed out of jail remained to be seen.

The bail hearing date hadn't been set yet, but with the papers now filed, it wouldn't be long before it was. I needed to broach another topic with Joan, and it wasn't going to be easy. Where did her husband stand on all of this? It wasn't idle curiosity on my part that made me ask; I needed to know because it was likely to come up during the bail hearing.

I explained it to Joan, who said that Dr. Shum was being an asshole—her word, not mine. He remained unmoved by Jenny's situation, steadfastly holding to his position that he no longer had a daughter. Joan confided that she was worried about the state of their marriage. She had never seen her husband so angry and so unwilling to consider any other opinion. He hadn't threatened her with divorce, but Joan believed it was certainly within the realm of possibilities. From the way she said it, I took it to mean that she might be the one filing for divorce.

Joan was doing her best to hold herself together, but I knew it wasn't easy, and she was clearly having a hard time of it. I excused myself, and in the office waiting room, I called Gracie and asked whether she'd mind if Joan had dinner with us. Gracie, understanding how things were, had no objection. So that night we had dinner together at one of Gracie's favorite sushi restaurants. It seemed like Joan loved sushi as much as Gracie. Why, God? What did I do to deserve having two women in my life who love sushi? One is more than enough, believe me.

We were almost done with dinner when I got the call from Mr. Fang.

CHAPTER 40

I normally don't answer calls during dinner. Gracie frowns on it, and she's right. Interrupting your dinner to take a call sends a callous message to your dinner companion. *I'm going to take this call because whoever is on the other end is either more important or more interesting than you are.* I'll bet you didn't think I could be so considerate of someone's feelings, did you? The truth is if I took a call during dinner with Gracie, I'm not likely to get laid for a couple of weeks.

But with Gracie and Joan chattering away while devouring what seemed to be half of a giant tuna fish, I don't think either would have noticed if I had set myself on fire. So I took the call, and I was glad that I did.

It was Mr. Fang in a state of panic. If Mr. Fang was panicking, the news couldn't be good, and it wasn't. Joey was missing.

Joey, against Mr. Fang's wishes, had gone out earlier for a little walk, promising to return within the hour. That had been seven hours ago. Mr. Fang had called around, but no one had seen Joey.

I excused myself from the table and went outside the restaurant. I told Mr. Fang not to worry, but to keep trying to locate Joey and to let me know if he was successful. Then I called Tommy and told him what was going on. Tommy said he'd check it out right away, and he'd get back to me as soon as he could.

Tommy hadn't said it, but I was pretty sure he was thinking, as I was, that guys from the Hip Sing Tong had snatched Joey. They were looking for the stolen bank money and with the Cha brothers dead, Joey was the only link to the money left. They obviously didn't know that Joey had no idea where the money was. Joey would tell them that, but I doubted they would believe it.

The Hip Sing Tong was merciless and when it came to torture, it was as inventive as it was cold-blooded. I was trying not to think about the stories

I had heard, but I knew If they had Joey, time was of the essence. Once they figured out Joey was telling the truth and he didn't know where the money was, he'd probably be dead or wishing he was dead.

As much as I hated to do it, I called Detective Chen. He was off duty, but the desk sergeant passed on my message, and Chen called me back within minutes. I explained the situation and asked if he had any suggestions. He said, "Pray."

I went back to the table and explained to Gracie that something important had come up, and I needed to go back to the office. Something like that doesn't happen often, but when it does, Gracie understands. She said that she'd take care of the bill, and she'd see me at her place later. I gave her a kiss, shook hands with Joan and rushed out of the restaurant. I didn't know where I was going, but I knew I had to be there quickly.

I was about a block away from the restaurant when Tommy called. He was on the street checking with his people, and so far, no one knew anything. He had a contact with Hip Sing connections, but he hadn't found him yet. He'd keep looking and get back to me if he learned anything else.

Having nothing else to do but being too worked up to do nothing, I decided to visit a couple of the clubs where Joey used to hang out. I recalled the name of at least two that Joey had mentioned during our first meeting, and I started with the closest, the Sunset Club.

It wasn't quite ten o'clock, so the place was nearly half empty. I don't know what I had been thinking, but at fifty-six years of age, I stood out in the crowd like a half naked stripper in a church choir. I'm sure they took me to be a cop, and they were avoiding me like I had the plague. I tried talking to the bartender but got nowhere. So much for my investigative skills.

With nowhere else to go, I went back to my office and waited to hear from Tommy, Mr. Fang or Detective Chen. Tommy was the first to call. He had finally found his Hip Sing guy who knew nothing about Joey being picked up. According to Tommy, that was good news. Everyone knew that the tong wanted Joey, and that they were paying a bounty for him, so if he had been caught, word would have gone out that the bounty was off.

Next to call was Detective Chen. He had his people out looking for Joey but no luck. It was coming up on midnight and a shift change, and he couldn't have the new shift tied up looking for Joey. If they came across anything, they'd be instructed to let him know, but other than finding Joey's body in an alley, Chen wasn't holding out much hope for finding him that night.

Then Tommy called and he said looking for Joey might be doing more harm than good. Rumor was now out that Joey was on the streets, so every wannabe gangster looking to make his mark with the Hip Sing Tong, was looking for him. Had I inadvertently created a monster? Just call me Dr. Frankenstein.

I was just about to give up and leave the office when Mr. Fang called. Joey was back. He had spent the day with one of his girlfriends in the Bronx. I was pissed, really pissed. Not just because Joey had disobeyed my instructions, but because it was sushi night, which meant Gracie and I would normally be having sex. But now it was too late. By the time I got to her place, she'd be sound asleep and, while that didn't bother me, it would probably bother her. So, because Joey had been having sex all day long, I wasn't going to have any that night. The world's just not fair.

Before closing up, I called Tommy and let him know what had happened. Then I called the desk sergeant at the Fifth Precinct and asked him to pass a message on to Detective Chen.

Walking from the office to Gracie's place, I didn't even bother checking to see if I was being followed or about to be mugged. I didn't care; let them take me. I was busy thinking of everything I was going to do to Joey next time I saw him.

By the time I reached Gracie's place, I had calmed down, and I knew what I had to do first thing the next morning. No, it wasn't having sex; it was to call my sponsor, Doug, and get myself to an AA meeting. Okay, maybe sex would come first.

CHAPTER 41

Little did I know when I awoke the following morning the problems Joey's little jaunt had created. It wasn't until I left the eight am AA meeting on Houston Street that I got the call from Tommy, who told me what was going on.

Apparently, the Hip Sing Tong had gotten word that Tommy and the cops were asking about Joey's whereabouts. Realizing he was on the loose, they were tearing up Chinatown looking for him. Neither Tommy nor I knew where Mr. Fang was hiding Joey, but that didn't mean we weren't in danger. More importantly, we didn't know who, except for Mr. Fang and Joey, knew Joey's location, so there was only one way to guarantee his safety. Have him arrested and kept in a NYPD safe house.

Joey wasn't likely to agree, but he had created the problem, and now he had to suffer the consequences. Besides, I was still mad at him for ruining my evening of bliss with Gracie which, if you're keeping score, wasn't rectified that morning. Gracie had a breakfast meeting, and I was still in a bad mood, which is always a sex killer. So, Gracie went to her breakfast meeting, and I took a cold shower, called Doug and went to my AA meeting.

Tommy met me at my office. After he filled me in on the details, I called Detective Chen. Chen knew what was going on, and you could say he was concerned. Actually, he was bordering on frantic because he knew if the Hip Sing Tong got its hands on Joey, Joey was dead and so was his career. So, when I suggested putting Joey in protective custody, Chen leapt at the opportunity. The only thing was that I couldn't guarantee Joey would go along.

The situation definitely called for Mr. Fang's input, so I called him and asked him to come to my office. But not before he chained Joey to a radiator or some other immovable object. Mr. Fang was no fool, and I suspected he knew what was coming when he said he'd be in my office in half an hour.

I called Chen and invited him to join the party and, of course, he accepted the invitation. If Chen had his way, he'd probably spend the next month handcuffed to Joey. I know from past experience that NYPD safe houses can suck. NYPD likes using flophouse hotels or tenement apartments in a slum neighborhood, which are neither safe nor sanitary. If the bad guys didn't get you, the bacteria or the vermin would.

Not to mention that every bad guy in New York worth his salt knows where the NYPD "safe houses" are located. If we were going to do this, I'd insist that Joey be kept in a federally-run safe house. I knew from personal experience that the FBI and the US Marshals have safe houses in Manhattan, as well as Queens and Nassau Counties, and they're a lot safer than the NYPD "safe houses."

So when Chen arrived, I told him to get on the line with his buddies at the FBI and arrange for one of its safe houses, preferably one that was as far from Manhattan as possible. Using whatever influence he had, Chen arranged to "borrow" an FBI safe house in Freeport, another place I've never been where I had no plans to visit. At least not until then.

When Mr. Fang arrived, Chen was still on the phone, this time making arrangements for around-the-clock watches at the Freeport safe house. I explained to Mr. Fang the problems we faced and suggested the only way to keep Joey safe was to have Detective Chen take him into temporary protective custody. Mr. Fang wanted to know where Chen intended to take Joey, but that question I left for Chen to answer. The less I knew, the better off I was.

Within half an hour the meeting was over. Mr. Fang had agreed that Joey was best off in protective custody, and he told Detective Chen where Joey was hiding out. Chen dispatched a couple of plainclothes cops to stand guard at the location until he and Fang arrived. After that, Chen and his plainclothes guys would transport Joey to the safe house where another team of detectives would be waiting.

Simply being out of Chinatown didn't mean Joey was safe. It just meant the Hip Sing Tong had a lot more area to search. Chen had warned me that if the heat didn't turn down in the next day or two, I could expect a visit from someone looking for Joey. It was no secret that I was Joey's lawyer. Chen had asked if I wanted a protective detail assigned, but I turned it down.

After Chen and Mr. Fang left, Tommy, who sat quietly during most of the meeting, said he was putting a man on me. I said that wasn't necessary, but he insisted. At least he hadn't offered to get me a gun, which is what he did in the past when he thought I might be in danger.

Actually, this time around I might have been more open to having a gun. Maybe I was starting to think like my friend who recently applied for a gun permit. In answer to the question on the application as to why he needed a gun, he replied, "Too old to fight." I don't think he's going to get the permit, but his reason has merit. If you don't think it has merit, you're probably too young to get it.

CHAPTER 42

I spent the next morning at the District Attorney's Office working out plea deals for a couple of my 18B Panel clients. It was the same ADA on both cases, and for some reason, he was in a generous mood that morning, so we wrapped up both cases in under an hour, which may have been a record. Plea bargaining is part art, part science and part luck. That morning luck played the biggest role. Why? Who knows? Call it karma; call it fate; or call it happenstance. I don't pretend to understand why things happen the way they do. Maybe I'm too dumb to understand, or maybe it's just simply chance, and there's nothing more to understand. It doesn't matter. Like they say, it is what it is, and that day it was good.

I dropped by Gracie's office and invited her to lunch, but she already had a luncheon date with Joan Shum. I thought maybe Gracie might invite me to join them, but she didn't, and for a moment I was a little jealous. I know that sounds stupid. I mean, what was I jealous about? That Gracie and Joan were becoming friends, maybe close friends, and I wasn't included? That could have been it. Thinking about it, it dawned on me that maybe Gracie might feel the same way about my relationship with Doug. But it was too early in the morning to get into something like that, so I kept the conversation light.

As I was getting ready to leave, Gracie said it would be nice to have takeout dinner and relax at her place that night, and I agreed. I think that was her way of making up for not inviting me to lunch. In case you hadn't noticed, Gracie's much more considerate than I am. A fact that hasn't escaped Gracie's attention. She claims that she has met serial killers more considerate than me. I don't think that's true; I think she was just mad at me when she said it. I mean, one serial killer maybe, but more than one, I doubt it.

I gave Gracie a kiss, told her to give Joan my regards and took off. I planned on grabbing a couple of hot dogs from one of the local carts before

I met Tommy, and we went for a final session with Professor Wu. But as I walked up Worth Street, I had a brilliant thought. Why not take another tour of the Wing Fat Arcade? I thought walking through the arcade could trigger some helpful thoughts. It was one of those ideas that seem sound when they first enter your mind. When you're desperate, you do desperate things, right?

The last time I walked through the Wing Fat Arcade, I had started at the Doyers Street entrance. This time I decided to start at the other end of the arcade, which is entered through the Wing Fat Mansion condominiums in the middle of the block on Chatham Square. Situated halfway between Doyers Street and Mott Street, it's only half a block down from the Citibank. But the Golden Wok, where the Houdini Bandits vanished, is another block and a half away on Mott Street. The arcade didn't run in a straight line, but there was no way it was anywhere near the Golden Wok. Besides, according to Joey, the tunnel was dark all the way from the Golden Wok basement to the building on Bayard Street. The Wing Fat Arcade is lighted, not well lighted, but lighted nonetheless. I was probably on a fool's errand, but if the rumors were true and there was a whole web of tunnels under Chinatown, the two tunnels might be connected.

The Wing Fat Mansion, built in 1920, was converted some time ago into expensive condominium apartments. Walking through the lobby to the Wing Fat Arcade turned out to be an adventure in itself. There were two burly doormen, both of whom bore a striking resemblance to Oddjob, the nasty henchman in the James Bond film *Goldfinger*. If you never saw the movie, trust me, you don't want to mess around with Oddjob.

As I walked by the lobby desk, I gave both a friendly smile, but neither smiled back. Instead Oddjob 1 walked out from behind the desk, stood directly in my path and asked what business I had in the building. Normally, I would have ignored the question and walked on, but that would have required a wide berth, as he stood about six feet five inches high and probably four feet wide. Besides, my sense of self-preservation told me I should give a more reasoned response. This was not a good time for my usual smart-ass comments, so I said simply that I was going to the arcade.

Oddjob 1 grunted, nodded his head and stepped aside.

Things didn't improve in the arcade. As I walked through the tunnel, I was getting some hard stares that were causing the hairs on the back of my neck to stand up. Nobody has ever explained to me why that happens, but in my experience it's never a good thing when it does happen.

At one point, two guys, who looked like they were a couple of gangbangers, stood blocking my path. I thought I was in trouble, and I might very well have been except, as I approached, they looked past me and abruptly moved aside.

Once past them, I glanced back and saw a guy the size of a refrigerator walking behind me. Our eyes met, and he smiled and nodded his head. I knew right away he was the guy Tommy had assigned to cover my ass. I hadn't liked the idea when Tommy proposed it, but now I was glad Tommy hadn't listened to me. I wasn't surprised because Tommy never listens to me.

By the time I exited the arcade at Doyers Street, I was convinced the Wing Fat Arcade was not connected to the tunnel that Joey and the Cha brothers had used during their escape. I was back to square one, and unless Professor Wu had something more to add about the tunnels, I was stumped.

CHAPTER 43

My visit to the Wing Fat Arcade left me feeling depressed, and since I didn't have time for an AA meeting before seeing Professor Wu, I did the next best thing. I stopped for pizza. I know, I said that I was going to have hot dogs, but when I'm feeling down, I prefer pizza. There's something very comforting about pizza, particularly when it's cooked in a coal fired brick oven. You probably think I'm insane, and you might be right. I mean, I'm an Irishman, so how come pizza is a comfort food for me? All I can say is that having grown up in Hell's Kitchen, I eat a lot of different types of food. The fact that my mother, God bless her soul, wasn't such a good cook also explains a lot.

As luck would have it, John's Pizzeria of Bleecker Street, was on the way to Professor Wu's office. Well, almost on the way. Let's say it was close enough to warrant a detour. Especially when you consider that the pizzas are made in a coal fired brick oven using the same recipe since 1929. How can you beat that? You can't.

I call it therapy on a plate because that pizza tastes so great that when you eat it, you feel good, and you forget everything on your mind. And the best part, for what you'd pay for forty-five minutes with a shrink, you can buy at least twenty medium size pizzas with toppings and get better results. At least that's my opinion. But before you go and quit your shrink and start buying pizza instead, you might want to bear in mind that I don't have high regard for psychiatry and psychology.

Leaving John's Pizzeria, I was naturally feeling pretty good. But then Chen called and said the Chief of the Police Department had nixed our plan to jackhammer our way into the escape tunnel in the basement of the Golden Wok. I really couldn't blame the chief for his decision. After all, the Special Services Division of the NYPD and the experts from the FBI had all concluded there were no entranceways through the foundation walls. Chen and I had nothing concrete to refute their conclusions. Frankly, we had nothing more than a hope and a prayer. So, it wasn't a surprise that the NYPD refused to underwrite the cost of the demolition and repair of the wall.

Unless Professor Wu came up with something definite on the tunnels, I'd be pretty much out of options. All I could think of was to approach Marty and hope he would be reasonable and accept the fact that I couldn't give him any more details about the escape. But first I'd talk with Professor Wu.

The meeting with the professor lasted under an hour, and what he said didn't make me happy. Since our last meeting, Professor Wu had done additional research on the tunnels, including a search of the NYC Building Department records.

Before a building is constructed in NYC or major renovations are made to an existing building, the contractor must file construction plans with the Building Department. Included in the required plans is a "Site Plan." If, during the construction, major changes are made such as a newly discovered tunnel or remnants of a tunnel, then the contractor would have to file "as-built" plans showing the changes.

It had been a great idea, but unfortunately it didn't bear fruit. The only plans Wu could find that referenced an old tunnel were the plans to seal off the tunnel that my previous client had used. Knowing the Chinese communities' disdain for regulations, I wasn't surprised. I knew old man Shoo's building didn't comply with the city's Building Code, and I doubted we'd find any plans on file for the changes he had made to the building. So the Building Department was another dead end.

Wu was convinced that the network of tunnels existed at one time. His interview and my own interview with the old man, Yue Ying Tso, had convinced us both that the tunnels did exist. Wu believed the tunnels still existed and were being used by the tongs and street gangs. But he had no proof. I didn't know what to believe, but unless I could show Marty something about the tunnels, Joey was in trouble.

After leaving Professor Wu, I called Marty Bowman and said I might not be able to come up with any information on the tunnels. After explaining why, I asked him to be understanding. But Marty wasn't understanding. He said a deal was a deal, and unless I explained and proved how Joey and the Cha brothers escaped from the basement of the Golden Wok, the charge against Joey would be upgraded to robbery in the second degree. When I pressed him and asked for a compromise, he said that he'd keep the charge at third degree if Joey gave up the stolen cash.

Since Joey claimed he didn't have the money, and I couldn't find the escape tunnel, we were in deep shit, and it looked like Joey was going to do some hard prison time. I had to find a way out, and I had to find it fast.

Walking back to my office after talking with Marty, I got a brainstorm. Maybe we didn't need NYPD permission to hunt for the tunnel entrance. First, I went to the Golden Wok Restaurant, then I called Chen and asked him if he could meet me at the Worth Street Coffee Shop right away. He asked what I had in mind, and when I told him, he said he'd be there in ten minutes.

CHAPTER 44

When Chen arrived, I explained my idea. I said we were making a mistake in thinking that we needed the NYPD to find the escape tunnel. I had spoken to the owner of the Golden Wok, and he had agreed we could jackhammer the basement wall as long as we repaired it. He didn't care who did the jackhammering; he just wanted assurances the wall would be repaired. If the NYPD wouldn't do it, we could find someone else to do it.

Finding someone with a jackhammer was easy; finding someone to pay the bill was the hard part. That was my brainstorm. Mr. Fang would pay for it. He had the money, and he was committed to doing everything possible to save his grandson from a long prison sentence.

Chen smiled and asked if I had already spoken to Fang. I said I hadn't, but if he agreed, I'd call Mr. Fang right away. Chen nodded, and I dialed. I explained the situation to Mr. Fang, and without asking how much it would cost, he agreed to pay for the work and the repairs. I said it was risky to which he replied, "It is foolish to refuse to eat just because of the chance of choking."

When I signaled Chen with a thumbs-up, a broad smile crossed his face. For the first time, we were both seeing light at the end of the tunnel. We had a general plan, and now it was time to deal with specifics.

Chen said his wife's cousin, Harry, was in the construction business, and he was sure he'd be able do the job. He'd check with him that night and get a cost estimate and a schedule for doing the work. He said, if possible, he'd have Harry meet with us at the precinct the next day. I said that was good, but I wanted to meet with Joey and go over the details before we did the work. I wanted to make sure we did the jackhammering in the right place. Chen thought that was a good idea and said after we met with Harry, he'd take me to the safe house.

Back at the office, I called Tommy and let him know what we were up to. Tommy said he had a question or two to ask Joey, so if it was okay, he'd ride along with us. I didn't see any harm in it, so I told him I'd call him when we had a time, and he could meet me at the precinct house.

That night, over our Indian takeout dinner, Gracie explained that she hadn't invited me to lunch with her and Joan because Joan wanted to talk about her marriage. Gracie said, in general terms, the marriage was on the rocks. That I had figured out on my own, but what I hadn't known, was the marriage was on shaky ground before Jenny disappeared.

Joan didn't think the marriage could be saved, and she was considering moving to New York permanently. She had contacted NYU about a teaching position, and she had an interview scheduled later in the week.

Hesitant to talk to me about the situation, she had called Gracie and invited her to lunch. After hearing the story, Gracie assured Joan that talking to me was the right thing to do. Joan agreed, but asked Gracie to talk with me first. After that, Joan said she'd talk to me directly.

It was funny how things were working out. I'd been practicing law for over thirty years, and suddenly I find myself in the construction business and the marriage counseling business. I think I liked it better when I was just in the criminal law business. At least I knew what I was doing.

CHAPTER 45

The next morning, Chen called and said he had spoken to his wife's cousin, and he could meet us that afternoon. I was on my way to court for a sentencing, which wouldn't take long, but to be on the safe side, I asked Chen to arrange the meeting for two o'clock. I told him after that, I was free to go see Joey. He said the timing was good by him, so unless I heard from him to the contrary, he'd see me at two at the precinct. I called Tommy and told him to meet me at the Fifth Precinct at two o'clock, and I went to the sentencing hearing.

That morning, Marjorie Collins, who had pleaded guilty to menacing in the second degree, a Class A misdemeanor, with a possible sentence of up to a year in jail, was scheduled to be sentenced. Ms. Collins, a rather large woman, weighing in at somewhere around three hundred pounds, was accused of repeatedly terrorizing her neighbor, Mr. Walter Gordon, and threatening him and his schnauzer with a knife. Mr. Gordon was a small man, maybe five feet three inches tall, and maybe one hundred and ten pounds soaking wet, so his fears weren't unreasonable.

Unfortunately for Ms. Collins, this was not the first time she had terrorized Mr. Gordon. In fact, it wasn't even the second or the third incident. It was the fourth, and all the incidents were spelled out in detail in the police reports. The first three times the cops had been called, they warned Ms. Collins to cease and desist. The fourth time they were called, they arrested Ms. Collins and charged her with violating Section 120.14 (2), menacing in the second degree. Under the statute, a person is guilty of menacing in the second degree when "she repeatedly follows a person or engages in a course of conduct or repeatedly commits acts over a period of time intentionally placing or attempting to place another person in reasonable fear of physical injury, serious physical injury or death."

When Joe Benjamin called me about the case, I thought at first it was a joke. But it wasn't a joke, and since I hadn't accepted a new assignment in a while, Joe insisted I take it. Of course, I wanted to meet Ms. Collins and find out her side of the story but, frankly, after reading the police reports, I didn't see where she had much of a defense. I was, however, relieved when Connie corrected my misconception, explaining that Mr. Gordon's schnauzer was his dog, not a part of his anatomy.

If we couldn't work out a plea deal, and I was forced to pick a jury, finding sympathetic jurors wouldn't be easy. I'd have to exclude members of PETA, as well as all males.

To make a long story short, Ms. Collins had no defense. She simply didn't like Mr. Gordon, and she didn't care for his schnauzer. So, whenever she saw them in the hallway, she ran after them, screaming and waving what she said wasn't a knife, but a soup ladle. The nature of the instrument didn't matter. In Ms. Collins's hands, a soup ladle could be just as deadly as a knife. I mean, this woman was huge and scary. I was afraid of her even without a soup ladle in her hand.

The best I could do for Ms. Collins was to negotiate a deal that kept her out of jail. If Ms. Collins promised not to menace Mr. Gordon and his schnauzer, the judge would order her on probation for three years. If she behaved herself during the three years, the record would be expunged. It was a good deal. Actually under the circumstances, it was a great deal. Only I doubted Ms. Collins had any intention of abiding by the deal. I say that because at the hearing, she kept throwing looks at Mr. Gordon that frightened even me.

I don't think the judge noticed the looks, and so the plea deal went through without a hitch. Once it was over and Ms. Collins was signing the agreement papers, Mr. Gordon took off like the building was on fire. I can't say I blamed him. If I were him, I'd grab my schnauzer and move.

When the hearing was over, I called Joe Benjamin and told him the case was concluded. Then I warned him that if Ms. Collins was arrested again, and he had any thoughts of assigning the case to me, I'd quit the Panel. I would have threatened to cut off his schnauzer, but I figured he knew it was a dog.

Finding myself with time to kill before I met Chen, I decided to hop down to the Financial District and grab some lunch from one of the many food carts. The food carts in New York City don't just sell Sabrett hot dogs. No, you can get all kinds of food from food carts. Halal, Greek, Middle Eastern, Asian, Indian, Italian and Caribbean.

That day, I was in the mood for Greek, so I went directly to the corner of Wall and Broad Streets and the Greek Street Meat cart. Like most other food carts in Manhattan, the Greek Street Meat cart is topped with a Sabrett umbrella. But there's more on the menu in addition to Sabrett hot dogs. I love those dogs, but I didn't go all the way to the Financial District for the hot dogs; I went for the shish kebab.

I had just ordered my lunch when I noticed the guy Tommy had shadowing me standing half a block away. At his size he was hard to miss. I mean, he stood out from the crowd like a NFL lineman standing in a class of first graders. Well, maybe that's an exaggeration, but not much of one. I waved to the man, and when he approached, I offered to buy him lunch. At first, he was unsure what he should do, but I guess he was hungry because after thinking it over, he ordered two gyros.

It was a long walk from Wall and Broad Streets to the Fifth Precinct, but I had plenty of time to get there, and I needed a good walk after my lunch.

Walking in Lower Manhattan at lunchtime on a weekday has always been challenging. The sidewalks are narrow and crowded with people moving in all directions, so there was always some unintentional jostling. But since the advent of the cell phone, walking in any part of Manhattan has turned into a human bumper car adventure. Too many people stare at their damn cell phones and don't watch where they're going. I hate those people, and I'm surprised they aren't killed walking into traffic.

What the hell could be so important that you have to stare at your cell phone continuously? If it rings, answer it; if it's not ringing, leave it alone. And what's with these text messages? The damn thing is a telephone; you're supposed to talk on it, not send cryptic messages using acronyms I don't understand. What does "LOL" mean anyway? You want to say something to me, call me, or talk to me like a human being. Don't send me a text message.

Okay, I guess I've done enough ranting, so before you tell me to call Doug or find a meeting, I'll move on.

Tommy, Detective Chen, Harry, and I met in one of the Fifth Precinct's interrogation rooms. Harry explained what needed to be done to uncover the tunnel entrance, and how he planned on doing the work. He seemed to know what he was talking about, and by the time he was done talking to us, we were all convinced he could do the job. However, before we committed to anything, I had to talk with Mr. Fang and get his final approval. I explained to Harry that before we could commit, I needed to know how much it was going to cost. Harry said it was difficult to give a hard estimate because he didn't know how long it would take to find the tunnel entrance and what conditions he'd encounter. He said he would do the jackhammering for $350 an hour, which included the rental cost for the jackhammer, his services and the services of a helper. When I pressed him, he said that knocking out a section of a basement wall, ten or so feet wide, and cleaning up the debris would take a couple of hours at most. That wasn't bad, but we still needed to add in the cost to repair the wall.

The cost for the repairs was a different story. Harry said until he knew what materials he needed and how big an area he had to repair, he couldn't give an estimate. However, he agreed to do the work on what he called a "time and materials basis." According to Chen, it meant he'd charge for the cost of the materials, plus a fifteen percent markup, and his time at $150 an hour. I still needed a figure to present to Mr. Fang, so I pressed Harry again.

Harry gave it some thought, then said if we had some idea where to look for the tunnel entrance, the demolition shouldn't involve more than ten to fifteen feet of wall and the total cost, including the repair, should be under $10,000. Of course, he didn't want to be held to that price because as he put it, "it was his best guess." Tommy, who had more experience in construction than I had, said it all sounded reasonable.

It was a gamble and a big one, but Chen and I were out of options. I called Mr. Fang and told him where we stood. Without asking a single question, he said to go ahead with the plan. Then he offered to bring the ten thousand dollars in cash to the precinct house. That was not a good idea, so I quickly said it wasn't necessary; I'd bill him when we needed the money.

Harry was available to do the work that coming weekend, but we needed to let him know by Friday, so he could rent the jackhammer. I was okay with Harry doing the work, but before giving him the go-ahead, I wanted to check with Joey and confirm his recollection that he had entered the tunnel through the wall just to the right of the staircase entrance.

Chen suggested that we take a ride to Freeport and see Joey right away. I had nothing else to do, and as much as I dreaded going to Long Island, the timing was right. Chen said if we left then, we could be back in the city by seven or eight o'clock. I thought that was a bit optimistic given Long Island's notorious traffic jams. But Chen reminded me that his car had a siren and flashing lights. As they say, rank has its privilege.

CHAPTER 46

Riding in cop cars wasn't new to me. As a young ADA, I had ridden in cop cars on numerous occasions, but that was years earlier when I was probably drinking heavily. It could certainly explain why I didn't remember being as terrified then as I was now riding in the car with Chen. With lights flashing and siren blaring, we weaved our way through traffic over the Brooklyn Bridge along the Brooklyn-Queens Expressway, and onto the Long Island Expressway.

Believe it or not, Chen's driving made me long for a New York City taxicab driver. Maybe it wasn't his driving as much as the fact that I was sitting in the front seat, which gave me a totally new perspective on near miss collisions. I found them much more terrifying when you're sitting in the front seat, and the only thing standing between you and certain death is a piece of glass. Not exactly the material I'd choose to protect me from being bashed into the bumper of a two-thousand-pound car.

At least in the backseat of a taxicab there's space and another seat to shield you from the impact.

I thought once we reached the Queens County border and entered Nassau County, which was out of Chen's jurisdiction, he'd shut off the flashers and sirens and slow down. But I was wrong. Chan said the only people we had to worry about were the local cops and since we were in an unmarked car, the locals wouldn't know it wasn't one of theirs or one of the Feds' cars. So we weaved and rocketed our way to Freeport while my life flashed before my eyes. It was like a bad movie, and it just kept playing over and over again.

The safe house was a small bungalow situated on a cul-de-sac at the end of a quiet dead-end street. The street was lined with similar small bungalows. It was the type of neighborhood where you'd expect to see white picket fences and people sitting in rocking chairs on their front porches. The only thing was that nearly all of the houses on this block were vacant and boarded up, having fallen victim to the great recession.

The safe house was positioned in the center of the cul-de-sac, so from the front window you could see all the way to the end of the street, making it impossible to approach without being seen. The back of the house was protected by a wide canal and a series of motion detectors. Anyone approaching by boat would set off the alarm well before they stepped on dry land. Motion detectors covering the side yards completed the electronic protection coverage. It was a safe house alright, so long as no one fell asleep at the switch.

No one had told Joey that Chen and I were coming to see him, so he was surprised when we showed up. Not only did he look surprised, but to me, he looked a little puzzled. I didn't think much of it at the time, but later on it made sense.

We took seats in the living room, and the two officers on protection duty left to give us privacy.

I have to say that Joey looked good and seemed more relaxed than he had been the last time I saw him. Being out of range of Hip Sing Tong apparently agreed with him.

During the ride, Chen had suggested that I do the talking, so once we were seated, I started. I asked Joey to tell us, in as much detail as he could remember, what happened when he and the Cha brothers entered the basement of the Golden Wok.

Joey thought about it for a minute, then he said that he recalled going down the stairs from the street. The door into the basement was closed but unlocked. Bobby opened the door, and after the three of them were inside, he told Joey and his brother to stand with their backs against the wall. I interrupted Joey to ask which wall. He said the wall to the right of the staircase. I wanted to be sure, so I asked him if it was the wall immediately to the right of the staircase after he entered the basement. Joey said, yes, that was the wall.

He did as Bobby instructed and put his back against the wall. Billy did the same, standing to his left. Bobby said for them to hold hands, then he closed the door. There were no lights, so it was pitch black, and Joey couldn't see a thing. He felt Bobby move past him. Then Bobby took his hand, and after telling him to hold tight to Billy's hand, he pulled him along the wall.

I asked Joey how far along the wall he was pulled. He said maybe five or six sideways steps, or maybe ten; he wasn't sure. After that, he heard a scraping noise, and light started coming into the room. The light was coming through a doorway.

I interrupted Joey again and asked how far from where he was standing the doorway was. He thought for a moment, then said maybe two or three feet. I asked if he was sure the doorway was through the wall he had his back against, and he said he was sure.

Bobby led the way through the door into the tunnel. Once in the tunnel, Bobby somehow closed the door. Joey hadn't seen how Bobby closed the door, nor was he paying attention to the door itself. That was about all he could tell us.

I looked at Chen to see if he thought we needed to ask anything else, and he just shrugged, so I figured we were done. But then Joey wanted to know why we were asking all these questions again. I said we were going to try to find the tunnel entrance.

Joey nodded his head, but a look passed over his face that said something wasn't right. The look had passed quickly, and maybe I read too much into it, but I wasn't about to let it go too easily, so I asked if he had any suggestions. Shaking his head, he said no, and since I didn't see the look again, I let it go.

On the way back to Manhattan, between fits of terror, I asked Chen if he thought Joey had reacted strangely when he heard we were looking for the tunnel entrance. He said that for a moment he thought that he saw something in Joey's look, but he didn't make anything of it. I figured since the two of us saw it the same way, it wasn't something I needed to worry about. Besides, I had bigger things, like a fatal car crash, to worry about.

Miraculously, with help from my Higher Power who I besieged incessantly during our trip, we made it back to the Fifth Precinct in one piece. Before we parted ways, Chen said he'd call Harry and tell him we were good to go on Saturday. Once Harry let him know the time, he'd pass it on to me.

Later that night, thinking back on the vibe Chen and I had gotten from Joey when I mentioned searching for the tunnel, I started to wonder if we had been too quick in dismissing it. I mean, if only one of us had gotten the vibe, that would be different. But both of us got it, which told me there was something to it.

Then again, I didn't want to make a big deal out of something that was probably nothing. If Chen was happy to let it drop, that was good enough for me.

CHAPTER 47

The next morning, I got a call from Sarah Washington. Jenny's bail application hearing had been scheduled for the following Thursday. Sarah wanted to know if I'd be ready, or if I wanted an adjournment. I asked her if, by chance, the District Attorney had had a change of heart and wouldn't oppose the application. Unfortunately, there had been no change of heart. I told Sarah I appreciated the call, but I didn't want to adjourn the hearing. There was no sense in delaying the inevitable.

That may sound strange since the only way Jenny was going to escape hard prison time was if I delayed her case until the heavyweight defendants pleaded out or were convicted. That's when the media would lose interest in the case, and the DA would look to clean up the remaining cases quickly. The reasoning was simple. There'd be nothing to gain from keeping the cases around, and since a case like Jenny's was marginal to begin with, why waste resources trying it? So if that was the strategy, why not adjourn the bail hearing?

The problem was the timing and how well Jenny would handle it. It could be months before the heavyweight cases were cleared, and if Jenny's bail application was denied, she'd have to spend the time at Rikers. I didn't want to see that happen, but if it did, I was convinced Jenny could do the time. It would come as a blow, but if she wasn't unrealistically optimistic about the bail, it wouldn't hit her as hard.

Therein was the problem. Since Joan had arrived, Jenny 's mood had improved, but now she was getting overly optimistic about the bail situation. I wanted her to be hopeful, but I needed her to be realistic, so if we lost, she wouldn't be crushed. The longer the bail issue went unresolved, the more optimistic Jenny was likely to become, and the more devastating it would be if she wasn't released on bail.

For me, it was a delicate balance. I had to keep Jenny's and Joan's spirits up, but at the same time, I had to make sure their expectations were realistic. It's pretty much the same with most clients and their families. No one wants to face the truth about themself, nor do their family members, so they all think things will turn out okay.

The exceptions are the sociopaths, the violent felon scumbags with no empathy and no feelings for anyone. Most times they know they're going away for long stretches, and they don't care. With scumbags like that, it's a rubber stamp proceeding, if you know what I mean.

Don't get the wrong idea; I do the best I can for all my clients. But when you have a guy caught red-handed beating and raping a woman, there isn't much I can do for him. If the scumbag has a record of violent crime, he's going away for twenty-five to life and deservedly so. I can argue all I want; I can even plead with the judge, but it's not going to do any good. That's why I call those cases rubber stamp proceedings.

Anyway, Jenny's case wasn't a rubber stamp proceeding, and I needed to prepare for the hearing. I called Joan and left a message on her cell. I knew she'd be at Rikers with Jenny as she was every day that the visitor schedule permitted. I needed her to free up some time so we could go over her testimony and plan our strategy.

I'd also have to prepare Jenny. She wasn't going to testify, but the hearing would be all about her, and it was important that she present herself in a good light. She needed to understand that her behavior during the hearing would weigh heavily in the judge's decision. No matter what was said, she had to remain calm and reserved. If she didn't, and if she made a scene, bail would likely be denied.

CHAPTER 48

I was on my way to Rikers to see Jenny when Chen called and said arrangements had been made to do the demolition work in the Golden Wok basement that Saturday. Harry and his helper would be at the restaurant by ten and ready to start jackhammering within half an hour. Chen planned on being there by ten o'clock, and so did I. There was a lot riding on the outcome, not to mention the fact that it was probably our best, and possibly the last chance to find the Houdini Bandits' escape route. I didn't want to think what would happen if it was a bust.

But there was no sense worrying about it then. Besides, I had a more pressing issue to deal with. I had to convince Jenny that no matter what happened on Thursday, she'd be okay. I didn't want her putting too much importance on the bail hearing because if we lost, it wasn't the end of the world. We could still follow our original strategy. While without bail it would be tougher on Jenny, in the end she would escape hard prison time. Believe me, lowering expectations is a lot harder than raising them, and Jenny's expectations needed lowering.

When I got to Rikers and arranged to see Jenny, I was told Joan was there visiting. That wasn't unexpected. I told the Corrections Officer that Joan was working with me on the case and asked that she be brought with Jenny into one of the lawyer conference rooms. I'm at Rikers enough that the Correction Officers know me, and since I don't give them a hard time, they'll do me favors on occasion. This was one of those occasions where I really needed a favor and, luckily, I got it.

I wanted Joan at the meeting that morning, but I purposely hadn't arranged for her to be there because I wanted the meeting to be spontaneous. Or at least seem that way. I knew Joan had been visiting Jenny every day, so I was sure she'd be there that morning. As I said, lowering expectations is a delicate thing, and I thought Jenny might take what I had to say better with

Joan present. I felt that knowing Joan was behind her, no matter what, would help Jenny accept her situation. I know that's easy for me to say since I'm not the one doing the time at Rikers.

There was one other factor playing into all of this, and I wasn't certain how to deal with it. During my last visit with Jenny when Joan was not there, Jenny asked how her father was taking all of this. I figured telling her the prick disowned her wasn't good, so I said simply that she should ask her mother. I never discussed it with Joan, so I didn't know if she and Jenny ever talked about it, but I didn't want it upsetting things.

Jenny struck me as a pretty sharp kid, so she had to know if her mother was moving to New York on a full-time basis that she was probably leaving Dr. Shum behind. Of course, not knowing, but suspecting, could be worse. Jenny had enough on her plate without worrying about her good-for-nothing father. He was a class A prick, and that was all there was to it, and she was better off without him. I couldn't explain that to her, but Joan could.

I won't go into details about our meeting that day. I'll just say it was enlightening. It started off with Jenny asking about her father. Much to my surprise and delight, Joan was brutally honest and revealed some details which I hadn't been privy to until that point. At first, Jenny didn't want to hear anything negative about her father, which I understood. But Joan didn't relent and for good reason. By the time the conversation ended, Jenny understood two things. First, her father wasn't the kind man she thought he was, and second, she wasn't the cause of her parents' impending divorce.

Then it was my turn to say my piece. Naturally, Jenny wasn't happy hearing that she might be spending another couple of months in jail, but she wasn't thrown by it either. During the discussion, Joan sat next to Jenny holding her hand. It was obvious that the session had been cathartic for Joan, and as importantly, it gave Jenny the assurance that no matter what happened, her mother would be there for her. It was from that assurance that Jenny would draw the strength to handle whatever was to come. Satisfied that Jenny would be fine on Thursday, I left. Joan and Jenny needed time alone.

On the way back downtown, I called Mr. Fang and told him what was happening with the tunnel search. I said he was welcome to come and observe the action on Saturday, but he declined. He said he had faith in me, and he didn't need to be there. He asked how Joey was doing and if he could visit him. I said Joey was doing fine, and as for visiting, it would be too dangerous. The Hip Sing Tong was probably watching and following him, hoping he'd lead them to Joey. He'd just have to be patient and wait a while. He said, "The longer the night, the more dreams there will be."

At times Mr. Fang sounded like a walking fortune cookie. But there was wisdom in his words; that much I had to give him. I just hoped for his sake, and all our sakes, we weren't on a wild goose chase.

I had something else on my mind that morning. It had to do with Gracie and our living arrangement. I spent almost every night at Gracie's place. I had most of my clothes there, but I still had a studio apartment on the East Side. A few years earlier, I had given up my larger one-bedroom apartment because I was spending so much time at Gracie's, it didn't make financial sense to keep it. But I needed to have a place of my own, so that was why I took the studio apartment.

Now the studio was becoming a financial problem, and Gracie said I should consider giving it up. Neither of us ever mentioned the "M" word for fear the other would run away screaming. It was just a topic that neither of us wanted to talk about.

Living together is different, so long as it's optional. Look, we're both crazy, okay? I know, and Gracie knows it doesn't make sense, but that's just the way it is. We both need to know we have options, and keeping my apartment gives us those options.

But now, with the rent going up on the studio apartment, we had a problem. Gracie said she had no issue with me moving in full-time. I already paid a portion of the rent, and if I gave up the studio apartment, I'd be able to pay half the rent.

On the positive side, we'd keep our separate bank accounts, and if we broke up, I'd agree to leave. I'd even put it all in writing if that made Gracie feel more comfortable. Of course, I'd want the agreement to include that I could leave without having my stuff thrown out the window. I don't handle divorces, but I've heard the stories.

I've talked to Doug about it, but he's been no help. He said that he's tired of me coming to him with the same old thing all the time. He claims it stems from my fear of commitment. I told him a hundred times that I'm not afraid to commit; I just don't want to be tied down. There's a difference. I have trouble articulating the difference, but I believe it exists. That's the point in the conversation when Doug groans and hangs up on me.

Gracie and I have to figure this out; I'm just not sure how we're going to do it. Probably over sushi, or if I'm unlucky, in the sack. I say unlucky if it's in the sack because, like most men, I'll say and do anything for sex, especially if it's right there in front of me. It's a biological thing. All the blood leaving the brain and heading to another organ keeps you from thinking straight.

CHAPTER 49

The next couple of days passed quickly. I had done everything I could to prepare for Jenny's bail hearing, so it was just a matter of waiting. Joan called daily, despite my assurances that nothing was going to happen until the hearing. The night before the hearing, Gracie, knowing Joan would be nervous, invited her to have dinner with us. It was a nice thing to do, and I'm sure it helped Joan. We spent the whole evening without once mentioning the next day's hearing. At the end of the night, I put Joan in a taxicab, then Gracie and I walked to her place. I wanted to talk about our living arrangement, but Gracie said I probably had bigger things on my mind, so the talk could wait. She was probably right; my head was focused on the bail hearing.

The bail hearing was scheduled for ten-thirty before Judge Collins. I liked Collins; he was a good judge. He was smart and fair, but in a close case like Jenny's, he tended to follow the District Attorney's recommendation. That would have been okay if Sarah Washington wasn't opposing the bail application, but she was so it could be a problem.

It was a tough case because even though Jenny had no prior criminal history, she had no strong ties to the jurisdiction. I intended to call Joan as a witness to establish her residency in New York and her intent to support her daughter, financially and emotionally through the trial. While Joan was absolutely committed to helping her daughter, she wasn't ready to say under oath that she intended to stay in New York permanently. I couldn't blame her for that. It was a big decision, and between Jenny's problem and an imminent divorce, she had a lot on her plate.

If Joan didn't testify that her move to New York was permanent, I'd be hard pressed arguing against a claim by Sarah Washington that Joan's recent residence was contrived, and there was no assurance she would remain in New York for the duration. That wasn't necessarily the worst of it. During

Joan's direct testimony, I'd avoid mentioning Dr. Shum, and Sarah Washington was savvy enough to suspect that something was there that she could exploit. I expected Sarah would ask during cross-examination if Jenny's father supported what Joan was doing. Once Sarah grabbed onto that topic, she wasn't likely to let loose. One or two issues raised on cross-examination wouldn't necessarily be fatal to the application, but what worried me was the cumulative impact on an already weak argument.

I had done everything I could to prepare Jenny and Joan for the worst, but I sensed they still thought bail would be granted. If it was denied, it was going to be a big problem. My greatest concern was that Jenny, in her disappointment, would revert to the arrogant indifference she flaunted when we first met, and I didn't think Joan would be able to deal with that. Not when she was already dealing with her marriage being over and the possibility of having to start her life over in Manhattan.

Joan didn't talk much with me about it, but she did confide in Gracie. Of course, Gracie kept the details in confidence, but from the little Gracie was able to say and from what I could tell by Joan's comments to me, I feared Joan might be nearing the breaking point. Good old Dr. Shum was being a class A prick. When Joan told him she wanted a divorce, he shut down their joint bank accounts and canceled all of Joan's credit cards. If Joan hadn't had her own money, we would have been stopped dead in our tracks. But Joan did have her own money, so the bastard couldn't stop her. But that didn't keep him from harassing her every chance he got.

I could only imagine the bastard's reaction if the bail application was denied. If, on top of that, Jenny reverted to her old behavior, I wouldn't blame Joan if she threw in the towel and walked away.

I've handled scores of bail hearings in my career, but none had as much riding on the outcome as this one. I like pressure; it makes me sharper. But the pressure on this one was a bit too intense even for me.

CHAPTER 50

The next morning, I met Joan at the Worth Street Coffee Shop, and we went over her testimony one last time. She was nervous, but she was more together than I expected. I figured if I was feeling the pressure, she'd be feeling it even more. Hoping to relieve some of that pressure, I told her not to worry. I was confident we'd win. But if we lost, it wouldn't be because of her testimony. It would be because we had a weak case.

When we got to the courthouse, I had Joan go directly to Judge Collins's courtroom, while I went down to the holding cells to see Jenny.

Jenny was in good spirits and wanted to know when she'd be released. I told her if things went well, it might be that afternoon or the next morning at the latest. I was going to caution her that things might not go well but thought better of it. I didn't need Jenny sitting in the courtroom in a funk.

Then I went upstairs and sat with Joan until Sarah Washington showed up. Hoping against hope, I walked up to Sarah and said, "I don't suppose the DA had a change of heart on the bail application?"

She said unfortunately not and as much as she hated doing it, she had no choice but to oppose the application. I wasn't surprised because I hadn't expected the DA to change his position.

The Court Officer who brought Jenny into the courtroom I knew from AA. When he saw me, he gave me a little nod, and I nodded back. That's what you do in those circumstances; you do a little nod. You don't shout out, "Hey, I know you from AA."

With everyone ready and in position, Judge Collins emerged from his robing room and took his seat. Glancing at the application, he told me to proceed.

Moving to the podium, notes in hand, I began by introducing Jenny and Joan. I said "*Jenny came to Manhattan, a confused young girl under the spell of an older man. Lured from the love and comfort of her family and taken thousands of miles from them, she became a lost soul. A young girl, more innocent than she was wise, intelligent but unworldly, and anything but street smart. Once here, she was abused, and ultimately she was abandoned by the man she had loved and trusted, the man she had given up home and family to be with. The man who, in her young mind, had become her entire world. Betrayed, ashamed and filled with guilt, she dared not call her parents.*

To survive, she found work. But having only the false identification given to her by her former boyfriend, there were no good jobs open to her. Left with no choice, she took what work she could find, and unfortunately, it led to her falling in with a bad crowd. Jenny has no criminal background and having lived her entire life until now in a solid upper middle-class neighborhood, she had no experience dealing with those types of people. In her naiveté and innocence and desperate for companionship, she accepted their friendship. That was how she happened to be in the company of Asian Dragons on the night she was arrested.

Jenny has no criminal record. There is no evidence that Jenny personally possessed any drugs or contraband. The entire case against her rests on guilt by association. Her mother, Joan, a college professor, is here in the courtroom and has taken residence in Manhattan as a first step to moving here permanently.

"I ask you, Your Honor, to look at Jenny Shum. Does she look like she is a threat to society, or does she look like the confused innocent child she is? With her mother here to keep her safe and to assure her appearance in court, what purpose is served by keeping this young woman in jail?

Having shown a nexus to the jurisdiction, the weakness of the People's case against Jenny Shum and her obvious lack of threat to the community, I ask the Court to set a reasonable bail."

I took my seat. Judge Collins asked Sarah Washington for the District Attorney's position. Sarah said simply that the DA opposed bail, but she made no argument and offered no rebuttal to my argument. I had no idea what was going on, but whatever it was, it was good for us, and I wasn't going to complain.

Judge Collins seemed as surprised by Sarah's statement as I was. For a moment, he said nothing, then he asked if I was prepared to present any witnesses. I said that I was, and I turned to call Joan to the stand when the judge said, "Wait a moment, Mr. Carney."

My heart stopped. I feared the judge, sensing something was afoot, was going to take Sarah to task for not offering any argument in rebuttal. But instead, he asked Sarah if she intended to cross-examine my witnesses. Under normal circumstances, the question would have been out of place, but circumstances were hardly normal.

Sarah stood and I held my breath. Then she said that she wouldn't be cross-examining any witnesses. I could hardly believe what I had just heard. Basically, it was a great big gift, wrapped in an enormous bow. The judge, understanding full well what was going on, said in that case he'd rule without taking any further evidence, and set bail at $25,000 cash or bond. We were done, It was over.

I wanted to hug Sarah, but I knew better. She had just done Jenny and me a huge favor, and her ass might be on the line as a result. Technically, she had followed orders and opposed the bail application. She just hadn't done a very good job of it.

I looked across the aisle at Sarah, smiled and whispered, "I owe you one."

She smiled back and said, "A big one. A really big one."

I turned to Jenny and told her we'd work on posting bail, and she'd probably be released sometime that afternoon, but for now she had to return to Rikers. Jenny smiled and gave me a big hug.

Joan came up behind us and gave Jenny a big hug and kiss. As the Court Officer was taking Jenny away, Joan turned and gave me a big hug. Then she sobbed and started to cry.

I assumed this was one of those happy cries, although I don't understand the thinking behind a "happy cry." That night, Gracie explained it as a release of pent up emotions which, to be honest, I didn't understand. Of course, I didn't say that to Gracie. I just nodded and tried to look like I understood what she said. Experience has taught me I'm better off when I do that.

By the time we left the courtroom, Joan had composed herself, and she wanted to know how to go about arranging Jenny's bail. Naturally, she wanted Jenny out of Rikers as quickly as possible, so I told her the best way was to use a bail bondsman. If she acted quickly, Jenny might be out by that afternoon.

To facilitate things, I suggested Joan use my friend Sal Martinez, at A-1 Bail Service. When she agreed, I called Connie and told her to start preparing the bail bond application. Then I called Sal and told him I had a client who was a friend coming to see him.

The bond was small, only $25,000, so it was no big deal. Sal usually requires the fee, which in this instance was $2,500 payable in cash, certified check or money order, but as a favor to me he'd take a personal check. Of course, if the check bounced, Sal would come looking for me to make it good. But that was okay. I trusted Joan.

As Joan and I were parting ways at the bottom of the courthouse steps, Sarah Washington was coming down the steps, and she called out to me. After thanking her again, I asked if she'd be in trouble for not arguing against the bail application. She smiled and said, "What my boss doesn't know can't hurt me." Meaning her boss would just chalk it up to a bad decision by the judge and wasn't likely to ask for a transcript of the hearing. He'd never know that Sarah had thrown the case.

Sarah made it sound like it wasn't a big deal, but I knew better. If her boss found out what she had done, she'd be in big trouble. Knowing that, I asked her why she had done it. She said that she felt for Jenny and her mother, and she believed Jenny's story. God knows she had heard enough stories to know the true ones from the bullshit ones. She said the DA was wrong in issuing blanket orders, and each case needed to be handled on its own merits. I agreed with that, but it still took a lot of courage to ignore a direct order from the boss.

Sarah wasn't done doing me favors. She said if she were me, she'd start making all sorts of motions to delay the case. Reading between the lines told me that plea deals and convictions were in the works, and my delay strategy would pay off. I asked Sarah if, when I made my motions, she would oppose them, to which she replied, "You bet. Of course, I might need added time for my reply papers." In other words, she'd delay the process as much as she could.

I asked Sarah if she was free for lunch, but she had to decline. I knew that I owed her a lot more than a lunch, but it's a touchy thing asking a single woman to dinner. Even someone like Sarah who I knew and had worked with for a couple of years. You can't be sure how a person will take something like that, so rather than risk putting Sarah in an uncomfortable position, I said Gracie would call her, and we'd all have dinner very soon. That seemed to please Sarah, so maybe I had done the right thing.

I had promised to call Gracie and let her know how the hearing went, and after telling her what happened, I mentioned my conversation with Sarah. Gracie said my instincts were spot on, and I had handled the situation perfectly.

It's not often that Gracie thinks my behavior is ideal, and rare indeed is the high praise she had just given me. I was basking in the glory of her praise and the win at the hearing. It called for a celebration, and I headed straight for the Sabrett hot dog cart. It was still a bit early for lunch, but what the hell? If he was selling, I was buying.

I was on a roll. If things continued going my way, on Saturday I'd be walking through the notorious Chinatown tunnels. Life was good.

CHAPTER 51

Whenever I would tell Doug that things were going great and I was feeling really good, he'd always say, "Don't worry; things will change." They usually did, and this time was no exception. The day after Jenny's bail hearing, I was feeling good when Connie announced Sarah Washington was on the line, and that's when things started going downhill again.

I had barely said hello when Sarah asked, "Who the hell is Shing Lew?" I had to think for a moment, then I remembered he was the creep boyfriend who had brought Jenny to New York. Not knowing what was going on, I decided it was best if I played dumb. I said I couldn't recall anyone by that name and asked why she was asking.

The little bastard had contacted the District Attorney's Office, claiming that Jenny Shao wasn't who she said she was, and he had information about her that he was willing to trade for leniency in another woman's case. Hell hath no fury like that of a woman scorned. But wait, he wasn't a woman, and he was the one who did the scorning.

It didn't matter; either way it wasn't good. Other than using false identification, I didn't think Lew had anything on Jenny that could hurt her, but I couldn't be sure until I spoke to her. In the meantime, I didn't want Sarah working any deals with Lew, so I decided to come clean and tell her what I knew.

When I finished, Sarah said she suspected all along that Lew was a con artist. He was just a little bit too slick for her liking. On top of that, the woman he was trying to spring had been arrested for running a scam with an as of yet unidentified Chinese man. Sarah figured Lew was that unidentified man.

From what I knew about Shing Lew, he was a lowlife who didn't care about anyone but himself, so why the concern for this con artist? Sarah explained that the woman had been offered a lighter sentence if she identified her partner, and she was considering it. If Lew didn't find a way to keep her quiet, he'd have to take off again or risk arrest.

I told Sarah I'd check with Jenny and get back to her as soon as I could. Sarah said she'd hold tight until she heard from me, but she cautioned that she couldn't wait too long.

As soon as I hung up with Sarah, I phoned Joan. She was out heading for a job interview at NYU, but she said Jenny was home and she gave me Jenny's new cell phone number. I didn't tell Joan why I needed to talk with Jenny; there was no sense worrying her over what I thought was nothing.

When I called Jenny, she seemed happy to hear from me, but when I told her why I was calling, her demeanor changed. In that moment, I knew we had a problem. Lew had something on Jenny, something she hadn't shared with me and something that might sink our case.

I didn't want to carry on the conversation over the phone, but I was afraid Jenny might take off if I didn't handle the situation right. I said whatever was going on, we could handle it, but only if I knew what I had to handle. Jenny got very quiet, and then she started to cry.

The Shums's apartment was a good twenty-minute walk away, and because of the traffic around Lower Manhattan, it wasn't a much shorter ride by taxicab. I was starting to regret having made the call. Then I heard Jenny say something to someone in the room. I held my breath, hoping to hell it wasn't Shing Lew. It wasn't; it was Joan. Concerned by my call, she had canceled her interview and gone home. I said we needed to talk, and she and Jenny should come to my office right away. Joan wanted to know what it was about, but I wouldn't say. I just told her to get to the office as soon as she could.

In less than twenty minutes, Joan and Jenny were in the office. Joan looked nervous, but Jenny seemed calm. I wasn't sure how to approach the topic, but I figured it was best if I was direct. Get it right on the table and deal with it from there.

I disclosed what Sarah Washington had told me. Then I told Jenny if there was anything to it, I would deal with it, but I had to know the truth. Jenny looked down and with tears running down her face, she said that she was about to reveal something she had hoped her mother would never know.

Jenny never struck me as a druggie and if she had been a user, she was clean by the time I met her. But I had represented enough young women with drug habits that I thought I knew where this conversation was probably heading. I asked Jenny if she wanted her mother to leave the room, but she said no, her mother deserved to know the truth. I had to admire the kid for her guts.

Jenny said when she and Shing had first arrived in New York, they were low on cash and needed money. Shing wanted her to sell herself, but she refused. He said she wouldn't actually have to go through with it, just get the john to go into a hotel room with her, and he'd take care of the rest. But she was too frightened and refused to do it.

That's when Shing said they'd have to sell some drugs. Jenny said she never wanted to get involved in drugs, but Shing said it was either sell drugs, or she'd have to work the streets. Scared, alone and afraid, she gave in.

Shing got a fellow Asian Dragon to front him some crack cocaine on a short-term basis, conditioned on them not selling in his territory. Shing then "borrowed" a van, and they drove to Brooklyn and sold the drugs. Shing set up a "safe house" in the van, and Jenny sold the drugs and did the running. That was it. She never got involved in selling drugs again.

It wasn't much but given her pending charges, it was bad.

I was confident Shing Lew didn't have evidence to support any of that, but I never underestimate an opponent. If nothing else, it meant Jenny wouldn't be able to testify on her own behalf if we were forced to try her case. Even without evidence to prove Lew's claim, the DA could confront Jenny with the claim on cross-examination. She'd be under oath, and, therefore, I couldn't let her lie. So, knowing the situation, I couldn't afford to put her on the witness stand. If we had to go to trial and Jenny didn't testify, her chances for an acquittal weren't very good.

I could see Joan was upset, but I think she was expecting something far worse, and she was a little bit relieved as well. Now that the story was out, Joan wanted to know how badly it would hurt Jenny's case. I had an idea how I might eliminate the threat entirely, but before I said anything, I needed to check something. So rather than answer Joan's question, I said simply there was nothing to worry about.

I'm not sure either Joan or Jenny believed me, but it was what they wanted to hear, so they didn't question my response. Of course, if my plan didn't work out, we'd have to revisit the issue, and when we did, my answer wouldn't be as optimistic.

CHAPTER 52

After Joan and Jenny left the office, I called Detective Chen to ask a favor. If what Jenny had told me earlier was true, there should be a warrant out for Shing Lew's arrest in San Francisco and if there was, Chen would be able to confirm it.

I usually don't ask cops for favors because doing favors is against department regulations. The only ones I could ask for a favor are friends, and the quickest way to lose a friend is to ask the friend for a favor that could cost him his job. But there have been times, like now, when I really needed a favor, and I had to at least ask. Chen wasn't exactly a friend; he was more like an acquaintance, but a close acquaintance if there is such a thing. I had a feeling the Houdini Bandits case had brought us closer together, and I was hoping the cooperative mood would carry over.

It did. When I explained why I needed the information, Chen said checking for warrants wouldn't be a problem, and he promised to have an answer later that day. Checking for warrants was a small favor, nothing you could call unethical and not something Chen could get fired for doing. But it was against department regulations, so Chen had a good reason to turn me down. The fact that he was willing to help me out meant a lot, and I owed him for it.

At three o'clock that afternoon, Chen faxed over a copy of a computer printout listing outstanding warrants issued against Shing Lew.

The list was longer than I expected and contained warrants issued in a number of jurisdictions. It looked like Shing Lew was a one-man crime wave. But Chen explained in the cover letter that the name Shing Lew was not as uncommon as you might think, so these were probably not the same person. That wasn't a problem. I was looking for one warrant in particular. A warrant issued for Shing Lew's arrest by the San Francisco Criminal Court around the time Jenny said she and Shing had come to New York. Halfway down the list, I found the warrant I was looking for, and it was definitely for our boy Shing.

I called Sarah Washington and told her Shing Lew was wanted by the San Francisco PD on a major drug charge, and I suggested she let them know that they could pick him up in New York. Sarah agreed it was a good idea and said she'd make the call right away. If things worked out as I hoped, our problem with Shing Lew would soon be solved.

An hour later, Sarah called back to tell me the San Francisco PD would be sending detectives to New York to pick up Shing Lew as soon as he was in custody. Just before calling me, Sarah had faxed a warrant for Lew's arrest as a fugitive felon to the NYPD Warrant Division and expected Lew to be in custody within forty-eight hours. With any luck, in less than a week, Shing Lew would be out of New York and back in San Francisco awaiting trial and out of Jenny's life for good.

Sarah also suggested I get busy on some motions to delay Jenny's case. She couldn't tell me anything more specific, but I got the idea it needed to be done quickly. That probably meant there was movement on the cases, and something big was coming down the pipeline.

Ah, the warm glow of victory returned again. How long would it last this time?

CHAPTER 53

Saturday morning, I was up early, excited over the prospect of finally finding the notorious Chinatown tunnels. I could see myself walking through the tunnels, pad in hand, mapping the corridors. A modern-day Magellan, charting underground Chinatown.

Gracie, knowing how I can get overly excited, warned me not to get my hopes up too high. I appreciated her concern, but my gut was telling me this was the day my questions would be answered. After all, we knew where the entrance was; it was just a matter of getting it opened. Since no one so far had been able to figure out how to open it, we'd just blast our way through and into the tunnel. It was simple.

That's what I kept thinking as I drank six cups of coffee, ate two toasted bagels and tried reading the newspaper. But I couldn't concentrate on the paper. I was too amped up to think about anything except the tunnels. Between the win at the bail hearing on Thursday, and the thought of walking in the tunnels that morning I was on cloud nine.

Finally, I couldn't sit in the apartment any longer. It was only nine o'clock, and the walk to the Golden Wok would take about twenty minutes, but it was a nice day, so I'd take the long way there and maybe tamp down my excitement. Or maybe find a place to buy an Indiana Jones hat.

I gave Gracie a kiss and said I'd call her as soon as I could, but my cell phone might not work inside the tunnels. She laughed and told me to be careful and not get lost. She also said that the Indiana Jones hat was a stupid idea. But what did she know? She never liked the Indiana Jones movies, so she couldn't appreciate the symbolism.

Walking in Lower Manhattan on a Saturday morning is a lot different than walking there during the week. There are a hell of a lot less people on the sidewalks on the weekends, and they're generally not in a big hurry to get somewhere. So it's a pleasant stroll, not a forced march. Of course, you still encounter the assholes on their cell phones who don't watch where they're going, but they're easier to skirt around when the streets aren't so crowded.

Halfway to Mott Street, I stopped in a Dunkin' Donuts and bought a cup of coffee. It was probably my sixth or seventh of the morning, but who was counting? The weather was too nice to stay inside, so I took my coffee and walked to Columbus Park. Columbus Park stretches for two blocks from Bayard Street to Worth Street between Baxter and Mulberry Streets. It was only a block away from Mott Street and the Golden Wok Restaurant, and it's a great place to sit and watch the world.

In the morning, there are always scores of elderly Chinese men and women doing tai chi exercises. Tai chi is a series of slow graceful moves, accompanied by controlled breathing and meditation. The purpose of the exercise is to increase your qi, or life force. With insufficient qi, you are dull and slow, but with abundant qi, you are full of life. Whatever its purpose, it's fascinating to watch people practice tai chi, and that morning was no exception.

I'm no stranger to the park and on more than one occasion, I've been invited by a kindly senior citizen to join in the exercise. That morning, I had two invitations, both from elderly women who seemed to take a shining to me. But I tend to be a bit clumsy, and I avoid exercise at all costs, so I declined both offers. Still, I enjoyed watching the groups go through their routines.

I wanted to move on, but it was only nine-thirty, and I had nowhere else to go. By that point, I had given up the idea of buying an Indiana Jones hat. Not because Gracie said it was a stupid idea, but because I don't like to wear a hat indoors. Okay, maybe on thinking it through, it wasn't my best idea, but I'm sticking with the "no hat indoors" reason.

I had thought about going to the office, but I had nothing to do, so I'd be as bored there as anywhere else. With nothing else to do, I called Doug and annoyed him for half an hour. I could have called Gracie, but she would have hung up on me in ten minutes. Doug, on the other hand, has the patience of Job, so I could count on him to stay on the phone with me. He didn't think much of my idea of wearing an Indiana Jones hat, but he was good enough not to call it a stupid idea. He just laughed, but it wasn't a malicious laugh.

At a quarter to ten, I impolitely told Doug I had to go and hung up on him. I don't know why the guy puts up with me, but I thank God every day that he does.

It was less than a five-minute walk from Columbus Park to the Golden Wok. As I walked down Mott Street toward the restaurant, I saw Chen approaching from the other direction. Parked outside the Golden Wok was a pickup truck, from which two men were removing tools. I presumed they were Harry and his helper. The only one missing was Tommy, which was surprising because he's usually early.

Chen and I arrived at the basement entrance at the same time and exchanged greetings. Then Chen introduced me to Harry. Harry was a big man, around six feet, two or three inches tall, and weighing well over two hundred and fifty pounds. His helper, who he introduced as Louie, was, by comparison, very small. He stood maybe five feet, eight or nine inches tall, and weighed no more than some one hundred and fifty pounds.

As Harry and Louie removed tools from the pickup truck with Chen and I standing by watching, Tommy came out of the Golden Wok. He had the key to the basement entrance. I should mention that two days earlier, I had delivered to the owner a contract allowing us to jackhammer his basement in exchange for $5,000 and a guarantee to repair all damage done to his satisfaction.

Tommy unlocked and opened the basement door. The rest of us followed him inside, where he found the switch and turned on the lights. Harry was carrying this big thing, and in passing I asked if it was the jackhammer. Apparently, I had insulted the tool, and Harry had to put me straight. It wasn't a jackhammer; it was a Bosch SDS-max demolition hammer. Now that I knew better, I wouldn't make that mistake again.

Whatever the damn thing was called, it looked heavy and dangerous. Louie wandered around the basement until he found an electric outlet into which he plugged a long heavy-duty extension cord. I presumed it was to power the Bosch SDS-max demolition hammer, but I wasn't about to ask. I try my best to limit myself to one stupid question a day.

Harry handed Chen a piece of chalk and told him to mark on the wall where we wanted him to break up the concrete. Using the notes I made when Chen and I had spoken to Joey, I measured off five sideway steps and had

Chen draw a line on the wall. Joey said he had gone another two or three feet, but I wanted to make sure we didn't miss it on the short side. Then I measured off another fifteen feet to account for the possible variations Joey had mentioned, and Chen drew another line on the wall. That line was only two feet from the corner of the basement, so I knew the tunnel entrance had to be inside the line.

Harry said the best way to go about finding the entrance to the tunnel was to chop a hole through the wall at waist level between the two lines until he found something besides dirt. Once he found something besides dirt, he'd chop out the rest of the wall to expose the tunnel door. It made sense.

When Harry finished setting up his equipment, he said if we wanted to stay in the basement while he chipped away the concrete, we needed to wear masks over our mouths and noses, and noise guards over our ears. I don't usually carry those items around with me, but fortunately, Harry had brought some for all of us.

Once everyone was geared up, Harry took the demolition hammer and went to work on the basement wall. It was slow, loud and dusty work. I was damn glad Harry had supplied us with the masks and noise protectors. After twenty minutes of hammering away, Harry had made a cut in the wall at waist level about a foot in height and four feet wide. Behind the wall there was nothing but dirt.

Harry took a break, but instructed Louie to take a steel rod that was about three feet long and drive it into the dirt every foot or so along the cut. The rod didn't hit anything solid; it was all dirt. Six feet to go along the wall, and I was starting to lose confidence.

Forty-five minutes later, the cut extended fully between the two lines that Chen had drawn on the wall, and there was nothing but dirt exposed. Louie drove the steel rod through the dirt every foot or so along the cut, but nothing. Chen asked if I thought we should widen the area of the cut, but where? It couldn't be any closer to the corner of the wall and at the other end, we were already close to the basement stairs.

No, we had been had. Joey was lying about a tunnel entrance, and that's why Chen and I got that vibe when we grilled him about it. I was pissed, and poor Chen was probably screwed. At that moment, I wanted to strangle Joey Chung. But the worst was yet to come.

Harry said it would take the rest of the day to repair the wall, and we were welcome to stay if we wanted. Needless to say, we all declined. I told Chen I needed time to process all of this, and I'd call him on Monday. Then we went our separate ways.

I had obviously misread Joey and probably the whole situation, and I needed time to think about it. I called Gracie, told her what had happened and said I was going to take a long walk, so she shouldn't expect me for a couple of hours.

At the moment, all I could think about was beating the crap out of Joey. As satisfying as that might have been, it wasn't going to help the situation. I needed to calm down and start thinking straight.

After an hour or so of aimless walking, my mind started to clear. It was now apparent Joey had lied about the entrance to the tunnel. Either it wasn't where he said it was, or it didn't exist.

I had deliberately re-questioned him about the location, so there'd be no mistake when we did the demolition. Both times Joey told the same story without hesitation or doubt. So where did that leave us?

The odds were that there was no tunnel entrance and no tunnel. So how did the three jerks escape? The Houdini Bandits, my ass. They got out of that basement somehow, and it wasn't by magic, and now I knew it wasn't by tunnel either.

I was thinking about that when my cell phone rang, and that's when things really got wild.

CHAPTER 54

On Saturdays when the office is closed, I have calls forwarded to my cell phone. Gracie doesn't like the idea, but I do it because I have to be available for the 18B Panel assignment clerk six days a week. But I don't like taking business calls, so Tommy's computer genius programmed my phone so that calls forwarded from the office have a different ringtone. That's how I knew when my cell phone rang late that Saturday afternoon the call was being forwarded from my office phone. For a minute I considered letting it go to voice mail, but then decided it might be important and answered it.

A man, identifying himself as Mr. Lee, said he and his associates were the rightful owners of certain property in the possession of my client, Joey Chung. In order to ensure its prompt return, they had taken Mr. Fang into their custody, and they were holding him as collateral.

There was no doubt in my mind that Mr. Lee was a member of the Hip Sing Tong, but it seemed that kidnapping Mr. Fang was a bit extreme. As far as I knew, we were only talking about the $325,000 bank robbery cash, and technically, the tong was only entitled to a percentage of the take. I asked Mr. Lee what property he was referring to, and he said that Joey Chung had $1.2 million dollars that belonged to him and his associates. Now I was really confused, not to mention concerned.

One thing was for sure; this was no hoax. I asked to speak to Mr. Fang, and after a moment or two, during which I heard a conversation in Chinese, Mr. Fang came on the line. I recognized his voice immediately. He was calm, but there was a tremor of fear as he spoke. He said he was fine, but if Joey didn't return the money, he feared that he would be killed.

He started to say something else, but Mr. Lee apparently pulled the phone away. Mr. Lee said I had one week to turn over either the money or Joey Chung, and if I didn't, Mr. Fang would pay the consequences, starting with the loss of his fingers. He didn't have to say more. I had heard enough stories of tong torture to know what would be coming next, and it wasn't pleasant.

I didn't have a lot of experience in dealing with kidnappers, but I figured the less I said the better. So I just asked Mr. Lee how I could get in touch with him. He gave me a phone number to call when I was prepared to turn over the money or Joey and said I'd receive further instructions at that time. Then he hung up.

I immediately called Chen and told him what had happened. We needed to move quickly, and I knew just where to start. I asked Chen how quickly we could talk to the two patrol officers who had chased Joey and the Cha brothers the day of the robbery. He said that he'd get to work on it right away, and he'd try to set something up for the next day. It was a Sunday, but this was one of those exceptions to the "no work on Sundays" rule.

I gave Chen the phone number Lee had given me, as well as the phone number from which he had called. Chen said he'd check them both out and get back to me. In the meantime, we agreed that we shouldn't talk to Joey until we had our ducks in a row. As it stood, Joey knew more about this than either of us, and that put us at a disadvantage. We needed to turn that around before we questioned him.

After hanging up with Chen, I looked at my watch. It was six-thirty. If I hustled, I could be at Gracie's place by seven-fifteen, plenty of time to take her for a sushi dinner during which I could break the news that I would probably be working on Sunday. I was almost sure Gracie would understand, but the sushi dinner was an insurance policy to hopefully get me laid that night.

During our sushi dinner, Chen called and said we could meet the two patrol officers at the Fifth Precinct at ten o'clock the following morning. Then he said the two phone numbers I had given him were burner phones. His detectives were out chasing them down, but he didn't hold much hope that they would come up with anything helpful. Burner phones usually lead to dead ends.

Gracie wasn't pleased with me taking the phone call while we were eating our sushi-sashimi combo special, and after I told her I'd be working the next day, she gave me the cold shoulder treatment for the rest of the night. When we got back to Gracie's place, she went into the bedroom to watch a chick flick on the Hallmark Channel. It turned out the sushi dinner insurance policy didn't pay off if the insured took a telephone call during dinner.

I got Gracie's message loud and clear and stayed in the living room. It didn't really matter anyway because my mind wasn't on sex, at least not entirely. I was thinking of everything I had to do over the next couple of days. After meeting with Chen, I had to decide what to do about Joey and come up with a plan to rescue Mr. Fang. Since Mr. Fang's predicament was tied directly to the Houdini Bandits case, we weren't likely to get help from the department. Not with everybody still ducking from the toxic media fallout. No, this was going to be basically a two-man operation.

I sure as hell hoped Chen had some good ideas because I didn't. This was one of those situations where in the old days, I'd simply close up shop and head for the nearest saloon.

Sinatra sang about, "a trip to the moon on gossamer wings." For me, it was a trip to the moon on wings of scotch. It was always a great trip, but the landings sucked.

I was sober nine years, but occasionally I still had thoughts about drinking. In one way, the mind is a wonderful thing; it drops the painful memories and keeps the pleasant ones. That's not always good, especially if you're an alcoholic because it makes you forget those crash landings.

That's why I still go to beginners' meetings, to keep the horrors fresh in my mind. In AA we call it, "keeping it green." I listen to the new people tell their stories, and it reminds me of my own story. Not the version sanitized by time, but the real one about the pathetic drunk who was living in the bottom of a bottle wasting his life.

I looked at my watch. I didn't have time for a meeting, but I did have time to read. I keep copies of the Big Book handy, and when I can't get to a meeting, I read it. To some it may sound too simple and maybe even stupid. But don't knock it until you've been there. The whole idea in AA is to keep it simple.

You would think that for a dummy like me, keeping it simple would be easy. It wasn't. In the beginning, I was looking for the quick way out. The cure, or some proof that I wasn't actually an alcoholic. It wasn't until I finally surrendered and admitted I was a drunk that things started to get better.

But enough about me and my drinking.

I had to quiet down my head, and with Gracie still mad at me, sex was not an option. It was a cold shower and some dumb late night television program. When things go bad, they go bad.

CHAPTER 55

The next morning, Sunday, Gracie was still giving me the cold shoulder treatment, so after a quick cup of coffee with the ice queen, I decided to head to the Fifth Precinct. I was an hour early, but Chen was already there.

Neither of us had any idea what the $1.2 million was about. As for the tunnel entrance, Chen questioned whether Joey could have made a mistake and really meant the wall to the left of the stairway instead of to the right. A good question, but I pointed out that the wall to the left of the stairway was less than six feet long, so he couldn't have lined up against it, then moved the distance he claimed. The wall just wasn't that long.

As for the side walls, the building was attached on both sides, and a careful search of the basements of the adjoining buildings produced no evidence of a connecting doorway. The back wall was eighty feet from the front wall, so an entrance there didn't fit in with Joey's story at all.

The logical conclusion was that there was no tunnel entrance in the basement, and the three escaped some other way. But how?

We still had forty-five minutes before the patrol officers arrived, so we took a quick walk through the Golden Wok Restaurant to have a look around. As I remembered and Chen confirmed, there was only one other way out of the basement besides the sidewalk entrance, and that was through the kitchen.

Walking up the stairs from the basement, we found ourselves in the small kitchen, facing the back wall of the building. Directly in front of us, maybe ten feet away, was a doorway. The door was locked with a key, but the restaurant owner opened it for us. He said the door was always kept locked, and the key was kept at the front desk.

The door opened onto a small fenced concrete backyard two steps down from the doorway. Ten, maybe twelve feet away, at the far end of the yard was a four-foot high cyclone fence. On the other side of the fence was a small yard and an old tenement building that faced Worth Street. Parts of the building were boarded up. Chen said the building had been under renovation, but the owner had been forced to stop the work when he ran into financial troubles.

We went back into the kitchen for another look. There were no windows in the back wall of the kitchen, and the back exit door was a steel fire door with no window. Someone standing in the kitchen had no view of the backyard.

The entrance into the kitchen from the restaurant's dining area was on the other side of the kitchen, away from the basement entrance. Looking at the layout, Chen and I concluded that Joey and the Cha brothers might have been able to race up the stairs into the kitchen and out the back door before the patrol officer got into the kitchen. But that would have meant the back door was unlocked, or one of the three had a key.

Back at the Fifth Precinct, we sat down with Officers Joe Coyle and Anna Pastore, the two patrol officers who chased Joey and the Cha brothers the day of the robbery. It happened to be their day off, so both were dressed casually, and I appreciated them being there.

Officer Coyle was younger than Officer Pastore, and I could tell by the way they interacted that he was the junior member of the team. He looked very Irish and very cop, if you know what I mean. Some Irish guys are born to be cops, and Coyle was one of them.

As for Pastore, I would say she was in her late thirties, maybe even early forties. She was attractive and in good shape. You could tell that in a physical confrontation, she could hold her own.

We got some coffee, then we got down to business. With Chen asking the questions, we went through the events on the day of the robbery, methodically, starting with when and how the two officers first learned of the robbery.

As Chen later explained to me, by going through the whole story in detail, it puts things in perspective which often helps in recalling details. I won't bore you will all the details. Suffice it to say that the most important part of the story, as far as I was concerned, started when the trio of jerks entered the basement of the Golden Wok.

Once the three suspects entered the basement, Officer Pastore recognized that further pursuit was too dangerous, and she ordered Coyle to stand down and keep watch. She called for backup, including a SWAT team. Then with the sidewalk entrance secured by Coyle, Officer Pastore ran into the restaurant to secure any inside basement access, thereby effectively trapping the three suspects in the basement. She estimated it was less than five minutes between the three suspects entering the basement and her entering the restaurant. Coyle said he had watched Pastore enter the restaurant and confirmed the timeline.

The owner of the restaurant was standing just inside the front door, and he told her there was a staircase to the basement through the kitchen and pointed the way. Unsure if the three suspects had assistance from anyone in the restaurant, she proceeded cautiously with her weapon drawn through the dining area to the kitchen door. After observing what she could of the kitchen through the window in the kitchen door, she entered cautiously, not knowing if the suspects had already made their way upstairs from the basement.

Inside, two cooks stared at her, apparently terrified by her drawn weapon. She saw a door in the back wall and assumed it led outside. There was another door facing the back door. Since it was the only other door in the kitchen, she knew it was the one to the basement.

She asked the two cooks if anyone had come upstairs from the basement, but the two terrified cooks apparently spoke no English. Using hand signals, she ordered them out of the kitchen, and the two quickly and happily fled. Later that day when she went looking for the two, they had vanished. The restaurant's owner gave the detectives the cooks' supposed names and addresses, but they turned out to be phonies. The cooks were probably illegally in the country, and by this time they were headed off to another location.

Officer Pastore checked the basement door and found it locked with a dead bolt. Later, the owner would say that the door was usually only locked at night when the restaurant was closed. He had no explanation why Pastore had found it locked.

After checking the basement door, Pastore then checked the back door and found it also locked, but with a key lock, so she couldn't open it to check outside. The restaurant owner would later say the back door was always locked, and only he and the manager had keys.

Satisfied that the three suspects hadn't escaped through the kitchen, she took up a protected position and kept watch until the SWAT team arrived.

Chen pressed Pastore for a timeline. This time he asked how long it was between the three suspects entering the basement and Pastore entering the restaurant's kitchen. Pastore said it was maybe one to two minutes at most between her entering the restaurant, talking with the owner and making her way to the kitchen.

Assuming Pastore's estimate was correct, there were five to seven minutes between the time Joey and the Cha brothers entered the basement, and Pastore reached the restaurant's kitchen. Enough time for the three to have escaped through the kitchen if they went directly from the basement to the kitchen. But that would have meant one of the three knew the layout and had a key to the back door.

The detectives were investigating that angle, but after Joey confessed and said they escaped through a tunnel, they changed their focus. Then when the Cha brothers were killed in the shoot-out, they closed that portion of the investigation entirely.

We had been at it for nearly three hours, and I figured we were about done with Pastore and Coyle. Chen must have thought so too. He asked if I had any more questions for the officers, and when I said no, he thanked them and told them they were free to go.

I asked Chen what he thought and as I expected, he now believed the trio had escaped through the kitchen. I thought so also. Now, what were we going to do?

Chen wanted to go to Freeport and confront Joey. I wasn't sure that was a good idea. We still had a bunch of unanswered questions, like how had a $325,000 robbery turned into a $1.2 million take, and why was the Hop Sing Tong saying the money was theirs? Any confrontation with Joey would go better if we knew at least some of those answers. Chen agreed but reminded me we were working under a deadline. He was right about that.

I suggested we think about it and meet again the next day to discuss our options. Chen thought that was a good idea, but he didn't want to meet at the precinct, so we agreed to meet at the Worth Street Coffee Shop at three o'clock.

After leaving Chen, I called Tommy and told him what was happening. Mr. Fang was a friend of old man Shoo, so Tommy had more than a simple business interest in the affair. He said that he'd hit the streets and see what he could come up with. I told him I needed whatever information he could get, and I needed it before my three o'clock meeting with Chen.

By the time I arrived at Gracie's place, she had thawed substantially. She was no longer giving me the cold shoulder treatment, but she wasn't exactly bubbling over with warmth. Between me rushing around and Gracie's mood, I hadn't found the time to tell her what was going on. Sensing that she wasn't quite yet in the mood to hear my story and hoping to soften her up, I suggested we go to Pino's for dinner. She agreed and after a nice antipasto, she started to loosen up. That's when I told her the whole story, and Gracie finally let me out of the doghouse.

CHAPTER 56

Monday was going to be a busy day. I had planned on preparing the motion papers in Jenny's case, seeking to exclude the drug evidence. The motion was a long shot, but I had a decent argument, and if nothing else, it would delay the case. But before I could think about the motion, I had to deal with Mr. Fang's problem and sort through a thorny ethical issue I was facing.

I wanted to do everything I could to help Mr. Fang, but I might be handcuffed since Joey Chung was my client. A lying, and possibly a scumbag client, but a client nonetheless. Even though Mr. Fang was paying the legal fees, he wasn't my client. If there was a conflict of interest between Mr. Fang and Joey, which seemed likely, I was duty bound to protect Joey's interests. But protecting Joey's interests just got a lot harder. His plea deal was contingent on him telling the truth, and since he lied about the escape, Marty could pull the deal out from under us, and there wasn't anything I could do to stop him. That was on Joey, and so was the situation with poor Mr. Fang. I was just stuck in the middle of an impossible situation. I wanted to help Mr. Fang, but I couldn't if doing so hurt Joey's case. Sometimes being an ethical lawyer sucks.

So far, I hadn't crossed any ethical lines. Telling Detective Chen about the kidnapping didn't violate any confidences, so I was alright there. But if I went much further, I'd definitely be approaching the line. I figured I'd deal with the issues as they came up, not knowing that the whole situation was about to take a radical turn and dump me into a quagmire.

It happened when Tommy came into the office and took a seat. He looked like shit. He'd been up most of the night working the streets and talking to his contacts. Word was out that the Cha brothers had ripped off the Hip Sing Tong for over $750,000 in drug money. No mention was made of Joey, but I was sure he was mixed up in it somehow, which explained why the Hip Sing

Tong was so anxious to get their hands on him. As if that alone wasn't enough to screw things up, it added another problem.

The rip-off obviously wasn't covered by Joey's plea deal, so if he was involved as I was pretty sure he was, I'd be exposing him to further prosecution if I told Chen or Marty about it. That in all likelihood was unethical. On the other hand, if I didn't tell Chen what I now knew, he might not attach much importance to rescuing Mr. Fang, figuring the tong wouldn't kill him simply over a small share of the bank robbery money. If the tong killed Mr. Fang because I never told Chen what I knew, I'd have a hard time living with myself.

Putting the information Tommy had picked up from his contacts, together with what we knew about Joey and the Cha brothers, it wasn't hard to figure out what happened.

Tommy had learned that two weeks earlier someone had killed a couple of tong bagmen as they picked up money from sale locations. Why were the Cha brothers the prime suspects? Because it was common knowledge that the Cha brothers had sold drugs for the tong and knew the operation. Not only did they know that the tong used bagmen, they knew who those people were and where they operated. All of it was information that was critical to the plan and available to only a few. Besides, no one but the Cha brothers was stupid enough to rip off the tong.

None of Tommy's contacts implicated Joey in the job, but I had little doubt that if he hadn't planned it, he at least knew about it. It had been a brazen but clever scheme. Billy and Bobby Cha were brazen, but stupid; Joey was the smart one in the group, which is why I believed he was involved. But the question remained as to why the Cha brothers didn't take off with the drug money, but instead hung around and pulled off the bank job. I knew they were crazy as well as stupid, but it didn't matter because they were now dead. If my theory was correct and Joey was involved, he was the only one left who knew where the money was hidden. The Hip Sing Tong had probably reached the same conclusion, and that's why they had kidnapped Mr. Fang.

All of it made me wonder if Joey turned on the Cha brothers so he could collect all of the stolen money himself. It wouldn't have been a bad play except you never want to mess with the Hip Sing Tong.

So now if my theory was correct, and I was going to help Mr. Fang escape torture and death, I had to share what I knew with Chen and probably Marty. That thinking was getting me awfully close to crossing the ethical line. In sharing what I knew with Chen, I'd be implicating Joey in another crime, and that would be working against my client's interests. On the other hand, if I didn't share the information, poor Mr. Fang was likely to be tortured.

Faced with this dilemma, I did what I usually do under those circumstances; I called my sponsor, Doug. I didn't call him for AA advice; I called him because he is a member of the bar's Disciplinary Committee, and is well versed in the Code of Professional Responsibility.

I explained the situation and after giving it some thought, Doug said New York Disciplinary Rule 4-101 (C)(3) allows a lawyer to reveal information about a client's intent to commit a crime. Unlike the rule in other jurisdictions, the New York Rule doesn't require that the crime involve a threat of physical injury or death. How I interpreted the rule and applied it to my case was up to me.

That's what I loved about Doug; he never gives me a straight answer. Whether it's a legal question or an AA question, he makes me come to my own conclusions. I sometimes call him Socrates, but he takes that as a compliment.

Anyway, I had the information I needed. As I saw it, Joey intended to make off with the stolen money, and that would be a crime. So I could reveal it to Detective Chen without violating my ethical responsibility to my client. Now all I had to do was figure out an ethical way to kill Joey.

I called Detective Chen, and we agreed to meet at the Worth Street Coffee Shop in an hour to plan our next move.

CHAPTER 57

It was still a bit too early for lunch when I met Chen at the coffee shop, but that didn't stop him from ordering a pastrami sandwich, a knish, onion rings and coffee. When I gave him one of my "What the hell are you doing?" looks, he said we should eat because we might not get the chance to eat again. It sounded ominous, but he only meant we were going to be busy the rest of the day,

Chen's informants confirmed Tommy's information. The Cha brothers had ripped off the Hip Sing Tong for over three quarters of a million dollars, and the tong was taking its revenge on Tommy's grandfather. Beyond that, Chen had nothing. No one seemed to know where Mr. Fang was being held, and if anyone did know, they sure as hell weren't saying.

Without more information and with the NYPD brass still playing duck and cover when it came to the Houdini Bandits, a rescue operation wasn't likely to happen. That left it up to Chen and me to figure a way out of this mess. Unfortunately, Chen didn't have any good ideas, and he wasn't keen on my idea that we throw Joey Chung off a tall building. I had to admit throwing Joey off a tall building wouldn't necessarily result in Mr. Fang's release, but it would give me a great deal of satisfaction.

After kicking around some ideas, we concluded it was time to visit Joey, which for me meant another terrifying ride with "Mad-Max" Chen behind the wheel.

The distance between Lower Manhattan and Freeport, Long Island, is somewhere between thirty-two and thirty-six miles, depending on the route you take. Given normal traffic conditions, which for Long Island is bumper-to-bumper traffic, the trip should take anywhere from an hour to an hour and a half. But "Mad-Max" Chen managed to do it in less than forty-five minutes.

During the ride, between my whimpering and begging for my life, we did work out a bit of a strategy for approaching Joey. Since he was my client, I would do most of the talking. Chen would interject at any point he felt was appropriate, and if need be, he'd play the bad cop. But if we got to the point that we were going to beat the crap out of Joey, then I wanted to be the bad cop.

Arriving unannounced as we did surprised Joey as we had hoped it would. Surprise leads to uncertainty; uncertainty leads to confusion; and a confused mind works to an interrogator's advantage. Lying requires concentration in order to maintain consistency, and confusion hampers concentration. Once a suspect, or a witness, starts making inconsistent statements, you can stick a fork in them because they're done. Their stories unravel faster than a cheap sweater with a pull. Chen and I had seen it happen over and over. He saw it with suspects during police interrogations, and me, I saw it with witnesses under cross-examination.

Joey knew from our last visit that we had planned on searching for the tunnel, but he didn't know if we had done so. That was the uncertainty that I hoped would keep Joey confused and eventually desperate.

We sat around the dining room table as we had during our prior visit. Pulling out a legal pad and pencil, I asked Joey to draw a diagram of the Golden Wok basement, showing the entrance from the sidewalk and the location of the tunnel. Joey drew the diagram, locating the tunnel entrance through the wall at the exact location he had told us. The same place we had jackhammered and found nothing but dirt.

Joey pushed the pad back toward me. Looking at the drawing, I asked if he was sure about the location, and he said that he was. He was starting to look a little nervous, so I asked him again if he was sure that was where the entrance to the tunnel was. This time he wasn't as fast answering. He looked at me, then at Chen, and then said, "I think so, but it was dark, so maybe I'm wrong."

Joey was a cool customer and no dummy. He knew where the conversation was heading, and he probably knew that we knew there was no tunnel entrance. I figured his mind had to be racing, trying to figure a way out. That was the idea, keep him nervous and guessing, and not let him get comfortable.

Rather than confront him right away, I asked if the tunnel wasn't along that wall, where could it be? I don't think he expected the question, and he seemed shaken by it. Before he could answer, Chen pulled out his handcuffs and put them on the table. It was a nice touch.

Joey stared momentarily at the handcuffs, then said, "I don't know, man. It was dark, and I was scared. Maybe I got disoriented. That could have happened. I just don't know."

Pushing the legal pad and the pencil off the table, I leaned into Joey's face and yelled, "There is no fucking tunnel, and you know it!" So much for Chen being the bad cop.

Joey blanched and stuttered, "No, no. There was a tunnel."

This time it was Chen's turn. But instead of yelling at Joey, he leaned close to him and said in a very calm voice, "Joey, we jackhammered that basement, and there is no tunnel entrance, which means you lied to us, so your plea deal is gone."

Joey looked to me with panic spread across his face and asked if that was true. I just nodded my head, and Joey looked like he was about to lose his lunch.

Now we had Joey where we wanted him, scared and having no idea how much we knew. It was time to drop the next shoe.

Looking at Chen, I said that I needed to talk privately with my client, and Chen left the room. It was all part of our strategy, but none of it was unethical. I was cooperating with the cops to keep my client from committing another crime. At least that was the rationale. The truth was that I was trying to save Mr. Fang's life.

With Chen gone from the room, I told Joey because he had lied, the plea deal had been withdrawn. Joey was no fool; he knew he was in trouble, and the look on his face confirmed it. He asked if there was anything I could do to get a deal back on the table. I said I couldn't do anything unless he told me the truth and the whole story.

With a half laugh of someone who knew he had run out of options, Joey told me the true story of the robbery.

CHAPTER 58

The story Joey then told me was as surprising as it was fascinating. Billy and Bobby Cha were small-time operators and not very bright, which I had already figured out on my own. Joey had met them at one of the nightclubs he frequented. They sold drugs, did a little loan sharking and committed an occasional burglary. The brothers weren't shy when it came to talking about their exploits, and Joey, who fantasized about being a master criminal, was an enthusiastic listener. Flattered by Joey's attention, the Cha brothers openly revealed more and more of their criminal activity to their newly found admirer. That was how Joey learned about Nancy, the bank clerk, and the cash payroll.

As it turned out, it was Joey, not the Cha brothers, who came up with the plan to rob Citibank. The story that he became involved at the last minute and reluctantly as a replacement was bullshit. Joey had been the brains behind the operation from the start. That made sense because the Cha brothers couldn't find their way out of a room with one door.

What I couldn't understand was how Joey went directly from being a decent, if mixed up kid, to a major felon. Most kids, who end up as major felons, generally get there in steps; they don't fall over the edge. It usually starts with drugs, and then they do small-time robberies or burglaries to support their habits. Until I met Joey, I didn't know anyone who had gone from law abiding citizen to bank robber in one step. As Joey explained it, he was bored, and his life lacked excitement. Even as a kid, he had fantasized about pulling off the perfect crime. He said maybe he needed a psychiatrist. I said he needed a swift kick in the ass, but it was too late for that.

Once Joey committed to the bank heist, he spent months planning the job. When Nancy, the bank clerk, reported that a cash payroll had been ordered, but not one big enough to warrant stealing, Joey would watch the bank from a coffee shop across the street to see what time the armored car delivered the cash. Then he'd wait to see when the payroll was picked up. After watching the process four times, he was satisfied that he had, what he called *his window of opportunity*. Then he visited the bank on five Fridays in a row at different hours between opening and noon to see when it was least crowded.

Joey and the Cha brothers rehearsed the robbery in Joey's apartment, practicing until they could pull it off in under five minutes. As for the escape, it had been well planned like the heist, but not as the mystery it eventually became. Joey's idea was simply to get out of the bank and out of sight as quickly as possible. In the first stage of the escape the three would mix in with the ever-present crowds around the bank. The bank's side door on Mott Street was the best option for the escape route, better than the main door on Chatam Square. Mott Street wasn't as busy as Chatam Square, but it had enough traffic for the trio to get lost by mixing into the crowd. Mott Street also offered better opportunities for what Joey called *the second stage of the escape;* getting off the street and into hiding.

Joey spent considerable time staking out possible stage two escape routes on Mott Street before finally deciding on the Golden Wok. Key to his decision was its proximity to the bank, and the fact that it was in one of the old tenement buildings with access to the basement from the sidewalk. It also had a rear door, which gave access to a building on Worth Street. When Joey found out that the building on Worth Street behind the Golden Wok was temporarily vacant and closed up, he knew he had found his escape route. But there was more work to be done. Joey had to scout out the basement of the Golden Wok, making sure there was access from there to the rear door, and more importantly, that he and his little band of thieves would be able to use it.

Since the Golden Wok was a very successful business, Joey assumed the owner would have no interest in aiding and abetting a gang of bank robbers. But that reasoning didn't apply to the staff.

After a dozen or so visits to the Golden Wok, Joey had befriended the restaurant's entire staff to the point that he could wander around the place without being bothered. He often followed a waiter into the kitchen and even managed to follow a busboy into the basement on a couple of occasions. That was how he learned that both basement doors, the one from the kitchen and the one from the sidewalk, were usually unlocked during the day.

The biggest problem standing in the way of his plan was the back door out into the yard. That door was always kept closed and locked, and you needed a key to unlock it, even from the inside. The key was kept on a hook beneath the cashier's counter at the front of the restaurant. Joey needed the key, and he came up with a clever plan to get it, or at least a copy of the key.

While chatting up the cashier, Joey took a picture of the key with his cell phone. Then, at a hardware store on Delancey Street, he bought a blank key that matched the shape and color of the key in the photo. So the key wouldn't stand out as a blank, he had it cut to match his apartment door key. His plan was to temporarily replace the real key with the one he bought at the hardware store while he had a copy of the real key made. He'd do it in the middle of the day when there would be no reason for opening the back door. As long as the key hanging on the hook looked like the real key, no one would notice it was a fake.

The plan worked perfectly, and now Joey had two keys to the Golden Wok's back door. With that problem solved, there was one remaining. They'd be seen going through the kitchen. But Joey figured it wouldn't be a big problem. He knew they had to pull off the job between ten o'clock, when the payroll was delivered by the armored car, and noon, when it was picked up from the bank. That meant they'd be going through the kitchen before the luncheon crowd hit the restaurant, and the only people likely to be in the kitchen at that time were the two cooks.

As with many of the cooks in Chinatown, these two were in the country illegally, which meant they could be easily manipulated by playing on their fear of deportation. But Joey was smart enough not to threaten them before he got what he wanted. Instead, he waited until he had word from Nancy that a big payroll was in the works. Word came from Nancy on Monday, and the payroll would be delivered on Friday. That gave Joey a week to put everything in place.

The next day he offered cash to the cooks to do nothing more than check every morning for the rest of the week to make sure both the street entrance to the basement and the entrance from the basement to the kitchen were unlocked. Since the doors were usually kept open during the day, it wasn't a problem for the cooks, and they happily accepted Joey's money.

On the Thursday before the robbery, he told them he and his friends would be coming through the kitchen the next morning. He didn't tell them why, and the cooks were smart enough not to ask questions. Joey said if they were asked whether anyone had come through the kitchen, they should just act dumb and claim they saw no one. He gave each cook a hundred dollars. It sounded cheap to me, and I asked Joey if he really thought a hundred bucks would buy their silence. He laughed and said he was never worried that the cooks would talk to the cops. He had figured when the cops came around, the cooks would be so frightened of being deported, they'd take off. The money was to help them disappear. As it turned out, that was exactly what happened.

The day of the robbery, everything was going as planned. The robbery went off without a hitch, and once they were out of the bank, Joey figured they were home free. That was until the two patrol officers came around the corner. Then all hell broke loose. Joey and the Cha brothers had crossed Mott Street, and they were on the south side of the street when the cops came around the corner from Chatham Square. With the cops so close, Joey realized their only hope was to keep the cops from crossing Mott Street. If they crossed the street, they'd have a direct view and line of fire to the three of them.

Joey ordered Billy and Bobby to open fire, forcing the cops to take cover behind the cars on the far side of the street. Then the three of them tried running to the Golden Wok, bent over behind the parked cars on their side of the street. The cops started to return fire, and somehow Billy got shot in the leg. It was probably ricochet, and it wasn't much of a wound, but it was bleeding a lot. That's when Joey told Bobby to keep the cops pinned down while he bandaged Billy's leg with a piece of Billy's shirt.

In telling me the story, Joey admitted he didn't care about Billy's wound; he just didn't want him leaving a blood trail. Joey was a real sweetheart.

With Billy's wound tightly bandaged and Bobby firing wildly at the cops, they made a break for the basement entrance. Joey didn't know if the cops saw them go down the steps, but he figured if they had, they wouldn't come after them because doing so would be too dangerous. But they'd probably check inside the restaurant for an exit from the basement.

With that in mind, Joey hustled Billy and Bobby quickly up the steps from the basement, through the kitchen and out the back door. As they passed through the kitchen, Joey noticed there was no one there except the two cooks, who looked terrified when they saw the guns Billy and Bobby were carrying. Using the key he had made, Joey opened the back door and they left, locking the door behind them. If the cops had gotten into the kitchen, they wouldn't be able to open the back door or to see the backyard until they had gotten the key from the front desk.

Joey kept looking behind them as they crossed the backyard, jumped the fence and ducked into the vacant building on the other side. Having seen no one open the kitchen door, he figured they were safe, at least for the time being. But as much as he trusted his instincts about the two cooks, he couldn't be sure they wouldn't talk. At least that was what he told Billy and Bobby when he said they had to move out quickly and separately.

The cops would be looking for three men, so they'd separate and meet later on when the heat was off. Bobby wanted to divide up the money right away, but Joey convinced him they didn't have time for that. He said he'd keep the money and call them later. Because Joey had convinced Billy and Bobby that they were in imminent danger, they reluctantly agreed to the plan, and the three left the building on Worth Street, heading in different directions.

It turned out that Joey was more of a prick than I thought he was. Smiling as he spoke, he admitted that he never intended to call Billy and Bobby that night. His plan had always been to roll on the Cha brothers and keep all the money for himself. So much for honor amongst thieves.

His plan all along was to play the role of the innocent dupe, and that was why he hadn't carried a gun. He figured with a good lawyer, he'd cut a deal by turning in the Cha brothers, and then after doing a short prison term, if any, he'd collect all the money for himself.

When the case received so much attention and became an embarrassment to the NYPD and the DA, Joey was smart enough to know his bargaining power had increased substantially. All he needed was a sharp lawyer, and that's where I came in. Joey needed a lawyer, and he wanted me, but he didn't want to hire me directly or too quickly. He knew that if he dropped enough hints, his grandfather would hire a lawyer for him. Knowing his grandfather was good friends with old man Shoo, and knowing my connection to Shoo, the odds were good that Mr. Fang would come to me.

Thinking we were done, Joey asked if I could still cut him a plea deal. That's when I dropped the other shoe and said, "First, you have to tell me about ripping off the Hip Sing Tong's drug money."

I don't think Joey saw that one coming because the look on his face was one of utter surprise. But he soon recovered his composure and said he'd tell me the story, but first, he needed to take a leak.

I watched him leave the room, never giving it a second thought. At least not until an alarm started blaring, and Chen and the two detectives came racing through the room, guns drawn, headed to the back of the house where Joey had just gone.

It took me a minute or two to realize what was happening, and by the time I did, Chen and his guys were marching back into the dining room with Joey in handcuffs. I must have looked bewildered because Chen found it necessary to explain that all the doors and windows in the house were rigged with alarms, and the backyard was fenced in with locked gates.

Chen pushed Joey down onto the chair he had just vacated. After sending the two detectives into the living room, he took a seat across the table from the still handcuffed Joey.

In the last hour, Joey had shown his true colors, and I was convinced he wasn't about to cooperate voluntarily, even to save his grandfather's life. He was that type of selfish piece of garbage. I could have been wrong, but I wasn't about to take the chance. I needed information, and I needed it fast. Ethics or no ethics, I had to force the issue, or Mr. Fang was going to pay a high price for his grandson's crimes.

CHAPTER 59

I don't like lying. I used to do it all the time before I got sober, so when I lie now, it takes me back to those days, and I don't like going there. But there are times you have to lie, and that night, sitting in the dining room of the safe house with Joey and Detective Chen, was one of those times.

Knowing it wasn't true, I said to Joey, "With your little stunt just now, you violated the terms of your bail, so unless we straighten things out fast, Detective Chen is going to take you to Rikers Island tonight."

Whatever bravado Joey had shown earlier was gone. Now he was just plain frightened, knowing if he went into the system, he was as good as dead. He asked what he had to do to get things straightened out, and I told him that he could start by telling us about the tong drug money.

Joey looked skeptical, and I could understand why. I said if the information he had was enough to link the money to the tong's drug operation, that would be worth a lot, and we could cut another deal. But he wanted to know why Chen was staying in the room. I said that it was so he could evaluate the information, but Joey shouldn't worry; we'd do the whole interview as a hypothetical conversation.

Hypothetical conversations are used when a suspect is offering information in exchange for a plea deal. Before agreeing to the deal, the DA wants to know what the suspect has to offer, but the suspect doesn't want to incriminate himself until there's a deal in place. Using a hypothetical conversation, the suspect can tell his story without admitting any wrongdoing. It's all a big charade, but it gets the job done.

Joey had to make a decision—tell us about the drug money or go to Rikers and get killed. It wasn't really a hard decision to make, and it didn't take Joey long to make it. Once he agreed to tell us about the drug money, Chen threw in a bonus and uncuffed him.

Ripping off the tong's drug money was another of Joey's brilliant schemes. He got the idea after the bank robbery was planned. Figuring he now had his own criminal organization, he might as well put it to use while he waited for the cash payroll.

Joey knew from the start that Billy and Bobby Cha sold drugs, but it wasn't until after planning the bank job that he learned the drugs were supplied by the Hip Sing Tong. What surprised Joey was the simplicity of the tong's operation. Every Thursday, the brothers used a burner phone to order their supply of drugs for the week. The next night the drugs were delivered to a prearranged location by two Hip Sing bagmen, who collected a cash payment on delivery. In the case of the Cha brothers, the delivery location was an alley behind one of the nightclubs.

I already knew from what Tommy had learned from his contacts that this was a totally different operation than the typical street sale involving runners and a stash house. In a street sale, the seller never knew who he was dealing with, so precautions had to be taken. But the tong operation was more or less a wholesale operation involving the same known customers. Besides, who would be stupid enough to rip off the Hip Sing Tong? That is, besides Joey.

After learning how the operating worked, Joey wondered if the same bagmen made multiple deliveries on the same night. Following the two bagmen one Thursday night after they left the Cha brothers, he found out they made nine additional stops carrying the same duffel bag to each stop. He didn't know where they had started, or how many stops they had made before the Cha brothers, but he knew where they ended, and he knew what was in the duffel bag.

Joey followed the bagmen for three weeks, and their routine never varied. He didn't know how much money they collected on those nights, but judging by how much the Cha brothers paid, he estimated it to be between one-half and one million dollars. From the looks of things, the two men weren't heavily armed, which wasn't surprising because no one in their right mind would try stealing from the tong. But Joey knew two guys who weren't in their right minds.

Billy and Bobby were stupid and greedy, a combination that made them particularly susceptible to Joey's manipulation. All Joey had to do was plant the idea that there was big money to be had, and the two brothers took it from there. Of course, their ideas of how to pull off the job were terrible and would have ended in disaster. It was Joey who supplied the final plan.

The key to success was to hit the bagmen between the last and next to last stop. Why? Because it had to be a sneak attack, and the last stop was too open and offered no opportunity for an ambush. The second to last stop was down a long dark alley, with narrow walkways along its entire length. When the bagmen were on their way out of the alley, they could be simultaneously attacked from the front and behind.

In addition, the two men wouldn't be missed for at least another hour, which was another benefit of attacking before the last of the night's deliveries. The longer it took the tong to find out they had been ripped off, the better it was for everyone.

Billy and Bobby loved the plan. They thought they'd pull off the tong robbery, and then after the bank job, they'd simply leave town. They had some crazy idea that if they went to Chicago, the Hip Sing Tong wouldn't find them. Joey knew that wasn't true, but of course, he never shared those thoughts with the brothers.

Joey didn't actually participate in the robbery. He was too smart for that. He convinced Billy and Bobby that it was a two-man job, and if there were any more people involved, things could go wrong. But he did agree to stand watch and then take charge of the cash. His reasoning being, if anyone saw what happened in the alley, they'd be looking for two men carrying a duffel bag. Joey was right about one thing; Billy and Bobby were stupid.

Billy and Bobby had killed the two bagmen, and Joey, knowing that was a problem for him, claimed he never suspected Billy and Bobby would kill the two bagmen. He simply told them the two men had to be stopped from identifying them in any way and from notifying the tong that they had been robbed. He said it wasn't his fault if the Cha brothers took this to mean they should kill the two bagmen. Now he thought Chen and I were stupid.

Joey must have figured that he had told us enough because he stopped talking. But he had left out the most important detail, where the money was, so I asked him where it was. The cops had searched Joey's apartment, and it wasn't there.

Joey wasn't surprised by the question; he knew it was coming, so he had a quick answer. It was in a storage locker in Brooklyn. I asked when and how it got there..

Joey said the day he disappeared from his grandfather's house, he hadn't gone to the Bronx to visit a girlfriend as he had claimed. He had gone and collected the money, which he had hidden in his apartment, and he took it to a storage locker in Brooklyn.

When I asked him for the location of the storage locker, Joey said he'd tell us that once he had a deal in place and in writing. It wasn't the answer I was looking for, and it certainly wasn't an answer I could accept.

I looked at Chen, and he nodded. It was time to tell Joey that his grandfather was being held captive by the tong. I figured there was no sense dragging it out, so I said straight out. "The Hip Sing has your grandfather, and they're going to kill him if you don't return the money you stole from them."

I had dealt with a lot of loathsome people in my career, real scumbags, but Joey took the cake. After hearing what I had just said, he smiled and replied, "When I get my deal in writing, that's when I tell you where the money is."

Still not believing what I was hearing, I told Joey we only had a day and a half to return the money and save his grandfather. Without skipping a beat, he replied, "Then you had better get that deal fast."

Without bothering to look to Chen, I lunged forward and grabbed the prick by his shirt, and dragging him to his feet, I said that he either told me where the money was hidden, or I'd personally drop him off to the tong.

Showing a little more panic than I'm sure he intended, he said I couldn't do that because I was his lawyer. I said that I didn't care, and if he didn't believe me, he could test me. Then Chen stood up, grabbed Joey's arms and slapped the handcuffs on him. He spun him around, and lowering his face until he was nose to nose with Joey, he said, "If Jake doesn't do it, I will."

I don't know which one of us he believed, or if he believed both of us, but Joey decided to tell us where the money was hidden. His only condition was that he be kept at the safe house until we were sure the tong was no longer interested in killing him. Chen agreed, but said he'd be held there under arrest and not simply as a material witness. That meant he couldn't leave on his own accord. Not having much of a choice, Joey agreed, and to make it official, Chen read him his rights.

Joey said the money was in storage unit 106 at Stadium Storage on Bridge Street in Brooklyn. It was a small place, and it didn't have twenty-four-hour access. As Joey remembered, access on weekdays was from eight in the morning until six in the evening. Chen said not to worry, he'd get us in. We just needed Joey to give us the key.

At first, Joey claimed to have lost the key, but when Chen grabbed him out of his chair and said we were heading back to Chinatown, Joey suddenly remembered he had a key with him. Chen uncuffed him, and Joey removed his right shoe, the heel of which twisted sideways, revealing a small compartment containing a key.

Chen took the key and after allowing Joey to put on the shoe, he cuffed him again. Joey asked him how long he had to stay cuffed, and Chen replied until he and I recovered the money. Joey groaned and looked to me. I just shrugged my shoulders. I didn't think that was the case, but I had no intention of making Joey's life any easier. Later on, I'd find out that Chen left instructions for the detectives to uncuff Joey once we had left.

Satisfied that we had everything we needed, Chen and I departed for Brooklyn.

CHAPTER 60

On the trip to Brooklyn, as I slumped in the passenger seat and watched my life pass before my eyes, Chen started to make phone calls. His driving with two hands on the wheel and not even distracted by his cell phone was frightening enough. Add the distraction and the one-handed driving, and the ride was beyond terrifying. If you're anything like Gracie, you're going to say that I survived the ride, so why am I whining? Because that's what I do; it's part of my charm; and if you don't like it, don't listen.

As much as I hate to admit it, Chen's calls did pay off. When we arrived at Stadium Storage, the owner was there waiting to let us in. Unfortunately, the search warrant Chen ordered hadn't yet arrived. But when Chen explained the situation, the owner agreed to let us open the unit provided we didn't remove anything until we had the search warrant in hand.

Unit 106 was on the ground floor not far from the main entrance. It was secured with a padlock, the same type of padlock as on all the other units. The owner explained that he provided the padlocks with the units. He said it was a good strong lock, and he was right. The only problem was the key Joey had given us didn't open that lock. It didn't come close to fitting into the lock. Fearing the worst, we had the owner check his records, and he confirmed the unit had been rented to the same person for almost four years. This wasn't Joey's locker.

Joey had screwed us again. Now we had to go all the way back to Freeport and threaten to kill the little prick once more.

I didn't think things could get much worse, but I was wrong. We had just walked out of the storage place when Chen's cell phone rang. I knew immediately from Chen's stream of obscenities that the news wasn't good, but I never guessed how bad it was.

Joey was gone. The two detectives at the safe house believed Joey learned from his earlier attempted escape how the alarm system worked, and knowing he couldn't escape through the backyard, he took a different route. He tossed a chair through the back bedroom window setting off the alarm and sending the two detectives on a search of the back rooms. Seeing the broken window, they assumed Joey had gone through it, and they raced out the back door and searched the yard; but all they found was the chair.

They now thought that after breaking the window, Joey had hidden in the bedroom closet and waited until they had gone outside Then he simply slipped into the hallway and ran out the front door. It didn't matter how he did it; all that mattered was he had done it, and he was gone.

It was a total disaster. I didn't have the money or Joey. What I had was a deadline a little over twenty-four hours away and nothing to trade for Mr. Fang. How quickly things had turned.

Chen was busy on his cell phone. He was making a lot of calls, and he seemed much calmer than I thought he'd be under the circumstances. When he finished making his calls, he said we should go back to the precinct house and wait. I asked, "Wait for what?"

Chen said, "For Joey to turn up on somebody's radar which should happen soon."

I must have looked puzzled, which I was, and Chen went on to explain. At the safe house, Joey's wallet, cell phone and money had been taken from him and locked away in a safe. They were still there in the safe, so Joey had no money, no identification and no cell phone. He was at least thirty-five miles away from his base with no way to contact anyone.

The two detectives from the safe house were out cruising around the area looking for Joey. Chen had alerted the Nassau County Police Department, and its patrol units had been issued a BOLO. A Bolo? What was that, some sort of fancy British hat? Chen gave me a dirty look and said it was an acronym for "*Be on the lookout.*" Live and learn.

The Freeport taxicab companies had all been contacted, as had the Long Island Railroad Police. It was more or less an interagency cooperative dragnet. Finally, Chen had ordered stakeout teams at Joey's apartment and Mr. Fang's place.

Chen and I were in his unmarked car heading back to the precinct when word came over the radio that Joey was in a taxicab on his way to Manhattan. Responding to the alert Chen had posted, the Freeport Taxi and Airport Limo Service had reported a young Chinese man fitting Joey's description had hired a taxicab at its dispatch office several blocks from the safe house. Joey paid for the ride with a credit card. He had apparently hidden it somewhere on his person when he was taken to the safe house. Perhaps in the heel of his other shoe. The name on the credit card was Joey Chung, confirming the passenger was our Joey.

Chen called the precinct on his cell phone, and gave the desk sergeant a series of orders. The cab Joey was riding in was equipped with a GPS, so the dispatcher had been able to give the police the cab's exact location. The taxicab was traveling westbound on the Southern State Parkway and being followed by a team of Nassau police officers in unmarked cars. Chen told the desk sergeant to have two NYPD patrol cars waiting for the taxicab at the New York City border, and as soon as it crossed into NYPD jurisdiction, to stop it and take Joey into custody and bring him to the Fifth Precinct.

I asked Chen why not just follow Joey into the city where he might lead the cops to the money? Chen said he'd considered doing that, but it would be difficult to follow the cab that far without being detected. If the cops were too cautious, they might lose sight of the cab, and if Joey thought he was being followed, he might jump out somewhere along the way. Besides, we didn't know for sure that Joey was going directly to the money. Chen preferred the less risky option of grabbing up Joey on the Parkway and interrogating him at the station house.

If things went as planned, Joey would be at the precinct house in about an hour. Chen and I were twenty minutes away from the precinct house, so we had plenty of time to get there before Joey arrived. But Mad-Max Chen insisted on using the flashers and siren. Surprisingly, I was getting used to Chen's driving, and I could even go a full five minutes with my eyes open.

I had read that you get over a fear by acknowledging it, embracing it and facing it, which seemed like good advice. The problem was, I couldn't figure out if I was afraid of riding in cars or afraid of dying. If I was afraid of dying, I didn't see any point in embracing it and facing it any sooner than I absolutely had to. Dying to get over my fear of death didn't appeal to me, and it didn't make much sense either.

CHAPTER 61

Forty-five minutes after Chen and I arrived at the Fifth Precinct, two uniformed officers delivered Joey to the interrogation room where Chen and I were awaiting his arrival. He didn't say anything, and he wouldn't even look us in the eye. One of the uniformed officers removed the handcuffs from Joey's wrists and pushed him roughly down on to a chair. Joey gave him a nasty look but said nothing.

Chen thanked the two officers, and they left the room. He took his seat at the head of the table, and I took mine across the table from Joey. Neither of us said anything. We just stared at Joey who didn't seem bothered by the silence or his circumstances. He sat there calmly, seemingly not bothered that his grandfather was held captive by a gang of vicious gangsters.

I wanted to grab him by the throat and slam him against the wall, but I knew that wouldn't do any good. Joey had played me from the start, and I had gone for it, hook, line and sinker. I wasn't about to give him the satisfaction of knowing he had gotten under my skin. I'd wait and sooner or later, I'd get the chance to get even. I just had to make sure it happened soon enough to save Mr. Fang's life.

Chen broke the ice by reading Joey his Miranda rights. Joey asked if he was under arrest, and Chen said he was. Joey asked about the charge, and Chen said robbery, possession of stolen property and felony escape. I think Chen made up the last charge, but it sounded good.

Joey seemed nonplused by the news. He looked at me and asked, "What do you think, counselor?"

I said, "Don't look at me. I'm not your lawyer on these charges."

Joey just shrugged.

It was time to change the dynamic. I took out my cell phone, checked the note in my pocket and dialed the number. Joey didn't seem interested, so I put it on speaker.

The phone rang four times before someone answered and said abruptly, "What?"

I said. "Mr. Lee, this is Jake Carney. I have Joey Chung here, and I'm ready to exchange him for Mr. Fang. Tell me how we're going to do this."

Joey was no longer calm and disinterested. He jumped out of his chair, and Chen had to grab him and slam him back down.

Mr. Lee said, "Excellent. You will receive instructions shortly." Then he hung up.

I looked at Joey and said, "In a little while I'm going to meet Mr. Lee, and I'm going to give him either you or the money in exchange for your grandfather. The choice is yours."

Joey looked from me to Chen, who smiled and said nothing. He was enjoying this as much as I was. Joey protested, saying he was under arrest and Chen had a duty to protect him.

Chen laughed and said he had escaped on two occasions, so a third escape wouldn't be suspicious. Joey, now clearly rattled, said he just wouldn't go. That was my cue to say that if he didn't come voluntarily, I'd drag his unconscious sorry ass to the exchange. In fact, I'd prefer it that way.

Would I really exchange Joey for Mr. Fang? Yeah, probably, but we'll never know for sure because the person on the other end of the phone had been Tommy, not Mr. Lee. Besides, I don't think Chen would actually allow me to exchange Joey for Mr. Fang; he was just going along with the ruse for the time being. Joey may have had the same thought, but he couldn't afford to take the chance that Chen would allow the exchange.

Whatever was going on in Joey's head, the plan worked, and Joey agreed to turn over the money. But that was just the first step in what was going to be a very complicated and dangerous arrangement.

Chen had gone along with the ruse so far, and he'd continue doing everything he could to save Mr. Fang, but there were some things he just couldn't do. One thing was turning over the stolen bank money to the Hip Sing Tong. Nor would he allow three quarters of a million dollars to go back into the drug trade. In other words, he couldn't allow the trade to actually take place.

It was a problem, but before we got to it, we needed to retrieve the money

.

CHAPTER 62

This time Joey said the money was in a storage locker at the Mini Storage Center on South Street. The building was less than a dozen or so blocks from his apartment and within easy walking distance, even from where we sat in the Fifth Precinct.

The shock of the telephone call with Mr. Lee was apparently wearing off, and Joey seemed to be regaining his composure. When I asked him for the unit number, he hesitated briefly, then said, "2014." I wrote it down.

When I asked him for the key, he hesitated again. But this time the hesitation wasn't brief, and it didn't end with an answer to my question. It ended with a demand that he get full immunity in writing before he gave us the key.

Chen laughed out loud, which didn't make Joey happy. He wasn't any happier when I grabbed him by his shirt and started dragging him to the door. He started yelling and wanted to know where I was taking him.

I said, "Over to the Golden Palace Restaurant on Pell Street, I understand that's where the Hip Sing bosses hang out." Joey knew that was true, and he turned to Chen looking for help.

Chen, still laughing, said, "Damn, looks like he's escaping again."

Joey isn't a very big guy, maybe five feet eight at most, and he weighs next to nothing, so I had no problem dragging him around by the collar. When I got him to the door of the interrogation room, Joey must have figured I was serious because he changed his tune and said he'd tell us where the key was.

Sitting him back down, I straightened his shirt collar and gave him a little slap on the cheek. It wasn't meant to hurt; it was simply to remind him I was still in charge.

Joey said the key was in his apartment, taped to the underside of the toilet tank in the guest bathroom. I was impressed; the man had a guest bathroom.

At my studio apartment, I barely had a full bathroom of my own, and he had a guest bathroom? But that wasn't the point, was it?

Joey's key to his apartment was still locked in the safe at the house in Freeport. I figured we'd have to wait for one of the detectives to retrieve it, but Chen had something else in mind. After depositing Joey in a holding cell, Chen and I drove to his apartment in Confucius Plaza.

I have to admit that sometimes the flashers on the unmarked car come in handy. Chen drove to the front entrance of Joey's building and parked right on top of the large bright yellow *No Parking* sign painted on the pavement.

When the doorman came out to greet us, Chen flashed his badge, and the man politely stepped aside while holding the door open. I think I'd like to have one of those badges. Not that I want the job that comes with it. I just want the badge.

Did you know the original New York City policemen wore copper star badges, and that's where the terms, copper and cop, come from? Just some more trivia from hanging out too much in gin mills.

But that's not important.

When we got to Joey's apartment, the door had two locks, and I had no idea how we'd get in. I had thought Chen would get the doorman to let us in, but obviously that wasn't in the plan.

That's when Chen really surprised me by pulling out a kit of lock picking tools. Imagine that, a cop with burglar's tools. I had a couple of smart-ass comments I was dying to make, but I didn't want to piss off Chen, not when he was doing me a favor.

It turned out Chen was a better cop than he was a burglar. It took him ten minutes to pick the first lock and almost equally as long to pick the second. But finally, we were inside the apartment. It was a nice place, messy but nice. And it was big, about fifty times the size of my studio apartment, and three times as large as Gracie's two-bedroom apartment.

I wasn't sure where to find a guest bathroom, but apparently Chen knew because he went directly down the hallway and turned right. I followed, and sure enough, it was a bathroom. Chen was kneeling by the toilet bowl and from my angle, it reminded me of my old days hugging the throne after too much booze.

After lurching around the bowl, Chen gave an *ah ha* and turned around, displaying a piece of gray duct tape with a key stuck to it. Hopefully, this time Joey was being honest, and this key would open the padlock on storage unit 2014.

Leaving the apartment, Chen pulled the door closed behind us, and I asked if it was locked. He looked at me and asked, "Do you care?"

What could I say? I didn't care. I don't even know why I had asked the question. I just shrugged my shoulders, and we both laughed.

It was a quick trip from Confucius Plaza to the Mini Storage building. But when we got there, we found out we needed an access code to get inside. We were debating whether to return to the precinct and beat the code out of Joey, or let one of the detectives do it, when a security guard showed up. Chen showed the man his badge and told him we were there to check a unit for possible weapons of mass destruction.

The guard looked confused. Chen nodded toward me and said simply, "Homeland Security." The guard looked at me, and I nodded, one of those grave nods appropriate for a terrorism situation. Then he let us into the building.

On the way up to the second floor, I told Chen if this whole thing went to hell in a handbasket, I wasn't going to jail for posing as a Federal Agent. He laughed and said that if things didn't work out, we'd be going to jail for worse than that.

For a mini storage facility, it was a pretty big building with a lot of corridors. There were signs which weren't particularly helpful. Plus, the lights were on a sensor system of some sort and came on automatically when you got close to one of the motion detectors. It was weird. As you walked down the corridor, the lights came on ahead of you and went off behind you.

Finally, we found a corridor lined with doors starting with number 2001. The doors were the size of the average closet door and spaced about two feet apart. Looking down the corridor, there must have been fifteen doors on each side. The odd numbered doors were on the left, and the even numbered doors were on the right. Unit 2014 was seven doors down on the right, a little less than halfway down the corridor.

Grabbing the lock with his left hand, Chen pushed the key into the lock. I held my breath. The key went in, and it turned. The lock opened. Chen removed the lock and opened the door. A light went on. The unit was really just a closet, four feet deep at most. But on the floor were two duffel bags.

Chen knelt and opened the first bag. It contained bundles of cash, all seemingly new bills neatly wrapped and banded. Chen looked up and said, "The bank money."

Then he opened the second duffel bag. It also contained bundles of cash, but these bundles were old bills held together with rubber bands. He didn't need to tell me that this was the drug money. The bag was a lot bigger and turned out to be a lot heavier than the first bag. I know because I wound up carrying that bag.

When Chen told me to carry the bag with the drug money in it, I objected. I said that as a Homeland Security Agent, I should decide who carried which bag. Chen asked if I wanted to be arrested there or at the precinct house. I got the point and carried the big bag.

CHAPTER 63

In the car on the way back to the precinct house, I had suggested we deliver the cash to my apartment, so I could have it handy when I made the deal with Mr. Lee. Ignoring my suggestion, Chen said we were going back to the precinct house to log the cash into evidence.

So now we had the money and Joey, but Chen apparently wasn't going to allow me to trade either one for poor Mr. Fang. That wasn't what Sundance and Butch Cassidy would have done.

I knew Chen wasn't going to allow the tong to torture and kill Mr. Fang, so I presumed he had a plan in mind. Since I was the contact person in the middle of this whole mess, Chen would have to share the plan with me at some point soon.

At the precinct house, a team of cops counted the cash and logged it on evidence vouchers. When they were done, two uniformed officers were sent to deliver the cash filled bags to the NYPD Property Clerk Division on Front Street, in Brooklyn. The bags would remain in the possession of the Property Clerk until needed as evidence in a trial or otherwise disposed of.

As for Joey, Chen was sending him back to the safe house in Freeport, this time under the watchful eyes of three detectives and with Joey wearing an ankle alert bracelet. Chen wasn't going to chance another escape.

I hated to admit it, but Joey was still my client, so before he left, I had a private conversation with him. I told him I'd do what I could to get him the best deal possible, but he had to understand he was in deep shit.

For the first time since his grandfather's kidnapping, he asked about the old man and whether I'd be able to help him. I hoped his concern was genuine, but given his track record, I had my doubts. In AA we say that we don't take somebody else's inventory, meaning we don't judge people. But as a lawyer I've been judging people all my professional life, and I've gotten pretty good at it. The fact that I couldn't tell if Joey's concern was genuine suggested to me he was a sociopath. But only time would tell.

When Joey had been carted away, Chen suggested we talk. It was nearly one o'clock in the morning, and I was beat, but we did need to talk. I asked Chen what he planned on doing about Mr. Fang.

He said we had six days left to work out a plan, but as he saw it, I was in the middle of this whole thing, so whatever the plan, I'd have to be involved. What he said was true; it was just a matter of how deeply involved I had to get.

Chen's general idea was to set up the exchange at a location where he could ambush the kidnappers. It sounded like a good plan, but we weren't dealing with amateurs, so it wouldn't be easy. That was why Chen wanted time to think about it and plot out some details.

There wasn't anything more we could do at that point, so Chen suggested I go home and get some sleep. It was a good idea. I was sure Gracie had gone to bed a long time earlier, so rather than going to her place and disturbing her sleep, I went to my apartment.

It had been a wild day, and I was still on edge. It was times like this when I missed drinking. A nice little drink of scotch would have taken the edge off and allowed me to fall asleep. That's the tempting memory. The memory that tempts you to drink again. But the memory is a lie. I never had a little drink of scotch. I drank it until the bottle was empty, or until I passed out. That was the memory I had to keep in my head.

Instead of a drink, I took a hot shower and fell asleep watching the Allied Forces invade Germany on the History Channel. I fell asleep before it was over, but I know how it ended. The good guys won. The good guys always win, at least most of the time.

CHAPTER 64

The next morning, I was working diligently on a new motion to dismiss Jenny's case. This motion was based on what I called a failure to properly Mirandize Jenny at the time of her arrest.

It's funny how words come about. Take "Mirandize," for instance. It's a verb meaning *to advise someone of their Miranda rights*. If you've watched any television cop shows, you've probably heard the Miranda rights given a million times. You know, the right to remain silent, the right to a lawyer, and so on. But do you know where they come from, and why they're called Miranda rights?

They're from the Supreme Court case of *Miranda vs. Arizona*, decided in 1966. Ernesto Miranda was one of four defendants whose cases were decided at the same time by the Supreme Court.

Ernesto Miranda had been arrested in his home in Arizona on the charge of kidnapping and rape and taken to the police station where he was identified by the victim. He was interrogated for two hours without having been advised of his Fifth Amendment rights against self-incrimination. Miranda confessed to the crime but later pleaded not guilty. At trial, his oral and written confessions were admitted into evidence, and he was found guilty.

The Supreme Court ruled that once someone is taken into custody, they must be advised of their Fifth Amendment rights before they can be questioned. As a result of the case, a standard set of warnings was developed and became known as the Miranda rights.

Ernesto Miranda was retried in Arizona, and even without his confessions being used, he was convicted and sentenced to twenty to thirty years in prison. Released early, he was killed in a barroom brawl in 1974. I'm sure Ernesto would be glad to know his murderer was read his Miranda rights.

Anyway, that's how the Fifth Amendment warning rights came to be called Miranda rights, and how Ernesto Miranda's name eventually became a verb. Weird, isn't it?

Getting back to Jenny's case, Jenny was arrested along with seven others at a local after-hours club. When a dozen cops burst through the club's doors, pandemonium erupted as people tried to escape the raid. The cops quickly located their targets and before anyone at Jenny's table could move, they were surrounded.

During the arrest process, the heavily armed cops tightly surrounded Jenny's table and read the seven seated at the table their Miranda rights. Knowing from past experience that Chinese suspects often claimed they didn't speak English, two Chinese cops read the Miranda rights in Chinese, while one cop read them in English.

I was claiming that in the confusion and intimidating circumstances that existed at the time of the arrest, having multiple police officers yelling Miranda rights in two languages did not constitute proper Mirandizing of my client. Each suspect should have been Mirandized individually when arrested. I was asking for a hearing to determine how, by whom and when Jenny had been advised of her rights.

I couldn't use an affidavit from Jenny because that would expose her to being cross-examined if the court ordered a hearing, and I couldn't take the chance of having her testify. That's why I had to dance around the issue, and it was also why I was likely to lose the motion. But even if the court didn't order a hearing, it would take at least four to six weeks to get a decision on the motion.

I was just finishing the papers when Connie announced that Sarah Washington was on the line. Sarah asked how the motion papers were coming and when I said they were just about done, she said to serve a copy on her office as quickly as I could.

When I asked Sarah what was up, she said she couldn't talk over the phone, but if I wanted to buy her a cup of coffee, she'd meet me at the Worth Street Coffee Shop in fifteen minutes. It was common knowledge that I often transacted business at the coffee shop, so I wasn't surprised when Sarah suggested we meet there.

Sipping her coffee and munching on a toasted bagel with lox which wasn't part of the original deal, mind you, Sarah told me what was going on. After weeks of haggling, threatening and negotiating, several members of the Zheng organization had flipped, and it had produced a domino effect. Of the group indicted in Operation Asian Dragon, the eighty-six illegal immigrants had been deported, and twenty-seven of the defendants had turned State's evidence and worked out plea deals.

The DA would announce the news the next day, and the twenty-seven would plead guilty over the next several days. All of that was sure to make a big hit in the press. The DA hoped that the remaining cases, which included Jenny's case, could be wrapped up quickly after that.

The DA expected to have plea deals in at least half of the remaining cases, and to set trial dates for the remainder. Sarah said that at least twenty of the heavy hitters were working out plea deals, and she expected the rest to follow suit shortly. With so many suspects having turned State's evidence, chances of an acquittal in any of the cases was practically non-existent. The only ones who would chance a trial were the hard-core dealers, who had nothing to lose by doing so.

Those cases were scheduled to go to trial soon, and it was imperative that Jenny's case not be in that group. The DA had already labeled the group as the worst of the worst and said there would be no plea deals in any of those cases.

But what would happen after that? Sarah assured me that once those cases were disposed of, the DA would lose all interest in Jenny's case, and we could cut a good plea deal. We might not agree on what constituted a "good plea deal," but it would be better than what we were facing now.

I told Sarah I'd serve the motion papers that afternoon, and she said she would ask for an extension of time to reply. With all of the other cases popping, she couldn't be expected to waste time responding to my ridiculous motion. Under other circumstances, I would have been offended, but truth be told, it was a ridiculous motion.

We finished our coffee and bagels, and I paid the bill. A small price to pay for the information Sarah had given me. On my walk back to the office, I called Joan and told her what I had just learned. I was careful not to sound overly optimistic because nothing was cast in stone yet, and a lot could go wrong before we were done. Still, the news was positive, and I figured Joan and Jenny deserved to hear something positive for a change.

The last I heard from Joan, she had filed for divorce here in New York, using her new apartment as her residence. In response, the prick had filed his own action in San Francisco. So as of the moment, there was a jurisdictional fight over which state would get to issue the divorce decree. Both states had no fault divorce, and neither offered a financial benefit to either party, so fighting over jurisdiction would do nothing more than make the lawyers a little richer.

I used to think that criminal defense lawyers were at the bottom of the heap when it came to the practice of law. Not all of them, you understand, but enough to give the group a reputation akin to used car dealers. But after listening to some of my colleagues who practice family law, I think divorce lawyers deserve that title more than criminal defense lawyers.

All of that thinking reminded me that I still had an ethical issue of my own to deal with in Joey's case. I had been more or less ignoring the situation all morning because I was uncomfortable not doing something to help Mr. Fang. But there wasn't anything I could do except wait for Chen to come up with a plan. As for Joey, until the situation with his grandfather played out, there wasn't much we could do.

CHAPTER 65

That afternoon, I was on my way back to the office, after having served the motion papers on Sarah, when Chen called and asked me to meet him at the precinct house.

When I arrived, Chen and four other officers were sitting in the interrogation room. I didn't recall having seen any of these men before and couldn't help wondering who they were. My curiosity was put to rest when Chen introduced them. They were from the SWAT team, and they were discussing a plan to rescue Mr. Fang. A plan that required my assistance.

Chen was certain that the tong would want me to deliver the money. They knew what I looked like, and they knew I wasn't likely to come armed. It was also probable that the tong wouldn't bring Mr. Fang to the exchange, but would agree to release him once the money was in their hands. That was a problem.

If Mr. Fang wasn't at the exchange site, the cops could put trackers in the duffel bags and bundle a couple in the money. But Chen didn't want to use the actual money in the exchange; he preferred using fake money which wasn't going to work. The tong guys were likely to check the contents of the duffel as soon as they left the exchange site and seeing the fake money, they'd take it out on poor Mr. Fang.

Chen was in a quandary. He could requisition the money from the Property Clerk to use in the rescue operation. But he had just gotten his ass off the firing line by recovering the stolen bank money, and he wasn't anxious to put it back on the line. I couldn't blame him for that. But the recovered drug money was something different. Yes, Chen had gotten some pats on the back from the brass, but Mr. Fang's life was at stake.

As for the bank money, I suggested we talk to Citibank and explain the situation. The cash wasn't needed as evidence because Joey had confessed to the robbery, so there wasn't going to be a trial. That meant the money would be returned to the bank. So why not ask the bank manager if we could "borrow" it for a little while? Chen thought that was a good idea. If Citibank agreed, the NYPD wouldn't be at risk, so the brass wouldn't give a damn what we did with the money.

Assuming all of the money was available, the plan was for me to call Mr. Lee and arrange an exchange. First, I'd demand to have proof of life, preferably a conversation with Mr. Fang. Then I'd demand that the exchange occur someplace public, and that Mr. Fang be there. Chen didn't expect the tong to agree to both conditions, but in refusing to bring Mr. Fang to the drop, they might give in on the location.

I wouldn't agree to the location right away. I'd say that I had to think about it. It was pushing the limits, but it would be up to me to decide when to stop pushing. Hopefully, we'd get a good location. But Chen suspected it would be a floating location, meaning I'd be sent to one place, then ordered to a different location, and maybe even other locations after that.

The money and I would be fitted with GPS devices, but Chen warned I'd probably be searched, especially if it was a floating exchange point operation. The SWAT team didn't want to be too close, but they couldn't risk losing the trackers and me.

Sitting there in Chen's interrogation room talking about the plan, it all seemed good and simple. That was because it was all hypothetical. I knew from past experience that I'd feel a lot different about it when I actually had to do it.

Step one was easy, and went off without a hitch. Chen and I visited the Citibank on Mott Street and after we explained the situation to the bank manager, he called the bank's corporate headquarters in Midtown Manhattan, and the use of the money in the rescue operation was approved.

They say success breeds success and, in this instance, it proved to be true. Feeling confident after our successful visit at Citibank, Chen and I visited his boss who agreed that Chen could requisition the drug money for the rescue operation. He wished us luck, but what he didn't say out loud, was if this operation went off the rails and the money got lost, Chen's ass was back on the firing line.

Now it was just a question of waiting a day or two while we planned what little we could before I called Mr. Lee.

That night at dinner Gracie and I had a lot of catching up to do. We hadn't seen each other in two days. Two very busy days for both of us. Gracie was preparing for a major rape case trial, and the victim, her main witness, was getting shaky. That wasn't uncommon in rape cases in which the victim can expect the defense to try and trash her.

Gracie was great at helping victims through those situations. She was kind, understanding and supportive. But once inside the courtroom, everything changed. She became a shark. Any defense lawyer who tried putting Gracie's rape victim on trial quickly learned he or she had made a big mistake.

Gracie knew how to read a jury and how to read a witness. If the defendant was dumb enough to take the witness stand, Gracie would reduce him to a pile of quivering crap in a matter of minutes. If you don't believe me, check Gracie's conviction rate; it's ninety-seven percent, best in the District Attorney's Office. Probably best in the state.

When I told Gracie about Mr. Fang and Chen's plan, she wasn't thrilled that I was going to be a part of it. She thought it was dangerous, and Chen should come up with another option. When I asked her for an alternative, she said it was Chen's job to come up with another plan, not hers.

You can't argue with logic, so I just let it drop. Besides, we were eating sushi, and you know what that meant.

CHAPTER 66

The following day, the District Attorney held a press conference to announce the convictions of eleven members of the Zheng Organization and ten members of the Asian Empire on drug trafficking charges. All twenty-one had pleaded guilty and would be sentenced later in the month. He also expected additional convictions in the coming days and promised to have all the matters related to Operation Asian Dragon concluded within weeks. It didn't hurt that twelve more of the defendants were determined to be illegal immigrants who had overstayed their visas and were in the process of being deported.

It was just as Sarah had said. Things were moving along nicely, and it was good news for Jenny. The news got even better when Sarah called and said the two detectives from San Francisco had arrived and were taking Shing Lew back to California on the evening flight. That was one more problem out of the way. If I could keep Jenny's case off the trial calendar for another five or six weeks, we'd be home free.

Now I had to deal with Joey's case. As much as I hated Joey at the moment, he was still my client, and I didn't have grounds to dump him, so I was ethically bound to represent him. If things didn't work out with the rescue operation, the Hip Sing Tong might kill him, but that wasn't my problem. My job was to get him the best plea deal possible, and that's what I planned on doing. If he got himself killed while I was representing him, it wasn't my fault.

I called Marty Bowman and invited him to lunch. He accepted, but he wanted to eat somewhere other than the Worth Street Coffee Shop. I suggested a nice dim sum restaurant on Mott Street, but he wanted to eat at Forlini's, an Italian restaurant on Baxter Street. He knew something was up, and he was upping the ante. The bigger the favor, the more expensive the meal. Forlini's, which has been around since 1943, is a white tablecloth joint with art work on the walls. It's no Worth Street Coffee Shop, but the food is good.

We met at the restaurant and ate at a table in the back corner. Over our Fried Calamari and Spedini Romana, Marty asked what I had learned about the tunnels. Between bites I said that I learned the Houdini Bandits didn't use the tunnels. Naturally, he then wanted to know how they escaped. Trying my best to save face for Chen, I explained how it all went down.

Marty had a good laugh over that one, but he said the deal was contingent on my client telling him about the tunnels. I corrected him; the agreement was contingent on Joey telling him about the tunnel he and the Cha brothers used to escape. Since they hadn't used a tunnel to escape, there was nothing to tell. Marty was chewing on that one when our main courses arrived. Veal Chop val Doslana for Marty, and Veal Scalloppini Pizziaola for me. Believe me, this wasn't a cheap meal, and we still hadn't looked at the dessert menu. But the more expensive the meal, the more I'd expect. At the rate Marty was eating, Joey might get a walk.

Of course, Marty wasn't aware of the tong drug money situation, and I wasn't about to mention it. Not that it mattered. Joey had been a coconspirator in the tong drug money robbery, but with both Cha brothers dead, there was no way to prove it. As much as I had used the threat of new charges to get Joey to turn over the money, there wasn't much to it. The worst he could be charged with was possession of stolen property, a more or less nuisance charge.

I assumed if Marty hadn't heard about the drug money, he didn't know the bank money had been recovered. That was my ace in the hole. Since the deal only required Joey to return his share of the money, returning all of the money was worth bonus points.

Over our espressos, and while Marty ate his Hot Zabaglione, I asked him what a return of all the bank robbery money was worth in a plea deal. He was intrigued. He asked what I was looking for, and I said our original deal, robbery in the third degree, a minimum sentence recommendation, and no further charges relating to the Cha brothers. It was a bit sneaky, but not something Marty wouldn't have done himself if given the chance.

Marty asked how soon the money could be returned, and I said just as soon as we agreed on the deal. He said okay and stuck out his hand, but just to be on the safe side, I pulled out a pen and wrote up the terms. Then after we both signed it, Marty asked when he could expect to receive the money. I said he'd have to ask Chen because the money was in the Property Clerk's Office.

I figured that wasn't the worst of the news, and it was best to get it all out, so I mentioned the drug money situation. I thought Marty might be upset, but he laughed and said, "You bastard, you got me again." Then he added that I owed him another lunch and not at the coffee shop. He was right about that.

CHAPTER 67

That afternoon, Chen called and asked me to drop by the precinct house. Tommy, who was sitting in my office at the time, insisted on coming along. I had filled him in on the events of the last couple of days, and he was concerned about this proposed Fang operation. I wasn't sure what he could do about it, but it wouldn't hurt to have him at the meeting.

When we arrived at the precinct house, Chen wasn't particularly happy that I had brought Tommy along. He didn't want him at the meeting, but I insisted he be present. It wasn't so much that I wanted him there as I hate being told what to do. It's one of the traits still hanging on from my old drinking days.

Chen finally relented, and the three of us took seats around the table in the interrogation room. I couldn't help but notice that the SWAT guys weren't in the room. When I mentioned it, Chen said we'd use them for tactical support, but before we got that far, we had to figure out some things ourselves.

According to his squad's confidential informers, the tong's push to find Joey was still on and going strong. Tommy confirmed his contacts were telling him the same thing. That meant the tong didn't know that Joey was in custody, and more importantly, that I had the money.

We still had four days to figure out what to do, but Chin thought it would be best if we made contact sooner, much sooner. Like within an hour. Tommy asked why, and Chen said if we turned down the heat, the rescue operation, as he was now calling it, stood a better chance of succeeding. The operation relied heavily on the element of surprise, and that required that the operatives be in place without drawing attention. With everyone on alert looking for Joey, going unnoticed was going to be a problem. But once the tong knew I had the money and was willing to trade it for Mr. Fang, it was likely to withdraw the reward for Joey's capture, and things should return to normal. Not that 'normal' guaranteed the operation wouldn't be breached; it just made it less likely to be breached.

Tommy didn't like the plan from the start, but he agreed it had a better chance for success if the heat was off, and letting the tong know I had the money would help do that. So it was just a question of what I would say when I called Mr. Lee. The idea was to put off the exchange for as long as possible without it seeming like that was the purpose.

Together we outlined what I should say, and then I rehearsed the call a couple of times until I felt comfortable. Chen set up a recording device, and I made the call.

Mr. Lee answered, "Yes Mr. Carney. Are you prepared to do business?" I recognized Mr. Lee's voice from our last conversation.

I didn't answer his question directly. I said only that I had the money. Then I waited for him to respond.

He said, "A good first step to start the journey. I will call you within the hour and tell you where to bring the money."

Things were progressing as Chen and Tommy predicted they would. It was the Chinese style of negotiation, and we had reached a critical point. I glanced at Chen and Tommy, and they both nodded their heads. I knew what to say.

"But first, Mr. Lee, we must agree on terms."

I think my brashness took Mr. Lee by surprise because it took him a minute to respond.

"Ah, Mr. Carney, terms are simple; you bring the money or Mr. Fang dies."

"No, Mr. Lee, if Mr. Fang suffers so much as a scratch, you'll never see the money."

Chen and Tommy nodded their approval. I was holding my own in these Chinese negotiations. But I was getting tired of the game. As you know, patience is not my strong suit.

It was time to shake things up.

"Mr. Lee let's knock off the bullshit. You want the money; I want Mr. Fang returned unharmed. So, here's the deal. First, I want to talk to Mr. Fang to make sure he's okay. Second, you bring Mr. Fang to a location of my choosing, and I'll bring the money. Third, you don't get the money until I see Mr. Fang is alive and well, and he's released. Those are the terms, Mr. Lee."

Chen was giving me the evil eye for having gone off script, but Tommy was smiling, so I figured I hadn't screwed things up too badly.

Mr. Lee gave a few *tsk, tsks,* and then he said, "Mr. Carney, what makes you think you can be so bold as to set the conditions?"

"Mr. Lee, I know you have a lot of wise sayings; well, we have a couple of our own. One is the Golden Rule; he who has the gold makes the rules. So if you want the gold, you follow my rules."

Then I hung up the phone. I thought Chen was going to go through the roof, but he didn't. He just looked worried. I asked what he thought, and he said that I had done okay, but I should expect one of Mr. Fang's fingers to be delivered to my office shortly.

I hadn't really thought about that, and I was starting to regret my little improvisation. But then Tommy chimed in and said it was better that I had taken a strong approach. It made me less predictable, and therefore, more dangerous to the tong. The tong wanted the money, and as long as I was unpredictable, they couldn't afford to piss me off by harming Mr. Fang.

Chen had to agree that made sense. So now we'd just have to wait for Mr. Lee to call back. At least we had accomplished one of our goals. The tong now knew I had the money. Hopefully, they'd call off the search for Joey.

Speaking of Joey reminded me I had to see him and have him sign the deal that I had made with Marty Bowman. As much as I hated the thought, I needed Chen or one of his detectives to drive me to the safe house in Freeport.

The things one has to do for a client.

CHAPTER 68

Chen said he'd take me to Freeport to see Joey, and along the way, we could talk about the rescue operation. The thought of riding out to Long Island with "Mad-Max" Chen didn't thrill me, but it was almost five o'clock, and I hoped the heavy rush hour traffic would slow him down.

I was about to give Gracie a call to tell her I wouldn't be at dinner when I remembered she, Joan and Jenny were having a girls' night out. I had no idea what that meant other than I wasn't a girl, and so I wasn't invited. That was fine with me. I had no interest in spending the evening listening to three women talk about whatever it is that three women talk about when they're together.

Much to my delight and Chen's annoyance, the ride to Freeport was slowed considerably by the rush hour traffic. On the way, Chen told me the SWAT team had been able to plant small GPS units in the linings of both duffel bags, and they were working on a way to plant microchips in the bands bundling the money. If they were able to do that, then the undercover units wouldn't need to be as close to the exchange location, and that would make their detection less likely.

Chen still didn't believe the tong would agree to a direct exchange of the money for Mr. Fang. He was certain they'd want the cash dropped and collected before they released him. He also believed they'd have me bring the cash to multiple locations before telling me to leave it. Which raised an interesting question. Seeing as how the two duffel bags were heavy, how was I supposed to jackass them around to all these locations?

Obviously unaware that I didn't have a driver's license, Chen said the department would provide a car. When I told him I didn't drive, he said that was even better. It put the tong in a tough position. If they didn't want to use a single drop site, they'd have to allow me to use a driver. Either way it would work out to our advantage.

My meeting with Joey took less than half an hour. He was naturally thrilled with the deal and happy to sign it. He wasn't so happy when I told him if anything happened to his grandfather, he'd be facing additional serious charges, and not only would I no longer be his attorney, I'd be a witness against him. He started to say something, but I gave him the middle finger salute and left him standing there staring.

I'm ethically required to represent him, but nothing requires me to like him or to be polite to him. Hopefully, that would be the last I'd see of the little punk until his sentencing.

We were halfway back to the city when my cell phone rang. It was Mr. Lee. I asked him to hold and put the phone on mute while Chen pulled off the highway and shut off the engine. I didn't want Lee to hear the engine or the traffic. The less he knew the better.

This time there were no pleasantries. Lee got right to the point. I would be allowed to speak with Mr. Fang once the other terms for the exchange were agreed upon. Mr. Fang would not be brought to the exchange, but he would be released as soon as the money was received. The drop location would be public but chosen by the tong.

Lee's tone was businesslike but not unfriendly, which led me to assume Mr. Fang would be keeping all of his fingers, at least for the time being. But to add a little insurance, I kept my own tone friendly.

I said that I'd consider the terms and get back to him, and then, not to be rude, I said goodbye before I hung up.

Chen, who had been listening in, was smiling and for good reason. He and Tommy had been right about how the negotiations would progress. Now it was just a matter of stringing Mr. Lee along a little while longer while Chen and the SWAT team worked out some tactics.

CHAPTER 69

The next couple of days I was able to devote time to my other cases while I waited to call Mr. Lee back. I didn't have anything pressing on the schedule which gave me time to attend a couple of AA meetings. When I first went to AA, going to meetings was a chore. But after a while, it became something I looked forward to. I still need to go to meetings, but it's easier going when you like to go.

After three days, Chen said he was ready, and it was time I called Mr. Lee back and negotiated the exchange terms. He wanted me to do that from the precinct house where the tech people had set up the recording system, and they would try to trace the call.

Earlier attempts to trace the calls hadn't worked. Lee was smart; he kept the calls short, so the trace couldn't be completed, and on the one occasion when the techs were able to trace the call, it was made from a crowded location. So, even if the cops arrived quickly enough, picking Lee out of the crowd would have been impossible. But there was no harm in trying. Maybe they'd get lucky. I called Mr. Lee and told him I wanted to speak with Mr. Fang and question him before proceeding. Lee agreed.

The technician trying to trace the call signaled me to draw out the conversation. I started to say something, but Lee interrupted, saying he'd call back shortly, and he hung up. He knew we were trying to trace the call.

Ten minutes later, my cell phone rang, but the incoming number wasn't the one Lee had been using. I answered it, not knowing what to expect. It was Lee; he said I'd be foolish to attempt tracing his calls. I said that I wasn't, and he laughed. Then he said that he would call back in an hour with Mr. Fang. All that was left was choosing the location of the money drop. I reminded Lee that the drop had to occur in a very public place. Lee said that wasn't a problem. Then he hung up.

An hour later, he called back, and this time he put Mr. Fang on the line. I asked him how he was, and he said that he was being treated kindly. At the suggestion of the NYPD psychiatrist who Chen had consulted, I asked Mr. Fang the day and date, and he answered correctly. I'd later learn that the purpose of the question was to gauge if Mr. Fang's cognitive powers were compromised by drugs.

Mr. Lee took back the phone and asked if I was prepared to make the exchange. I said I was once he told me where it was going to take place. We all held our breath. Mr. Lee said he hoped I understood that he couldn't tell me the location, but I had his word it would be someplace very public. As odd as it may sound, the word of a tong member is generally considered good. So with a nod from Chen, I asked when and how.

He said in two days. He would call that morning with instructions, but he wanted to know how the money was packed. I told him it was in two duffel bags. He asked how large, and I told him. Then he hung up.

The next day, Chen, Tommy and I met with the technicians and the SWAT team, and we planned for the drop. The meeting took most of the day, and when it was over, I was exhausted.

At dinner with Gracie later that night, she looked worried when I told her the plans. She said that she didn't like the idea of me being essentially on my own. I said that I wasn't on my own, and I'd be in constant contact with Chen and the SWAT team. But Gracie reminded me these were the same people who concluded Joey and the Cha brothers had escaped through a tunnel. She had a point.

I thought that was the perfect opportunity to lobby for sex, so I said if my life was in danger, we should spend what time I had left making mad passionate love. Gracie said my time would be better spent making a will. She was kidding, of course. She knew I already had a will. I said if she wanted to stay in that will, she'd better think seriously about my request.

Gracie, never at a loss for words, asked if having sex with me to stay in my will, would make her a hooker. I said no, and given the present state of my finances, no money would be changing hands. She should consider it as an act of mercy with the possibility that her kindness might be rewarded sometime in the future. When Gracie laughed and said to call her Sister Mercy, I got her message, and I signaled the waiter to bring the check. But

Gracie pointed out we hadn't yet been served our dinners. When there's sex involved, I've been known to jump the gun.

CHAPTER 70

With one day left before the scheduled exchange with Mr. Lee and the tong, the news on Jenny's case got better. The District Attorney announced additional guilty pleas and convictions in the Asian Dragon cases, and he promised to have the whole matter wrapped up in a matter of weeks.

After hearing the news, I called Sarah and asked where we stood with Jenny's case. Sarah said that between the guilty pleas and the deportations, there were only a handful of cases outstanding. Most of those involved suspects who had turned State's evidence, and they would be getting favorable plea deals once the media attention died down. That left only seven cases, including Jenny's, that were going to be scheduled for trial. Sarah expected plea bargains would be worked out in most of those cases over the next couple of weeks.

If I could keep Jenny's case off the trial calendar for another month, Sarah was sure she could push through a deal involving nothing more than possession, which would carry no jail time. That was great news.

Sarah said she'd help out by asking for another adjournment of my motion to dismiss on the Miranda warnings issue. The motion calendar was jammed at the moment, so an adjournment was likely to push the motion date off for at least three weeks. If Jenny's case couldn't be cleared by then, I'd just have to convince the judge to grant a hearing which would add another couple of weeks, after which waiting for a decision could take even longer.

Things were definitely looking good for Jenny. I called Joan and told her the good news. As we spoke, she passed on the word to Jenny who I could hear laughing in the background. Joan had good news of her own. She had a second interview for a professorship at NYU, and her chances of getting the job looked good.

After a quick lunch with Tommy at Shoo's Restaurant, I spent the rest of the afternoon with Chen and the SWAT team. Chen had requisitioned the two duffel bags, and they were setting there in the interrogation room. They had been fitted with tiny GPS units and ready to go. Fearing the tong might try grabbing the duffel bags early and not wanting Gracie involved, I said that I'd spend the night at my apartment on Henry Street. Chen thought that was a good idea and said he'd send someone to watch over me. I reminded Chen it was a studio apartment, and he said that he'd make sure to send a man. I told him to make sure that the guy brought a cot.

Gracie and I had dinner at Pino's. I tried to stay upbeat, but I have to admit I was nervous, and it probably showed. I can hide my emotions from everyone but Gracie and, most times, Doug. With Gracie, it's like she can read my mind and my soul. I could never keep anything from Gracie, not that I would.

Anyway, we had a nice dinner, and then we stopped by Ferrara's for cannoli and espresso before parting. We've spent nights apart, and I don't think either one of us even thought about it when we did. But that night it was different. Gracie gave me a kiss and made me promise to be careful. I said I'd call her when I could to let her know what was happening. She said not to worry; she had Tommy's number, and she knew I was going to have my hands full.

When I got to my apartment, Detective Salerno was there with a cot. We shot the breeze for a while, then he went to sleep. I was debating whether to call Gracie when the phone rang, and it was Gracie.

Salerno was on his cot snoring so loudly that Gracie thought we had a bad connection and wanted to call back. I explained the noise was coming from my bodyguard, who Gracie observed was apparently not doing a very good job at keeping watch. I said to be fair, she had a rough day. Gracie laughed and said if that noise was coming from a woman, I was welcome to her.

We talked for half an hour and said goodnight. Salerno was still snoring, but somehow I managed to fall asleep.

CHAPTER 71

The next morning, Salerno and I were up before six o'clock. After showering and shaving, I made us some coffee and waited for the rest of the team to arrive.

By seven o'clock, everyone was in place. The Mobile Command Unit was set up and operational. The SWAT team and undercover cops were on standby, ready to move into position on command. The NYPD taxicab was parked around the corner from my building with an undercover cop sitting at the wheel waiting.

Inside the apartment, a team of technicians were outfitting me with a number of miniature GPS transmitters and something called an earbud. It was a little thing that plugged deep into my ear, allowing me to hear instructions from the Mobile Command Unit.

The techs assured me that no one else could hear the transmissions, so I didn't have to worry about anyone overhearing them. Better than that was the fact that the little bug enabled the Command Unit to hear me. I don't know how it worked, and normally I'm not crazy about things like that, but under the circumstances, I welcomed anything that enabled me to call in the cavalry with our prearranged safe word, "brother."

My cell phone had been rigged so that all my calls would be monitored in the Mobile Command Unit and broadcast to everyone working the operation. It was like an open line for all the good guys. Hopefully, the bad guys couldn't hack their way into the conversation.

When you're sitting around waiting for something like this exchange operation to go down, everyone is on edge. I was on my fifth cup of coffee. I was definitely nervous, and to be truthful, a little frightened. Waiting was the hardest part. Or maybe not. If I was lucky, waiting would be the hardest part. The Hip Sing Tong is well known for its merciless brutality. There was no guarantee that once I dropped off the money, I wouldn't be killed on the spot. But why focus on the negative? As a wise man once said, *A coward dies a thousand deaths; a brave man dies but once."*

Chen and Tommy were in the Mobile Command Unit, a seemingly dilapidated U-Haul truck with enough electronic equipment inside to launch a space shuttle. I had ridden in the thing a couple of times, so I was familiar with its operation. Chen must have been nervous because he kept testing the communications equipment. Finally, I told him that he was driving me nuts and to knock off all the testing.

Finally, at nine-fifteen, Mr. Lee called; it was showtime. Lee asked if I still had the money in the two duffel bags, and I said that I did. He then told me to take the two bags to the Columbus Park Pavilion on Bayard Street and to call him when I arrived.

Having the NYPD taxicab parked around the corner was brilliant. As I exited the building and reached the curb dragging the two duffel bags, the taxicab rolled into sight.

It was a short taxicab ride from my apartment to Columbus Park. Columbus Park has a long checkered history. Located between Mulberry Street on the east and Baxter Street on the west, it runs from Worth Street north to Bayard Street. This area was part of the infamous Five Points neighborhood, home to several immigrant groups and known for its violence. The first park on the site opened in 1897, and it was called Mulberry Bend Park, after the bend Mulberry Street takes at Pell Street.

Renamed Columbus Park in 1911, it's now used mostly by the Chinatown community as a gathering place and somewhere to practice tai chi. At the north end of the park at Bayard Street stands the Pavilion. Built as part of the original park, the open-air Pavilion had fallen into disrepair and wasn't used much until it was renovated in 2007.

As my taxicab pulled up in front of the Pavilion, I called Mr. Lee. He said for me to take the two duffel bags through the front entrance of the Pavilion and down the back steps to the entrance to the storage room below the building. The door was unlocked, and I should take the duffel bags inside and wait. Then he hung up.

Chen thought this might be the drop, and he had his teams on ready. I hoped it was the drop, but I thought it was too simple, and I didn't like the idea that I had to go inside a storage room out of everyone's sight. What if the tong guys were waiting for me in there, or maybe there was an entrance to one of the tunnels I hadn't been able to find? But I was just being crazy.

Following instructions, I half carried, and half dragged the two duffel bags through the Pavilion and down the back steps. Next to the staircase was a double door entrance to what I assumed was the storage room. I dragged the duffel bags inside and waited.

The room was big and filled with maintenance equipment and what looked like supplies for the park. Next to the door was a big cardboard box that seemed out of place. I was about to examine it when my cell phone rang.

As if he had been reading my mind, Lee told me to open the cardboard box. Inside was a huge Perry Ellis rolling duffel bag. I more or less figured out what was coming next. But just to make sure Chen and the SWAT team were on the same page, I said to Lee, "What am I supposed to do with this big duffel bag? I like Perry Ellis and all, but I'm not crazy about the tan color."

Lee was no fool, but hopefully, he'd let my comment pass as another one of my smart-ass remarks. But Chen was happy with it and warned me not to take any more chances. I assumed it was out of concern for my well-being, not out of fear that I would blow the operation.

Lee, ignoring my comment, said to transfer the money from the two duffel bags into the new one. Then he hung up. Short calls can't be traced.

When I opened the new duffel bag, I found it had been roughly lined with a silver material. I suspected it wasn't originally part of the bag and probably something Chen needed to know about. I didn't know if the room was bugged, so I couldn't chance simply telling Chen over the earbud. Instead, I pulled one of the edges of the plastic silver lining, tearing it away, and then I called Lee.

When he answered, he asked if I had transferred all of the money, and I said I hadn't yet because there seemed to be a problem with the bag. Lee asked what the problem was, and I explained that the silver plastic lining was torn and asked if that was okay. He hesitated for a moment, then said it was fine and to load the bag.

As I was transferring the money, I heard a technician tell Chen over the radio that the plastic silver lining was probably a signal blocker that would block the miniature GPS units in the bands wrapped around the money. Not good news.

The good news, if you want to call it that, was the new duffel bag had wheels which made it a lot easier to move. Of course, that meant I was going somewhere else, only this time none of the little GPS units carefully hidden in the linings of the two duffel bags were coming with me and the GPS units in the money bands weren't going to work. I was now the only GPS unit connected to the money.

Mr. Lee called. There was a taxicab waiting for me in front of the Pavilion. The driver had been instructed where to take me, and the fare had been paid. I said that I hoped he had included a big tip because I had a reputation to protect.

CHAPTER 72

I knew it was a pipe dream, but I had hoped that the tong was using the NYPD taxicab I had left outside of the Pavilion. But, of course, that wasn't the case. The NYPD taxicab was gone, replaced by another taxicab which I was sure was not being driven by a cop.

My new driver was Chinese, so I had to assume he was either working for the tong, or the cab was bugged. In either case, I couldn't risk communicating directly with Chen. Instead, I started a conversation with the driver. According to his license, his name was Howard Chow, which probably meant he was American born and spoke English.

Surprising as it may seem, my fear of riding in taxicabs was apparently overridden by my fear of being killed by the tong. I say that because I was amazingly calm as Howie raced up FDR Drive, weaving between lanes. I kept up the nervous chatter so that if I had to pass a message to Chen, my talking wouldn't come as a surprise. I was careful not to say anything that might be interpreted as a message. I kept my comments to light bullshit, so if someone was listening, they'd hopefully get bored and lose interest.

When Howie exited the highway at East 42nd Street, I figured tail cars might not have been able to keep pace, so I'd be wise to let Chin know where we were. I said, "Wow Howie, you really scared the crap out me. I didn't think it was possible to go from Chinatown to 42nd Street that fast." Howie had no comment.

As Howie pulled to the curb in front of the entrance to Grand Central Station, my cell phone rang. Mr. Lee said for me to open the small zippered compartment on the side of the duffel bag where I'd find a Metro card I could use for the subway. I was to take the duffel bag and go to the IRT Number Seven subway line and board the local train to Flushing. Lee hung up.

Chen confirmed he had heard the conversation, and he was sending people to the station. He just wasn't sure he could have someone there soon enough to be on the train with me.

Following Lee's instructions, I rolled the duffel bag through Grand Central Terminal to the subway platform for the Flushing bound train. I was familiar with the IRT Number Seven subway line, having ridden it to Shea Stadium a few times to watch the Yankees play the Mets, and having recently ridden it when Tommy and I visited Yue Ying Tso to talk about the tunnels.

When I reached the station platform, my cell phone rang. Lee told me to take the train that was pulling into the station. Obviously, he had eyes on the situation. I had hoped to stall to give Chen's people more time to arrive, but that wasn't going to happen. Grand Central Station is the last stop in Manhattan before the Number Seven train goes under the East River to Queens. If Chen's people hadn't made it onto the train, their next chance to do so would be in Queens on the other side of the East River at Vernon-Jackson Avenues.

I looked down the platform as the train pulled to a stop and the doors opened. I had no idea what any of Chen's people looked like, but I scanned the boarding passengers anyway, praying that one or more of them were cops. For instance, I thought about not boarding the train, but knowing Lee was watching me, I decided that wasn't a good idea. Left with no other choice, I boarded the train.

Cell phone service in the subways is basically limited to the stations, and even there it's spotty at best. But once the train went under the river, there was no cell phone service. The last thing Chen was able to tell me before we lost contact was that his guys missed the train. I was on my own, at least for a while.

I had to assume Mr. Lee was either on the train or had some of his people on the train. At that time of morning, there weren't many people traveling from Manhattan to Queens, and the subway car was relatively empty.

Looking around the car, I noticed several Oriental men, but that wasn't unusual given Flushing's large Asian population. Most of the men were middle age or older and didn't look to me like Hip Sing Tong guys, although I had no idea what a Hip Sing Tong guy looked like. Of the three younger men in the car, one was carrying schoolbooks and definitely didn't look like a gangster. The second was with a girl, and they were making out. The third, who had boarded the train with me at Grand Central Station, was sitting across from me. He looked as though he was sleeping, but that could have been an act, and I decided he was Lee's man.

As the train rumbled through the tunnel, I couldn't help wondering if Sleeping Beauty was going to kill me and take the duffel bag when we pulled into the Vernon-Jackson Avenues Station. I didn't dwell on the thought because I hate contemplating death, particularly my own.

When the train began entering the station, I held my breath, hoping to hear Chen's voice in my ear. But no such luck; the bug was silent. Looking at my cell phone, I saw there was no signal, so I assumed that I wouldn't be hearing from Lee either. The good news was that Sleeping Beauty hadn't opened his eyes or moved. I figured I would live at least until we arrived at the next station.

When the doors opened at the Vernon-Jackson Avenues Station, the young couple that had been making out got up to leave. On their way past me, the girl dropped a folded piece of paper on my lap. Either she was a litterbug, or I was a lousy judge of people, and it was a note from Lee.

You guessed it; it was a note from Lee. I was to exit the train at the next station at HunterspointAvenue, walk to the exit at the end of the platform and wait. I was beginning to see where this was heading, and if I was right, it was a brilliant plan. Lee must have suspected that the cops would have me and the money wired with some sort of GPS and communication devices, and he had figured out a way to neutralize them. Had Lee forcibly removed the devices, Chen would have no choice but to abort the operation and have his undercover teams move in. Instead, Lee simply disrupted the communications in a way that Chen wouldn't consider a threat to my well-being. Chen knew I was on the train and that there was no signal, so while he may have been concerned, there was no need for him to panic. He'd simply wait for the communications to resume once the train left the tunnel after the HunterspointAvenue Station stop.

But when the train left the tunnel, I wouldn't be on it. Exactly where I'd be, or if I'd even be alive, was the question.

CHAPTER 73

As the train pulled into the HunterspointAvenue Station, I had a choice to make. Follow Lee's instructions and get off the train, or stay on the train and hope we reached the end of the tunnel, and I could communicate with Chen before someone killed me. There was no guarantee that following Lee's instructions wouldn't get me killed, but it might save Mr. Fang's life. If the Hip Sing Tong didn't get the money, I had no doubt that Mr. Fang was going to be killed.

I'm no hero by any stretch, and I don't mind telling you I was scared, but I had to decide and quickly. When the train doors opened, I stood but didn't move. Then I figured, what the hell "you have to die somewhere," and I walked off the train. I listened, desperately hoping to hear Chen's voice, but there was only silence. Not sure what was going to happen next, I walked slowly toward the end of the platform, pulling the duffel bag along behind me. The few people who had gotten off the train with me all passed me by and made their way up the stairs to the street exit. By the time I reached the end of the platform, the train had left the station, and the platform seemed empty. But I knew someone could be hiding behind one of the steel support columns waiting for the right moment to put a bullet in my brain. Part of me wanted to drop the duffel bag and make a break for the exit, but I didn't. I stood there at the bottom of the stairs and waited.

Shortly, a man in a hooded sweatshirt came down the stairs. He had the hood pulled over much of his face, but from what little I could see, I thought he was Asian. He handed me a walkie-talkie and kept walking. The walkie-talkie squawked, and I heard Mr. Lee's voice. He said I had done well, and we were almost finished. The man who had handed me the walkie-talkie would take the duffel bag, and I was to wait for the next train and take it as far as I wanted.

My heartbeat rate that had reached stratospheric levels was returning to normal, and the pounding in my head was starting to ease. Maybe I wasn't going to die on the Hunters Point Avenue Station platform.

Having hung around with cops, I knew how to work a walkie-talkie. I pressed the talk button and asked Lee about Mr. Fang. He said in twenty minutes Mr. Fang would be released unharmed in Chinatown. I asked where in Chinatown, but Lee refused to answer. He simply repeated that he'd be released unharmed. The last thing Lee said was for me to return the walkie-talkie to the man in the sweatshirt.

Moments after the walkie-talkie went silent, the man in the sweatshirt came back, took the walkie-talkie and the duffel bag, and walked up the stairs to the street exit.

I was tempted to follow him, so I could at least alert Chen to what had gone down, but I figured that wouldn't help, and it might wind up getting Mr. Fang or me killed. So I sat down on a nearby bench and waited for the next train.

When the next train arrived a few minutes later, I got on board and took a seat. There was still no signal showing on my cell phone, and the bug in my ear was silent. The next stop was the 45th Road Courthouse Square Station. As I recalled, the train came out of the tunnel almost immediately after leaving the HunterspointAvenue Station, so I'd get a signal soon. It was probably too late to do anything about the money, but you never know.

Within minutes after the train started moving, I saw sunlight filling the car ahead, and I could hear static in my ear. The bug was starting to connect. By the time my car had cleared the tunnel, I could hear voices. I yelled, "It's me; it's Jake!"

Then I heard Chen's voice. He was yelling to someone, "It's Jake; he's alive!" I yelled back, "Yes, I'm alive!" Naturally, my sudden outbursts caught the attention of the other passengers in the car, but they quickly looked away, figuring I was just another nut talking to myself. I didn't care. I was just glad to be back in communication with the team, and I started explaining what happened.

When the train pulled into the 45th Road Courthouse Square Station, I raced out of the car and headed for the exit. At that point, the Number Seven line runs on an elevated structure above the street. As I ran for the exit, I could hear Chen and Tommy talking excitedly.

When I reached the street, an unmarked police car with its siren blaring came to a screeching stop in front of me. Chen and Tommy jumped out of the car and ran toward me. Tommy grabbed me in a bear-hug, while Chen wrapped his arms around both of us.

Tommy kept asking if I was okay, which didn't surprise me. But Chen wasn't saying anything, which did surprise me. I figured he'd want to know what happened to the money, and he'd have a million questions for me. But, instead, he gave me a big grin, got on his cell phone and walked back to his car.

I asked Tommy what was up, and he said Chen would explain it all in a couple of minutes.

As Tommy and I walked to the car, it dawned on me that Chen and Tommy had arrived in an unmarked car, not the Mobile Command Unit. So where was the Mobile Command Unit, and how had Tommy and Chen gotten to Queens so fast? The closest access to Queens from Grand Central Station is through the Queens-Midtown Tunnel, which is always jammed with traffic.

I had just gotten seated next to Chen when he took his phone away from his ear and turning to me, he said that Mr. Fang had just walked into the Fifth Precinct station house and was fine. Then Chen got back on the phone, and I heard him say, "Okay, hit it!" After that, he peeled out, and we raced away like a bat out of hell.

As I fumbled putting on my seat belt, I asked Chen where we were going and why the hurry. That's when he really surprised me by saying, "We're going to pick up the money."

CHAPTER 74

If you're wondering what the hell happened, you know how I felt at the time.

As we went racing through Long Island City to God only knew where, Chen explained it all.

When Howie, the cabbie, headed up the FDR, Chen decided to take the Mobile Command Unit uptown. But commercial vehicles like the Mobile Command Unit truck are banned from FDR Drive, so they had to take the local streets.

In the meantime, since the signal from the GPS units in the duffel bag was blocked, the unmarked cars had to keep pace. But with all the taxicabs on the FDR at that time of the morning, they had lost track of my cab.

It was my comment to Howie about how fast he had gotten from Chinatown to 42nd Street, that enabled the unmarked cars to catch up. Everyone heard Lee tell me to take the Number Seven subway train, but unfortunately, none of the undercover teams made it to the platform in time to board the train with me.

Still struggling to get uptown in the Mobile Command Unit, Chen decided it was better if he went to Queens, but not in the Mobile Command Unit because it would take too long. So they detoured to the East 34th Street Heliport and had an NYPD helicopter pick them up there.

Not sure where Lee would have me exit the train and fearing it might be before the train emerged from the tunnel, Chen ordered a second helicopter to assist in keeping an eye on things. When the first train exited the tunnel and there was no signal from my transmitters, Chen knew I was still somewhere in the subway system, most likely at one of the underground stations on the Queens side of the river. He had considered sending undercover cops to cover those stations, but there wasn't enough time and, besides, he was worried they'd be made.

Then things took a turn for the better. The second helicopter, hovering high over the HunterspointAvenue Station, was using a telescopic lens to watch for passengers exiting the station. When what seemed to be the last passenger exited, the pilot asked if he should relocate. Chen was about to have the helicopter move on to the next station when his gut told him to have the pilot hold his position. Chen's instincts proved to be good because shortly after that a man in a hooded sweatshirt emerged, dragging a tan duffel bag. The detective riding in the helicopter remembered my comment about a Perry Ellis tan duffel bag and pushing the telescopic lens to its max, he saw the Perry Ellis logo on the bag.

While the helicopter hovered high above watching, a black limo had pulled up, and two men had put the duffel bag in the trunk. The helicopter had followed the limo, reporting its location, while a squad of marked and unmarked police cars had moved into position to overtake it.

Satisfied that the money was safely within reach, Chen had waited to give the arrest order until Mr. Fang was released as promised. Then, fearing I might have been killed on the subway station platform, Chen ordered the helicopter to land, and he commandeered a local precinct unmarked car. With Tommy on board, the two were racing toward the HunterspointAvenue Station when they heard my voice over the radio, and they changed course and headed to the 45th Road Courthouse Square Station.

Just as they were arriving at the station, word had come that Mr. Fang was safe, and Chen had given the order to stop the limo and arrest the occupants.

The limo, three men, and a duffel bag, filled with over a million dollars in cash, were on the shoulder of Brooklyn-Queens Expressway a couple of miles from the Brooklyn Bridge. And, of course, "Mad-Max" Chen was racing to get there. My suggestion that it would all be there whenever we got there, so there was no need to rush, fell on deaf ears. I must admit that I did share some of Chen's excitement over the prospect of the arrest and recovery of the money. It meant his ass was saved, as was Mr. Fang's and my own. That was three asses saved with one arrest. It might have been a record.

That night, drained of adrenalin to the point of being nearly comatose, I celebrated with Gracie, Chen, and Tommy at Shoo's Restaurant. I don't remember much about the celebration, but I know I was happy that the Houdini Bandits case would soon be finally closed.

CHAPTER 75

Over the next week, things moved quickly. It turned out that one of the three men in the limo was Mr. Lee, or I should say, Long Hai, his actual name. Long Hai was the number two man in the Hip Sing Tong, and he was charged with kidnapping, extortion and money laundering. Over the DA's strenuous objection, he was granted bail, although he was required to surrender his passport. Not that it mattered since you can buy excellent forged passports in Chinatown as easily as you can buy a dim sum meal. Shortly after being released on bail, Mr. Lee, or Long Hai, or whatever name he was using, fled to China. Marty, who handled the case, suspected there had been a payoff involved, but he was never able to prove it. Nailing a crooked judge is harder than nailing a crooked cop.

With all of the stolen money safely returned and the bank's share back in the bank, we moved forward with Joey's plea deal. The DA had no evidence tying Joey to the drug money, so no new charges were brought. Marty kept his word, and Joey pleaded guilty to robbery in the third degree. However, Marty did draw the line at recommending a light sentence, and frankly, I didn't argue with him that much. Joey deserved to do time and the more, the better. But even without the recommendation from Marty, the judge went easy on Joey.

Mr. Fang was in the courtroom when Joey was sentenced, and he sent Joey off with his blessing and forgiveness. Mr. Fang is a bigger and better man than I am. As for me, I sent Joey off with a goodbye and good riddance. I never understood what made Joey tick. Maybe the death of his parents had something to do with it, but as far as I'm concerned, nothing could justify what he did to his grandfather.

With Joey's case out of the way, I concentrated on Jenny's case. I made motions that I knew I had little hope of winning, and as expected, they were all denied. But it delayed the case, and that was the objective. Finally, after another two months had passed, the rest of the main target defendants plead out their cases, and the public interest in the Asian Dragon cases finally died. Two weeks after that, I cut a plea deal with Sarah. Jenny pleaded guilty to possession of a controlled substance in the fifth degree, a Class D felony. It was a felony, but since it was a first offense, and with Sarah's recommendation, the judge sentenced Jenny to one year in jail, but he suspended the sentence and placed her on one year of probation.

With Jenny's case finally closed, it was back to my usual 18B Panel cases until someone else interesting walks through the door.

EPILOGUE

All of that happened two years ago. I see Mr. Fang every now and then, and he always thanks me for what I did for him and Joey. As for Joey, he did his time on the burglary charge, but I haven't seen him since his sentencing. Honestly, if I saw him coming down the street, I'd cross to the other side.

Detective Chen survived the Houdini Bandits episode. I thought he should have gotten a citation. After all, three Hip Sing Tong members were taken off the street; the bank's money was recovered; and three-quarters of a million dollars was taken out of the Chinatown drug trade. But Chen was happy just to have his job. When I said he had unrealistically low expectations, he said that I owed him a lunch. I think he proved my point.

He and I have lunch about once a month, and most of the time I pay which is okay.

As for the tunnels, I don't know if they exist or not, but I wouldn't bet they don't. I learned from Professor Wu's history lessons that Chinatown is a mysterious place, never to be taken lightly.

As for Joan and Jenny, I wish I could tell you that everything worked out fine, but it didn't. Joan got the job as Professor of Economics at NYU, and Jenny was admitted to the University as a freshman. Everything seemed to be going along smoothly. Gracie stayed close to Joan and helped her get through a messy divorce from doctor prick. But when the divorce was finally behind her, and Joan's life was settling down, Jenny, who hadn't completed her year of probation, took off again. No one knows for certain where she went or why she left, but Joan suspects there was a young man involved. I guess some people never learn, or at least never learn easily. I'm probably a poster boy for that proposition.

I still wonder if Jenny had told Joan and I the truth about what she had done while living with Shing Lew. I had my suspicions that she hadn't told us the whole story, and she was just damn lucky that Shing got hauled back to San Francisco before he could spill the beans. I've never shared that thought with Joan or with Gracie, for that matter. As you might expect, Jenny is a sore topic with Joan and Gracie, so you can understand my reluctance to talk to either of them about her. Jenny has caused Joan a lot of anguish, but things have a way of evening out. Jenny is still on probation, and technically, she's in violation, but nobody really cares. Of course, if she gets arrested again, it'll be a problem, but it'll be her problem, not mine, and hopefully, not Joan's.

As for Gracie and me, nothing has changed, and hopefully, it never will. We talked long and hard about me moving in with her on a full-time basis, but in the end we decided that we liked things the way they were. I got a smaller and cheaper apartment, if you can call two hundred and fifty square feet of space an apartment. It's apparently all the rage in Manhattan. The chic call them "micro apartments;" I call them closets with toilets. But it suits its purpose, and I only spend a few nights a month there.

I'm sure, at some point, we'll talk about me moving in again, but probably not soon. Maybe we're afraid of what might happen if we change things. Right now we're happy, and in this life you can't ask for more than that.

AUTHOR'S NOTE

As with all my books, the stories and characters in this book are fictional, the product of my imagination. However, the history of Chinatown is mostly, if not entirely, factual. I say mostly factual because in my research I discovered historical accounts differ on minor details. As this is a novel and not a historical account, I chose the versions that best fit the story line.

As for the tunnels, it is well documented that they existed during the late 1800s and early 1900s. But the story told by the old man is, of course, fictional. Do the tunnels exist today? All I can say is that the Wing Fat Arcade does exist, and it is said to be part of the original tunnel network. As for the existence any other tunnels, I leave it to you, the reader, to make up your own mind. Perhaps if you find yourself in New York City's Chinatown with time to spare, you might do your own exploring.

Made in the USA
Las Vegas, NV
11 February 2024